Immortal Reborn

Book 1

Arianna's Choice

A Children of Angels Novel

Natalie D. Wilson

DEDICATION

The story of Alexandria and Arianna began in my mind years ago when I heard an instrumental composition, and I asked myself what story would evoke the emotion behind the melody. Through the years, I slowly developed different aspects of the tale within my imagination, but I always knew from the very beginning what the last scene of the last novel would be. Writing to that point seemed a daunting task to one who was new to writing her own stories, as I was. But no journey, such as mine has been, is without love and support. And it was through the encouragement of my dear, sweet husband, Will, that I finally decided to put my thoughts to paper and create the world of the *Nephilim* that I saw in my mind. For his honest appraisal of the story, his willingness to go without sleep so that I could keep the light on to type, and his unwavering devotion, my dream has been made real. For it all, Will, I thank you from the bottom of my heart.

To the sister of my heart, Catherine, I also extend my most sincere thanks. It was she who was the first to read the initial two chapters, and it was she who told me that there was indeed something there that sparked her interest and curiosity. Hearing that positive feedback did propel me forward, and I shall always be grateful for the hope she brought to my journey.

When the initial draft was complete, I turned to my dear friend Danielle, asking for her input, honest opinion, and constructive criticism. Danielle was able to cut through the sheer emotion I felt after writing the final page of the first novel, and helped me fine tune many scenes, so that they were what I had truly intended them to be. And her unwavering support and love of the characters gave me a kindred soul to confide in. For the quotes she shared to keep me rolling, and the constant texts which bolstered my spirits, I must humbly say, "Thank you."

For the final readings, I enlisted Nicole, Sally and Eileen. They also read through the first novel in record time and quickly asked for the second in the series. With that request, I knew that others could, and did love my characters as much as I did. And for any author, I would imagine that the sheer elation one feels when you receive that kind of validation, was the soaring high that I experienced. So ladies, thank you for loving Alex and her friends as much as I do.

And finally, I have to say a special thank you to my true Father. I prayed and worked towards using my words and ideas to glorify Him, and I hope that my readers will see and feel the love I always experience whenever I think of the Lord. It is no small thing to feel as inspired as I have felt, creating these stories. And I can honestly say that there were many moments when I felt as though His words were coming through more so than my own. And the story is all the better for that inspiration, I think.

So readers, I sincerely hope that you will enjoy the first installment in this new series. I hope that it will entertain you, inspire you, and perhaps make you laugh a little, too. I certainly know that Rohan helps me laugh quite often. Enjoy, until the next story, my friends.

Natalie

CONTENTS

ACKNOWLEDGMENTS

Cover Photo: Quiet Moments by Michael Drummond

All characters appearing in this work are fictitious. Any resemblance to real persons, living or dead, is purely coincidental. Actual locations are referenced solely to lend realism to the story. No negative connotations to real locations are implied or suggested.

They are here. They have always been here, living amongst us. Remarkably, mankind has always *known* of their existence, yet failed to fully articulate and acknowledge when our paths cross theirs. Tales of angels, immortals, warriors, heroes, even 'the Wandering Jew' persist through time, religions, and mythologies. You may call them what you will – but they *are* here.

What makes the truth so hard to believe? What is truly amazing is one little biblical verse gives the secret away, actually spells it out. But humans, as we are so apt to do, are slow to convince and even harder to compel to bear witness to the truth, even when it is right before our eyes.

Genesis 6: 1-4 (¹ When human beings began to increase in number on the earth and daughters were born to them, ² the sons of God saw that the daughters of humans were beautiful, and they married any of them they chose. ³ Then the LORD said, "My Spirit will not contend with ᵃ humans forever, for they are mortal ᵇ ; their days will be a hundred and twenty years." ⁴ The Nephilim were on the earth in those days—and also afterward—when the sons of God went to the daughters of humans and had children by them. They were the heroes of old, men of renown.)

Prelude

It began long, long ago, before recorded history, when the first angel, Ganymede, asked The Most High for permission to linger here on Earth a bit longer. He asked for a little more time to breathe the fresh, untainted air, and to experience time in the humans' way. He was intrigued by their development and he felt drawn to the spark of the Father within each one.

He was granted this unique opportunity, hearing the Father's voice tell him that he would walk the earth until his true purpose was fulfilled. Though not knowing what the Lord's plan was for him, Ganymede had complete faith that his life would be used to glorify the Lord, so he graciously accepted the Father's permission. Travelling over the land gave him the opportunity to marvel at the Father's creations, and to befriend those ever developing groups of people that he encountered.

After a great time, Ganymede wanted more than the solitary roaming that had become his existence and he chose to settle in a small village nestled in lush, green hills that was brimming with life and possibilities. The sea rose up before the village and offered its inhabitants not only a fresh food source, but also the future promise of travel. Ganymede could look long into the future and see the vessels that would one day traverse the seas and dock along those shores.

As time went on, Ganymede became an integral part of the village, helping to heal those who were injured or sick and leading their spiritual growth with stories of the Father and promises of the next life. His neighbors felt as though there must be one God, instead of many, because they could feel the energy and purity radiating from Ganymede and knew that he was no false profit living among them.

Ganymede continued to meditate and commune with the Lord, and blessed generation after generation in the ever growing village. When he thought that it was surely time to return to his Heavenly home, he noticed someone that had previously escaped his acute attention. A young maiden, named Maireid, had become of age, and when she came to listen to him speak of holy things, he felt moved for the first time in the way he had seen every married man and woman react in all the time he had lingered on this earthly plane.

He found that his heart felt a bit lighter when she spoke, and he longed to be near her just to watch her breathe. Not knowing how he should respond or react to these startling new feelings, he entered a period of deep meditation and sought guidance. It was on the second night of his meditation, as he sat prostrate on his knees in the courtyard behind his dwelling, that he finally heard the Lord's voice.

The Lord told him that He was greatly pleased with all the good works Ganymede had accomplished in the Father's name while walking and living among humans. And before his time was done, he was to truly know the human experience by marrying and having a human family. For the first time, Ganymede's mind roamed over the possibilities of what it might feel like to be loved in that way, as a husband and as a father, and the possibilities seemed hopeful and full of promise to him.

Early the next morning, he bathed and dressed simply, and went to the home of young Maireid and her family. He tentatively knocked on the door and was received by her father, who did seem a bit surprised to see the young man who never aged at his home's entrance. For the first time, Ganymede understood the nervousness of courtship and he had to chuckle at himself. He offered Maireid's father a basket of warm bread and asked if he might come in and have a conversation with him.

After a very short exchange, Maireid's father, Enote, was all too happy to see his daughter with one so respected, but he was concerned about how she would age and Ganymede would not. The angel replied that he could not know how this new phase of his life would progress or develop, but perhaps he would finally age alongside her.

Throughout the next weeks, Ganymede was allowed to sit and talk with Maireid and take short walks with her. Her mother and aunts always walked along behind the two, and he could hear their conversations behind them as they passed the time while they guarded over her. But Ganymede used the time to establish a deeper friendship with her during their visits.

He learned that she liked the early hours of the morning, when the day was still new, fresh, and quiet. When it held such promise, that it gave her hope of good things which might come to pass. Maireid also confessed her love of animals, and how she detested the moments she had to help prepare birds for her family's dinner table. And she loved the color blue, from the sky and the water near their village.

He eventually took her hand in his one afternoon and felt her squeeze his fingers back in return. When he looked down into her warm, green eyes, he saw the spark that made his heart rejoice. The angel thanked the Lord for allowing him such a new and heartfelt gift.

After a month, Ganymede walked with Maireid in her parents' garden and asked her if they might sit along a low, wooden bench. She blushed, but agreed. He told her of his conversation with the Lord and that of all the young maidens he had ever known, none had moved his heart as had she. Ganymede asked Maireid if she felt the same and when she answered that she did, he asked her to be his wife. Her bright smile and sudden hug was all the answer he needed, but she did find her words and told him that she wanted him for her husband for the rest of her days.

The courtship did not last long after that, and finally Ganymede and Maireid were joined as husband and wife. The village came out in its entirety to celebrate this most magical union, and to wish the two well. Ganymede felt as if he had just begun to live for the first time, after all the ages he had spent traversing the world. Every time he knelt in prayer he asked for a little more time to walk alongside Maireid. He knew the joys and utter brilliance of basking in His presence, yet he found that he also wanted to share a lifetime, a human lifetime, with Maireid.

For Ganymede, her lifetime would have been but a blink in time, or lack thereof, which he was accustomed to. But here on Earth, taking the slow path meant that he would not suffer the loss of one of her breaths. He would not miss one flutter of her heart, or one smile that spread and colored her cheeks when she looked at him. It was the light within her heart, mirrored in her eyes, which lit his heart aflame and captured him, day after day.

As it had been decreed, he lived out her days with her; and most unexpectedly, their lives were blessed with a daughter a little more than a year into their time together. Arianna, half human, half angel, was a joy to her parents and a source of comfort to their little village. Her laughter, flitting through the small houses and lifting on the breeze, made everyone feel safe and just a little happier, content. She was a balm to their homes, and they were captivated by her.

Arianna grew knowing that she was quite different from the other children and even adults that she encountered. She could see and hear things that other people could not, from long distances away, or from the person's mind sitting next to her at the hearth of her parents' home. It was always her parents' sustaining love and easy acceptance, though, which made her feel wanted and a part of the human experience.

And like her father, Arianna could heal anyone, no matter what the injury or illness was. Though this amazing gift was able to cocoon the family for a significant time, there eventually came a day when Maireid faced what all humans do. Maireid aged, and reaching the end of her body's days, she finally breathed her last.

Arianna and Ganymede grieved their mortal loss together, leaning on one another for the strength, love, and courage needed to see them through. And though they loved their home and the people around them, Ganymede understood that he could not let them remain there forever. He would have to return to the Lord's presence soon, and Arianna would have to learn to navigate the world, for better or for worse, without him constantly by her side. Ganymede knew that he would always be able to visit her and counsel her, but he would no longer be with her every waking moment. And the human world could often be a terrifying place.

So it was with a very heavy heart, on a crisp, cool spring morning, that both Ganymede and Arianna bade farewell to the villagers who were their extended family. The hugs and gentle way the women squeezed her hands reassured Arianna that she would always have a 'people' to call her own and a place to return to in the future. The elders of the small township promised Ganymede that their story would be told and that the villagers' descendants would know their names, so that they would always be welcomed back, whenever or if ever they chose to return.

And though Ganymede graciously accepted their pledge and love, he knew that within a few generations their story would fade from memory. Mortals would think the story of one who never aged too difficult to believe, if their eyes could not bear witness to such a truth. He and Arianna would fade from the villagers' minds and become but a whispered bedtime story. And it was for the best, he thought. For Arianna would not know just one people in one place, but all peoples in all places during her long life.

As they walked along the winding road that led away from the only structures she had ever known, Arianna turned just once to look over her shoulder and whispered, "Good-bye," to her home and to her mother. When she turned her head to look forward, Ganymede gathered her in his arms and the two stepped ahead, united as she faced her future.

1

To say she was extraordinary would not do justice to the fair-haired, angelic creature who danced through the manicured and meticulously planned garden which ran behind the large stone Manor House. She was the very breath that caused the flowers to sway and the boughs to sigh. Wherever she walked, skipped, or ran along one of the pebbled paths, anyone who witnessed her meander about found that they held their breath involuntarily until she passed.

It was as if they knew, subconsciously, that something or someone quite remarkable had just crossed paths with them, and in the face of one so – '*other*' – than themselves, nature asked a still and immovable reverence be shown. In her wake, she always left a feeling of contentment and a smile lingering on each person's face.

Alexandria, or Alex as her parents called her, was indeed a miracle child. Her mother, Lady Juliana, had given birth to two boys, Wallace and Conner, just two years apart, and then lost two more babies within a five year period. She and her husband, Lord Errol Fitzgerald Groaban, had resigned themselves to the fact that they were not to be blessed with any more children. They settled into a comfortable pattern with their sons, and were beyond shocked when Juliana's doctor confirmed three years later that there was to be another chance, perhaps her last, to become a mother again.

Lady Juliana received the best care, and after nine months a daughter came into the Groaban family. They all doted on her and vowed to watch over her, her older brothers more than anyone else.

Through the years, Lord Errol served in various ambassadorial roles for the British government, and though the family traveled along with him, they always returned to the Manor House for holidays and rest. It was the one place that they felt they could truly relax and refresh their spirits. It was also a place for their beloved butler, Edmund Jameason, to finally feel his way around a properly organized household.

"Nothing," he told them quite often, "is as satisfying as seeing everything in its place, and order restored to the soul."

Jameason traveled with the Groabans wherever Lord Errol served as ambassador, and he kept not only the household in order, but also served as nanny, mentor, and at times, disciplinarian to the three Groaban children. Wallace and Conner gave him a good run for his money some days, as the two were constantly trying every new experiment or stunt they could to see if they were as invincible as young adolescents often think they are.

But Jameason seemed to be the rock on which the family was built, and the glue that kept them bound together. He had not one, but several pairs of eyes in the back of his head, and try as they might to get things past him, Jameason always knew what his young charges were up to.

Wallace and Conner reveled in the travel and opportunities they were afforded. Tutors were always coming and going throughout the children's lives, and each new home or country they lived in was a canvas for their global experience. As their father took up the position of ambassador to Egypt in the late 1990's, Wallace and Conner were more than ready to explore tombs and scale pyramids.

Alexandria, however, seemed to eerily make instant connections to each new foreign land they found themselves in. She would occasionally see an artifact or a painting and her brothers could tell from the gleam in her eyes that she was '*hearing the echo*', as that was what the two of them called it. For Alex, her remembrances and the emotions she experienced were all encompassing and took her completely to another time.

She would cease to see what was actually around her and find herself standing amid a world that had long since passed by and been forgotten. Alex never knew where the visions would take her, and she sometimes found herself standing in the midst of a very frightening scene of some past battle or she might find that she was witnessing the last moments of a person's life. At other times she was simply a silent witness to a person's day to day routine, almost seeing the people walk right through where she stood as she watched the scene play out.

Wallace and Conner knew the look well, and made a deliberate point to circle the wagons and protect her until a vision cleared. When she was very young, Alexandria would actually talk her way through the visions and describe what she was seeing, alarmingly in whatever language the scene played out in. But as she grew older, she learned that this terrified anyone outside of her immediate family, and she became aware of the danger she placed them in when she allowed outsiders knowledge of the images, even her mind could scarcely comprehend. So, Alexandria quickly learned to attune herself to the first signs of an impending recreation of the past, and steel herself against any reaction within sight of possible witnesses.

She would feel slight vibrations in the air and begin to smell and taste the new environment that was bearing down on her. She had learned to school her face into as serene a mask as she could muster and then allow herself to be pulled away. It was not easy for her parents, her brothers, or for Jameason to see her suffer, and in an effort to protect them, she often would keep the most horrific details to herself. As she grew older, she began to keep more and more of the experiences to herself, much to the disapproval of her brothers. They honestly thought that it was not productive or healthy for Alexandria to keep it all bottled up within.

While in Egypt, Alexandria found she had to keep her hands in her pockets quite a bit, because touching an object was sure to swirl her into the past, seeing into various images and scenes from the object's history. While Wallace and Conner were always touching obelisks and stone passageways, Alexandria would try to walk around the stones, marvel at their size, and then step quietly into alcoves to witness history in her own way. Though this seemed the best way to avoid the encounters she experienced, she was dismayed to find that she really could not keep the old voices at bay.

It was on a hot, humid night there in Egypt that Alexandria, then only eight, learned her life would take a drastically different path than the one she thought lay before her. She was lying in her bed, reading The Chronicles of Narnia, when she noticed the air off to the left side of her bed begin to shimmer. She felt the familiar tightening in her chest and shortness of breath that came when she knew her world was about to shift.

Not taking her eyes off of the air, she carefully laid her book down on the bed and placed her hands on either side of her so that she could push herself into an upright position slowly. When she was two or three, she would have called for Wallace and Conner, even her parents, but not anymore. She tensed all over and tried to ready herself.

A soft hush came over the room. Alexandria could not hear the sounds on the street near the house her family rented, nor could she hear the clock ticking on her bedside table anymore. Her heart sounded loud enough in her ears to wake anyone in the house, but she knew no one else could hear her distress.

The air seemed to move in waves now around the room, almost as if it were water moving along a shoreline. It was not moving any objects around the room, only congealing and coalescing into something far thicker than air should be. Alexandria had never seen the atmosphere become so charged and wondered if it would feel any different to touch. Hesitantly, she reached out her left arm and let her fingers skim the edge of the nearest swirl.

Instantly, her body was thrown back on the bed and she found that, in her mind, she was no longer on the bed, but standing on a beach looking up at a sky filled with stars. She drew in a long, shaky breath, and saw it puff out in front of her face as she exhaled. Turning completely around, Alexandria beheld no lights from civilization in any direction. The sounds of the waves lapping and night birds competing to be heard over a din of insects, were the only ones her ears could detect. Rather than just wait to *see* what was coming, she felt compelled to speak.

"Hello," she called out tentatively, wary of how shaky and magnified her voice sounded.

Though she perceived no new sound, Alexandria knew without a doubt that if she turned around again, she would see someone standing right behind her.

"Don't be a coward," she thought to herself, "just turn around and face this."

To her surprise, a warm, melodious laugh filled the air around her, stripping away her fear. The laugh manifested itself into a voice that instantly reassured and welcomed her.

"Oh, Alexandria! You have never been, nor will you ever be, a coward," said a man's voice.

She turned and found herself staring up into eyes so vivid and blue, that they almost seemed clear. A face of perfection smiled down at her, with distinct dimples and curly locks of golden hair.

"Quite the contrary, my dear," he said. "You are more powerful and formidable than any warrior who has ever lived. I do not think that your character would ever allow you to run from any challenge you encounter. You are, in the simplest of terms, extraordinary."

Alexandria was stunned, and after opening and closing her mouth several times, she could not help but speak the thoughts that were burning their way through her mind.

"You can see me? And you can hear my thoughts? But, how? No one has ever noticed me before?"

"Well," chuckled the stranger, "I sincerely doubt that anyone has ever failed to notice you. I am quite certain that you are frequently noticed and the topic of much discussion."

At this last comment, Alexandria's cheeks flamed scarlet, and she lowered her eyes. She knew that people whispered about her constantly, and she noticed complete strangers openly gawking at her far too frequently for her own sense of comfort. She knew that she had nothing to be embarrassed about, but she still felt tears pricking her eyes despite her desire to keep them at bay.

The golden man stepped forward and placed a finger delicately under her chin, then ever so gently raised her young, wounded eyes up to meet his. In a voice that seemed barely above a whisper he said, "No, no sweet child. I am not making fun of you in any way. If my words seemed too sharp, I most humbly apologize."

"You must know that most people find you to be such an enchanting and beautiful child, that they are in awe just a bit. But I do not think that they find you lacking in any way."

"Thank you, sir," Alexandria breathed out, as she cleared her throat.

"Let's sit for a while, shall we?" the stranger asked, and when she nodded her agreement the two walked over to a large piece of driftwood that lay beached on its side.

At first Alexandria looked to the stars for some small reassurance that there was still something familiar and known about the place she now found herself in, but beyond that, she could not stop herself from turning to concentrate completely on the gentleman at her side. She had been taught again and again not to talk to strangers, and she certainly knew that she was never to leave with an unknown adult. But, she wondered if those same rules of safety that her parents and brothers had drilled into her time and time again, applied in a world apart from her own. She had never had reason to consider it before that night.

The golden-haired man was also looking up at the stars, but a slow smile spread across his face.

"Alexandria, I can promise you on my life and all that I hold dear that you are in no danger from me. Not on this night, nor on any other."

He slowly turned his head down to gaze at her, and she knew within her very core that this man would never harm a hair on her head.

7

She was very safe, and though she could not explain it, she even felt love emanating from him.

"I forgot that you can hear my thoughts," she said. Scrunching up her nose and shaking her head at him, she asked, "How are you doing that?"

He laughed and the sound pealed gently across the air between them.

"You can do it too, you know. I am surprised that you have not started reading my thoughts to find out the answers to all of those questions racing around in that little head of yours. Why don't you give it a try? See if you can tell me my name, little one?" he encouraged her.

"You're joking, right? I cannot really read your mind," scoffed Alexandria.

"Oh yes, my dear, you most certainly can. It is a talent not easily mastered, but one that I think you will find comes with relative ease to you. Go on, concentrate. What is my name?" he pressed gently.

Alexandria slowly pulled the salty air into her lungs and stared into the man's warm eyes. She began to hear and feel a pulsing within her own ears, and at first she thought that it was her own heartbeat echoing too loudly. But then she became aware of the difference in the new pulse from her own. She was hearing his heartbeat and feeling the rhythm. Her breath began to keep time with his body's current and she started to feel pulled in by that flow.

She could sense the fact that he was slightly hungry, and that the hairs on his arms were beginning to rise. She knew that his left ear itched and that he wanted to scratch it, but that he dared not lest he interrupt her concentration. His eyes seemed to urge her onward and she felt her mind reach out like a slowly twirling ribbon. It gradually snaked away from her and it found a similar ribbon of thoughts within him that hers could travel along.

She gasped as her stream of consciousness began to flow along his. She saw him walking with a billowing robe and sandals on, along a road that looked quite ancient, pausing to look back at her, his hand outstretched. Then she caught a glimpse of him by a doorway to a small, thatched home in a lush, wooded area beckoning her inside. Finally, she heard a woman's voice call out to him that their evening meal was prepared, and laugh as he scooped her up for a kiss. She whispered, "Ganymede," as he held her.

Alexandria pulled back, and shock flooded her system. She was panting as if she had just run a race with Wallace and Conner, but the man was still smiling down at her, with no sign of exertion whatsoever.

"You're Ganymede?" Alexandria asked, almost reverently. She reached up to push her long, golden hair out of her eyes.

He slowly nodded his agreement.

"Very good, Alexandria. I am indeed Ganymede, and I must say that I am quite impressed. You took a very direct route to ferret out the information you needed. You did not waver, only traveled along a memory strand of mine until you ended with what you sought. In fact, you accomplished that little task so quickly it makes me wonder."

"Wonder what?" asked Alexandria pensively.

"Wonder why you have not tried that before," replied Ganymede. "Have you never once taken a peek inside someone's thoughts to hear what they were contemplating? Never once been tempted?"

Alexandria would have thought that he was joking had she not just plucked information directly from his mind, and felt the accompanying sensations of capturing that information.

"No, sir," she said, shaking her head to confirm her innocence. "I've never even known that any of this was possible!"

He tilted his head to the side and furrowed his brow at her.

"Any of what, dear one?" he asked.

"Any of what's been happening tonight," breathed Alexandria. "I have never talked to anyone in any scene from the past I've been trapped in and I have never, ever listened in on someone's thoughts. That would be wrong, wouldn't it?" asked Alexandria, not knowing if she was giving him the answer that he sought, but hoping that the truth was the correct path to take with Ganymede.

And for just a moment she saw a twinge of sadness in his eyes as he refocused on her face.

"I am sorry that the remembrances make you feel trapped, Alexandria. Although, now that I think of it from your perspective, I am sure that you have been very afraid on occasion haven't you?" As he asked this, he reached out one hand to her offering her his open palm. She laid her hand in his and felt warmth spreading quickly from his hand into her arm, then chest, and before she could draw another breath the feeling had spread to her toes. Her eyes widened at the sudden contentment she felt.

"Thank you for letting me comfort you little one. I know that this is a most unusual night for you," he said, letting his eyes roam over her face.

Alexandria slowly took her hand from his, and feeling less alone in all the madness she had experienced in her short years, she asked, "Are you my guardian angel, then?"

Ganymede chuckled, "Something like that Alexandria, something very much like that indeed."

He looked at her with the same love and sadness that she sometimes glimpsed in her own parents' eyes when they did not realize that she was watching them talk about her. Though they cherished their daughter, they were uncertain of her future in the world and they worked diligently to shield her as much as possible.

Alexandria had become so accustomed to holding everything in, she was actually eager to continue her conversation with Ganymede, even if he was just a figment of her imagination. Funny, she thought, that the one person who would understand was someone that only she could see.

"Are you here to help me with the things that I see?" she asked, praying that he could relieve the fear and anxiety she lived with each moment of each and every day.

Ganymede looked back up to the stars as if they would give him the right answer. "Yes, Alexandria, I am here to help you. Though not in the way you mean. I can give you a choice tonight, and you must think long and hard before you make it, my dear."

"A choice?" she held her breath, afraid to wish for the impossible. But Ganymede could read her silent pleas, and again she noted the twinge of sadness in his eyes as he looked at her.

"Yes," he breathed out, as if it cost him something to speak these words to her. "You can choose to be just as you are today, a young girl, maturing, who will continue to learn and grow into the abilities that are meant just for you; or you can choose to put those gifts to the side for a time and live without them."

At first, all Alexandria heard was that she could lay down the burden of seeing into the past and be like her brothers, untroubled and carefree. She could go to a real school with other children, and not have tutors keeping her sheltered at home. Her parents would not have to worry about when and where she would lose her focus, and try to explain the odd occurrence away as seizures or epilepsy.

"Normal," she thought to herself, "I could just be a normal kid!" But slowly, that latter part of Ganymede's offer filtered into her thoughts, "For a time," he had said. Rather than speak aloud, Alexandria simply thought her question while pointedly looking into Ganymede's eyes.

"If I take a break from all of this, when do I have to start again? Will I have a choice, or will it suddenly hit me when I am in a school surrounded by other children, or a public place with people all around?" she asked him within her mind.

Ganymede shook his head and said, "You will never *have* to do anything that you do not want to do, Alexandria. But taking away a vital part of who you are does not come easily, and it can only be held at bay for so long. Imagine for a moment, that I told you I was going to take away Wallace's mischievousness or Conner's inquisitiveness, their exuberance for life. Can you picture the lads they would be without those traits?"

The thought of her brothers altered thus, made Alexandria shiver. She knew that without those qualities both boys would have the light within dimmed to a point that she would not know them as her brothers anymore.

"No," she spoke sadly aloud. "And I would be that different too, if I could not see into the past, or look inside people's thoughts?"

"Yes," Ganymede shook his head, "you would seem very different to your family. Not so different that they would not love you, or care for you, but they would always wonder what had changed and how that change had come about. But even their fears could be laid aside for a time, if you so choose to have a respite from all that you are currently enduring. You would be letting part of you lay dormant for a time, but it would always be within, because your abilities are truly a part of who you are, Alexandria,"

Ganymede said gently, as he reached forward and tucked a loose lock of hair behind her ear.

"Is it bad to say I want it to stop, even if only for a day?" she asked him, hoping that her question was not making him think less of her, or disappointing him.

She thought it odd that she wanted to please Ganymede so, having just met him, but she really did want to make him happy. And at that thought, he smiled widely at her with an internal light that she could feel vibrating all around her.

"As I should have told you before, you cannot disappoint me. I am very proud of you, Alexandria, and I know your answer now as well. You shall have a nice little rest from all the voices and faces that intrude upon your days, until you are a little older and more prepared for what is to come. And more mature for a choice that you will be called upon to make. I must admit though, that I am worried the time spent away from who you are, will make it all the more difficult on you in the future. But I am willing to concede that you need a break. For now, at least."

"Will you decide when my abilities come back, or is that for me to choose?" asked Alexandria, hardly believing that this could be happening to her.

"That will be for us both to decide, in time. I will be watching and waiting until you are ready to begin again." Ganymede reached out a hand and gently stroked her hair.

"Will I see you again?" she silently wondered, as a feeling of lethargy and tiredness spread through her limbs.

"Indeed, my sweet Alexandria, we will meet again. But I think that I have tired you out enough for this evening and I would be remiss if I kept you away from your home much longer. Close your eyes now and sleep little one."

And though sleep was pulling her under quite forcefully, Alexandria tried to keep her eyes open. She had so many questions that she had somehow not been able to voice. But her eyelids betrayed her, and sleep came on quickly. The last thing she could make out was the sound of the waves breaking along the shore, and when she moved her hand out beside her, she felt the smoothness of her bedding under her fingertips.

Alexandria sat up and looked around her bedroom. It looked the same as always; her lamp was still burning brightly, and her novel remained turned face down on the bed beside her. Only the gauzy curtains moving with a slight breeze made the room feel animated by something unseen. Unexpectedly, the door to her room opened and her eldest brother, Wallace, stuck his head in.

"Hey, you okay in here? I thought that I heard you talking to someone," he said, letting his eyes roam around the room to make sure she was alone and safe.

Alexandria tentatively stretched her legs out and smiled. "Yeah, Wallace, I'm good," she said shakily. "I just had a strange dream that's all."

He angled his head to the side, studying her more intently now, and then walked over to the side of her bed and sat down.

"Wanna talk about it?" he asked, hoping to tease some information out of her. It had become much more difficult for Wallace or Conner to get details from Alexandria in the last few years, and though he was ten years her senior, he usually could not brow beat anything from her once she had decided to close down. But to his surprise, she nodded.

"Wallace, I know you won't believe anything I'm about to say, but I think I'm free," said Alexandria, as she raised a shaky hand to push her hair out of her eyes. She gave him a smile that lit up her entire face, and he saw such a trusting look of joy in her eyes, that he dared not make fun of her statement.

"Well, I think that I need a little more information to go on there, kiddo. Free in what way?" he asked.

"Free of everything!" cried Alexandria. "I visited with someone tonight who gave me a way out of seeing into the past all of the time, and I can just be like you and Conner now," she gushed.

Try as he might to follow her train of thought, Wallace seized on the one bit of information that any big brother would.

"What exactly do you mean when you say you visited with someone? Would that be a male someone, and how did he get in here?" Wallace could feel himself tensing up and was ready to walk over to the windows to test the latches, but Alexandria stayed that action by reaching over and holding his hand.

"Wallace, look at me," she said quietly. Just as Ganymede had predicted, her family would question the change and be alarmed. Her mind raced feverishly to find the words that would both calm and reassure her brother that all was well, and would hopefully continue to be so for the foreseeable future.

"What I am telling you is true. I had a, well I guess you could call it another vision. I was here the whole time, but somehow I went somewhere else." Wallace's face indicated that he was trying to believe her, but having a hard time. "I met someone, who I think is my guardian angel. He promised that for a while, I can just be a normal kid; no echoes, no memories from another time or place, just the chance to be, well, me. I know it doesn't sound real, but truthfully, has anything with me ever sounded real to you?" she smiled tentatively, hoping that Wallace could sense the faith and happiness she felt through her words.

Wallace let out a long, slow breath and shook his head. Then he started to chuckle. "Well, if you put it that way, I'll concede that you saw someone that I couldn't have. Heck, squirt, if you say he was here, I will back you all the way. He really told you have an escape clause from everything?" Wallace sounded as though he still needed a bit more to go on, but Alexandria simply nodded her head. Her smile said it all, and he exhaled as he nodded.

Wallace shifted his weight and stood beside Alex's bed. He reached over and smoothed her hair off of her forehead, then leaned in to give her a goodnight kiss. When he straightened he had his usual lopsided, mischievous grin in place. He walked over to the door of Alexandria's bedroom and paused at the threshold before leaving.

Alexandria knew that he had something he wanted to say, and she giggled inside as she waited for one of her brother's quirky or witty quips. But instead he looked around the room one last time, and then back at her before saying, "I love you, Alexandria, all of you. Remember that, okay, kiddo?"

"I will. I promise," said Alexandria, smiling up at him.

The door closed after Wallace, and Alex settled back on her pillows for what she hoped would be uneventful dreams and slumber.

2

Alexandria was coming home. All of the family was gathering at the Manor House for Christmas, and she was returning after almost eleven months away. Jameason had insisted on driving down to London to meet her, even though she had begged him not to over the phone, thinking that the drive might tire him out too much.

Surely her father could have a car delivered and waiting in the airport's parking lot for the drive from Heathrow to Oxford, she had thought. But Jameason had simply scoffed at the notion over the phone, stating that the day he was not able to take care of one of his charges, would be that day that he would meet his maker again, so Alexandria acquiesced.

The two chatted about all that had been going on with her new position at the United Nations in New York where she worked as an interpreter for multiple language divisions. After Alexandria entered boarding school when she was thirteen, she discovered that she could quickly grasp any language she heard, so she had fed this new found talent feverously. To the current date, she had mastered twenty-two currently spoken languages. She only confessed to speaking fourteen fluently, hoping that the additional languages would pay off at a later time in her career. She was determined not to show all of her cards to anyone just yet.

The drive from Heathrow would take them a little under an hour and a half in the heavy traffic, but Alexandria was glad for the time to unwind and breathe before she saw her family. Life had become exceptionally busy for Alex and her brothers, as each pursued their own career. But they always made time to chat through Skype each week, and texted often through their phones. Alexandria never felt alone, no matter how far across the pond she was.

As the car traveled on, rocking her gently to and fro, Alexandria absentmindedly trailed her finger along the weather stripping of the car's window. She moved her finger forward and higher onto the glass, feeling the cool texture beneath her skin. Without thought to what she was doing, her index finger began to trace slow, looping infinity symbols over and over again.

"I wonder what travels that finger is leading that little mind on tonight," mused Jameason, breaking through her mental wanderings.

Alexandria chuckled. "Just thinking about being back here after such a long time away. And honestly, Jameason, wondering how long before I can take a long, hot shower."

"Ah, yes, the restorative properties of hot water. I believe it won't be long now, my dear. But something tells me there is a bit more lurking behind this pensive silence that has come on in the last ten minutes," probed Jameason.

Alexandria turned her head slowly towards Jameason and gave him a leisurely smile. "You never miss a thing, do you Jameason?"

"Miss something?" scoffed the old man. "My dear, I haven't missed a thing about you or your brothers since the day you were brought from hospital to your parents' home. Now tell me, what has you so anxious, Alex?" asked Jameason, trying to sound nonchalant, but instinctively growing concerned over the worry that was painted clearly across Alexandria's forehead.

Alexandria drew a shaky breath into her lungs and ran her hands up and down her thighs, while she contemplated how much she should disclose to Jameason. She knew that this man was her greatest confidant and had always held her best interests at heart. If she could confide in anyone, it would be him.

"Jameason, I have always been able to tell you anything, even more than I was ever able to tell my parents, so I know that I can trust you won't mention this to anyone…," she trailed off, holding her breath for his confirmation.

Jameason took a hand from the wheel and placed it over his heart in an attempt to look mortally wounded. "Oh, I think my heart will recover sometime this week. When have I ever told anyone anything regarding you that they did not need to know?" he pursed his lips and looked over his glasses at her.

That stern look melted the last of her resistance, and she shook her head.

"Never, sir, not once. I'm really alright, I just feel a little uneasy and I cannot really explain why," sighed Alexandria. "It's just the last two days, a growing sense of disquiet that has made me a little jumpy and sad. That sounds peculiar, doesn't it?" asked Alexandria, chuckling nervously as she ran her hand through her long hair.

Once again, Jameason glanced over his glasses at her and slowly shook his head. "Nothing you notice is ever odd or out of place, Alexandria. You know that. You learned early to trust your instincts enough to know that your body sends you signals forewarning of events to come. Though you've had a long period without incident, you told me that the mysterious figure who visited you so long ago promised that your abilities could return one day. I suggest that we watch carefully, and prepare for whatever the days ahead shall bring."

"Of course," said Jameason after a brief pause, "it could be that you're just nervous about the inevitable hazing your brothers are surely planning to dole out, or enduring yet another round of your mother's incessant matchmaking."

Alexandria and Jameason looked at one another and then burst out laughing simultaneously. Gracious, her mother's matchmaking, she thought. Now that was enough to have the stoutest warrior quaking in his boots,fr looking for any means of escape. It felt so good to let the tension ease away, and Alexandria was content to leave the worry behind along with the kilometers they were traversing.

The house was ablaze in lights and Alexandria could see at least three Christmas trees twinkling from various windows as the car made its way up the pebbled drive. Candles flickered in all of the front-facing windows, and an oversized wreath of fresh cut evergreens hung on the Manor House's large, oak door.

"Home, sweet, home," she thought to herself.

Though she was pursing her life in New York, if the truth were told, she had yet to make any real connections to the place. She had a very comfortable routine established, and the apartment that her parents had helped her purchase on the Upper East Side was not large, but comfortable and safe. She enjoyed walks in the park and weekends spent perusing the stacks at the public library. But try as they might, her colleagues had yet to pull her into their social goings on, as Alexandria still felt far more comfortable in the company of Jane Austin or Charles Dickens than a rowdy group at a night club or bar.

"You're old before your time, girl," Suzi often teased her.

Suzi was a receptionist in the offices where Alexandria and six other interpreters worked. She was a sparky, giddy lady with spiky red hair who kept them all abreast of the latest office gossip, whether it was true or not. Alexandria had at first tried to refute the observation, but finally found it easier to agree and play the part to staunch any unnecessary time arguing with Suzi over the finer points of her not so outgoing personality. Sometimes it's just easier to give them what they want, she often thought to herself.

Alexandria climbed out of the car and stretched her hands high above her head, rolling her head and shoulders as she tried to work out the kinks. She walked to the back of the car, and began helping Jameason with her luggage. She had packed too much as usual, four large checked bags and two carry-ons.

"What the heck did you bring home with you, half of your flat, Alex?" shouted Wallace from the top step.

"Right on cue," mused Alexandria, aloud to herself. Before she could stifle her smile, she was swept up into an all consuming bear hug. She squealed with delight and held on for dear life.

"Put me down, Wallace!" she implored, but her attempt at earnestness was stifled by the fact that they were both giggling. As soon as her feet had brushed the ground she was soundly handed off to Conner, who had come out right behind Wallace, and he happily swept her up as well, and hugged her warmly.

"Hi, sweetie, how are you?" asked Conner.

"Good, and you?" she smiled up at her brothers. She was always in awe of how tall and handsome they both were. Wallace, dark haired and hazel eyed, and Conner, fair haired like herself with sparkling blue eyes. No wonder ladies were always trying to get them to glance their way.

"Oh, you know, tired after a long flight, but happy to be back," confirmed Conner. He had recently been to Washington, D.C. to share some of his archeological finds with a rather large symposium and had just arrived back across the pond as well.

She stepped forward and hugged them both again, then soundly slapped their arms. "Come on, we can't leave Jameason to get all of these bags by himself," she said, turning back towards the car.

"Bossy as ever," smirked Wallace, but he was smiling as he began to banter with Conner over who would carry the heaviest bag in.

Alexandria chuckled to Jameason, who stood arching an eyebrow at the three. "Hopeless," he sighed, "I tried, I really did, but…, absolutely hopeless!"

Coming inside the Manor's immense foyer, Alexandria paused and breathed in the smells of Christmas at home. Her mother had every available surface richly decorated. The entire entryway was decked out in fresh evergreens, mistletoe and several small Christmas trees were flanking each side of the grand staircase that led to the two stories above. Alex smiled and turned to her brothers as they stepped inside behind her.

"How many this year?" she mused, biting her lower lip to keep from giggling aloud.

Wallace just shook his head, "I think I stopped counting at around thirty trees this morning."

"Yeah," sighed Conner, "nothing like an understated Christmas back home, huh?"

They all started laughing at once, just as their parents walked in, happy to welcome Alexandria back home again. As they hugged and chatted, the family made their way to a large sitting room that served more as a den, and was their traditional gathering spot. An enormous fireplace which anchored one wall was ablaze, its mantle layered thick and deep with candid shots of the family through the years.

Large couches and overstuffed chairs were arranged for conversation and gathering throughout the space. Several large rugs made the hardwoods more comfortable to walk on, and her father had placed quite a few bookcases filled to the brim around the walls as well. Even though the Manor boasted an impressive two story library, Lord Errol felt it important to keep literature close at hand wherever he relaxed, so books were an integral part of each gathering room's décor. The room's ceiling soared over thirty feet in height, yet it felt warm and cozy to those lounging. They spent the next hour catching up with one another, and Alexandria felt herself relax in the warmth and safety of her caring family.

Jameason came to the doorway and called them all to dinner, and they rose to walk to the spacious dining room still talking as they made their way down the hallway. Lady Juliana and Lord Errol walked on either side of Alexandria, and her mother gently stroked her back, while Alex described a new neighbor in her apartment building who played music too loudly often late into the night. Wallace looked back over his shoulder and told her to play her own music and drown out the pesky neighbor's, but

Alex and their parents all pursed their lips at Wallace and shook their heads in admonishment.

As soon they were settled, Lord Errol asked one and all to pause as they bowed their heads and joined hands to say grace together. Once the meal and fellowship were blessed, Jameason came and took his seat at the table, passing platters of food around so that each person could take what they wanted. It was how they had always dined when they were alone as a family, and Alexandria loved the lack of formality they enjoyed in one another's company.

She remembered once, when she was eleven, her Uncle Benedict dropping by unannounced during the dinner hour and asking why Jameason was sitting with them at the table. Her father had quickly subdued his impertinence, when he told his youngest brother that Jameason was at their table far more than most family members, and he was just as much a part of their set of loved ones as was her Uncle Benedict. Her uncle had humbly apologized and then asked if he, too, could join them.

Their conversations continued to flow throughout the shared meal, and Alex smiled over her brothers' and Jameason's topic of choice. Though they all knew it to be mischievous, both Wallace and Conner sought to brush up on the local goings-on with Jameason whenever they came home to Oxford. Lady Juliana caught Alex's eye, and the two shook their heads at one another. Alex felt herself chuckle over her brothers' need to stay tapped into what was truly none of their concern.

After dinner, Alexandria made her way to her bedroom fully intending to curl up with a book and one of her family's Labrador retrievers. Most likely Dudley, as he seemed to be attached to her more than anyone else when he had his pick of the entire Groaban clan. She knew the following day would be a fun-filled one, with lots of family coming for Christmas dinner and the exchange of gifts. So, Alex hoped to get a little rest before the crush descended.

She had just come from a long soak in her bathtub, deciding the bath would help her more than a shower would, when there was a knock at her door and her mother peeked her head in.

"Mind if I come in, sweetheart?" she asked, smiling.

"No, of course not Mother, what's up?" Lady Juliana walked over to Alexandria and gazed lovingly at the youngest of her children. She reached over and tucked a strand of wayward hair behind Alex's ear, something she had done a thousand times before.

"I just wanted to check in on you and make sure that you're all settled. Did you remember to bring everything you needed, or did you forget anything darling?"

Alexandria loved how thoughtful her mother was, but it had ingrained in her a fastidious need to always make a list for every event, trip, or occasion and to check it at least four or five times. She rarely forget anything, but she knew her mother liked to fuss over her, so she answered that she might have forgotten an extra pair of tights for the Boxing Day ball to be held in two days at Lord Lenley's. An annual tradition, it was the event of the season that her family never missed if they were in country.

"Well, that's no worry; I'm sure there are several pair still in your wardrobe, so you should be fine. Did you bring one or two gowns?" her mother asked.

"Oh, two of course. I wanted to have a backup in case something happened to the first, or if I had a change of heart about which one I wanted to wear," replied Alexandria.

"Sounds as though you're prepared. Oh, it's so good to have you home, Alex," her mother sighed, and pulled her into a warm embrace. "I know you're a grown lady now, but you'll always be my baby. You know, don't you?" Lady Juliana smiled, as she asked her question.

"I know, Mother. And trust me, as tired as I am right now, I'd be happy to be tucked in for a long winter's nap," laughed Alex.

"Quite right, my dear. Well said. You and Dudley get into bed, and I'll leave you two to dream of sugarplums and brightly colored packages. How about that?" she laughed at her own words.

Dudley, hearing his name, jumped on the bed and began to beat out a steady rhythm with his tail welcoming Alexandria under the sheets. She hugged her mother goodnight once more and then climbed atop the bed. She looked over at the happy, yellow lab who was intently staring at her.

"You know, Dudley, I think we'll skip the book tonight. I really don't feel up to reading, how about I just tell you a story?"

This was a habit that Alexandria still held onto from her childhood. She would pick an object or random thought and then build a whole story for it, and tell the tale to a family pet or just to herself. For Alex, it was another way to deal with the visions that had so invaded her mind as a child. By telling the tale herself, she felt in control. And that had, at times, seemed her only lifeline.

Dudley thumped his tail once and leaned his head to the side, as if answering her question.

"Story it is then," she confirmed.

She settled herself beneath the covers and began to slowly stroke his coat, unwinding and letting her mind wander. All she could think of was the incredible amount of Christmas trees in their home that season, so she began with a tale of a little tree who longed to be brought indoors for the festivities. He had to wait for many a season until he was mature and robust. Only to find that when he was large enough to be a Christmas tree, he preferred to stay outdoors where he was a part of the landscape and a home for many animals.

Dudley seemed content too, and he laid his head near her and slowly closed his eyes. Alex could feel herself fading, but she closed her story before slipping off to sleep.

"The tree finally learned, Dudley," she yawned, "that sometimes it is better to choose to be who you really are, not who you think others expect you to be." And with that last thought, Alexandria fell into a sound slumber.

3

Christmas morning had dawned with new fallen snow and the promise of more to come throughout the day. Alex, her parents, brothers, and Jameason gathered to open stockings after a filling breakfast, and laughed at the witty or funny gifts that they found within. They always went for clever ways to rib each other, even on Christmas morning. The morning of the holiday was always reserved for her nuclear family and Jameason, and Alex appreciated the special time they all shared with one another.

As her grandparents had already passed away, they were usually joined by two aunts, three uncles, and six or seven cousins who arrived in the late afternoon, and regularly stayed through dinner. Alexandria helped to greet and welcome each one for the festivities. Food was plentiful and the fellowship joyous. Alex thought several times to herself throughout the gathering that Christmas was the one day of the year when time seemed suspended and everyone seemed to crave peace and happiness. If just for the one day.

The extended Groaban family watched the Queen's annual Christmas address together, exchanged gifts afterwards, and then convened in the formal dining room for Christmas dinner. Roasted turkey and goose, smoked salmon, green beans, roasted parsnips, Brussels sprouts, cranberry sauce, chipolatas, bread sauce, roasted nuts, and pudding and cake for desert were served to one and all. Alexandria marveled that she could still fit into her clothes after consuming as much as she had. But then she had always had a ravenous appetite, and could easily eat more than her brothers at any meal they shared.

After dinner, Alex and Conner volunteered to walk the three labs out back. They each stepped into a pair of tall wellies, which could always be found by the mudroom door, and slipped jackets and scarves on. As soon as the door was open, the dogs bolted into the white landscape.

"I think we're going to have a heck of a time getting them back inside," chuckled Conner.

"Yeah, I think you could say that," agreed Alexandria. "Don't worry though, they just need a chance to run and let off steam. They haven't had their supper yet, so they'll come back. So tell me, how is the dig going?" she asked.

Conner told her of the most recent finds at the archeological dig he was leading near Brading, on the Isle of Wight. He and his team were uncovering an ancient Roman structure complete with detailed mosaics, and artifacts from Viking conquerors who set foot on the island long, long ago. It was grueling work, but he felt such a sense of fulfillment and accomplishment when he was painstakingly recovering history.

Alex was looking out at the romping dogs, listening to her brother, when Conner's mobile began to ring.

"Sorry, Alex, gotta take this," he said apologetically, as he turned and walked back towards the house.

She returned to watching them play, as she continued to meander along where she knew a pathway lay hidden under the snow. Alex was letting her mind wander when she heard a strange sound coming from the left edge of the garden path before her. It did not sound like the trees creaking from the weight of too much snow, but rather a chittering sound that was not like any animal she had ever heard before.

Normally, Alexandria was curious about and unafraid of animals, but something about this sound called to an instinctual fear that ran deep within her and made all of the hair on her arms stand on end. Something was very wrong, and she felt the alarm all the way to her core.

She refused to take her eyes off of the area before her, but she began to back slowly towards the house. Before she could call out to the Labradors, they seemed to sense the danger as well and were rapidly making their way back over to her. The sound began to increase in volume and Alex was moments from calling out, when the dogs reached her side and began to bark in unison at the origin of the noise.

Alex was more afraid that they would be hurt defending her, so she softly called them to follow her as she continued to back towards the door. Just as she thought she would suffer the same fate as the old man in The Tell-Tale Heart, the sound suddenly ended. She heard the snow crunching behind her and dared a quick peek over her shoulder, only to find Conner coming back to her side.

"What's got them so wound up?" asked her brother.

"I don't know, Conner, but we're going inside, right now," Alex insisted.

One look at his sister's face and Conner knew not to question her further. Something had left her terrified, but she had her eyes trained on the same spot as the dogs and refused to look away. He saw that she backed towards the house, so he put his hand on her arm and helped guide her safely to the door, so that she would not trip. He walked her up the steps, then opened the door, leading her to the security and warmth inside.

Alexandria made sure that all three dogs were inside with her, before she sank to the cushioned bench underneath the mudroom's large window, and drew a shaky breath into her lungs. All three were crowded around her and whimpering as if to tell her that they, too, had been frightened by whatever was making the sound.

"Good boys," praised Alex, as she soundly patted each head turned towards her face.

Finally, she lifted her eyes to Conner who had said nothing, but was watching her intently.

"I'm glad you came back when you did, Conner. I don't know what spooked us, but I'd rather not go back out tonight," she unsteadily voiced her request.

Conner stepped forward between the labs and knelt on one knee in front of his sister. He cupped her face with one hand and stared at her, concern etched across his brow.

"Are you alright, Alex? I haven't seen this look on your face in a long time, and I'm worried about you. What did you see?" he questioned, as his eyes searched hers.

Alexandria shook her head. "I didn't see anything, but I heard a sound that was not one I could place, and it scared the living daylights out of me. It sounded like a high pitched, garbled babbling that became increasingly louder. I didn't feel like I could turn my back on it, whatever it was. Thank goodness, you and the labs were there!" she breathed. "I'm okay, I just want to go back to the sitting room and be with everybody."

"Well, I can't imagine what would make that sound, especially on such a cold night, but I want you inside with us, too. Safety in numbers, right?" he asked, as he dropped his hand and patted her knee.

"Let's give these guys some much deserved food, and then catch up with the family. Tomorrow morning, Wallace and I will go out and take a look around; see if we can't spot some tracks or some evidence that points to what made the noise all of you heard. How's that sound for a plan?"

He was reassuring her and giving her a methodical and logical course to follow. How thankful she was for Conner, protecting her and not making her feel foolish.

"Sounds like a plan," she agreed.

Conner stayed by her side as they fed and provided fresh water for each of the dogs. When it looked as if they were happily occupied with their fare, he took her hand in his and led her to the large sitting room. Silently, he guided her over to a sofa so that they could sit together. Wallace arched an eyebrow at the two, taking note of Conner's protective stance immediately. Alex noticed Conner slightly shake his head in Wallace's direction, as if to tell him not to initiate a discussion at the present in front of so many other family members. It was a familiar movement she had witnessed her brothers make more times than she could count.

Alex sighed and looked out before her at the various loved ones gathered there that night. She knew that her unusual childhood was an unspoken thing amongst her extended family. They were all so focused on the present, that it was a welcome respite from the strange looks many of them had leveled at her when she was so very young. Now, they were all content to see her living the life they expected from someone her age.

She sat back against the sofa's soft cushions, and crossed her legs at her ankles. Alex watched as Conner did the same and she looked from his outstretched legs to hers, finding a small smile present itself despite the fear that was still surging through her body. Though she had always thought of herself as tall, when she was around the men in her family, she was anything but. Alex stood at the height of their shoulders, and she was constantly having to crane her head back to look them in the eye, even her father and Jameason.

Conner looked down at Alex and watched her for a moment, until she turned her gaze back to his. He winked at her and squeezed her fingers. She smiled tenderly in return, silently thanking him for being by her side when she needed him most, as he and Wallace had always done through the years. Alex's eyes then turned back to Wallace, and she found that he still observed the two of them. He nodded in her direction, and she sent him a small smile in return to reassure him she was alright.

The rest of the evening was uneventful, and when it came time to turn in, Alexandria invited all three Labradors to sleep with her. She did not have to ask twice, as they clambered up the stairs ahead of her. She quickly showered, and found Dudley laying on the tiles when she opened the curtain to reach for a towel. His tail thumped a steady beat and his eyes stayed on her face.

"I love you, old boy. You know that, don't you?" she asked. His tongue rolled out of the side of his mouth, giving her a grin as her answer.

Dutch and Buddy were lying on the bedroom floor when she came out of the bathroom, and both had taken positions watching the closed

34

door which lead out to the hallway. An image of the lions guarding the public library's entrance in New York came to her mind. She could not explain how she knew, but without a doubt she felt certain that they, too, were still thinking of whatever had made that sound, and were afraid that it might return.

Alexandria climbed into bed and called all three up onto the mattress with her. Dutch and Buddy thumped their tails, but chose to remain where they were, acting as sentinels for the night. Dudley bounded atop the bed with her and laid his head on the pillow next to hers. She chose to leave her bedside lamp on low, and snuggled deep in the warm bedding.

"Thank you guys, for staying," she told the labs. "Keep me safe." And with that last plea, Alex allowed herself to sleep, though it was fitful at best.

4

Alexandria stood in front of her floor length mirror, making sure that everything was in place. Her long, sapphire gown suited her eyes perfectly, and made her pale skin stand out. She had chosen to leave her hair down, but curled it so that it cascaded down her shoulders and back. Earlier in the afternoon she had borrowed her mother's sapphire earrings, necklace and bracelet set, and if she had to admit it, she thought she might actually turn a few heads at the ball.

Thankfully, the morning had been uneventful. She rose early, but found that Wallace and Conner were already up and walking the gardens at the back of the house, looking for tracks or any sign of animal disturbance. Nothing could be found. Both of her brothers agreed that she and the labs had heard something, but neither had the faintest idea what it was or what had caused it.

As they had done when she was younger, they filled her day with activity without leaving her alone for too long. They all took an invigorating horseback ride after breakfast, walked and talked about their busy lives, played cards with their father, and napped on the couches in the sitting room. And if it had not been for the near hour long nap, Alexandria doubted she would have had the energy to go the ball that evening.

"Hey, squirt, you coming?" Wallace questioned her loudly from the hallway.

She laughed and opened the door. "Well, when you put it so nicely, how can I refuse?" She took a moment to acknowledge that no matter what she wore, she would have a hard time ever coming close to how attractive her brothers were, especially when they were in a tuxedo.

"How have you managed to stay single for so long?" asked Alexandria, bewildered by Wallace's perpetual bachelor status.

"I could ask you the same thing," he frowned down at her.

"What?" asked Alex, looking worryingly down at her gown.

"Hell! Conner and I are gonna have to beat 'em off with a stick tonight! And here I was planning on having a nice, boring evening, just smiling and making Mother proud," he grumbled. They both laughed at that thought.

"The only way we're going to make her proud, is if we all end up married this year," chuckled Alex.

Wallace visibly shuddered. "Ugh, let's get going. The sooner we're there, the sooner we're home."

Jameason drove Alexandria's parents in their Jaguar, ahead of the Range Rover that she and her brothers traveled in. The men were talking in the front seat about some of the latest gossip they had picked up from Jameason earlier in the evening, and Alex was letting her mind wonder in the backseat. Try as she might, she could not stop thinking about the sound that she had heard in the garden the night before.

It was threatening and imposing, as if trying to exert a feeling of imminent danger. Initially, it had rooted her to the spot, but surprisingly she broke the trance and willed herself to start moving. She was thankful that her legs had obeyed her command to move away.

The Rover pulled up in front of Lenley Hall, and a footman stepped forward to open Alexandria's door, while her brothers climbed out. The footman stood staring at Alexandria, until Wallace walked up behind him and tapped him on the shoulder.

"Keys are still in the ignition," said Wallace, in a steady but firm voice.

The footman, who looked to be Alex's age, recovered and turned towards her brothers. He paled a bit further, looking up at the two, but remembered himself and handed Wallace the ticket he would need to recall the vehicle later in the evening. As the footman drove the Rover away, Alex narrowed her eyes at her two brothers and swatted Wallace's arm.

"Be nice, you scared him," she chastised.

"If he hadn't, I would have," said Conner.

"Damn right," agreed Wallace.

Before she could scold them further, her parents joined them to enter together. Her father reached forward and straightened Alexandria's wrap, then kissed her forehead.

"You look lovely, my dear. Ready to go in?" his eyes crinkled as he smiled down at her.

"As I'll ever be, Father. We don't have to stay too long, do we?" asked Alex, hoping this would pave the way for an early exit if she so desired one.

"Oh, no you don't," scolded her mother. "The three of you will find this evening a refreshing distraction. And besides, I understand Henry is back from university and I know he would love a few dances with you."

Henry. The one young suitor that neither Wallace nor Conner would ever help scare away, because they knew that there was no chance Alexandria would agree to anything serious with him. He was one year older than Alexandria, and as the son of one her mother's dearest friends, Lady Juliana was sure they were a match made in Heaven. Alexandria was sure that she would never last more than a day with Henry. He was sweet, but so boring that she found watching peeling paint a more interesting focus for her attention.

"Yeah, let's go see Henry," smirked Wallace.

She just rolled her eyes at him and turned towards the stairs that led to the estate's entrance. Alexandria's parents led the way, and she followed behind flanked by Wallace and Conner. As they were announced, several family friends began to come forward and greet them. Everyone seemed happy to welcome her parents, and Alexandria looked on with pride. Her parents were such good, kind people, and she was glad to see them warmly received.

When they all emerged into the main ballroom, Alexandria felt self-conscious, but hopeful that the night would move quickly and not drag by. It was a worry she need not have had, because young gentlemen were soon pressing to fill her dance card for the evening. She allowed several to secure a dance, but was successful at keeping her card from filling. Unfortunately, Henry also found her and asked for three dances, but she negotiated it down to two.

As the night wore on, so did her tired feet. She was happy to see her brothers dancing with several young ladies. It was obvious that all of them hoped to catch her brothers' attention, but she knew that it would take more than just a pretty face to turn their heads. Wallace and Conner wanted the same thing she did: a marriage like their parents had. One built on mutual friendship, love and passion, which could see two people through a lifetime together. And until they each found someone they truly loved and respected, none of them were willing to flippantly enter into a relationship. She knew that both her brothers had dated different young ladies through their years at school and university, but none had really been 'the one'.

After one particularly long turn around the ballroom, Alex found herself with a nice gap in her card. She made her way out onto one of the large balconies to take in a bit of fresh air. As she stepped into the clean, crisp air, she saw several couples huddled together in different places along the balcony, hoping for a moment of privacy both from the crush and probably from their parents. Such events were family affairs, but most of the young guests would rather be with their peers at clubs, Alex thought to herself.

Alexandria smiled and turned her attention towards the well lit grounds below, watching people mingle in the paths where snow had been cleared earlier in the day. Hiding behind a hedge, she mused, really did afford one privacy. The thought made her chuckle to herself, and she shook her head. She turned, leaning her back against the railing, and thankfully so, because she saw Henry inside obviously looking around hoping to spot her.

She slowly inched along the perimeter of the balcony until she came to a door leading to another room, and made a hasty exit before he saw her. She walked out of the parlor she found herself in, and entered a hall.

Alex was unsure where she should head next, but she was stopped by a young lady, working as a server for the evening, calling out her name at the end of the hall. Alex approached her, answering that she was indeed Alexandria.

"Thank you, Miss. You have a call. I was told to find you and tell you that you can take it in the office two doors down on the left." Alex responded with her thanks and entered the office.

She had been in the room before, on a tour of the house when she was a very young girl. She remembered the heavy, antique mahogany desk with its intricate carvings of angels along each leg flanked by a wall of bookcases that went from the floor to the ceiling. She saw the phone sitting on Lord Lenley's desk and made her way over to it. As she picked up the receiver, she heard the lock of the door click into place behind her, and cold, unadulterated panic flooded her system.

Alexandria did not dare turn around; hoping that the element of surprise could be on her side, rather than on the side of whomever had just sealed them inside the room. She pretended to answer the call, while she reached forward with her other hand to pick up the large mail opener which lay on the desk's leather pad. Alex could feel her breathing and heart rate accelerate, but she tried desperately to sound normal when she spoke into the phone.

The phone line was dead. She knew that the longer she delayed, the closer the unknown and silent person behind her would come. Her brothers had always told her to never be taken or go down without trying to defend herself, and Alex knew she had little time and no real choice if she wanted to get away.

"Now or never," she thought, and she twirled with the opener pointed away to protect herself.

The man had gotten closer than she realized, because when she spun he clasped a strong hand down on her right forearm and forced the opener out of her hand quickly. Though disarmed, Alexandria was not going anywhere without a fight. She brought her left hand down and scored his face with her nails, as she tried to bring her knee up to his groin at the same time. He grabbed her left arm as well, and angled his right leg to block her attack.

Using his leg, he swept her feet out from under her, and pushed forcefully against her arms as he released her, using the momentum to propel her to the floor. She fell hard against the wood planks, and felt the wind rush out of her lungs. Alex began to struggle up on her elbows when he pounced. He was astride her so quickly that she fell back and hit her head once more on the floor. Her eyes clouded with tears, but she willed herself to breathe and see. She knew she could not afford to lose consciousness now.

She got a clear look at his face then. He was beautiful in form, with wavy dark hair that touched his collar, but his eyes were devoid of any compassion, hard and unyielding. The evil she sensed within him came off in waves that felt suffocating to her. He had her legs and arms pinned, but seemed in no hurry now to do anything more. Alex began to fight again, but he pressed on her limbs and she was completely immobile, so strong was he. His eyes roamed over her face and searched her eyes.

He began to chuckle, and it was a deep, menacing sound that set her teeth on edge.

"Well, well, Arianna. Fighting like a girl! A human girl no less. I can't believe that you would stoop to such antics," he said in an understated and lethal tone.

Arianna? Alexandria looked desperately into her attacker's face. She shook her head ever so slightly, praying he would realize his error.

"No, you've made a mistake. My name is not Arianna, it's Alexandria. I don't know who you are, but you've got the wrong person. Please, let me go," she breathed out.

"Let you go?" he hooted incredulously. "I think not! I've been looking for you for a long, long time. I knew that you weren't dead. There was no way you were defeated, much less dead. No, you're coming with me, and you can be damn sure I will be well rewarded when I produce your pretty face to the council."

He quickly shifted her arms above her head, pulling them painfully together and locked them in a vise-like grip with his left hand. She tried desperately then to buck him off and kick her legs, anything to remove his weight. He was so strong, that she doubled her efforts. But she was rewarded with a sound slap from his right hand, and then his hand moved to squeeze her cheeks, forcing her eyes to look at his.

"I don't know what you're playing at, but this is fun! Keep it up. We don't have to go anywhere just yet, we could have a bit of fun," he whispered, and lowered his face so that his lips hovered just above hers.

Bile rose up in her mouth as she realized what he was threatening to do to her, and she took in a deep breath preparing to scream to anyone within the sound of her voice. He sensed her intent and moved his hand from her cheeks to her throat and clamped down hard. He squeezed and lifted her head up long enough to slam it back down on the hardwood. He repeated this once more, and then moved in such a swift and unnatural way, that he had them both on their feet with her neck still in his hand. Alex felt him lift her slightly, and she registered that her toes were just barely touching the floor.

Alexandria was sure that he could snap her neck if he wanted to, and she knew that she did not have the physical strength to remove his hand. She also doubted now that her voice could produce a scream, and what if her brothers or someone else did hear her? She refused to let this monster hurt anyone else due to a case of mistaken identity and misplaced rage. There was only one thing that came to her mind, one word that suddenly became a litany, a prayer, a plea – *"Ganymede!"*

Alex began to scream his name out in her mind, knowing that he could hear her that way just as well as if she had spoken it aloud. Her assailant was squeezing her throat so hard that she was beginning to lose focus on his face, but she heard his sharp intake of breath, and felt a tremor begin in his arm.

"No," he hissed, and turned Alexandria, so that she was positioned between himself and Ganymede.

He was there in the room with them, and he was real.

Alexandria was so happy to see him, that new tears formed in her eyes, but they were tears of gratitude. She could feel the man behind her shifting nervously and inching them closer to the window. His intent was clear; he hoped to make a dash for it. Whether he intended to take her along with him remained to be seen.

Ganymede kept his eyes locked on the man's face, never once looking into her eyes.

"You cannot win, Bertrand. What you have done here will not be allowed, and will not go unpunished. Release her." His words sounded calm and measured, but they reverberated around the room with such force that several crystal frames and vases shook. His words were a command that could not be denied, and Bertrand quaked at the authority Ganymede wielded like a sword.

In a desperate attempt to save himself, Bertrand threw Alexandria across the room into a table as if she were a ragdoll, knocking it over as she and the table hit the ground. The table splintered, and she was sure she had broken something within herself too. A blinding light filled the room, and she heard a strangled scream that ended in a gurgling crunch. She heard the window breaking, and glass flying outwards into the shrubbery.

Ganymede was at her side then, holding his hand under her head. He pulled it back for a moment and observed the blood that thickly covered his fingers. Alexandria smiled up at his face, perfect and young, just as it had been so many years ago.

"You came," she squeaked, unable to get anything more from her throat.

A sad, slow smile crossed his lips.

"Yes, I am here, dear one. I am so very sorry that I was not here sooner." He shook his head with regret as he looked down at her. His eyes quickly swept over her body, taking stock of all her injuries. Tears welled up in her eyes once more and she began to feel cold all over.

"Hush, now," he crooned. "All will be well again. Close your eyes and let me fix this, Alexandria. All will be well," he whispered again, as he leaned forward and placed his forehead against hers.

What she felt was unlike any sensation she had ever experienced before. It felt as though warm, melted gold had been poured into her head, and it slowly swept down throughout her body. She felt her skull fuse back together, ribs meet back up in her chest, and her leg, which she had not noticed sticking out at an odd angle, set itself. Though this should have caused her more pain, she only felt warmth. She lifted her left hand up to his shoulder and patted him, to let him know she was experiencing the healing he was bestowing on her.

He stayed like that, forehead to forehead for another minute as if in prayer, then he pulled his head back and looked into her eyes. A warm smile graced his lips, and he brushed her hair out of her face.

"Thank you. Oh, thank you so much," whispered Alexandria, as fresh tears came unbidden to her eyes once again.

"Shhh, do not cry, sweet child," he whispered back, as he began to rock her in his arms. "I am just sorry that I was not aware of his presence sooner. This should never have happened. Never."

"Who was he, and why did he call me Arianna? I don't understand any of this," she hiccuped. She was trying to retain what shredded bit of composure she had left, but it was quite an internal battle. She had never had anyone lay hands on her before, and certainly not one so determined to hurt her so badly.

Alex and Ganymede could hear voices in the hallway, getting closer and closer. It was her brothers looking for her. "Dear Lord," she thought, "what do I tell them? How do I explain this?" She looked into Ganymede's beautiful, clear blue eyes, hoping for answers and reassurance.

"No, there is no need to speak of this now. You are not finished healing, so close your eyes and rest, dear one." She was so afraid that he would bring on sleep as he did that night so long ago in Egypt, that she spoke urgently.

"No, please not yet. Please, I need to know how he found me and what just happened. Please, Ganymede, I don't want to sleep," she pleaded. She could hear someone working on the lock. It would not be long now, before her brothers gained entry.

"Ganymede, please," she breathed out, and shook from her shock and still flowing tears.

He placed a finger over her lips. "I promise Alexandria, you will have answers, but you must sleep now." His last word resonated within and she could feel her eyes growing heavy.

"No," she whimpered, "no, I don't understand."

Her tears were almost Ganymede's undoing, but he held fast and made sure that she succumbed to sleep before releasing her. He knew that the door was almost open, but he lingered for a last few seconds to look down at her. His eyes flashed with anger over what had happened there, and he turned from Alexandria. Time had run out for him, but it was all just beginning for her.

"I'll not leave you," he quietly vowed, and with that he vanished from the room.

Time seemed to stand still for Wallace and Conner. As soon as they managed to get the door open, they could not process what their eyes took in. Broken furniture was strewn about the room and Alexandria lay in the middle of what used to be a small side table. She was completely motionless, and it was obvious that she had battled for her life in the small confines of the office. Both brothers rushed forward and fell to their knees on either side of her, unsure if it was wise to move her, or foolish to leave her lying on the floor for another moment, fearing that she needed immediate care.

Their eyes locked, as they reached a silent agreement. They both lifted her and began to carry her down the back hallway which led out to the area where all of the guests' cars were parked until they were recalled. They shifted her into Wallace's arms, so that Conner could open doors and make sure the halls were clear of people who would love to grab on to anything they thought could be used as a tasty bit of gossip.

Conner had asked the servant who helped them enter the office to summon Lord Lenley and their parents as well, and then to come back and stand guard at the room's entrance. Neither brother wanted their parents to see the room, and they knew that Alexandria would not want the other guests to see her in her current state. There would be too many questions.

"What has happened?" Lord Lenley questioned the brothers, as he caught up with them. "Is she alright?"

"No, she's not alright," seethed Wallace, through clenched teeth.

"Did she faint?" he pressed.

"No, she was attacked, Lord Lenley," responded Conner, "in your office. We asked a servant to let us in once we realized she was trapped inside. And we've asked that same person to stand outside the door, keeping people away until we sort this out, once she finds our parents."

"Dear God! I'll keep the room completely sealed. Do you want me to call a friend I have at MI-5? He'll handle this quietly, if that's what you want," suggested Lord Lenley. Both Wallace and Conner knew that would work in everyone's best interest, because none of them wanted the scandal.

"Yes, do that. Our parents are being discretely led this way. We'll take her to hospital and then call you from there. Make sure your friend goes over that room with a fine brush. I don't want one piece of evidence comprised." Conner's tone brokered no argument, and Lord Lenley quickly agreed.

"I pray that she's alright, boys," he said. Wallace gave him a tight nod, and they turned and continued on their way to the SUV.

5

Beeping. The slow steady rhythm of machines called to Alexandria, but coming to the world where they existed seemed so very hard. She was sure that she could make out her parents talking in hushed tones to other unfamiliar voices, maybe a doctor or a nurse, she just could not be sure. Then, she knew she heard Wallace arguing with someone that they were not doing enough to bring her around, while Conner tried to calm him down. How badly she wanted to reach out and tell him she was there and that Ganymede had already healed the worst of her injuries.

Ganymede. Even in this strange, disconnected state, she could see his face. It was the one image that rang strong and true. Those clear blue eyes, so perfect and so kind. What was happening? Ganymede had called the man Bertrand, but was he a man? There was something unnatural about the way he had lifted them both into a standing position, while still gripping her neck. His movements had been fluid and fast, but not quite right. Oh, she could not hold on to the thought. And Ganymede. How could she explain to her parents, to her brothers, to investigators? Surface, she willed herself. Surface and find the answers! But her mind met her with blackness again.

The beeping was finally becoming loud enough that she could hang onto it and not lose it. The fog that had kept her unconscious was receding and Alex slowly lifted her eyelids. They felt heavy and they tried to close on her several times before she could make them stay open. The room she found herself in was a little out of focus, so she squinted and continued opening and closing her eyes until she could really see her surroundings. She was most definitely in a hospital room, all sterile and white, she told herself.

A tower containing a monitor stood to the left side of her bed and another held a bag of liquid, its tubes snaking down into the back side of her left hand. She moved her head slowly, looking around, and beheld her parents. They were both asleep, and leaning into one another on a couch in the corner of the room by a large window. Soft light filtered in, giving her no indication of what time it might be.

Tentatively, she lifted her right hand to push her hair out of her eyes, and was surprised that such a slight motion could make her feel dizzy and winded. She pushed herself up just a little more in the bed, but that movement woke her parents. They were both on their feet then, and her mother was the first to reach her side.

"Oh sweetheart," she breathed. "Thank the good Lord!" Tears welled in her eyes, as she settled herself beside her daughter.

"No, Mother, don't cry. I'm okay. How long have I been asleep?" asked Alexandria, hoping her question would distract her mother from her sadness.

Her father reached forward and brushed her hair off of her forehead, while her mother placed Alex's right hand between her two palms and began to stroke her daughter. Alexandria knew that her mother and father needed to touch her to make sure she was still there with them. And the gentle gesture reassured her as well. It was her father who spoke and answered her question.

"You've been asleep since last night. It's almost four in the afternoon, so not quite twenty-four hours. Alexandria, we want to know what happened, but only when you're ready to tell us. We want you to know that we'll not rush you, darling." The anguish in his voice was her undoing, and tears began to run unchecked down her cheeks. Her parents cocooned her while she quietly let her grief run its course.

Alexandria knew that whatever had been within her and a part of her childhood - the strange occurrences, the differences that no one could account for, had finally caught up with her. She had been running away for so long, almost in a desperate flight to 'be normal', but she had always known that eventually she could not run anymore. And her time had most assuredly run out the previous night, she told herself.

"Shhh, baby," crooned her mother, "it's alright, everything's going to be alright." They stayed like that for a long while, the three of them just soaking up the comfort and love that was freely offered and so easily received.

Finally, her father broke through the quiet, saying, "I suppose I should let the doctors know that you're awake, Alex. I'll be right back." Her father walked slowly from the room, as if reluctant to let the two of them from his sight.

As he left the room, Alex squeezed her mother's hand. "I'm so sorry, Mother. I've no idea why this happened, but I'm just so sorry."

"No, you will not place the blame for this on yourself. I forbid it," her mother said, with steel in her voice. "Whoever did this to you is solely responsible, Alex, no one else. And we'll make sure the filth is caught and dealt with."

Alexandria had not seen Bertrand's demise, but from the furry in Ganymede's eyes and the sounds she heard in Lord Lenley's office, she was sure he had not only been killed, but wiped from existence. Alex doubted that anyone would ever see any piece of him again. But this was not something she ever intended to share with her mother. No matter how strong and supportive her parents were, she just did not know how to tell them about Ganymede. She really did not understand, herself.

"Where are Wallace and Conner?" asked Alex, realizing that neither was present.

"Oh, we sent them home a few hours ago to rest. Wallace was constantly creating a commotion with the doctors here, so we thought it best to make them leave for a bit. Hopefully, we'll be heading home soon, and you'll see them there," her mother answered, still gently stroking Alex's hand between hers.

The door to her room opened and her father re-entered followed by two doctors, one much older than the second. She drew a deep breath in. She knew the older doctor's face. She could not place where or when she had met him, but she knew him. Her mother mistook the breath for pain and worryingly looked at Alex.

"Well, well, she is indeed awake," said the senior doctor, looking intently at Alexandria. She wondered if he was looking for any sign of recognition.

"Alexandria, I am Dr. Holbrook and this is Dr. McLaren. We are in charge of your care while you're here. Your parents have been quite anxious for you to wake. Let's take a look, shall we?" he said in a friendly enough tone, but one that reeked of authority and brokered no argument.

Alexandria's parents moved back to make way for the two doctors. Dr. Holbrook led the examination, which was brief but thorough. He asked her to touch her fingers to her nose and follow his finger back and forth. He asked questions that showed she could recall long-term information. He then reached forward and felt along the back of her skull and pressed on her ribs gently.

Alexandria's eyes never left his and once he was finished he looked directly into her eyes. Why could she not remember how she knew this man, she asked herself. He smiled and stepped back to allow Dr. McLaren access to her leg, the one that Ganymede had set back in the office. Dr. Holbrook turned and began talking with her parents. He told them that if she continued to improve through the night he would release her in the morning, but he wanted her to rest one more evening under their observation.

"A sound knock on the head is nothing to play with. Lord Errol and Lady Juliana, would you please follow Dr. McLaren to his office? I would like for him to go over some possible complications of a head injury, which we would like you to help us watch for once she's released into your care. I don't foresee any problems, but I want to be prepared," Dr. Holbrook advised them.

He looked over the rim of his glasses at her parents when he said this, and they reluctantly agreed to leave her. "Don't worry, I'll wait here with Alexandria until you return. She won't be alone." This final reassurance settled the matter.

"We'll be right back, dear," said her mother, and they followed the young doctor out of the room.

He turned his eyes towards her and smiled again. Dr. Holbrook walked back over and sat down on the side of her bed, sighing.

"Well, well, Alex. What a pickle we're in now, huh, sweetie?" he chuckled.

Alexandria's mouth dropped open and then she snapped it closed, unsure what response to give. Was he talking about the obvious, or did he know what really happened in that room, she wondered to herself. How could he, she asked?

As if in answer to her silent question, he patted her leg. "It's alright, dear. I know all about it," he sighed again and shook his head. "I know about Ganymede, and I know about Bertrand. This was never supposed to happen, but now that it has, I think it's safe to say we have a lot to discuss." He angled his head at her silence, and waited for her to say something to him.

"Who are you? You're not really a doctor are you?" Alexandria grabbed the bed's control and used it to move herself into a sitting position. She did not know if she would need to be ready to make a run for it, but lying down did not seem like the best way to protect herself.

"Stop for just a moment, Alexandria, and feel. You know what I'm talking about. You can sense who is friend and who is foe. I mean you no harm." He now looked at her over the rim of his glasses, his bushy grey hair falling forward as he tilted his head towards her.

She breathed in slowly, staring directly into his eyes. She allowed the long hidden ribbon to slowly unfurl from her mind, and she felt it inching towards the doctor who was sitting still and patiently waiting on her. He seemed to anticipate what was coming and he exhaled just as her mind connected with his.

Alex saw scenes from his past, before his hair turned grey, laughing and running with another young man, as if in a race. She saw him tending to wounded soldiers on a battlefield that looked like World War I trenches, and then her vision skipped to him helping emaciated Jews leave a concentration camp. "Thank you, John," the man wheezed out between labored breaths. This man was good to his core. She had nothing to fear, and she withdrew her connection to him and once again looked up into his eyes.

She raised a shaky hand to her forehead and noticed that it was damp with sweat. "Good Lord, what is happening? I want answers and I want them now. You will start talking, and you will explain why I almost died last night!" She realized she had all but roared her last words as a command. "Please," she added a bit less loudly, deciding that being rude to the one person before her with answers probably was not the best approach to take.

"Yes, ma'am," he laughed, as his eyebrows darted up. "First, I want you to know that I have nothing to hide from you, and I will make sure that you get all of the answers you are looking for, whether you know the questions to ask right now or not. In time, you will have all the information you seek. I'm not going anywhere and I have every intention of making sure you are safe. In fact, your safety is our primary objective now."

Alexandria held up her hand, "Wait, you said, 'our' not 'my'. Who else is with you?"

"Oh, there are many who have a vested interest in your safety. Not one of them expected Bertrand to find you and come after you the way he did, but we cannot change what has happened," he said heavily.

"And now, whether for better or worse, you are on the edge of a great precipice, Alexandria. You say you want answers, and answers you shall have. But understand that by calling Ganymede and asking for these answers, you cannot go back to ignorant bliss."

"You will know who and what you are, but knowledge comes at a price. Not a price you cannot pay, but a price that may make demands on you. You may have to rise to the challenge of those demands. I cannot ask you if you are prepared for what lies ahead, because you have no frame of reference right now, but are you willing to concede that this knowledge may change the course your life has been on up until now?" he asked her gently.

Alexandria drew in a long, deep breath. All of her past questions, feelings of insecurity and bewilderment, and the sheer terror she felt at Bertrand's hands culminated in one clear thought, the only decision she thought she could make at the crossroads where she now stood.

"I understand things are about to change, John, but I don't think I can live like this anymore. I want to know who I am and what is happening." Alexandria was proud that her voice did not betray the fear that she really felt deep down inside. Yes, she admitted to herself, she was out of time and out of options. If information could help her protect herself and those she loved in the future, then it was answers she wanted.

"My brave, sweet girl," smiled John, "I am so proud of you. I know that you're scared to death, but bravery in the face of insurmountable odds is the mark of a truly courageous soul. And you will find that deep within you beats a heart that's true and gallant. All those faced with such choices as yours either decide to run and cower, or face it head on, and face it we shall together. You'll not be in this alone, Alexandria, that I swear to you," he promised, and Alexandria gave herself over to the trust that he was extending to her. Holding onto it, as if it were her new lifeline.

"What can you tell me right now? I have a feeling there is more for you to share than what one conversation can hold."

"Indeed, Alexandria. I can share some bits of information with you now, and the rest will come as you indicate you're ready to hear more," he said.

Alex began to shake her head, "No, don't patronize me, please. I don't want to be spoon-fed information; I want to understand and I want to know everything. Don't treat me like I'm a child who cannot handle what you have to tell me. If I could live through last night and all that happened around me when I was a child, I can hear the truth now. I'm twenty-one years old; I am an adult." The last thing Alex wanted now was to be patted on the head as if she were five.

Dr. Holbrook chuckled, "No, I don't suppose you want to be treated like a child. I'm not denying you what you need, Alexandria. But trust me, too much information will overwhelm you, possibly even frighten you, and that is what we don't want to do." He looked out of the window for a long moment, then turned back to her and gave her a quick nod as if he had just made a decision about something.

"Now, what I can tell you is this: Ganymede is indeed real. He has been by your side from the day you were born and he will be with you until your last day on this earth. He loves you and has only your best interests at heart. He will come to your aid whenever you call for him, but our goal is to get you to a point where you can take care of yourself, defend yourself and protect those you love, so that you won't have to rely on Ganymede to do that for you." He was looking at her face closely as if gauging her reaction to what he was saying so far.

"Is Ganymede an angel?" she asked. She was pretty sure she had worked this much out, unless of course he was some sort of alien. If that were true, she decided she might not want to know anymore after all.

"Yes," he smiled warmly, "and he is a very powerful angel at that. Ganymede was one of the first and he has been our Lord's companion and emissary for longer than either of us can imagine."

"Go, on, please," encouraged Alex.

He cleared his throat for a moment before he spoke again. "Bertrand is, or shall I say, was, the antithesis of Ganymede. He and his kind abhor all that is good about this world and the next. They do not want to see any of us dedicated to the side of *right* succeed in the work that we do. They're a constant hindrance and a constant danger," he said, his lips twisting sourly. "That's why we have to make sure you are prepared for his kind."

"Why single me out? What makes me different enough that they would even be aware of me?" asked Alex. This was what she had wanted to know for so long – why was she different than everyone else she knew.

"Yes, that gets to the heart of things, doesn't it? And that, my dear, is an answer that I hesitate to give you today," he said, holding up his hands to stop Alex, as she was already opening her mouth to interrupt him.

"You are different, Alexandria, more so than you can even imagine. You are a very unique young lady, even in our world. I want you to know that I am not trying to hedge your question, but that is the one question I cannot, or rather, should not answer, as it is not my story to tell, but yours and Ganymede's. He should be the one to explain."

"So I should summon him again, is that the way of it?" She knew she sounded exasperated, but honestly her nerves were stretched to the breaking point, and once she had made the decision to know the truth, by

goodness she wanted all of it and quickly. Enough with the constant
skirting of the truth.

"No, Alexandria, you should not call on Ganymede right now,
because your parents and someone called Jameason are on their way back
to us. There is an investigator coming in about thirty minutes to question
you, and unfortunately, your parents have also employed security who will
be arriving shortly and we'll have to deal with that."

"How do you know all of this? Are you sensing it somehow?"
asked Alexandria, astounded that he had rattled off such a detailed list of
who was coming and when.

"No, dear," he laughed, "I have been in and out of this room since
last night and I have overheard your parents' plans. I also happen to know
how long it takes to walk to Dr. McLaren's office from your room and I
think that they should be returning shortly. So as I said, more information
is coming, but first we need to get you out of here and deal with the
investigator's questions which may be a little tricky to get around."

Alexandria looked over at the window for just a moment. "Okay,
Ganymede, I know you can hear me," she thought. "I'll wait a little longer,
because I don't think my parents can handle this right now, but please stay
with me and promise me I'll understand soon."

She looked back over at Dr. Holbrook. "I'm not angry with you, I
just want to know," she sighed. "So how then do we talk to an
investigator? I don't think you want me telling him an angel came in and
saved me from an attacker with supernatural powers, do you?"

"Alexandria," he admonished, "this is nothing to joke about.
Indeed, you will omit any reference to Ganymede or Bertrand. You will tell
them that you received word that you had a call, entered Lord Lenley's
office and heard an assailant lock you in. You fought, but his face was

masked and you never actually saw him. Tell them that he called you Rebecca, and when he heard your brothers approaching, he threw you down onto the table and broke through the office's window so he could escape."

As John was giving her an acceptable accounting for the assault, Alexandria saw the attack flash before her eyes, and she closed them tightly hoping it would help her block out the graphic images. She could see Bertrand's face inching closer to hers as he whispered menacingly, *"We don't have to go anywhere just yet, we could have a bit of fun."*

"Alexandria, look at me," implored John. "You are safe now. I know these images are going to resurface for a while, but no one else is going to lay a finger on you. We have many in place now protecting you and your family. Try to concentrate on that feeling of safety, and perhaps it will help just a bit."

"Thank you," she replied, nodding her head slowly to reassure him that she would try. At that last comment, the door to her room opened and Jameason walked in carrying a small, soft cooler. He smiled warmly at his young charge, and came over to the side of her bed.

"Well, what's all this?" asked Dr. Holbrook, gesturing to the bag.

"Good evening, doctor," replied Jameason crisply. "This is a bit of soup and fresh baked bread for Alexandria. Would that be an acceptable dinner?" Always proper, mused Alex. She smiled up at Jameason. Lord, how she loved this man she thought to herself. He was like a grandparent to her and she was so happy to see him, safe and dapper.

"Oh, I would think soup would be just fine." He stood and looked down at Alex, back in charge of the room. "Start with the broth and if that stays down, you can try a bit of the bread, alright? I'll be back in a few hours to check on you for the night, Alexandria." He smiled at them both and then took his leave.

Jameason began setting the small hospital table for her supper and when he was finished, he helped her sit up a little more and placed a napkin in her lap. She ate while he distracted her with small talk about Dudley and the preparations for New Years' Day. About halfway through the meal her parents joined them and they all avoided the elephant in the room, so Alexandria could enjoy the food.

After dinner, just as Dr. Holbrook had predicted, two investigators came to ask Alexandria for her account of the previous night's attack. Harris Wilborough and Nigel Hughes, both of MI-5, had been called upon to handle the investigation in hopes that their expertise and discretion would help to solve the case quickly and quietly. Alex's family had already worked with a few close and powerful friends to make sure nothing about the story made it to the papers or the Internet.

Her parents and Jameason remained in the room during the interview, and Alex hated that they had to hear a description of someone hurting her, but she repeated the story that John had asked her to tell. It was really the only one she could tell. She focused on a small spot on the bed's blanket and told the story to that spot, so that she would not have to see the pain in their eyes. When the two were finished recording her statement, they asked her several questions, and she could easily tell they were trying to verify her story and look for holes. She held fast to her version and did not waver.

"Well, I can tell you that his prints are known to us," Agent Wilborough told her parents. "He has quite an extensive file with Interpol and our agency, as well. We can't give you false hope that he's still in the area. This one's quite good at slipping away quickly, but we hope that knowing he's looking for a Rebecca, who most likely matches your daughter's description in this area, will help us catch him when he resurfaces."

"If you will agree, we would like to place agents with you here and at your home until he's apprehended," asked agent Hughes. "Knowing his history for violence, we want to make sure that he doesn't come back to finish what he started, even though your daughter didn't see his face."

Alex thought that this was probably something they would normally just do, but out of deference to her parents, they were asking for permission. She silently prayed they would refuse. She did not know how she would meet with John and the others he spoke of, if she were being watched.

"No, thank you, gentlemen," her father said, shaking his head. "We've already employed security both at our home and here. If you like, you can come by the Manor to make sure they're properly set up, but I have hired a top firm's best men and I think we'll be well protected. What I would like, are frequent updates."

Alexandria could tell the two agents were not happy with her father's decision, but they agreed to stay in contact with him. They also pushed to come to the Manor that same night to inspect the net the security detail had established for the family.

Her father agreed and as they took their leave, Agent Wilborough paused in the doorway of the room and told Alex how sorry they were that she had met up with her assailant. He vowed they would do everything in their power to find him. She thanked him, but also silently thanked Ganymede for obliterating such a venomous creature. He would never hurt anyone else again, and that was the only thought that allowed her to get some sleep that night.

6

After a few more tests and several walks up and down the hospital corridor, Alexandria was released the next morning. Jameason had taken the night watch in order to allow Alex's parents to go home and rest. Two security gentlemen were posted outside her room and others were inconspicuously scattered around the hospital grounds. Even the MI-5 agents had to begrudgingly admit, that her father had indeed hired a firm who took their clients' safety seriously.

The lead guard, Mr. Jackson Campbell, was young but he was the point man on the assignment. He was one of the two who stood vigil outside her room throughout the night, and all others, both at the hospital and the Manor, reported to him. After a quick shower, Alex dressed in the soft sweats that Jameason had brought with him and prepared to leave. Jackson came in the room when Dr. Holbrook returned with final instructions, and John reminded Alex that he would see her within the next day or so at home to check in on her.

If Jackson thought this odd, he did not let on. He just stood quietly in the corner of the room taking it all in. Jameason also had no comment, as he was used to people showing great kindness and consideration to the Groabans. She heard Jackson speaking quietly into a small communication device that she could not see, but one that he obviously had in his ear, preparing everyone for their immanent departure. But before they could leave the room, Wallace and Conner entered looking relieved to see her standing and walking unassisted.

"What are you two doing here?! I thought you'd been banned from this hospital?" laughed Alex, shaking her head.

"I'd like to see them try to keep me out of this place," said Wallace. He walked forward and gave her a gentle hug. "How are you, sis?"

"I'm doing alright, I think." Alex kept her right arm around Wallace and extended her left hand to Conner, who stepped forward and clasped it.

"Thank you both for getting me out of that room. Mother told me that you came in and found me." Alex shook her head sadly. "I wish you'd not seen me like that, but thank goodness you came."

Conner stroked her head and he shushed her. "No dear, we're sorry that he had enough time to hurt you. But you can rest assured that we won't let anyone come within a kilometer of you again. We just need to get you home now."

Wallace smiled at her, but she could tell it was a little forced. "You ready to get out of this smelly place?" he asked.

"Absolutely!" she nodded.

They left by a rear exit, the security team monitoring their every step. They were flanked by six guards, three in front and three in back as they walked. Alex was further cushioned by Jameason at her side and her brothers behind her. Even though she knew that an ordinary human would have trouble breaking through the wall of testosterone, she did not doubt for a moment that were Bertrand still alive, he would be able to quickly subdue all those around her and reach her with little or no effort.

That thought was sobering. She did not want anyone there or at home to get hurt if someone or something came for her again. But how could she give her family and the new security team the slip, Alexandria wondered. In her heart, she could not do that to them at present. Her family seemed so fragile right now, because in a way, they felt the effects of the attack as well.

She knew that if anyone told her that Wallace or Conner had been savagely beaten, how sick and furious she would feel. Alex wondered if her family would ever let her out of their sight again. At some point she would have to return to work and life as it was before, and that, she decided, would be her best opportunity to meet with John and the 'others' he had mentioned.

Her brothers and Jameason climbed into their Land Rover and Jackson took the wheel. The rest of the team climbed into two other SUVs and put one in front and one behind the Rover. She smiled at Jameason, because she knew he hated for anyone else to drive him anywhere. But he was not given the option, and he did not raise the issue at all. He sat quietly up front with Jackson and surveyed the road ahead.

The drive home was, thankfully, uneventful. They turned off of the main road onto the long, winding drive that led to the Manor. She noticed several additional security men scattered throughout the trees and hills and wondered how many were on the property. There were just too many guards to call Ganymede to her side for answers, she thought.

Then she thought back to that night so long ago in Egypt, when he had taken her mind somewhere else, while leaving her body in her bedroom. Perhaps she could ask him to do that again, she pondered. Then, she considered to herself, her family would never suspect her leaving the grounds.

This was what Alexandria did not want. The more she thought about all of the security she saw, the more trapped she felt. She never liked it when her father had hired security personnel before, but some of the locations the family traveled to in the past had warranted extra protection. She knew that she would have to deal with this for now, because her family needed it more than she did.

She looked up and caught Jackson watching her in the rearview mirror. Their eyes locked for a brief moment before they each looked away. Uncanny, she thought, that he would look back when she was planning ways to handle his presence.

Once they pulled up to the front of the house, Jackson stepped out while a man from the rear SUV came forward and climbed into the driver's seat. Her brothers opened the rear doors on either side of her, and she slid out on Conner's side because it was closest to the Manor's front door. Her parents came out, and enveloped her in tender hugs.

Her mother and Jameason began to walk her inside. But Alex looked briefly back over her shoulder, and saw her brothers and father in deep discussion with Jackson and another older guard. All three SUVs drove off towards the garage, while the men continued talking and planning. Planning, Alex thought, of how to keep her there and safe.

The rest of that afternoon and the next two days were spent napping, reading and watching movies indoors. Her parents had a nice collection of classic films and Cary Grant seemed to dominate the screen. After one too many black and white films, Wallace finally had all he could stand and purchased, "something with explosions," as he put it. Both Wallace and Conner frequently stepped out to take calls on their mobiles, trying to stay in touch with those they worked with. Both were expected back on their jobs within the next two weeks, and Alex was both relieved and deeply worried.

Wallace had recently been promoted to the position of director for the World Diamond Council, and he was needed regularly in London and Africa in the organization's campaign to stop conflict diamonds from making their way to the global black market. Conner's team would be reassembling shortly at the dig site on the Isle of Wight after the holidays, and as the leader of the project, he could not be tardy.

Alex lay back in her cushy chair as the sounds of aliens and bombs detonating filled the room around her. She twirled the remote between her fingers as she wondered how she could get John Holbrook to the house, sooner rather than later. John spoke of others, so surely those others could help look after her brothers too. Was that too much to ask, she wondered. She just did not know, because she really did not know John or the others.

A loud crash sounded on the screen and an alien bounded over a large vehicle to pin an actress to the ground. He turned his head in an all too familiar motion. It moved exactly as Bertrand had when he inspected her while she was trapped beneath his body. She felt chilled to the bone, as she saw Bertrand's face flash before her eyes, lowering towards hers. *"Fighting like a human!"* His words echoed viciously in her mind again. She was startled out of the memory when the remote clattered to the hardwood floor.

"You okay, Alex?" asked Conner from a chair off to her left.

"Yep! Just gonna go to the bathroom for a moment," she covered, and quickly made her way out of the room. Conner gave her a concerned look as she passed by, but she evaded any questions he might have had.

After visiting the restroom in her bedroom upstairs, Alex did not want to go back to the movie. It was just too surreal, and she felt raw inside. For the last two days she had been quite efficiently handed from one family member to another so that they could keep perpetual watch over her. She was never alone, and she was beginning to feel like she was rapidly approaching a breaking point if she were not allowed some space. Even when she was able to evade her brothers, Jackson showed up and would silently stand guard. It was just too much.

She grabbed a coat and made her way down a back staircase and headed outside. Just before she opened the door, she paused and silently asked Ganymede to be with her. She had not talked to him since returning home, instead using the past few days to heal, rest, and reassure her family that she was okay. She opened the door to find three expectant labs wagging their tails and ready for a walk.

Alexandria smirked, "Well, guys. Ready to try it again?" And she followed the dogs out into the crisp, winter air, drawing in deep cleansing breaths into her lungs.

7

Alexandria walked quietly along the back garden paths for almost an hour. The solitude was both refreshing and invigorating. She stopped occasionally and threw a stick for one of the dogs to chase, or scrubbed their heads before they ran away to play again. Finally, she brushed off snow from a bench and took a seat just to let her mind wander. There was so much to think about, so much to process. The one thing that came back to her mind, time and again, was how easily Bertrand had lifted her and thrown her. That was a feeling she never wanted to be on the receiving end of again. She wanted that power. Not to dominate and hurt, but to shield herself and her family.

Looking out over the frozen landscape, she vowed that no matter what she had to go through to get it, she would figure out how to have it and wield it. She would *never* be a victim again.

"Never again," she whispered aloud.

At the utterance of those words, she noticed that the already still surroundings became even more quiet, felt more brittle. Alexandria stood slowly and looked around, but spotted nothing. The dogs were close, but still playing, certainly not raising an alarm as they had before.

"Ganymede," she thought, "I know that you're here. And I know that you hear me. Come and show me the way. I'm ready."

Alexandria felt as if a long suffering weight rose from her shoulders, at the utterance of those words. She felt relief all over and a small sob escaped her lips. She sat back down hard on the bench and gripped the edge with her hands, leaning forward as a surge of dizziness swept through her body. Her vision became a little blurry around the edges and she was sure that she was about to faint. Alex took slow breaths attempting to hang on to consciousness.

As she looked around, Alex saw that the world took on a green hue. Snow began to melt and she smelled the fragrance of the earth in the spring. She heard birds calling to their mates and saw butterflies flitting about bushes along the pathway. Her eyes quickly searched for the dogs, but they had vanished. Alexandria rose from the bench slowly and looked around. Just like the night on the beach so long ago, she felt Ganymede near her before she saw him. She turned slightly to her left and there he was. He was beautiful as before, and smiling at her.

This time Alex did not wait for an invitation, she simply strode forward and walked into Ganymede's outstretched arms. Hugging him felt so natural and serene. Ganymede rested his chin on the top of her head and rocked her slowly back and forth. She knew that she could stay like that forever if he would allow it. Nothing could touch her there, no one or nothing.

"As much as I would love to hold you forever, I do not think that we could stay this way and watch the world pass us by, dear one," he chuckled.

"No, I suppose not, but what say we give it a try? Just for a while?" mused Alexandria, still not releasing him.

"Alright," he laughed once more. Alex could feel the rumble of laughter from his chest reverberate in hers and she felt totally content. Yes, she thought, she could stay like that for a long while.

Finally, Ganymede straightened and smoothed her hair out of her eyes with his hands. He held her at arm's length and took in her appearance, as if to reassure himself that she was fully healed and whole. She looked up into his blue eyes, so trusting and so benevolent.

"I have waited for this day for many years, Alexandria. I deeply regret that Bertrand's aggression brought about your decision to call me. But we are here together, and together we can face anything." He spoke with the hint of a question in his voice, as if he was unsure whether she really wanted him there or not.

Alexandria took a step away from Ganymede and looked out over the now lush countryside. The world just awakened for spring held so much promise, new wildlife and new growth just waiting to come forth. She looked back at Ganymede and shook her head slowly.

"I cannot pretend to know why Bertrand came at me with so much hate and violence, but nevertheless, I am not going to run and hide. Ganymede, you told me when I was a child, that I was brave and incredibly gifted. I'm ready to know what you meant. I have a feeling that things are about to get a lot more complicated for me, but I cannot ask anyone else to place themselves in harm's way on my behalf. If something happened to my family, I would never forgive myself," she exhaled heavily, and shook her head at the image her mind was painting.

Alexandria was deeply afraid that her family would suffer from some unknown threat which she felt to be looming over her now. Even though she had no idea how she could fight off Bertrand or his like, she was willing to learn. She caught Ganymede's slow smile and then remembered that he could hear every thought and whisper her mind could form. Looking him in the eye then, she thought, "Tell me, Ganymede. Please."

Ganymede took Alexandria's hand and asked her if she would sit with him on the bench in her parents' garden. Together, hand in hand, they took their seats and Alex steeled herself to hear what he had to say. He turned toward her just as he had on that piece of driftwood so long ago and looked down into her eyes, blue meeting blue.

Slowly, he began rubbing his thumb across the back of her hand as he spoke. "Alexandria, you and I have known each other for a very, very long time. I have been with you since your birth and I will be with you until the end of your days. But this has happened before, you see, you and I. Long ago, there were angels who were given permission to marry humans. Humans whom they loved and respected. Those marriages and unions often begat children who were incredibly gifted, powerful, and strong."

Alexandria drew in a quick breath. She had heard of such children before, in church of all places. "They were called the heroes of old weren't they? And they had a name that started with *neph...*, or something like that," she said.

Yes, she remembered thinking that Hercules could have been real when she was a young girl, and was a little disappointed that her brothers did not agree with her way of thinking.

"Yes," he smiled, "when humans told their stories, they often referred to these children as the *Nephilim*. They were unlike any other human children, and humans knew them for what they were. If the immortal children did not take precautions to limit or alter their interactions with humans, problems sometimes arose." His eyes took on a faraway

74

look, as if he were remembering times long since passed and challenges that she could not fathom. He refocused on her face and continued.

"Many *Nephilim* children were born, and still there can be some born today. They are very unique and most are gifted with long life, and abilities far beyond what most humans are capable of. Some have been here for millennia."

Alex's eyebrows rose sharply at that last statement. How could a being possibly live that long, what with disease and cellular deterioration, she wondered. Ganymede reached forward with his index finger and tapped the end of her nose.

"Sharp as ever, my dear," he praised her.

Alexandria felt herself blush from head to toe.

"There are ways for the *Nephilim* to sustain their bodies through the ages, but life is not always easy for them. In today's world, they must work diligently to avoid detection from authorities and unwanted attention. They are quite adept at living amongst humans and assuming identities which allow them to help their fellow man, to be an asset to the world. As the children of angels, most want to love, protect, and heal as many humans as they can. They understand that there is a greater good to be served while they walk this earth."

"You said, 'most', but some don't, like Bertrand. He was too fast and strong to just be human. So he was a *Nephilim*, just a very misguided one, huh?" Alex mused aloud. She shivered all over when she thought of him.

"Yes, Bertrand was also a *Nephilim*, but not of my kind," said Ganymede sadly, and for the first time, Alexandria saw deep sorrow and hurt in his eyes. She took in a slow breath, because she could feel the chasm of sadness that spanned from his grief, and it felt as if she would be swept away by his feelings of disappointment and be consumed by them.

"Oh, Ganymede," she whispered, "I'm so sorry." Alexandria did not know what she was apologizing for, but she was sorry that he felt such anguish.

"No, sweet child," he shook his head at her, and brushed her hair behind her ear. "This was all set in motion long ago, and it will continue for some time to come. You see, there are angels who serve the Lord, and want only to please Him and take care of all that He loves. They delight in what is good and what is right. I am one of the first angels. Along with Gabriel and Michael, I have been at the Lord's side from the beginning, and I have served Him faithfully from the moment I was created."

"Sadly, there are those who wanted more power, usurpers to the Lord, who were cast out for their disobedience and defiance. The denial of the power they sought made them bitter and angry. But they left still with a great amount of power, and their leader wanted to see the perpetuation of his followers. He allowed *Nephilim* to be born of his fallen angels as well." Ganymede was watching her as a hawk watches its prey; carefully, as if she might bolt at any moment and he might have to lay chase.

Alexandria paled all over. She tried to speak, but her voice sounded dry and thin. "You're talking about Lucifer aren't you, Ganymede?" She was afraid to give voice to his name, as though he might suddenly appear before them once summoned.

"Yes, Alexandria. There are many names associated with him. Some call him the Devil, Beelzebub, Lucifer, or Iblis. I knew him by another name, when he was filled with radiance and integrity," lamented Ganymede. A look of deep sorrow filled his eyes again. He slowly shook his head.

"He was a dear friend at one time, and all of us still want to love him as a brother, but this is not something that he welcomes. He still rejects the love that the Lord freely offered him, and he is determined to cause mischief and chaos amongst the humans who walk this earth. As long as he turns away from our Father, he will feel the loss of that love and Light, and his heart will remain hardened. It is a terrible burden to bear, but it is one of his own choosing."

Alexandria reached forward with her left hand and laid it atop Ganymede's hands, which still held her right palm. She squeezed his hands from both sides and tried to will her compassion and affection into him, to help him combat these dark memories. He smiled at her comfort and drew his hand to the top of the pile and patted her.

"Yes, it is a sadness, my dear, but I digress," he said solemnly.

"Through the ages, many have wrongly believed that all *Nephilim* were evil or descended from angels who were cast out. This is not true. Those angels who still serve the Lord have, throughout the millennia, walked on this earth with His blessing. We have carried messages to humans, healed them, and at times lived amongst them. I have done this for thousands of years, coming and going as the Lord determines, providing aid and comfort to His people. Once, many thousands of years ago, I was given permission to marry a human woman who was a blessing I never thought I would receive. She was a true joy and I will be forever the better for sharing her life with her."

Alexandria could actually see her face. As he spoke of her, she saw the two of them laughing and walking together hand in hand. When she was little, she remembered dreaming of this lady and she remembered her laughter. Warm and ebullient, it made her feel safe. She looked at Ganymede questioningly.

"I see her. Oh, Ganymede, she was beautiful. But I've seen her before, in my dreams when I was a child. How is that possible? Were you sharing your memory of her with me even then?"

"Yes, and no. She is always with me, as is the child that we had together. Her name was Maireid and she blessed me with a beautiful daughter. We called her Arianna." Ganymede let this last statement hang in the air between them. His eyes bore into hers, as he waited for her to react to his last words.

Alexandria pulled her hands away from Ganymede and stood quickly. She immediately took a step back.

"Arianna?" she whispered. Alex felt as if the air was leaving her lungs too quickly and not enough was returning to them.

"What are you telling me? Your daughter was the same person Bertrand was looking for when he found me? What does that mean? I look like her and I, I, what? We're so similar that you can talk to me, too?"

She found herself stuttering and floundering. Alex felt as if a dark shadow was creeping over her and preparing to engulf her like a tidal wave.

"What are you telling me, Ganymede?" she whispered, and kept a little distance between them while she stood and waited for his response.

His eyes never left hers as he stood slowly and stepped towards her.

"Please, Alexandria, do not be afraid. This is a hard truth, one I have wanted to share with you since you were a child, but I was not allowed to until you wanted the information in your own time and for your own reasons."

"Arianna lived for a very long time. She was the first of the *Nephilim* and she grew to be very powerful. Her life was devoted to the care and preservation of human life. She became a teacher and a healer to the other *Nephilim* which followed her. She guided them on a path of righteousness." Ganymede's eyes glowed with pride and love, the look a parent has for their child.

"You're speaking of her in past tense. Where is she?" Alexandria asked tentatively. "Did she die?" She felt like an intruder asking this question, but she could not stop herself.

Slowly nodding his head, he answered her. "Yes, she did perish, but she has returned."

Neither said anything for several minutes. They just stood looking into each other's eyes, waiting for those words to compel one of them into motion. Alexandria knew then, that this was what she would have heard back in Egypt when she was eight. How would she have processed it then, she asked herself. Better than right now? Or could there have ever been a moment when she heard Ganymede's proclamation and felt prepared for the ramifications?

"Returned? Do you mean I am Arianna? But I know who I am! I am Alexandria Grace Groaban. I have parents and brothers who know me. Jameason has helped raise me from birth. How can I be Arianna, if I know that I am Alexandria?" Her voice strengthened with each question as if she was holding on to them as proclamations of her person.

"Arianna was greatly missed by the *Nephilim* she left behind here on earth. She was and is needed. But her life had come to an end and she finally knew peace, such as she could never have fathomed. When the others pleaded for her return, I was allowed to give her the option. I did not expect that permission to come, but He knows better than I do how His plans can best be fulfilled."

"Arianna was reluctant to leave Paradise behind, but finally she agreed to return here if her soul could return first as a human. She wanted to know once and for all what it felt like to live as a human with no extraordinary powers or abilities. Just to be human for a brief time. She found that in you, Alexandria. You were chosen to be Arianna's vessel and path back to earth."

"But it didn't work, did it? This plan that she had," said Alexandria, feeling the color rise in her cheeks. "Some things couldn't be held at bay, and they've been seeping in throughout my life. All the visions and voices, all of the times I knew I wasn't quite like everyone else. Even my parents used to look at me as if they didn't understand what I was." She sat back on the bench and put her elbows on her knees, then supported her head in her hands.

She rocked back and forth, trying to find some comfort or peace in what he was telling her. "Ganymede, who am I?" She sounded so forlorn and pitiful, that he sat quickly next to her and pulled her onto his lap. He rocked her gently, trying to expel the fear he felt running rampant through her body and mind.

"You are my child, Alexandria, and you always will be. Yes, you are Alexandria Grace Groaban, and that will never change. Your mind is your own and you know yourself as the person you are. It is your soul which stretches back for millennia, and that is the part of you which I call my daughter."

"When your soul lived as Arianna before, we had time to learn our way through this together. Now, there are so many other immortal children to help you, perhaps we can find our way this time with their assistance. It will make it easier on you, to have others who are like yourself guiding you and teaching you." He continued to rock her and sooth her as he spoke. She thought she must look silly, sitting there on his lap, but at that moment it seemed to be what she needed.

"But I am still not like them, am I? I mean they have always been half human and half angel, never completely human and immortal at the same time. How will they know what I'm feeling and going through? How can you?" She leaned back in his arms and looked up into his eyes, searching.

"Yes, you are unique Alexandria, but then again you always were. You were the first and the most powerful of all *Nephilim*. You paved the way for the rest and that path is still there, *if* you want to follow it."

"If I want to?" Alex asked, both shocked and perplexed. "How do I have a choice, Ganymede? I mean, avoiding this truth for all these years has made me a target. How can I hide now?"

"Alexandria, I made sure that Bertrand never had the opportunity to go and relay to anyone else that he had found you. Though you do look as you did before, we have kept you shielded for all of these years. We could still do that for you. I believe now that Arianna knew exactly what she was asking for when she requested to come back as a human. She always wanted a choice in her destiny, an alternative view, if you will."

"There are challenges which immortal children face that can wear on a soul over time. As the oldest, she did become weary at times, and wanted an end to much of the violence and heartache she witnessed," he said sadly, while he looked over her head now as if he was seeing into the past and looking at Arianna once more.

Alexandria sat up straighter in Ganymede's arms, causing him to refocus on her face. "Ganymede, how will this work for us? I don't know what to say to you or what to do? I mean, I do feel a connection to you, I always have, but I have a father and mother. How do I just leave them and come with you, if that's what I want to do? And right now, I'm not sure if I should agree to embrace this or not. I feel shocked honestly, but I cannot lie to you and give you false promises about the future."

He smiled warmly at her as he said, "Thank you for your honesty, Alexandria. It means more to me than you know. I think the best thing for us both, is for you to meet with the other *Nephilim*, get to know them and allow them to introduce you to some of the possibilities open to immortal children. Then, after you feel you have a good idea what it means to accept this life, you can make your choice."

"But I do have a choice still?" she questioned him, pressing to make sure she had this verified.

"Of course, my dear. You have free will, and you can choose which path you want to follow. No one, not an angel, not an immortal child, no one would dare to interfere with the free will that the Lord promises to all of His children. He does not force humans or *Nephilim* into any choice or path in this life or beyond. He loves us all as His children, and therefore He wants us to be free and happy, not under His direct control pining away for freedom." Ganymede looked as if he wanted to add more, but held back for some reason.

"Oh," Alexandria whispered.

So she still had a grace period, a chance to bow out if she needed to. But would she want to once she met the others, Alex wondered. She thought again of her brothers' laughter and easy banter. She thought of her parents sitting inside and Jameason's plucky, sassy leadership of their household. She owed it to them to find a way to keep them safe. All of the unconditional love they had shared through all of the years, meant something profound to her. She would lay down her life if it came to that to ensure their continued happiness.

Alexandria scooted off of his lap to sit beside him once more, and looked from her home back up to his face. "I'm through with the what ifs for now Ganymede. I said I wasn't running and I will hold to that. How do we go about a meeting with the other *Nephilim?* I don't know how I will get around my parents or their security guards. In fact, I'm not sure how I've been allowed outside alone for so long this afternoon."

She wrinkled her nose at him and gave him a wry smile. "You wouldn't have had anything to do with that, would you now?" They both chuckled then, knowing full well he had orchestrated their privacy.

"Oh, sweet Alexandria, that is a sound I love to hear. And I hope to hear more of your laughter and happiness in the future." He leaned forward and cupped her cheek and chin in his hand. Earnestly he looked into her eyes, imploring her to hear his every word.

"As we move into the days ahead, I want you to know that I am placing no expectations or demands on you, Alexandria. You please me by just being here, and whatever choices you make about your future, I know that you will choose the path and destiny you feel is right. You only have to follow your heart and conscience, and that will be enough. Do you understand?" He held his breath as he waited for her to agree.

"Yes," she breathed out, "I do understand. Thank you for skipping the guilt trips. I don't think I could stand the weight of them, honestly. I think it would be too much for me right now."

"There is no pressure from me, I promise," he smiled, and released her chin. Alexandria remembered something he had mentioned earlier in the conversation.

"You said the other immortal children wanted and needed Arianna back. Are they expecting me to be her when I arrive?" She knew that would be a huge burden to bear right from the start.

83

"No," he said, vehemently shaking his head. "They and their immortal parents understand what is at stake here. They will not frighten you away by expecting what was. They know that we are embarking on a new journey, together. They want that as much as I do, so they will accept you for who you are, Alexandria."

"Okay," she smiled tentatively up at him. "I can agree to a meeting on those terms. When and how shall I go?" Alex chewed her bottom lip, waiting to hear how it all might play out.

"I have asked John Holbrook to come to your parents' home this evening. He will suggest a retreat for you to go to before heading back to New York. The place you will travel to has served as a meeting place for the immortals for numerous years, and many other *Nephilim* will gather there to greet you. They are anxious to see you, dear one. As for the security team, well, you will see that our powers of persuasion can be quite effective," he added, with a twinkle in his eyes.

Alex chuckled and shook her head at him, as if in reprimand. But the truth was, she was glad to have his help. She had tried to imagine how her family was going to handle her leaving after the holidays, but with Ganymede's and John's help, perhaps it would not be too painful a parting for them.

"Thank you for coming once again, Ganymede. I'm glad to know who you really are now, and I look forward to learning about our past together." She patted his hand, amazed at how much she seemed to be touching him that day, and how he allowed it. It seemed that he was hungry to reconnect with her as well. Well, if she was his child in some way, he must have missed talking to her like this, she mused.

"Will I see you at this retreat? I know that by the time I get there I'll have a million more questions, but my head seems kind of full right now. You've given me a lot to think about." Alex hoped that he would be there, because she really trusted Ganymede, and she wanted him close at the moment.

"My dear, I am always a breath away. You need not fear what is to come. You are safe and protected. Go and meet with them, and then yes, you will see me again," he reassured her once more.

"Now, I must take my leave," he said gently, as he stood. He leaned over and placed a kiss on her hair, then smoothed it back over her shoulders. "Alexandria, I love you and I am proud of you. Remember that, always."

Ganymede took a step back from Alex and she noticed that the ground around them was slowly becoming covered in snow once more. She could no longer hear the birds, and the butterflies had disappeared. Ganymede himself was becoming harder to see.

"Thank you," whispered Alexandria, and with that he was gone.

8

"Alexandria, are you alright?" Jackson asked, standing over her and looking a little worried. She opened her eyes to find that she was lying on the garden bench with Dudley licking her left hand, which was hanging off of the side.

"Um, yes, I'm fine. I was just napping, that's all." She sat up feeling ridiculously self-conscious, and she could feel the heat in her cheeks.

"I'm sorry if I startled you," he apologized, looking as embarrassed as she did. "I just wanted to make sure that you were okay. It's kind of cold out here. Wouldn't you rather sleep inside?"

She narrowed her eyes at him as she asked, "Which one of my brothers put you up to coming out here?" Alex knew that Jackson probably had been told by everyone in the household to come outside and get her. She had been with Ganymede, but to the outside world, she had slept. She looked around disoriented. "How long have I been out here?" she quizzed him further.

"Well, about two hours, but you've only been asleep for the last forty-five minutes or so. And to answer your earlier question, no one in your family told me to come and get you. I offered and they acquiesced. It's what I do," he said, sounding a little shy. Had she embarrassed him, she wondered. Surely not.

Alexandria stood up from the bench and felt cold to her core, but she was not about to admit that to Jackson or anybody else. She decided to walk a bit more to get the kinks out before returning to the house.

"I think I'll take another turn around the garden before I go in. Is that alright with you?" She waited to see if he really had no deadline by which she had to be indoors. To her surprise he agreed and offered to escort her if she would allow it. How polite they were being, she thought.

As they strolled around the frozen landscape, she decided to find out more about the quiet, controlled man by her side. "So, Jackson, can you tell me where you're from?" She looked out at the path in front of them, not wanting to look into his eyes, in case he looked put off by her question.

"Sure, ma'am. I'm from a small, but growing town in Georgia called Evans. It was smaller when I was a boy, but it's growing like wildfire these days." Wildfire! She chuckled over his choice of words. "Are you laughing at me?" he asked, feigning shock and indignation.

"No, I just like your phrasing, that's all. So you're an American from Georgia. Why are you here, then?" That last question popped out before she could stop herself. Perhaps this was too personal and not her business to know. But he did not hesitate to answer.

"After college, I joined the Marines and served a couple of tours in Iraq and Afghanistan. After that, I decided to put my talents to work in the private sector. I knew some people from the service who had already crossed over to contract work, and they encouraged me to make the change. Still getting to do something I like, just not quite so dangerous as the front line in an active war zone," he explained.

She stopped walking and looked up at him. She was deeply humbled and embarrassed that she had made him explain such a personal account. He looked questioningly at her.

"Did I say something to upset you, Alexandria? I know that not everyone is a fan of what's going on in the Middle East." He looked concerned, and she wanted to apologize.

"No, no, that's not it at all," she said, shaking her head. "I am sorry I intruded, but please don't mistake my reaction for disapproval. I have nothing but respect for your service. In fact, I am in awe that you chose such a dangerous occupation. Isn't your family worried sick about you?" There, she had done it again! She had asked a personal question, and this time about his family. She had to stop before she made a complete idiot of herself.

"Not as much as they were before I entered the private sector. My parents and grandparents are proud that I served. Heck, my little brother thinks I'm like James Bond. If only he knew that most of what I do is stand, watch, and listen. Not so glamorous," he said, smiling down at her.

And for the first time, Alexandria really took a good, long look at Jackson. He was over six feet tall, just as her brothers were. He kept his blonde hair cropped short, but it was still given to curl around the edges. A straight nose and a sculpted chin set off his face, and he had beautiful blue eyes with little laugh crinkles around the edges. He was a very handsome man, and she admonished herself for noticing. In fact, he looked like he was aware she was noticing him, and that could not be good for either of them, she decided.

Alexandria tore her eyes away from his and started walking again. Alex pretended that she was watching the labs running up and down the long stretch of lawn. Neither said anything else for several minutes. Finally, it was Jackson who broke the silence.

"If it would be alright with you, Alexandria, maybe we could head back inside? Your father told me that Dr. Holbrook had called to say he was coming by, and there's a good chance that he might already be here." He looked down at her expectantly, but was surprised to see all of the color drain out of her face.

"Alex, are you okay? Are you feeling ill?" he asked, alarmed at the change in her complexion. He reached out and grabbed her elbow in case she was about to faint.

"Yes, I'm fine," she replied, not sounding as sure as she had hoped she would. "I'm just tired. Perhaps we'll go back now and see Dr. Holbrook." She tried smiling up at him to reassure him, but the smile did not quite reach her eyes, and his keen eyes saw that it did not.

"Okay, let's turn back." And he guided her in the direction of the house, studying her every so often through wary glances.

"Now or never," Alexandria thought. This would be an interesting conversation. She wondered how John was going to convince her family to let her leave with him. She hoped that he would be telepathically communicating with her, so that she could help him establish the case for her departure. But the sooner she got away from her family, the sooner they would be safe. She just did not know how to extricate herself from them so soon after Bertrand's attack.

As she and Jackson entered at the back of the Manor, Jameason was waiting in the mudroom to give her his famous, hands on hips and eyebrows crinkled up, wilting glare.

"Just where have you been, young lady? It is too cold out there for you to take your beauty rest on a frozen bench. The next time you decide to give yourself pneumonia, I am coming out there with a switch. Have a made myself clear?" Boy, he was in a state, Alex thought to herself. Alex did not dare laugh, but she could not help the smile that began to spread across her face.

Jackson looked from Alexandria to Jameason and back again, trying to make sure she was not about to be throttled by the old man.

"Yes, sir. Love you, too," she giggled, and leaned up on her toes to kiss him on the cheek. "Is Dr. Holbrook here yet? Jackson said he was coming." Alex hoped to distract him from his tirade, but he was not completely derailed by her affection.

"You're lips are like ice! And, yes, Mr. Campbell is correct, Dr. Holbrook has already arrived and he's with the rest of the family in the main sitting room. Hurry along and don't keep him waiting. I want him to see how blue your skin looks," and with that last command, he swatted her with a newspaper that had been lying on a nearby bench to get her moving.

Alexandria laughed and moved in the direction of the sitting room, with Jackson right on her heels.

"Has he been with your family for a long time?" he asked.

"Yes," she smiled back at him, "since before I was born. He's like our butler, nanny, and grandfather all rolled into one. He keeps us all straight."

"Yes, I can see that," agreed Jackson. "Oh, and you can call me Jack. Most of my friends do, and if we're going to be together for a while, you might as well."

Alex stopped short in the hallway and Jackson almost bumped into her. She looked up at him suddenly confused. "Just how long do you think we're going to be in one another's company?" She had hoped only for the remainder of the week while she was home, but honestly knowing her father, she should have counted on a more drawn out affair.

"I'm with you until you're safe, Miss Groaban, or until your father decides our services are no longer needed. I'm in his employ, so he will decide the when and the where. I hope that's alright with you?" As soon as he added that last question, he was kicking himself internally. Why would it matter to him whether she wanted the security detail there or not? His firm was working for her father, and as long as he was keeping protection tight, Jackson knew he should not worry about his team's presence.

Alexandria studied Jackson for another moment and then pursed her lips together. She slowly nodded in his direction to let him know she understood she was not included in the chain of command, and turned to head down the hall. Jackson regretted the look of hurt in her eyes, but he chose to remain silent and followed along in her wake.

They entered the sitting room to find Alex's parents and brothers listening to Dr. Holbrook. He was explaining a new aspect of the residency program he was currently overseeing, and he had their rapt attention, even Wallace's. Alexandria was shocked. She walked over to her father and kissed him on the cheek, then turned her attention to John. Jackson stood to the side of the doorway, looking bored and detached.

John finished his last statement, then turned his intense gaze towards Alexandria and shifted the focus to her. "Alexandria, you look well. How are you feeling?" Oh, she did not want to conduct a medical interview in front of her family. She wanted to shift the focus somewhere else, quickly. She caught John's smirk and knew that he was playing with her.

"I feel really well, thank you. I'm less sore today too, after a long walk. So all in all, I think things are going well," she said aloud, but she pointedly looked at John and sent him a silent message. "What are you playing at? I don't want to do this in front of my family," she admonished, but to her surprise he did not back down at all.

"Yes, we'll do this here and now and, forgive me, but my next line of inquiry will be your ticket out of here for the next few days." She heard him loud and clear in her mind, but she had a hard time schooling her face at his words. What was he thinking?

"Very good, my dear," he said, aloud. He paused for a moment and leaned his head to the side a bit, considering her. "Can you tell me how you're sleeping at night? Any flashbacks, Alexandria, during the day or night?"

No, no, no! She definitely did not want to have this conversation in front of her loved ones. Alexandria paled, and sat back on the edge of one of her father's desks which was in the room.

"You're going to hurt them, John! Stop now!" she shouted in her mind.

"No, Alex, they have to be able to let you go," he countered, his internal voice calm and steady. He was not going to relent.

Wallace walked over and sat next to her, putting an arm around her shoulders. "It's okay, Alex, you can answer Dr. Holbrook. We're all here for you," he encouraged. She looked up into his eyes and saw only love and encouragement, not pity or judgment.

She turned back to John and slowly nodded her head. "Yes, I have had flashbacks since coming home and bad dreams."

"Hmmm, indeed. I know that this is new territory for you, Alexandria. Can you tell me how often they are occurring?" John pressed her further, tapping a lone finger on his chin.

She gave him the coldest stare that she could manage and said, "Constantly."

The word hung in the air for what seemed like an eternity. Alex had to remind herself to breathe. Her mouth felt dry and she wanted to run from the room and hide. This was not what she had expected and not what she wanted. Dear Lord, what had she agreed to, she wondered.

"Be patient, Alexandria," John spoke to her mind. "This would be the natural course after any kind of attack. They need to know you're in need of more specialized care than you can get here at home."

Wallace squeezed Alexandria close to him and looked pointedly at Dr. Holbrook. "What can we do to help her? Will these pass in time, or is there something we can do to help her with what that bastard did to her now?" he asked, as his voice shook. Alex lifted her left arm and rubbed his back, trying to sooth his anger away.

"Well, what I suggest may not sit well with everyone here, but I think that meeting with a team of specialists I know quite well, may help to begin the healing process. Alex, when a person experiences what you have, there are many residual feelings of hurt, anger, betrayal, and even sorrow. Sorrow for innocence lost and anger at feeling so helpless in the face of a stronger, dominant opponent."

"I think it would help if you talked with some very skilled colleagues of mine, just to start to exorcise some of these intense emotions." He looked at her alone when he explained his intentions, and she knew that he was not just giving her a way out of the house, he was hitting on a very raw and real issue that she had not discussed with her family yet.

She was angry that Bertrand had gotten the upper hand so easily, and she was mad as hell that she had felt powerless to stop him. Her father broke through the silence by clearing his throat and walking over to Alexandria. She looked up into his face and saw how moist his eyes looked.

"No, Father, don't cry," she whispered.

"I'm sorry, sweetheart. One day, when you have children of your own, you'll understand. When they hurt, you hurt." He gave her a sad smile. "I think Dr. Holbrook has a good point, Alex. You're healing well on the outside, but you haven't even begun to heal the inside."

He turned away from her to face John again. "I think your idea is a sound one, doctor. Where are these colleagues of yours? Are they in Oxford?" her father inquired.

"No, Lord Groaban, I am afraid not. They're not here. Their retreat is slightly outside of Rochester in Northumberland. In my opinion, it is one of the best facilities in the world to help with emotional trauma. It won't take us long by helicopter, and I could set that up if you all decide to pursue this." He stood and walked towards the doorway. "I'll just step out for a few minutes while you all talk this through."

Once John left, Jackson stepped out into the hallway as well, giving the family the room. They all took turns telling Alex why they thought she should go with Dr. Holbrook, and she had no rebuttal. She silently agreed that she must go and not just to meet the other immortal children, but to perhaps meet another who had experienced a run in with a fallen *Nephilim* before and understood what she was grappling with.

"Alright, I think I'll go with him and perhaps find a way to cope with this before I go back to New York. I guess I should call and ask for more time off. Do you think they'll agree?" she asked her father. She highly doubted she could ask for more leave, because she had barely been there a full year.

"Don't you worry about that. I'll call Donald and he'll sort it all out for us. Time off should be the least of your worries right now." Alex thought that sometimes it really did help to have a father who knew the right people to call at the right time. He had managed to keep all of what had happened out of the papers; he could surely get her more leave with an old friend at the U.N.

They all moved together and hugged one another in a group hug that started tightly and almost desperately, but ended in giggles and all out laughter when Wallace accused Conner of stepping on his new shoes. As she was wiping the happy tears from her eyes, her mother moved forward and hugged her again.

"I love you, Alexandria, always." She leaned back and looked into Alex's eyes, then smoothed her hair away from her forehead. It was a calming gesture, one that Alex had loved since she could first remember.

"I'm going to be okay, Mother. It's just going to take a bit of time, that's all." Her reassurance gained her another hug and then they heard a discreet cough from the doorway.

John re-entered and they told him that Alexandria would be traveling with him. "Very good," he said, rubbing his hands together. "I can call them and set everything up this evening. I shall come at ten in the morning to collect her. Will that be satisfactory?"

"Yes, that sounds just fine," agreed her father. He looked back at his daughter, and asked, "Is that okay with you too, Alex?" She appreciated that he was asking her rather than telling her what the plan was. She felt more in control.

"Sounds good," she smiled back.

"Oh, John, if I may call you John?" her father asked, and received Dr. Holbrook's nod. "I plan to send Mr. Campbell and his team with Alexandria. I want her to still retain some security while she's there. Can you see to accommodations for them as well?" This left them in a unique situation. Everything was going according to John's plan, but Alex had not considered her father would not want her to travel alone.

"No, Father. Mr. Campbell and his team don't need to come too. I'll be just fine in Northumberland. Who's going to look for me there anyway?" asked Alex, sounding more eager than she had intended. Wallace and Conner both studied her expression, trying to determine what might be on her mind.

"Alex, I think Father is right." said Conner. "We would all feel better if we knew security was tight." Alex looked over at John whose face was unreadable. He looked almost bored.

"Help me with this," she pleaded silently to him.

"Lord Groaban, I can assure you that this retreat caters to people who expect their anonymity to be preserved. Security is already very strict at this facility. The best I've ever beheld."

"I appreciate that John, but if she's going, then so is Mr. Campbell, at least. Just one guard shouldn't cause them too much discomfort. I'm afraid this is non-negotiable for us." Alexandria held her breath, and was beyond shocked that John finally agreed.

"I understand completely, Lord Groaban. If she were my daughter, I would demand the same for her. I'll set it all up. Well, Alexandria," he moved forward and extended a hand to her, "until tomorrow morning." And with that last sentiment, he walked with her father and mother out of the room.

Alex could feel her brothers still watching her and she looked up, surprised to see Jackson studying her as well. She had not heard him re-enter the room. She would have to be very careful to watch for him in the future, she told herself. He moved too stealthily for her own comfort.

"You don't feel railroaded here, do you, Alex?" questioned Wallace. His concern was misplaced. She had no idea how Jackson could possibly go where she was headed, and no idea why John was allowing it.

"No, I just want to make sure I have privacy, and not an audience when I go there." She looked past her brothers at Jackson. His cheeks and ears colored at her pointed remark, but he shook his head at her.

"No ma'am, I won't be intruding, I promise. You won't even know that I'm there. Remember, I'll just stand, watch, and listen, that's all."

"See," interrupted Conner, "he'll just be in the background, so don't let it worry you for another moment. You just concentrate on you, we'll handle the rest."

"Alright," she quietly agreed, but her eyes drifted back to Jackson who was still intently studying her.

9

The next morning, Alex felt strung out and tired. She had barely gotten any rest, and what sleep she did get, was filled with images of Ganymede and Bertrand fighting, scenes of her parents from her childhood, and old adventures with her brothers. It seemed that her mind was trying to flit through her memories, eager to settle on what she needed to see the most. Now, she just felt exhausted.

She finished packing a large suitcase and an overnight bag, trying to downsize from all that she had brought with her from New York. Luckily, two of her pieces of luggage had been filled with presents, so she had much less to go through now. She showered, taking longer than she needed to let the water cascade over her body, to warm and restore some color to her skin. She dressed and applied a little makeup under her eyes, which she never normally did. After a final look around her bedroom, she headed out of the door for breakfast.

They all enjoyed easy banter with one another and even Jameason seemed relatively calm, despite her imminent departure. Dudley had positioned himself at the end of the table, hoping for scraps, or perhaps just to say good-bye. Alex eyed him speculatively, and finally determined that he was begging for food. She quietly handed him a piece of bacon under the table.

"I saw that," said Jameason, but he did not sound angry. They all chuckled at his non-effective reprimand.

Promptly at ten o'clock, John arrived with another younger man who was their driver to Oxford's Kidlington Airport. He introduced the man as Heath, but Alexandria had that same peculiar feeling she had felt when she first met John, that she knew this man. An image of him running, as if in battle, through an old wooded forest came unbidden to her mind, and she blinked to clear the vision. He was smiling down at her with his hands clasped behind his back, studying her in return. He looked to be in his late twenties or early thirties, but his eyes looked quite ancient. She knew without hesitation that he was an immortal child.

He stepped away from her to take her bags from Wallace and Conner and broke the spell she felt she had been under. She hugged all of her family and promised that she would call often. John promised to check in with her father once she was settled, and put him in contact with the doctor who would head up her care at the retreat. With one last kiss and hug, Alexandria joined John, Heath, and Jackson in the large BMW sedan, and set out.

Driving along, Alex realized just how little she knew about these people she was traveling with. She knew where Jackson was from, but almost nothing about John or Heath. She knew only what she had glimpsed in her brief connections with their memories. But she trusted her instincts and she trusted in Ganymede. She had agreed to this, so she steeled herself inside, hoping for the best.

Once they arrived at the airport, Alex wondered which helicopter was theirs, and had to stifle her surprise when Heath pulled up to a brand new burgundy and black Sikorsky S-92. She knew exactly what this was, because she had seen several at the U.N., and she had a good idea how much they cost.

"Whose is this?" she said quietly to John. Heath and Jackson were loading luggage into the sleek machine, so she hoped they could not hear her.

He chuckled and looked down at her. "Oh, Alexandria, you have so much ahead of you. And it is going to be so much fun seeing you learn." He shook his head, still laughing.

She pressed him again, "You didn't answer me, did you charter this or did my father?" She was actually worried about how much her father might be billed for the excursion.

"Don't worry about your father's accounts, Alex. We did not have to charter this, it's owned." There was an odd twinkle in his eye.

"Whose is it?" whispered Alexandria, again.

John angled his head to the side, then leaned in a little closer to her face. "Why, my dear, it's yours."

Alex abruptly closed her mouth and leaned back. John was still laughing as he turned and left her standing there, gaping at his last statement. How could this brand new helicopter be hers, she questioned. Maybe they had purchased it for her, perhaps that was what he meant. But no, she thought, she had no reason to need something like this that would carry so many people in style.

"You coming, dear?" called John from the S-92's steps. Alex shook her head slowly and dutifully followed.

They were underway now, headed due north, and Alex was still reeling from John's statement. Heath was serving as their pilot for the trip, so she, John, and Jackson were in the spacious accommodations alone. The interior of the machine was amazing. Pale cream leather seats were scattered around the cabin giving passengers several different gathering and conversation areas. There was a sofa near the back, and beyond that a restroom. Light colored wood was appointed both functionally and artistically throughout the space, and she had noticed three flat screen televisions thus far.

Alex caught John watching her intently, and so she got up and moved to a seat closer to his. She was still extremely wary of Jack learning too much, so she addressed John with her mind in an effort to keep their conversation a private one.

"John," she began, but he mentally interrupted her in answer.

"Yes, Alexandria?" he asked silently, still smiling a bit too much.

"Okay, you know you have to explain what you said to me before we lifted off," she insisted.

"I believe I was quite clear. This is your helicopter. We frequently use it for business to and fro, but it is yours."

"But how could I own something like this? It must cost millions!"

"Oh, yes, it did." He sounded downright jolly about the expenditure. Maybe because he was not spending his own money on its purchase, she thought.

"I will explain more over the next few days, Alex, but as the first immortal child, you were here for a very, very long time. You learned quickly that humans placed importance on material goods. They wanted to barter, trade, or purchase things and the more one possessed, the more power or position one had."

"Although we have a myriad of abilities that set us apart, we needed shelter, food, and transportation just as ordinary humans did. And as the world evolved and technological advancements progressed, the investments we made enabled us to do a lot for our fellow man," he explained.

"We've followed your lead and continued your financial plan, Alexandria, and amassed a fortune that the world could never fathom. We can provide for those in need, when help is needed most. To get from point A to point B, we also need transportation, so we invest in vehicles that help us get around. You will see soon enough, but know that we view our things as just that: things. They don't make us better than anyone else, they just provide comfort for us and those we are charged to help and protect."

Alexandria was humbled by his words, and the respect she heard in his voice when he spoke of Arianna. She still thought of Arianna as someone else, a separate person. She was not ready to start owning Arianna's story as her own just yet.

Alexandria looked out of the window closest to her and let her mind wander, thinking about all that the immediate future might hold. So many possibilities, and so much promise. If she were honest with herself, she did feel a little bit excited, and she vowed that she would not harden her heart to what was to come. She would stay open to the possibilities that these immortal children, these *Nephilim*, offered her.

She looked back over at John and continued to speak with her mind.

"John, why is Jackson here? How can he possibly be around us while we're discussing angels and immortals? I feel like we're taking an innocent human into dangerous territory," she slowly shook her head with regret at her last thought.

"I understand your reservations, Alexandria; I felt them initially as well. I was planning to use a bit of suggestive power with your parents and brothers, but Ganymede halted me in my tracks. He feels it is better for you to have a human with you, someone a little more removed than your parents or brothers, but someone who can help you look at your choices objectively."

"Wait, so he is going to have full knowledge of the *Nephilim* and the fact that I might be one? John, I don't really know this man at all. I've only just met him. How do we know that he won't run straight to the press or worse yet, try to call my parents and have me committed to a real facility for mentally damaged or ill people? I don't understand how this can work?" Alex was worried that this was a recipe for disaster, and had no idea how to handle Jackson in the midst of all that she was poised to encounter. He did not seem to be a man that would allow anyone to manipulate or control him.

"Watch and learn, Alexandria. I'll handle Jackson before we land and help him adjust to what he's seeing. And, quite frankly, so can you. You'll both be experiencing this world of the *Nephilim* for the first time and you can both be of help to each other. You always were a nurturer, and I suspect you'll look out for him. Besides, there are humans who know about our existence."

"What? You allow humans to know who you really are?" she asked incredulously.

"Well, of course," he mentally scoffed at her. "We work and live amongst humans. Sometimes we trust one enough to tell them who we really are and what we're capable of. Sometimes we fall in love, and then we certainly share the secret. Close your mouth, Alex," he teased silently. "Of course we love. Do you really think we could go through the ages without a companion, without someone to share our lives with?" John's eyebrows rose up into his hairline with his last question.

"I, well, I haven't really thought any of this through yet. Of course, you all love during the span of your lifetime. Do you sometimes marry humans or other *Nephilim*?" she asked, really out of her depth now.

How stupid, she admonished herself, of course they were not celibate monks or priests. Gosh, she thought, her own angelic father had married a human, so of course the *Nephilim* could too. Then her cheeks reddened when she remembered John was listening to all of her thoughts, not just those she pointedly directed towards him.

"It's alright, Alex. You can think or ask anything of me, or the others for that matter when you meet them. Nothing is taboo to talk about, so don't feel embarrassed. Yes, we can marry whom we like, whether they be human or *Nephilim*. You know what they say, 'Love makes the world go 'round.'" His eyes danced at his own joke, and Alex could not help but smile at him.

"And we'll teach you how to stop other immortal children from eavesdropping on your thoughts. None of us are too keen on having our minds laid bare for all the others to peruse."

John spoke aloud now so that both Jackson and she could hear him. "If you'll both excuse me, I'll head to the facilities. There are refreshments in the refrigerator right over there if either of you gets hungry." He smiled politely at Jackson as he passed by and left the two of them alone. Alexandria turned and found Jackson's eyes on hers. She gave him a tight smile and got up, heading in the direction of the fridge.

"Would you like something, Jackson?" she offered. Her manners were ingrained deeply in her, and they were often a comfortable fallback when she felt nervous or uneasy. "Water, juice, or hmmm, looks like spirits are available, too," she looked back at him, hoping that she had not sounded as silly as she felt.

"Water would be just fine, thanks," he quietly answered her.

She snagged three water bottles, and placed one on the table closest to John's seat, then walked back to hand Jackson his. He gestured for her to take the seat opposite him, so she did, not wanting to seem rude.

"Alexandria, please call me Jack. You don't have to stand on formalities with me. We're going to be together for a little while, so you don't have to address me so properly. Okay?" he asked, as he leaned his head to the side and smiled at her.

Her eyes were trained on his cheek. Gracious, he had dimples when he smiled, she silently mused. She admonished herself, because she definitely should not be noticing his dimples. She dragged her eyes back to his and agreed.

"Alright, I'll call you Jack, sometimes," she qualified, "if you'll call me Alex, sometimes. My brothers started that nickname when I was a baby. They thought my name was too long, so Alex worked for them." She started kicking herself again. Why was she telling him this? He really did not need to know. Or maybe she was being polite by making small talk, who knew?

"Okay, Alex it is. Can you answer a question for me, Alex?" he put the emphasis on her name and tapped his index finger to his lips as he stared at her attentively.

"Yes," she agreed.

"What were you and John talking about over there?" Alex sat back hard in her seat. They had not uttered one word aloud, so what made him think that they had been talking to one another?

"I don't know what you mean?" she stammered out.

"Well, if you're making plans for after our arrival, I need to know so that I can plan appropriately for your safety. It would help a great deal if you would speak aloud, but I understand that you might want to uphold your privacy. Still, I think it's just a tad rude to do that in front of me and not expect me to be curious about the topic of conversation." Jack let the words hang between them, waiting on Alex to be the first to speak.

"How did you know?" she was so flabbergasted, she could not think of an appropriate denial. He had clearly been aware they were conversing, and she had not paid him the least bit of attention throughout the whole exchange.

Jack chuckled and shook his head, "So you *were* talking telepathically? If I hadn't seen it with my own eyes, I wouldn't have believed it."

Alexandria was shocked. "Wait, you didn't know for certain until I said something just now?" Now she really was mad at herself. Give her one human being, and she already could not hide what was within her.

"No, though I had been warned to look out for such things. Seeing is definitely believing." He was really smiling at her now.

"Who have you been talking to? Who warned you about me?" Alex could feel herself getting angry and scared at the same time. Her fight or flight response began to kick in, and she felt a surge of energy pass through her body that made her feel energized and hyper-aware all at once. Jackson seemed to sense the change in her as well. He held his hands up, palms facing Alexandria, to indicate he meant no harm.

"Alex, calm down, please. I am not a danger to you, I swear. I'm still Jackson Campbell from Georgia, and I'm still here as a bodyguard. Wallace and Conner had a long, frank discussion with me last night. They were not trying to betray your confidence, but they wanted me to have some inkling of where you're coming from and what to watch out for."

He took a breath to continue, but Alex bolted straight up from her seat. "What to watch out for?" she whispered incredulously, as she stared down at him. "You make me sound like some kind of science experiment!"

He stood then and reached out for her, but she pulled away from him and glared up into his face. "Don't patronize me, Jack. I don't like it when people look at me like that. Like I'm some kind of freak, like I don't belong. I'm fine, thank you very much." Tears were welling up in her eyes, and she was furious with herself for allowing that kind of angry reaction to Jack's words.

His eyes were filled with concern, not disgust, and Alex did at least admit that to herself.

"Alex, no, that's not what I meant, and you know it. I don't think there's something wrong with you; I think there's something very special going on with you. Your brothers seem to think so too, and they made me promise on my life that I would see you safely through this trip. They aren't fooled for one minute that you're just going to a treatment facility to deal with the attack that happened a few days ago. They think it all ties back to what was going on throughout your childhood, and they want me to make sure you come back to them in one piece, both physically and emotionally."

He reached for her again, and this time she did not pull away. He held her arms in his and looked imploringly into her eyes. "Trust me, Alex; I'm not the bad guy. I just want to bring you back home to your family again, safely. I promise not to make fun of or judge whatever I see. I can't and won't ever tell anyone anything that you don't want repeated. I swear it." His impassioned speech was her undoing. Tears started to run down her cheeks and all she could do was nod at him.

Her dear, crazy, sweet brothers. They were not mad at her or angry that she had not told them the full truth about all that had happened since Christmas Eve. They still were looking out for her well-being and trusting this stranger to bring her back home. Wallace and Conner were always such good judges of character. They always saw through people's facades and when they made a friend, it was someone they could count on for life. If they had decided to trust Jackson, then perhaps she should do the same.

"I see you two have worked through some sticky issues," laughed John, as he passed by them. He startled Alex and she jumped back from Jack's arms to put some distance between the two of them. She could not bring herself to look him in the eye, so she glared at John instead. John walked down the aisle and picked up the water bottle Alex had left out for him, and returned to where they were standing.

"Let's have a seat shall we?" he said, gesturing to the cluster of leather seats beside them.

John took his time getting himself settled in his seat and opening his bottle. He took a long, slow drink then finally looked at Alex then over to Jack.

"Now, Mr. Campbell," John began, looking over his glasses at Jack, "I have been unsure how to proceed with you, but it seems Alexandria's brothers have broken through the proverbial ice for us. Alex is indeed a very unique young lady, and I am glad to see that you already are looking at her non-judgmentally. We are going to a place that is both steeped in history and generally closed to the outside world."

"You have already signed a confidentiality agreement with her parents, but you must now pledge the same to us as well. Alex will not be harmed, but she will hopefully grow and learn while she's with us. To do that, she needs to absolutely put her trust in all of us, and that includes you now, sir. She and I need to trust you implicitly, both in your words and your deeds. So, do I have that promise from you now that you'll not betray her in any way as we proceed?" John's tone brokered no argument, and Jackson nodded his agreement.

"You have my word, Dr. Holbrook," and he extended his hand to John for a firm shake. He looked at Alex next. "Alex, where I come from a man's word is his bond. As a Marine, I would never dishonor myself by going back on my word or betraying someone I'm charged with protecting. I've got your back," he smiled, so that the corners of his eyes crinkled again.

"Besides," he added, "if I didn't take care of you, I don't think I'd have to worry about John or Heath here. I think that your brothers would tear me limb from limb once we returned."

"Oh, don't worry about my brothers, Jack. Worry about me," said Alex, and she meant it. She was through letting her brothers fight her battles for her. She knew that Jackson meant what he said, but she could take him on if she had to. That thought made her smile.

"Remember, I grew up in house with both of them. I think I can handle just one of you," she said smugly, as she crossed her arms over her chest.

"Of that, I have no doubt, Miss Groaban," Jack countered, and they all three had a good chuckle.

10

"Alex, we're almost there," said Jack softly. After their revealing conversation, John had suggested she stretch out on the rear couch and sleep while she could. Once they landed, she was going to have a lot to process, so he thought a little extra shut-eye could not hurt.

She sat up and stretched, feeling like a few more hours would really do her good. Alexandria rose from the sofa, folded her blanket, and walked to the restroom, still amazed at the sheer size and luxury of the helicopter. She took time to brush through her hair and wash her face. She looked a little too pale for her own liking, but she finally just shrugged and walked back out into the cabin.

"Alex," called John, "come on up here and buckle-up. We're going to be landing soon." She moved to the seat opposite John and Jack. They had, apparently, been sitting together and talking while she napped.

Her seat swiveled towards a window, so she looked out on the landscape around them, startled that she really saw no houses or buildings below.

"John, I thought you said we were heading towards Rochester. Where's the town?" She looked back at him, to see his nod.

"Well, we're near Rochester. Actually, slightly northwest of the town to be exact."

"But that's national park land. How are we heading there?" asked Alex.

"There are some homes and buildings in the national park, but we're actually going to a place situated between Kielder Water and Forest Park and the Northumberland National Park. It's a little place we carved out for ourselves a long time ago, and well, it's still ours," he shrugged a little apologetically.

"Can't people find you through satellite or GPS? How do you stay hidden in today's world?" she marveled aloud.

"It's actually not as difficult as you might think. We decided long ago that no one would know of this place, so no one has ever really looked for it. People hike right by us all the time, but we're just slightly out of sync with the rest of the environment around us. It makes us pretty much a lost little colony." He smiled slowly at his young charge. "Try not to analyze it too much, Alexandria. You'll give yourself a headache."

She and Jackson laughed at John's brashness and she shook her head. The S-92 began to bank to the left and she noticed the ground coming closer. She could make out sections of a huge estate that dwarfed her parents' home and surrounding grounds. Little colony, she scoffed to herself.

Once they had completed their touch down, and gotten the all clear from Heath, John moved to open the door and release the steps so they could all exit. John turned back and extended a hand towards Alex, giving her the support she needed to leave the cabin. She stopped short of the door and took in a deep breath. This was it. She felt Jack right behind her.

He placed a hand on the small of her back in case he needed to propel her forward.

John squeezed her hand, "Ready, kiddo?"

Alexandria stood straighter and squared her shoulders. Her chin went up slightly and she nodded her answer to John. She walked down the steps slowly and beheld her surroundings. She was stunned into silence as she titled her head back to take in the enormous estate before her.

Alexandria's entire field of vision was filled with a colossal earth-colored stone castle, which rose from the ground like a beautifully carved mountain. It looked as if it had always been a part of the landscape, there longer than the surrounding trees, fields, and the small lake which sat off in the distance. To say it was immense or vast did not do justice to the structure. There were so many sections to the castle, and her eyes roamed over its many widows, artfully angled sides, and ornate spires and edges along its rooftop. It was four stories tall in most places, but she could make out a portion at the far right end which rose to five stories in height.

She slowly turned in a complete circle and beheld a dense forest behind, fields with grazing sheep, cattle, and horses, and gardens to the rear which obviously meandered around the side of the castle out of view. They were so expansive, that the gardens were terraced and partitioned with stone walls to give them a sense of purpose and privacy. Alex beheld lines of fencing that separated the various pastures and noticed that jump gates were integrated into them, allowing horse and rider the freedom to leap over the barriers if they felt so inclined.

How this place, this refuge, had remained hidden, was almost incomprehensible. Alex looked back at John in wonder.

"We like to call it home," he smiled.

"It's just a tad too small, isn't it?" mused Jack.

"No," said Alex, "it's amazing! Just brilliant!" Both John and Jack shared a smile over her head.

"Well, amazing or not, it's home for us from time to time. So glad you came, Alexandria," said Heath, giving her a wide grin as he came down from the S-92's steps. He held out his elbow to her, and said, "Shall we?" She gave him a firm nod and linked her arm in his.

They walked away from the helipad along a pebbled walkway leading them in the direction of the structure's main entrance.

"We'll go in through the front door this time like civilized people," said John, "but there are many doorways in and out. We'll give you a tour in a bit, Alex, but first there are a few gathered who would like to see you."

Upon reaching the immense wooden doors that led into the principle entryway, Heath patted her hand. "Welcome to Aeoferth Hall, Alexandria Groaban. I hope you'll feel at home here."

"Thank you, Heath," she nodded, and smiled up at him.

John moved forward and held the right door open, so they could all enter. Once she stepped inside, Alex let go of Heath's arm and moved slowly ahead of all three. She looked around the opulent and expansive foyer that opened before her, and beheld a grand staircase that would render her father speechless. It was so artfully crafted, with such attention to detail. Tiny little cherubs were carved along its spindles all the way up four flights of twists and turns. How appropriate, she thought.

Alexandria tentatively continued further in, and saw a crystal chandelier larger than any she thought he had ever beheld directly above her. Her eyes began to roam over the space now, hungry to drink it all in. She counted four hallways branching off from this central point, and there were many rooms feeding off of the corridors just from the initial glance she chanced down each. Alex saw small tables, a few upholstered chairs, and several low, cushioned benches in the foyer as well.

As she walked around the space looking at mirrors and paintings, she reached out to touch the frame of an oil landscape hanging to the right of the staircase. But the moment her fingers made contact it stopped her short, and she felt her vision blur and the air around her being sucked away. She reached for Heath to steady her, but he was gone, as were John and Jackson. She knew what this was, another vision from the past. However, this one came on quickly and with no preamble as they had before.

Alex looked around and saw two men walking past her, talking about a horse that was about to foal. They continued their conversation through the length of the entrance and down a hallway to the left of the staircase. She stepped away from the wall and listened to see if anyone else was approaching. The hair on the back of her arms began to stand on end, and she slowly turned to see a man with thick, wavy black hair which was turning grey at his temples, walking not around her, but straight towards her.

"Good evening, Arianna," he said, with a slight Mediterranean accent, nodding in her direction. He had his hands clasped behind his back, and he stopped just a foot away from her and rocked back and forth on his heels, looking her over from head to toe. "Something tells me this is an unexpected visit," he added, as he waggled his eyebrows at her.

"Um, yes it is. How are you this evening?" she asked, hoping that simple conversation would keep him talking until she could discover who he was and what time she had landed in.

"Why Arianna," he tutted at her. "I should think you would know better than to think that loudly in my presence without shielding your mind from me," he admonished. "So here you are, child. Arianna certainly, just not the Arianna of this time," he added, as he took in her clothes and eyed her watch.

She moved her arm bearing the watch behind her back and used her other hand to brush her hair back behind her ear, out of her face. He noticed this small, familiar gesture and smiled warmly at her.

"As it would seem that you no longer know me, allow me to introduce myself. I am Archimedes, someone that you should know very well. But you, I would recognize you anywhere. Tell me how you've come to be larking about in the entrance looking as though you are as lost as can be?"

"As you can hear me thinking, I suppose it would do no good to evade your questions, eh?" she laughed nervously.

He shook his head slowly and pursed his lips at her. He was actually enjoying this exchange she realized, and that helped her relax a little bit more. If things were changing, she would have to get used to the idea of people interacting with her when she was thrown back in time she supposed.

"Completely futile child, so tell me."

"I am actually known as Alexandria now, so Arianna doesn't really *fit* me, if you will. I'm visiting Aeoferth Hall for the first time in my lifetime, and well, I just touched a picture frame and here I am. Lost, I hope not, but I'm certainly not in my time. What year is this?" she asked.

"What year?" he hooted. "My, my, this is a treat. I do love surprises, you know. Well, I suppose you don't know yet, but you will. You are in the year of our Lord, 1747. And what year have you just arrived from, Arianna?"

"No, please call me Alexandria. It is almost 2011 in my time, Christmas has just passed and New Year's is just a day away." She paused at the incredulous look on his face. "Why are you looking at me like that? Have I said something amusing?"

"Not, at all, Arianna," and he held up a hand to stifle her protest. "Now, enough of this nonsense. You are Arianna, or I am a toad. I don't care what anyone else has told you, but that is who you are indeed. Even if I couldn't see you, I would *feel* you, your presence, your aura and essence, and know you a million times over. So, you're returning to us, hmmm? That should tell you something right there," and he put a finger to his nose tapping it at her, chuckling as he did so.

"I'm trying to decide if I want this life, but I really don't know what it will encompass. That's why I'm here, to decide. Okay, stop laughing, this isn't funny," she tried to scold him, but failed miserably and found herself laughing with him until they both had tears running down their cheeks.

"Oh, dear child, this will be fun for us both. I will get to see what this journey in 2011 entails for you, and hopefully we'll have a good laugh about it together. Perhaps it is best if the few others who share this particular gift with us do not see you tonight. Let's not expose them to this future; it just might prove to be information they do not need. I shall look forward to your arrival, Alexandria."

And with that last sentiment, he blew her a kiss and she felt herself being pulled rather forcibly back into the present. She opened her eyes to find that she was lying on a bench near the picture she had touched, with John standing over her, and Jack kneeling by her head. Heath was just coming back into the foyer with a large glass of ice water headed straight for her.

"Nice trip?" grinned John. Alex began to sit up and had to take it slowly because the room wanted to tilt and spin on her.

"Easy does it," cautioned Jack, looking very concerned.

117

"I'm fine. I just need a minute. So, John, who is Archimedes?" she asked, happy to see him finally at a loss for words.

She reached forward and thanked Heath for the water and took slow, small sips. She turned back to John waiting on his response which seemed slow in coming. Finally, he cleared his voice and answered her.

"I take it you met the esteemed Greek when you left us, just now?" Now it was her turn to be amazed.

"You mean he was the real Archimedes?" she asked, astounded that this could be so.

"One and the same, *Alexandria*," said a voice from a hallway straight across from her, heavily emphasizing her name. Archimedes walked into the foyer and gazed down lovingly at her. He extended a hand in her direction and she rose to shake it.

Jackson backed up to let her pass, but moved with her to greet this new person. "I suppose others have used my name, but this is who I have always been. The name suits me, don't you agree?" he asked her playfully.

"This is so surreal!" Alex exclaimed. "I just saw you, but it was hundreds of years ago for you. And you," she gestured at his person, "I thought that Archimedes perished thousands of years ago, yet here you are," she marveled at this amazing possibility.

"Oh, we've had to sometimes come and go throughout recorded history to keep humans from becoming too suspicious. Keep them off the trail, and all that. It's so nice to meet you, Alexandria," he said, as he opened his arms to welcome her. She stepped forward and was enveloped in his warm embrace. She felt so loved and supported, so cherished. Waves of contentment seemed to roll off of him. If she had harbored any doubts about coming there, they were being quickly dispatched.

"Close your eyes," he leaned forward and whispered into her ear, and she did as he asked. She felt a slight breeze lift her hair and she saw herself walking with Archimedes along the lake outside in clothes reminiscent of the early 1500's. They were discussing a new sailing vessel that he wanted to build and take across the Atlantic Ocean, to see the 'New World' everyone was talking about. She was telling him about her earlier travels there that were never recorded, and about the native peoples he would encounter.

The scene changed on her and she was in Rome with him a few hundred years after his supposed death, helping him add scrolls to a large library by transcribing texts from their memories. Again, the scene shifted and they were with a group of orphans who were deathly ill with the plague in what she knew to be the south of France in 1349. They were methodically healing these children one at a time, and ridding their little bodies of the contagion. The air hung thick and heavy with the smell of sickness and death. Still, the cries of those they had yet to heal were hard for her to hear.

Alex's eyes were wide pools in her face as she pulled back and looked into Archimedes eyes. "Oh my," she breathed, as her eyes welled up with unshed tears.

"Yes, my friend. You've done so much good, so much, that there can never be enough written or told to convey all that you have beheld and accomplished. And I for one, believe that there is more yet to come."

"Perhaps," she said, not willing to say anything more. She knew that if she followed the emotional pull of images such as those Archimedes had just shared, she would agree to embrace an immortal life without critiquing all aspects of her choice. Would that mean that she would be following her heart instead of her mind, she wondered.

Ganymede had said, "You only have to follow your heart and conscience, and that will be enough," in her parents' garden just the day before. She knew she would have to work hard to strike a balance. She was already overwhelmed and she had not yet left the foyer.

"Thank you, Archimedes, I think that I'd like you to show me more, soon. Maybe later tonight or tomorrow?"

"Of course," he smiled, rocking back and forth on his heels just as he had in her vision. The movement was now familiar and it made her smile. Before she turned back to look at John or Jackson, she squinted her eyes up at him and really studied his countenance. She *knew* the line of his nose, the high rise of his cheeks which were tinged pink, and the way his hair flowed off of his forehead.

She stepped a little closer and placed the palm of her right hand on his cheek and looked into his warm, brown eyes. Archimedes inhaled sharply and his eyes grew wide at her touch. She definitely knew this man, like she knew the back of her own hand. Alex smiled and whispered, *"Haley o' thoway."*

Without summoning them, she began to see flashes of him in a myriad of different garments and settings. Time was flitting past her at an alarming pace and still she held fast to his cheek, not wanting to look away. Suddenly, she saw him standing before her, in the present, and they both took a deep breath in at the same time.

"Hello," he breathed out.

Alex dropped her hand as she slowly smiled, pursing her lips. "Hello," she answered. "I've known you for so very long, haven't I?"

"Yes," he replied, and she heard such conviction in his voice when he answered her. "And I am so glad you are here with us again, my dear, dear friend." He squeezed her arms as he spoke. "Shall I take you to meet some of the others? Do you feel up to that?" he asked, with no trace of coercion in his tone. Alex knew it was completely up to her, but she was eager now. She wanted and needed to see more.

They turned and Archimedes smiled broadly at John, and he returned it in full. They seemed to have both taken a collective sigh of relief. This would be alright somehow. Neither knew for sure what the days ahead would hold, but the biggest hurdle of getting Alex there of her own accord had finally come to pass. The rest would come. They had all faith that it would.

11

"Alex, we are gathering in the ballroom this afternoon before a late lunch. Not everyone will be there to begin with. You'll meet more of us over the next few days. We don't want to overwhelm you, but honestly we won't know your limits. You will have to guage your emotions and your body's response to us and let us know if all of this becomes too much, alright?" asked John.

"Okay," Alex nodded her agreement.

"Wait," said Jackson, before the group went any further. "She just said something to you." He looked in the direction of Archimedes. "What did it mean, *Haley...*, something or other?"

Archimedes smiled at Jackson, "It is from a very old tongue. One never recorded and not often spoken amongst even us. It meant, 'Greetings of our kind, be upon you always.'" He looked back down at Alex. "I'm very encouraged that you spoke in our tongue. It was you who taught the language to me, you see."

"Now, Mr. Campbell, there may be many languages spoken amongst us, but we're not trying to keep anything from you. Just simply ask and we will interpret. I'm sure Alexandria can help you with that," he finished.

Alex looked at Jack nodding her agreement, "He's right, Jack, it's what I do at the U.N. I can understand about twenty languages."

John, Heath, and Archimedes all started to laugh.

"Oh, Alex," corrected Archimedes, "you speak far more than twenty."

"Well, how many do you think I speak?" she looked perplexed at him, wondering if he somehow knew she had been keeping the last few she had mastered from her superiors at the U.N.

"Why, all of them, my dear!" he chuckled once more. He tapped his finger to his nose again as he had done in her vision of the past. "Yes, we're going to have so much fun. Now, we're heading to the ballroom, can you lead us to it?"

Alex looked at all four gentlemen before her, unsure if Archimedes was teasing or serious.

"Oh, he's serious," said Heath, grinning. "You used to live here, Alex. You built this home. Just feel your way through, and I bet it'll come back to you. Come on, give it a try," he encouraged, nodding at her as if that would get her moving.

Alex turned her back to the four and closed her eyes. She imagined herself walking in through the main doors sometime in the past, and she started to see a hazy image of herself in a riding dress with large hounds flanking her. She was walking towards a table that no longer sat in the entrance and depositing her gloves there. She turned and started walking off to the left of the grand staircase. Alex decided to follow herself and the dogs. It felt correct to go left.

One of the dogs sprinted ahead, and she heard herself laugh at the hound's playfulness. It was happy to be home. Alex was aware that all four men were following her, and that none of the *Nephilim* had corrected her direction yet. They continued down the corridor, past several drawing rooms, a music room, and a study to a set of ornate double doors. She saw herself and the dog, which had remained at her side, go through one of the doors, as it had been left open in the vision. Alex reached forward and slowly turned the door handle. She glanced back once at her companions, noting that they all seemed to be smiling. Well, she thought, Jack looked stunned and amazed, but he was slightly smiling at her.

She turned and walked into the grand ballroom, stopping just inside its entrance. It was immense in size and proportion. It looked to be almost as large as the Hall of Mirrors in the Palace of Versailles, which she had viewed as a child on a tour her family had taken. Now, she was sure that she had seen the Hall as Arianna during an earlier visit, too. But this ballroom was not as ostentatious and heavily decorated as the Hall at Versailles.

Its understated elegance was delicate and regal, gentle on the eyes and senses. Pale blues, yellows, and creams adorned the room. Numerous chandeliers hung around the area, giving light overhead and windows all along the left wall allowed natural light to soften the space. An expansive mural stretched across the entire length of the ceiling, depicting scenes of angels and humans working and living side by side. Its floor was an intricate pattern of wood, perhaps the original parquet, she mused. Couches and chairs were arranged along the sides of the cavernous space to allow for rest and conversation, and stone statues and busts were scattered in and around the seating areas.

One particular statue caught her eye, and she walked over to it and let her fingers trail down the sides of the little faun's figure and back up to his reed flute that he was happily playing. She thought of her childhood fascination with *Narnia* and Mr. Tumnus, wondering how long she had enjoyed the stories of mythical creatures. She looked up when she heard a door at the far end of the ballroom open, tensing a little at the unknown. Jack moved forward and came to stand beside her.

One after another they came, slowly filing into the room with her until they numbered forty-two. With each new face, Alex noted something familiar, something that she recognized. The way one's hair stood straight up, the gait of another, the dimple of yet another. They all had some quality that made her feel a tentative familiarity. It appeared to Alex that they hailed from every continent on the earth. *Nephilim* of all races and both genders had come to welcome her. She smiled at this, because to her, it meant that the angels had found beauty in all of God's people, and it made her proud.

The first to break away from the group was a tall, muscular man with light brown hair and a mischievous glint in his startling green eyes. He approached her and extended his hand, trapping her palm between both of his as he shook it gently.

"Alexandria, I am Elrick. It's so good to finally see you." His Scottish brogue was extremely thick, but she understood him perfectly.

"Thank you. I'm glad to be here," she responded in kind. "Have we known each other for long?" she asked, hoping that he would not take offense at her lack of memories.

"Oh, you could definitely say we have, yes, indeed!" he laughed, a big booming sound that caused many others around him to laugh as well.

"You've been saving my hide again and again for hundreds of years. I wouldn't be here today if it weren't for you. Can't wait to have a little sparring match with you again," he grinned crookedly at her. Sparring sounded dangerous and scary to Alex. Perhaps he would go easy on her, she hoped.

Elrick's boisterous tone broke through the reverie, and others began to move forward. A stunning, raven haired lady approached her next and rather than shake her hand, she gathered Alexandria in a tight hug.

"Oh my, I never thought we'd get this chance again! Welcome back!" she said softly. When she pulled away, her eyes looked moist and Alex could tell she was trying hard to keep her tears at bay. "I am Sabina, dear friend." She reached forward and pushed Alex's hair off of her forehead and smiled into her eyes.

Alex began to see images of herself with this woman helping slaves they had freed from a Roman market make their way out of the city. She saw them strolling through a street in Jerusalem, and Sabina was animatedly talking with her hands as if she was trying to convey something of importance to Alex.

"I remember you," said Alex, nodding her head slowly. Sabina's eyes shone brightly with her pleasure and delight that she was still somewhere in Alexandria's collective memory. Sabina glanced encouragingly over her shoulder at this small victory.

"Do you remember me, too?" asked a man with red hair, pale skin and freckles. He was tall and lean with very intense eyes. He moved forward and stood before Alex expectantly. From his accent she knew him to be Irish, but flashes were not coming of their own accord with him. She looked directly into his blue eyes and concentrated on the set of his jaw and the way his eyes narrowed as he stared down at her.

She began to remember something about his eyebrows. They were in a small row boat and she was teasing him that they were too long and bushy, suggesting that he trim them. She then saw him standing with her and several others on the deck of a ship discussing how they should hold the approaching bad weather back to protect their mortal crew. She heard someone call his name from starboard, 'Benen'. Ah, this one likes water, she thought to herself.

"Benen? That's you?" she asked. His intense gaze melted into a relaxed and grateful smile.

"Yes, I'm Benen," he confirmed, reaching out to touch her shoulder.

And with that, others wanted to find out if Alex remembered them as well. They began to come closer and she could tell that they were trying to contain their excitement, but their anticipation got the better of them. She looked at each one in turn and began to recall names.

With each remembered immortal, Alex found it easier and easier to bring forth the memories. Each one seemed to need to touch her as well, as if to reassure themselves that she was real and actually with them.

"Tabor," she named a stocky and slightly shorter man, who she remembered actually laying stone with on a wall behind Aeoferth Hall.

"Nikolaj," she said, to a man with dark blonde hair who could have easily passed for a model, he was so stunningly beautiful.

"Conleth, I remember you falling from a large steed at full speed. You broke so many bones that day!" she exclaimed, over the painful memory she had glimpsed.

"Yes," he nodded, "and you helped set every one before I healed incorrectly. You're quite good at that. You'll see," he encouraged her.

Ughh, she thought, hoping she would not be called on to do such an unpleasant chore anytime soon.

"Iain," she named a particularly tall and handsome man, who smiled disarmingly down at her. He chuckled and took her hand in his, and then made quite a show of bowing over her palm before he released her and backed away a step.

More and more she saw and called their names as they came to her. Guymon, Rawley, Weldon, Paulus, Youko, Sibel, Jaqen, Daiki, Abdalla, Reuban, Porcia, Abeo, Malkia, Nassor, Ahadi, Flynn, Braddock, Albion, Tomoko, Lena, Urvine, Makoto, and so many more. Alex was in a vortex, caught between a past that seemed vast and deep, and the present sea of faces before her.

While Alexandria recalled as many *Nephilim* as she could, she felt like she was just barely skimming the possibilities of what her mind was capable of. It felt like there was a tangible film or mental block that was keeping more of the memories from flooding in. She was working on recalling a particularly eager young immortal's name when she felt a slight shift in the atmosphere. Another had entered the room, and he was taller still than all of those assembled.

Easily six foot five or more, a *Nephilim* entered who effortlessly pulled her attention in his direction. Alex had no doubt that he would have been one of the 'heroes of old'. He stood a little behind the crush, but his eyes pinned hers and she focused on him rather than the man before her. The others near her noticed him now as well, and turned, parting to the side and allowing him to advance.

She saw this man in battle, with armor on, leading a group of humans on horseback across a green field not yet littered with the gore of warfare. She saw him picking up a man and holding him by his shoulders

129

off of the ground so that his feet dangled wildly in the air. He was shaking him with anger because of the small bruised and battered boy who lay at his feet on the ground. And she saw him laughing at a long, well worn dining table, singing much too loudly after consuming too much ale.

Alex saw herself pointedly reprimanding him and calling him back to her, even though he looked like he would rather do anything else than listen to what she had to say. Finally, she saw him coming to her aid when she was lying on the ground after receiving a rather hard blow that should have ended any mortal being. He was lifting her and carrying her back to her horse.

"Rohan," she breathed. She knew she had nothing to fear, but this immortal radiated pure power and she could feel the tension rolling off of him.

His voice sounded gruff and hoarse at the same time, but he cleared it enough to speak her name, "Arianna."

Archimedes stepped forward in an attempt to chastise him. "Rohan, you know we cannot call her by that name. We all agreed."

"No, you all agreed. I never did." He turned his scowl back to Alexandria. "I mean no disrespect, but I cannot call you by any other name. You are Arianna to me, and I won't play false witness to my friend, not now, not ever," he said, shaking his head at her to emphasize his words. The entire assembly collectively held their breath, unsure what direction this would take.

Jackson, who had remained quiet thus far, stepped closer and placed his hand on the back of her left elbow, letting her know that he was still there. John started to interject, but Alex stayed him with her hand. She took a step forward and craned her neck back to look Rohan directly in the eye.

"In this lifetime, this is my first meeting with you, yet I know you are as surly and brusque as you ever were. Have you not softened a bit with age yet, Rohan?" she chuckled. Her laughter helped to ease the tension that had built around Rohan's displeasure. Alex reached out and touched his arm, and the two felt a distinct jolt surge through their bodies.

"I know myself as Alexandria. But I am here willingly to learn, so don't scare me away, okay?" she grinned and angled her head, hoping that she had him on her side.

"I am on your side, I always have been," he said, his voice thick with emotion. Alex's eyebrows went up at his statement. So he was one of the immortals who could hear her thoughts, she thought to herself.

"I sure can," he grumbled.

Alex threw caution to the wind and opened her arms, enfolding his broad chest in a hug. She could not reach all the way around him, but she squeezed him with all her might. His hands shakily patted her back, then he too was hugging her and she thought she might not be able to breathe if he squeezed any tighter.

She felt the rumble of laughter in his chest, before she heard the surprising sound. It was filled with such mirth and joy, that it briefly took her breath away. He picked her up and swung her around, burying his face in her hair, then finally settled her back on her unsteady feet. He smirked as he looked down at her.

"It's really good to have you back," he said soberly.

Alex nodded at him, not liking the lump that now sat in her throat.

The emotions were running thick and heavy with everyone now, she could feel it. She looked at Archimedes, then to John for help. She finally needed a few minutes to herself.

"Say no more," said Archimedes, smiling warmly at her. "I think I speak for everyone gathered here today, when I say we are more than pleased to have you with us, Alexandria. We welcome you, dear one." He held up his hands to the assembly as he said, "Let us adjourn to the dining hall, and Alex will join us in little while, once she has had a small respite. Everyone," and he gestured towards the doors putting his request into action.

Many of the *Nephilim* moved in to hug or touch Alex as they walked out of the ballroom, and finally John came over to speak to her.

"Alex, there is no hurry. You and Jackson take all the time you need. You can stay in here or go up to the third floor to your bedrooms, or just meander about. I think you can find yours, Alexandria; it's the one that has always been yours when you stayed here. Jackson, we have placed you right across the hall from Alex, and your luggage has already been taken up for you both."

He squeezed Alex's arms and patted her. "I am very proud of you, you know? You exceeded all of our wildest hopes for this first meeting." And with that he leaned forward, kissed her forehead, and then headed out with the others. Alex looked up into Jackson's eyes and found that he was looking pretty pleased with her too. She shrugged her shoulders at him, because she did not know what to say. She just felt like she was running on pure adrenaline and emotion at the moment.

"Would you like to sit down or walk it off for a bit?" Jack asked, gesturing to the seats lining the space.

"Hmmm, I think I'd like some fresh air, if you can stand the cold."

He chuckled at her suggestion, "No worries, I think I can stand it, if you can."

The challenge, once issued, was all the agreement she needed. Alex nodded at him and headed for the large windows, which were actually glass doors at the bottom. She thought that the room must be lovely on a cool day in late spring with all of the windows flung open. But before she connected with another memory thread, she pushed the thought from her mind and walked outside with Jack.

12

The two strolled outside for almost thirty minutes in companionable silence. Alex was lost deep in thought, trying to process the experience of meeting so many immortal children. They were so beautiful in so many different ways, not only physically, but from within as well. There was something shining through from each one's eyes that drew her in like moth to a flame. She wondered if humans were as fascinated by them as well. Then she remembered Jack at her side.

She glanced up at him, and he caught her movement out of the corner of his eye and turned to look down at her. His hands were clasped behind his back as he walked, which she was learning was a position he seemed comfortable with. Jack had appeared impressed by the proceedings, but he had yet to look star struck by the immortals.

He raised an eyebrow at her, "You feeling okay? Want to sit a moment?"

There were gazebos and benches placed at strategic positions throughout the gardens, so that a person could rest and meditate while enjoying their time communing with nature. The gardens were not heavily sculpted, though it was obvious that meticulous planning had gone in to the different themes for various sections.

Instead, there were whole areas where Alex could tell wildflowers were permitted to grow of their own accord and nature was allowed to plan its own course, rather than bend to the dictates of a gardener. She imagined it would be hard to tear her away from this land in spring when the earth had come back to life and flowers were in full bloom.

She let Jackson lead her over to a gazebo, and she sat back extending her long legs and reclining her head on the back of the seat. She glanced over at him and noticed he seemed just as lost in thought as she, while he gazed out across the grounds.

"I'm sure you have a million questions. How are you with all of this?" she asked hesitantly.

"I think I'm actually doing quite well, all things considered," he smirked down at her. That dimple was back in his cheek, and she looked down to study her fingers instead of him. She needed to ask him a question, but she did not know if he would answer her.

"Jack, if I ask you a question, would you promise me you'll answer it truthfully?" Now his eyebrows really did arch high on his forehead.

"Alex, I don't have anything to hide from you. While I am with you, I am completely on your side, so I'm not going to be keeping any secrets from you. Ask away, and I'll answer as best I can," he nodded, to add emphasis to his declaration.

"Okay. What exactly did Wallace and Conner tell you before we left?"

"Ah, they told me you would want to know as soon as we were alone, and they were right! They know you very well," he said, appraisingly.

"Better than anyone," she confirmed.

"Well, they told me that you were a very gifted, bright, young lady. They told me about the visions that presented themselves when you were young, and how you could describe in detail what you were seeing in any language that you heard while witnessing the scene. They told me how you methodically shut down over the years, until, according to Wallace, you shared a vision with someone you called your Guardian Angel, and then the voices seemed to quiet themselves."

"Conner also spoke of how you seemed to be in a race against time after that fateful night; trying to live as normal a life as you could, and trying to soak up the human experience as if you might run out of time and miss an opportunity. And even though it appeared you had indeed been granted a reprieve, you experienced constant anxiety not knowing when time would run out on the freedom you were gifted with."

"Both of your brothers felt like the assault you experienced at Lord Lenley's affair entailed more than you let on, but they wanted you to tell them when you were ready. Nobody's going to force the story from you, not even me, Alex. When you were napping on the helicopter, John told me what and who the *Nephilim* are. He spoke of Arianna and Ganymede, and told me briefly about what might transpire here at Aeoferth Hall."

"And yet you came," she whispered, astonished that he had not called them all nuts and bolted for the nearest door.

"Yes," he laughed, and it was a warm, genuine sound, "I came. John told me if I couldn't handle this or if I tried to betray their confidence in any way, they would wipe any memory of this trip or of you from my mind and deposit me back in London. I'll admit, I thought he might be joking, but he was dead serious. I didn't want to leave you in this on your own, and I certainly didn't want to forget you ever existed." His ears and cheeks began to color pink at his admission, and Alex felt her cheeks warm as well.

She looked back down at her fingers, unsure of what to say. But words came unbidden from her lips. "I'm glad you came. I don't really have any friends, you see. It's kind of hard to explain to anyone what I have experienced or what might come crashing back in. I've just kept people at the surface, nothing too deep." Alex was amazed at how her confession made her feel like a weight was being lifted. It actually was nice to talk to someone who was not judging, only listening. He nodded to indicate he understood.

"Well, it seems to me, that you have an entire house, if you can call that gargantuan structure a house, full of folks who want to be your friend very badly. You may end up with more friends than you ever thought you'd have out of this before it's over, Alex. And that seems like a really good thing, if you ask me." Jack's quiet confidence reassured her and gave her strength.

"What do you say, we go back in and see what kind of spread these folks put on? I don't know about you, but I'm just a bit hungry." She appreciated his light-hearted tone and could easily see that he was trying to put her at ease.

Jack stood and held out his hand, and she placed her palm trustingly in his. He gave her a light squeeze, and she rose to walk back into the castle with him.

When they reached the dining hall, food and fellowship were already flowing heartily. She and Jack were beckoned forth and placed near one another at the center of an immense mahogany table. An ornate fireplace taller than Jack anchored the wall behind them, and it was alight with a crackling fire. Alex let her eyes roam over the heavily paneled room, taking it all in. She noted three large chandeliers lighting the space, and Alex gave up counting chairs lining the table when she reached one hundred.

Alexandria and Jack remained in the expansive dining hall for over two hours, laughing and talking with some of the same immortals Alex had recognized earlier, and additional new faces that she had not spoken to previously. They regaled her with tales of Arianna's past, and to Alex it seemed as if she were the backbone of their congregation.

Why then had she perished, Alex began to speculate. It sounded as if she knew no limits, could physically and mentally subdue any opponent, and had the foresight to avoid situations which would cause her pain or injury. What indeed had happened to Arianna? As she wondered this thought to herself, she noticed several *Nephilim* had stopped talking, eating, or drinking and were staring intently at her.

"I know you can all hear me," she thought pointedly at those who shared this ability. "I am curious how one so powerful, one so wise, could allow herself to be driven from her body and this mortal plane. Who will tell me?"

At first no one answered, not telepathically nor aloud. They all seemed to be stunned that she had already reached the point where she felt ready to ask this most important of questions.

"Come now, that is why I'm here, right? Something very significant happened in Arianna's life, something that she was unable to combat, and it cost her, her life." Alex let that statement hang in the air, hoping one of them would break their silence and answer her.

"Alexandria, to this day we don't know the full scope of Arianna's last few moments, but we do know what led up to her demise. We have a core group of twelve which help lead our kind. Most are here tonight. Let us adjourn to the library after dinner and we'll share with you what we know. Will that be sufficient?" asked Archimedes, through his mental connection with her.

"Yes, thank you," she mentally agreed, nodding in his direction. Alex noticed Rohan nod once in her direction as if he approved of her bold question. The other immortals sensed something was afoot and began to wind down the celebration.

Jack leaned over and whispered, "Anything I need to know about?"

"You're very good at this, you know," she chuckled. "We'll be heading to the library when we leave here. I want you to come along too, if you don't mind. I've asked a question that needs answering before we proceed much further. They have agreed to talk, but there'll be just a few of us."

"Alright," he said.

As the bulk of the gathering made their way out of the room, Alexandria counted eleven immortals left in the dining room. She had met all of them either in the ballroom or during the meal. They stood one by one and began to head out in the direction of the castle's library. Jackson rose, then pulled out Alex's chair for her so she could stand as well. John waited by the doorway, and walked with them down the long corridor.

Alex noted the many pieces of art which hung on the walls or stood on pedestals and niches. "You collected many of these, you know," he remarked gesturing to the impressive collection. "This is only a small sampling, mind you, but you always had a knack of discovering artists before the rest of the world could see their gifts manifest."

One particular oil landscape caught her eye and she stopped to marvel at it. "Please tell me this isn't by the artist I think it is," she breathed out.

John stopped and looked along with her. "Oh, you mean Monet? Indeed, he quite liked you. You were one of the few he allowed to call him Oscar, and if you hadn't used your powers of persuasion with those who held sway over the French cavalry at the time, he might have languished and died in Algeria. And then the world would have never witnessed the genius that was just waiting to blossom." John smiled and shook his head, then turned and continued on down the hallway.

Alex promised herself that she would make time while she was there to take in the expansive collection. If only Conner were with her to look at the historical items held within these walls, she mused.

"Perhaps, some day, Alex. Perhaps," called John over his shoulder.

They finally reached a junction in the hall and turning left, John entered the first door on the right. Alex and Jack quietly followed. Once inside, Alex stopped and gazed around in sheer admiration and wonder. Now she wished her father were there.

The library rose a full three stories in height, and books lined the walls on sturdy, dark wooden cases that soared from floor to ceiling. The right wall of the cavernous room had large, stained glass and clear paned windows interspersed amongst that wall's cases to allow light in. Rolling track ladders made it easier to retrieve any volume from the bookcases, and Alex noted that there were scrolls, as well as books, stored on the shelves.

There were many desks scattered around the floor with chairs alongside, but some were so piled high in books and papers that the wood was completely obscured from view. Still other chairs and sofas were positioned throughout the room with accompanying lamps so people could sit and read, study, or nap. Alex noted several game tables set up between chairs as well, holding intricately carved chess sets with games already in progress. Other tables held such games as Mancala, Mah Jongg, Draughts, Go, and an early form of chess, called Chaturanga.

Like the ballroom, the library's ceiling was one expansive mural, displaying various images of enlightened minds bent in study, others debating hypotheses with colleagues, measuring, inventing, or pondering. The images were a collage of scientific and mathematical geniuses, with literary and artistic greats comingled in the airy exhibit. Alex spotted Isaac Newton, Plato, Socrates, da Vinci, Copernicus, Pythagoras, Euclid, Muhammed al-Khowarizmi, Ptolemy, Aristotle, Michelangelo, and to her astonishment, Archimedes.

She turned her eyes away from the ceiling and they fell onto Archimedes' face. "Brilliant!" she exclaimed.

"The ceiling or the collection?" he asked, trying to play coy but failing miserably.

"Oh, you know I love it all. How do you ever get anything accomplished? I would never want to leave this room!" She gestured up at the mural, "Which master created this, Archimedes?"

"Ah, that would be Sinjon. He's very good, but often lacks the confidence to really embrace his talent. He's coming along though, and as the years progress, he does hone his talent. One of the benefits of an extraordinarily long life, which I am sure many of the masters wish they had been given a fraction of. It gives one time enough to patiently nourish their innate abilities, until they become perfected."

"Sinjon misguidedly thinks he is far from having perfected his talents, though perhaps that drive to better himself, is what keeps him interested in the work," he mused aloud. Archimedes began to rock back and forth on his heels again, as he contemplated his last statement.

The sound of Elrick clearing his throat brought Archimedes, Alexandria, and Jackson's attention back to the smaller gathering of immortals and they walked forward to join the group. Rohan and Benen were pulling chairs together so that they could sit in a circle and see one another clearly. Jack stepped forward and helped bring two more over, causing Rohan to give him a startled look. Jack simply smiled back at him.

"Alex," gestured John, at a soft looking leather chair. She inclined her head and took her seat, looking around the circle to see who was a part of the elite gathering. Archimedes sat immediately to her right and from there the circle progressed. He was the first to speak to the group once they were all settled.

"Tonight we shall make an effort to speak aloud, so that Mr. Campbell will not be excluded from our talks. Though it is most unusual for a human or even another immortal to be called to join us, we will honor Ganymede's request that he be present with Alexandria."

"I ask that each of us introduce ourselves once more for Jack's benefit and if we so choose, claim the land we hale from."

Each *Nephilim* gave voice to their name as if they were calling role. "John of England," "Elrick of Scotland," "Ahadi of the Kingdom of Kush, now Sudan," "Tomoko of Wa, known today as Japan," "Sabina of Rome," "Nikolaj of Siberia," "Benen of Ireland," "Nassor of Arabia," "Rohan of Germania," "E-We of the Cherokee," and finally "Archimedes of Greece." Eleven immortals faced Alexandria and Jackson, and she could feel the power and collective knowledge radiating out, touching her mind and spirit.

She gasped, and Jackson, who was seated to her immediate left, reached out to her. Several frowns followed his arm, but he did not pull back.

"Hey, you okay there?" he asked, as he searched her face.

"Yes, thank you," she reassured him. There was no way to describe what she felt, so she refrained from saying anything.

Archimedes drew her attention and Jack let his hand fall back to the arm of his chair. "Alexandria, as you have been told, this is all new and uncharted territory for us. You are here at last, and it is our sole intent to give you whatever information you seek, so that you can make an informed decision about your future. Several members of our council expected you to become acclimated to our kind at a slower pace, but others here thought that once the dam sprung a leak, the water would find a way to push forth. I think after what we've witnessed tonight, it is safe to assume the latter to be true."

"To the best of our ability, we will try to explain what we know to you about Arianna's demise and what led up to her last moments. But first, we need to tell you a little information about what led up to that day." He gestured for Sabina to proceed with the account.

"Arianna was my most treasured friend for over three thousand years. After my father left this earth and returned to the Lord's presence, I was placed in her care, as were most of us here. As the first *Nephilim*, Ganymede took centuries training her and helping her learn how to control the vast power that resides within a child born to an angelic parent. We could easily wipe out our mortal brethren if we were not mindful of how we use our talents. As long as we seek a path of peace and righteousness, we are allowed to continue here on earth. The Lord would not abide us if we were an abomination or threat to His peoples," she said solemnly.

"Even when I met her so long ago, Arianna had already walked this earth for thousands of years, like her father. She saw the Egyptian, Mayan, and Aztec pyramids go up, she traversed the globe before others were daring to take ships across the great seas, and she was helping humans establish towns and villages that would leave their marks throughout mankind's history. She healed and inspired many noteworthy people to strive for more information, more inspiration, and more tolerance," Sabina said, gesturing towards the ceiling.

"But her work did not go unnoticed, and not everyone approved of her determination to help humans advance." Sabina bowed her head for a moment and Nassor continued for her.

His voice was rich and commanding as he began. "Often when one is doing good, those who abhor what is right, take notice first. They seek to destroy that which they fear most, and for us that means the children of the Fallen."

Alexandria thought back to her conversation with Ganymede in her parents' garden. He had told her Lucifer allowed his Fallen angels to mix with humans as well. She thought of Bertrand and shivered from head to toe. Jack reached over and touched her hand again, and this time she noticed Rohan's eyes tracking the movement with thinly veiled anger. She smiled her thanks at Jack, and moved her arm off of the chair into her lap to break contact. Jack might not care about Rohan's opinion, but she was not looking forward to a possible feud between the two.

"There came a time when the Fallen's children became embolden by their successful destruction of human life, peace, and ingenuity. They targeted us, and looked for ways to undermine our efforts. When they grew bored with that game, they sought to wipe us from the earth. Arianna knew their plot before they did, and had already started to seek us out, train us and form us into a cohesive group. Together we are much stronger, and more protected than if we were out in the world alone." Nassor looked at Archimedes after he spoke, and a silent exchange passed between the two. Both looked pensive and saddened by whatever thought they were sharing.

"Needless to say," added Elrick, "we became very strong and determined. Arianna formed this council of twelve to monitor the whereabouts and work of all of the others, and to help mentor and guide the newest of our kind. She was always the first one a new *Nephilim* would work with after their angelic parent returned to the Lord, and since her passing there has not been another new immortal child born."

"Wait," interrupted Alex. "Not another one born? How long ago did Arianna die?" She looked around the group expectantly, and it was Rohan who answered.

"One hundred and twenty-one years, three months and four days ago," he said, evenly. Alexandria did the math quickly and looked back at him sharply.

"She died one hundred years ago to the day I was born?" she asked, astonished.

"Yes, Alex," responded John. "You came to this world exactly one century after Arianna passed. We had hoped to see you sooner, but our parents believed it would be better to let some time pass before they requested you be allowed to come back. I have often thought of how the last century's technological advances would have excited you. Oh, I'm sorry, I misspoke," he admonished himself. "I meant her."

"It's alright," she reassured him, and marveled at the authoritative tone she heard pass through her lips. Alex looked back at Elrick and directed her next question to him. "You said she formed a council of twelve, yet there are only eleven of you here tonight with me and Jack.

Where is the twelfth member?" This time no one seemed ready to answer her.

Finally, E-We spoke and her voice sounded like soft rain pattering across the cool stones of her native Appalachian mountains. "There is another who could not be with us tonight. Sometimes our work keeps us from always being ready for council business, and many of us are currently tracking children of the Fallen and cannot leave their posts. Our twelfth member is tasked with such work and is not able to join us at this time." She nodded solemnly at Alex, letting her know that she was finished speaking on the topic.

Benen spoke next, drawing Alex's attention from E-We's stillness and quiet reverie. "As Arianna was our first and most powerful, so too was there a counterpart amongst the Fallen's children. A leader who tried to mimic Arianna's organization and instruction amongst his own kind. And though he sought to collect his brethren into an elite fighting force, they rebelled even within their own ranks. They fought one another for power and control. And they pulled away, not wanting to be under anyone's authority or command. It is their reluctance to befriend one another that has worked to our advantage time and time again."

Alex felt the hair on the back of her arms and neck begin to rise. She felt her heart rate accelerate, and she began to draw in shallow breaths. She tried desperately to hold on, not wanting to be swept away from this most important of discussions. She dug her nails into the leather arms of the chair trying to anchor herself to a tangible object. But try as she might to fight the undertow, the room in front of her darkened and disappeared from sight and she saw that she was standing on a cliff overlooking a rocky shore below. Water foamed and cascaded over the rocks as the current pulled it to and fro.

Wind and mist whipped her hair around and she reached up to brush it back behind her ears. She found herself facing a man whose back was turned towards the cliff. He was beautiful, with deep brown, wavy hair, light hazel eyes, and a thick muscular build. He stood much taller than she, and he had a look of absolute anguish on his exquisite face.

"No!" he screamed. "You cannot do this to me; you cannot take from me what is mine! What gives you the right?" he laughed bitterly, the sound landing harshly on her ears. "You cannot fix everything and everyone, Arianna. I'll be damned if you will succeed with me!" And though he yelled and rebelled against her, she moved closer to him.

Alex could feel Arianna's pulse quicken as she came increasingly closer to this being who was eyeing her warily, and inching closer to the sheer drop behind. He held up his hands in warning for her to stop her advance, but she kept coming. Finally, she was within reach, and she lifted her hand laying it aside his cheek. Tears began to run unchecked down his face and he shook his head in denial at the love and forgiveness that flowed from her to him.

"I do not believe all is lost for you and your kind, Kronis. If I did, then I would be ready to give up and join my Father. God forgives all, and that includes you. Do you think yourself above His mercy? Do you think yourself so far removed from His grace? He can wipe you clean and heal you, if you will only let Him! Do not turn away from this redemption. Call all of your brothers and sisters together, and join us," she pleaded, throwing all of her regret for the lost ones and affection for them into her palm. She felt a surge of white hot power leave her and enter him.

His pupils dilated and he opened his mouth in shock and wonder. He gasped loudly as her energy spread throughout his body. And then she saw it is his eyes, his reaction to the wonder of this new feeling of enlightenment and pure unadulterated love.

"Yes," she whispered, nodding at him. She realized she, too, had tears streaming down her face. He fell to his knees and she went with him, so that that they were still looking into each other's eyes.

"I never knew," he choked out. "Oh, God! What have I done?" His eyes looked panicked and he searched hers wildly. "All this time, all that I have destroyed! Why? Why did you seek me out? Why not leave me to rot?" His words sounded like a plea to her, begging for release and understanding.

She smiled sadly, because she knew all of his transgressions. She knew of the human and *Nephilim* deaths he had either inflicted personally or helped to orchestrate. She knew of the chaos that he had masterminded, and of his continued determination to undermine all that she worked to create and uphold.

"Because, there but for the grace of God, go I, Kronis. We are all of us half human. We all feel temptation, the desire to interfere with humans' choices, the need to alter their paths. The pull of the power within us is a heady and potent enticement, and we have to constantly will ourselves to resist. It would be so easy to give in to it and play God. But we are not Gods, nor are our parents. They are only servants to the one, true God."

"You were raised to believe your path lay only in one direction, one that leads to pain and suffering. I have seen humans with the same twisted message from their parents or owners too many times. The damage that such indoctrination can do to a child is so hard to surmount, but it can be, if one has the will to change. You have to want it so badly, that you overcome what you were raised to be. Do you want the Light enough,

Kronis? Can you see now what we could accomplish together, if we were no longer fighting each other?" Please, she thought to herself, please want this!

There was still such a raw look of pain and internal struggle reflected in his eyes. Could he triumph over the parentage of a Fallen angel? She had no way of knowing, but she had tired of wondering. After all the ages of war and threat, she was ready to find out. She had pushed Kronis to the edge, quite literally, and there was no way out for either of them now.

Arianna had finally succeeded in trying to show one born of darkness the Light. A Light that was cleansing, but also terrifying to one such as he, for it held up a mirror to all of the sins he had committed through the ages. The weight of that alone might crush him, and dash her hopes of reconciliation. She had not told the other *Nephilim* that she was meeting Kronis there. They had made it clear to her that they thought the plan too risky.

But she had believed that Light would always chase away the darkness, and so she had secretly arranged the meeting. She had searched deeply within herself in the days leading up to their rendezvous, and found that this core belief was what had sustained her through the thousands of years she had tread the earth. She could not abandon that truth now in the face of such insurmountable odds. What was even more surprising, was that he had indeed come to the abandoned and lonely cliff top to hear her words. That was no small victory in her mind, and it gave her hope.

"I cannot give you the words, Arianna," he breathed out. "A part of me wants to, now more than I ever thought possible, but I cannot. This is too new, too much!" He clawed at his chest with his hand as if he could tear this new sensation from his breast and hide from the tidal wave of emotion threatening to engulf him. His eyes wildly looked around for a means of escape.

"Kronis, you do not have to answer me today. You do not have to pray and be forgiven today. You have at least felt what is possible, and you know the path you have to choose to make that feeling your own. What you do now is your choice, of your own free will," Arianna shrugged slowly. "What I want you to do, well, you understand, really understand now, too."

"Recognize that I walk away with a heavy heart, but I am here to help you follow a different destiny if you will only take what I offer. Grace and forgiveness are freely given, yes, but you will feel the weight of that choice and have to reconcile yourself to the changes such a life will bring. No more death, no more destruction. But pain, yes, there will be pain. No one can do what you have, for as long as you have and not feel it. I will take my leave, but you can come to me whenever you are ready." She removed her hand and began to unfold herself so she could stand, but his hand shot out and clasped hers, stopping her.

"No, stay, for just a while longer, please," he pleaded. She was startled, but nodded her agreement. She sank back to her knees and squeezed his hand, which was still grasping hers as though it were a lifeline.

"Shall we pray?" she whispered.

His wide eyes reminded her of frightened child, one not accustomed to kindness, but hungry for it all the same.

As Arianna began to pray quietly, Alex felt the familiar tug that drew her back to her own time. Only this time, she resisted. She wanted to stay with Arianna; look out of her eyes a while longer. Actually feel what she was feeling, and *be* her. Alexandria looked down at her fingers, and Arianna's were hers. They were one and the same. The struggle was too much though, and she lost her connection to her past, twisting and swirling back to the present.

13

"Alex, open your eyes if you can." She heard Archimedes' voice and it sounded so far away, but her consciousness grabbed onto the sound and she used it to make her way back. Her eyelids fluttered open and she saw several faces close at hand, the others standing not far away looking worried and pensive.

To her surprise, Rohan had collapsed his large frame on the floor near her and was holding her head in his lap and hands. Jack was also on the floor at her side with a wet cloth in his hand. John had moved to her former seat and was staring down at her, concern etched across his brow.

"It took you a while to return. Where were you this time, Alex?" he asked.

Her eyes widened in wonder. "I was Arianna, John. I mean, I felt at one with her. I felt her emotions, felt her anguish, and felt her desperation. She, or I, was with Kronis on a cliff overlooking the sea."

Rohan's hands brushed her hair back and he looked worryingly into her eyes. She tried to sit up only to realize how shaky and clammy she felt all over. Rohan moved to put his hands behind her back and he steadied her, supporting her weight so that she did not fall back and hit her head on the hardwood floor.

John and Archimedes shared a long look, then they both turned towards her. "We knew that she met with him, but only after the meeting had taken place. It was the most risky thing Arianna ever did, I think. But she believed that if she could bring Kronis to the table, then all the others would follow eventually," said Archimedes.

"Some of us didn't agree," said Rohan behind her.

"You're angry with her, I understand, Rohan, I do. But if you could have seen her on the cliff, on her knees with Kronis, and felt the love emanating from every fiber of her being…," her voice trailed off, as a thought suddenly occurred to her. Arianna was within her, so if she could see this, then she should be able to show all of them what she saw through her connection to them.

"What are you doing?" Rohan eyed her warily.

"Please, let me try," she asked tentatively, as she stretched her hand out in front of her. She concentrated on the memory she had just experienced. All of the emotion behind it began to come forth, and she used it to push the memory outward, going back through every second of it with each *Nephilim* in the room. Some widened their eyes, while others closed theirs and concentrated on the vision. Each in turn slowly released their breath as she began praying with Kronis and the memory left her, signaling her release on those around her.

Alex noted that her hands were shaking violently and she felt cold all over. Rohan's hands had not left her back, and though he looked stunned by what he had just witnessed, he reached around her and began to rub her hands, letting his chest warm her back.

"Thank you," she said, through clattering teeth.

"Hmph," he huffed.

She looked up into Jack's eyes and they were shining brightly. Had he seen the vision too, she wondered. From the look in his eyes, she felt that he had.

No one said anything for several minutes as each tried to assimilate the new information into their established timeline of memories and history. Elrick shook his head sadly and spoke first.

"I never understood why she did it. When she came to us and told us that she had met with Kronis, I thought she had finally lost her mind. I mean…," he seemed to be searching for the right words as he ran a frustrated hand through his thick hair, "I couldn't imagine why she would want to meet with something so vile and evil. But seeing him like that, humbled and penitent. I, I just don't know. Maybe she was right to try." He looked around to gauge his fellow immortals' thoughts.

"Doesn't change a thing," said Rohan through clenched teeth. "He still killed her."

Alex sat up then under her own power and whirled around to look up into Rohan's face. "What?" she mouthed.

"Yes," he said, giving her a stern, no nonsense glare. "He waited a year after that meeting and he killed her. When he attempted to draw in a few others to the possibility of change, they turned on him like a pack of rabid dogs. He lost his standing amongst them, and the only way he thought he could get it back was to kill her."

Alex reached out and squeezed Rohan's hand. "I'm so sorry, so very sorry." She did not know what to say that could ease his heartache. It was obvious that he was using his gruffness to hide the deep pain he was still experiencing from the loss of his friend. Alex looked around the room and saw the same haunted look on many of their faces. They were remembering her death, their mentor, their guide.

She began to think back through what had transpired in the last few days. So many changes, so much to process, and digest. Before Ganymede intervened, the words Bertrand had threatened her with came unbidden to her mind in that moment. *"I knew that you weren't dead. There was no way you were defeated, much less dead. No, you're coming with me, and you can be damn sure I will be well rewarded when I produce your pretty face to the council."* Alex looked back at Jack, now aware that he was about to hear a different version of her attack than the one she had recited to investigators.

She regained their attention by rising slowly and looking around at each one. "On the night of Lord Lenley's ball, I came face to face with one of Kronis' ilk. Bertrand threw me around like a ragdoll, and would have taken me with him had Ganymede not come to save my life. He said he wanted to present me to the council to prove that I was not dead and receive a reward. What council was he referring to?" Her tone left no doubt as to where her mind was running with the thought.

"Certainly not our council, Alex," Ahadi vehemently interjected. "The Fallen's children tried to emulate us, remember? They have a council of six, more or less, depending on how well they're getting along at the time. If Bertrand threatened to take you before their council, he might have been trying to unseat Kronis again and claim the victory for himself in a bid for more power," she added speculatively.

"Which means that Kronis will be coming for you," said Rohan, standing now too, and looking directly at Alexandria.

"I agree," said Benen. "Kronis always knew what his brethren were up to, just as Arianna always knew where we were and what we were doing. It's possible, that if Bertrand was making a power grab, he may have enlisted the help of a few others hoping for success."

"Or, he may have kept his plan quiet hoping the element of surprise could truly be on his side. He might have been worried that someone else would betray his confidence to Kronis," speculated Nikolaj.

"So you think Kronis is coming to finish this once and for all?" asked Alexandria softly.

"Unfortunately, it would seem so, Alex," Archimedes said regrettably. "He may come alone or with help, we've no way of knowing. It's possible Bertrand had allies that will want to finish what he started too, so we may have multiple assaults from different fronts before this is over.

She looked alarmingly at Jackson. "What? What's the matter?" he asked, picking up on her fear.

"Jackson, they'll come for my family. How many people do you have watching them?" she asked, breathing heavily.

"We've got plenty guarding your family, and some will follow your brothers when they return to work," Jack tried to reassure her.

Alex looked to Rohan next. "And how many do you have watching them?"

"Many," he said, sounding sure of himself.

"We should fortify everyone for what's to come, and prepare Alex," Benen said, nodding in her direction.

"Yes, I concur," replied Archimedes, walking over to stand directly in front of her. He reached out and squeezed both of her arms and smiled warmly at her. Though this was a tense moment, his unruffled reassurance helped to calm her swiftly beating heart. "Alex, I think you will agree, that you need to know how to defend yourself, now more than ever. Will you embrace this and allow us to train you? Will you reconnect with what was, and still is within you, child?"

She had sworn to herself never to be a victim again and to protect those she loved while in her hospital room and parents' garden, before she knew the broader picture. And she had made that vow before she had so many others to care about and protect. But looking back on the assemblage of faces in the ballroom earlier that night and the core group gathered there before her, she could not shirk her duty and leave them to the wolves who were circling.

This was her duty, and this was her task, however daunting, to see through. She had once offered Kronis absolution and he had taken her life in return. If her soul had been the one to call him to the table, then those she loved could not pay the price for that decision. She knew there had to be more to the story, and why the mental block persisted, she did not know. It was keeping all of Arianna's memories at bay, but the ones she had experienced thus far, had felt like her own, not someone else's.

She was beginning to see that in time, she might be able to completely embrace the life of the *Nephilim*. The less she fought the memories, the less she felt confused and torn between these two lives. They were coming together, now rather forcibly, and she would have to find a way to meld her present being with who she was before to reign victorious over Kronis and his kind. And if that was what she had to make happen so that they could all be truly safe, then she would rise to the challenge.

When she spoke, her voice reverberated with power and conviction. "I will, Archimedes. And I will protect what is mine. My family, and that includes all of you, will not suffer because of a choice I offered a lost soul long ago. I'll not leave; I'll stand and fight." She looked around and made eye contact with each one giving them each her pledge.

"Well done, Alex," praised Archimedes. "Tomorrow is New Year's. I cannot think of a better way to start fresh, than to put this plan into action. Why don't we all retire for the evening, and we'll convene after breakfast to begin your training? What say you all?"

It was unanimous and slowly the library emptied of the *Nephilim* council. Each gave Alex a warm embrace or squeeze as they departed, until it was just she, Jack, John, and Rohan.

"Alex, how are you feeling after your vision?" inquired John, ever the doctor.

"I can't honestly tell you, John. I've never had this many visions in one day before, although I suppose I should stop calling them visions. They're memories aren't they?"

"Yes, they are, and some are directly Arianna's. Others are tied to your ability to see into the past. But, we'll delve into that later. You've had enough for one night, so off to bed with you both. We have placed some light food and refreshments in your rooms in case you grow hungry, and should you desire anything more substantial, help yourselves to whatever you want from the kitchen. What is ours is yours. Goodnight to you both," he said gently. And with that last sentiment, he patted her arms, then turned and left the library.

"I'll see you in the morning," Rohan stated, and turned to take his leave as well, but not before giving Jack a long look.

"I'm not sure he likes me. Whatcha think?" he asked, smiling down at her.

"I think he's just being overprotective, that's all. Nothing for us to worry about," Alex reassured him. "Shall we?"

As they passed through different hallways and followed the main staircase's twists and gentle turns, both were silent, thinking back on the incredible day they had just experienced. Nothing could have prepared Alex for all that had transpired since she rose from bed in her parents' home that morning. She did not even begin to know how to process all of the information she had gleaned, and her head was now throbbing persistently.

They finally reached a door that felt like hers, and Alex paused in front of it tracing the wood with her fingertips.

"This our stop for the night, Miss Groaban?" asked Jackson teasingly. "That must mean I'm in here." He stepped across the hall and opened the door directly opposite the one she stood in front of. Jack found his luggage at the foot of his bed, and a substantial fire burning in the fireplace. "Wow, a real fire! They sure do go all out, don't they?"

"It would seem so," she acknowledged quietly.

"Come on, let's have a look at your place." Jack stepped back over and opened her door, walking into the room first and he proceeded to look all around her apartment. He made no secret of his intentions, as he left her standing just inside the doorway while he went and looked in the adjoining sitting room, watercloset, and walk-in wardrobe. He even looked under the bed and opened the double French doors, despite the cold, and looked out onto her balcony.

Alexandria stayed rooted to the spot until he was satisfied that she was alone and safe, not due to fear, but from fatigue and exhaustion. She discovered that she was actually swaying on her feet, so she did not chance any forward momentum. Jack came over and stood directly in front of her, lightly gripping her shoulders until she looked up at him.

"Hey, I know you're running on empty. Why don't you get a shower or hot bath, and then call it a night? If you need anything, anything at all, all you have to do is call and I'll hear you, I promise," he nodded slowly at her in order to secure her agreement. But she did not trust her voice, afraid if she spoke a dam would surely break inside and she would start to cry, so she nodded her concurrence.

Though he looked worried about her, Jack took his leave, slowly closing the door behind him. Alex took a tentative step further into the room and felt the first crack in her armor. A sob escaped her lips and she drew the back of her hand up to try and stifle the onslaught, but it was of no use.

She began to cry in earnest then, her whole body racked with sobs stemming from the heartache she had felt for so many throughout the day. She cried for her family's pain of seeing her hurt and in danger, for the *Nephilim's* loss of Arianna, for Ganymede's loss of his daughter, and for her own vulnerability and loss of safety. She could not stop the flow now if she tried.

Alex doubled over, placing her hands on her knees trying to catch her breath, but the tears kept coming. Just when she thought she could not take any more, she felt strong arms lift her and cradle her. Jackson had heard her and gathered her up. He stood for several minutes just slowly rocking her, and then he moved over to a leather sofa by the fire and sat down with her in his strong embrace.

"It's okay, Alex. You cry all you want," he whispered, and rocked her until her tears were finally spent.

She felt completely rung out, and could not summon the words to thank him. She stayed there in his arms trying to regain her composure, but each time she tried to speak, she would feel a knot in her throat. One of his hands, she realized, was slowly caressing her back and the slow circles were making her drowsy. She finally gave up the fight and dozed off, taking comfort in the steady beat of his heart close to her ear.

14

Alex awoke with a start and looked around, trying to orient herself. She was in bed, still in her clothes minus her shoes and the sweater she had worn over her long-sleeved shirt. The fire had banked down, but it was still glowing softly. And Jackson was sleeping on the sofa nearest the embers. He had a blanket over him, but it had slipped off of his legs; leaving his feet, still in their socks, exposed. She glanced at the clock on the mantle and saw that is was 6:35 in the morning.

She pushed the covers back and got out of bed as quietly as she could. She started across the room hoping to adjust the blanket back on Jackson's feet, but the floorboards creaked and he shot straight up from the sofa with his Glock at the ready. He immediately turned the barrel towards the ceiling when he registered that it was Alex he was looking at, then reached over and laid it down on the table nearest the sofa.

"Sorry, about that. Hope I didn't scare you too bad," he said, yawning and rubbing his eyes.

"No worries. I'm good," she responded, and they both laughed at her poorly veiled attempt to brush it off. She came over and took a seat adjacent to the sofa and smiled gratefully at him.

"Jackson, I don't have the words to thank you for last night. I'm so sorry you had to babysit me through the evening and didn't get to sleep in your own bed."

"Hey, no problem. I've had to sleep on the ground a lot in my lifetime. This couch is not bad at all," he said, patting the cushions to convince her. He sat up then and scooted down to the end of the sofa closest to her. He reached out and took her hand in his.

"Alex, look at me. When I told you I was here for you, I meant it. I don't scare easily, so I doubt a few tears are going to have me running for the hills, okay," he said, and he winked at her.

"A few! I'm sure I ruined your shirt last night. Jack, I'll try to hold it together a little better from now on, I promise."

He began to shake his head at her, and she wondered what he was disagreeing with. Surely he liked to have his clothing salt water free.

"Wrong. You don't need to hold anything back from me or any of the others here, Alex. Don't try to be a martyr or a saint. If you are a *Nephilim*, then you're still half human. And that means you get to experience the full range of human emotions. So if you need to cry, then you cry, okay?"

"Okay," she exhaled and nodded.

"Now, I'm going to step across the hall and grab a quick shower, and I'll see you after you do the same. Then we'll go downstairs and see what's for breakfast. Sound like a plan?" he angled his head at her, waiting for her agreement. As if in answer, her stomach grumbled loudly and they both laughed again.

"Sounds like a plan," she smiled.

Once Jack had taken his leave, she headed into the watercloset and found an enormous steam shower with more heads than she knew what to do with. She thought to herself that technology had certainly improved the castle, and she was grateful for it. Alex stood for what seemed an eternity in the large stall, letting the water wash away the fatigue and cleanse her body and mind.

The day held the potential to be a huge step forward, and it would take her focused concentration and energy to see it through. She finally stepped out of the water and finished getting ready, choosing thermal exercise pants, a fleece turtleneck, and running shoes. She dried her long hair and secured it behind her head in a braided ponytail. Before she left her room, she took out her mobile and called her family to wish them a happy New Year's. Hearing their voices only solidified her resolve to protect them, but she still made sure to threaten to lay hands on Wallace and Conner when she next saw them.

She was just ending their conversation, when Jack knocked on her door. "Coming," she called, and met him at the door. It seemed he had a similar idea about the day's activities, and had dressed himself in a rather expensive looking black track suit, and new trainers.

He noticed her appraising his new outfit, and shrugged, "Got this from my Mom for Christmas. Trust me, she'll be asking if I wore it soon enough, and this way I can say yes, and mean it." Looking down at the phone in her hand he asked, "Did you call your family?"

"Yes, they all sounded really good. I wished them a Happy New Year's and threatened to pummel my brothers, so I'm good to go." He laughed at her wicked grin and they left together in search of food.

Once they arrived in the kitchen, it was obvious breakfast was already in full swing. Alex opted to eat at the huge butcher block island that looked like it could seat at least twenty-five around its perimeter. There were stools down one side, so she and Jack sat alongside several others and ate there, rather than head for the more formal dining hall.

Jack was still talking to two *Nephilim* after they had eaten their portions, so Alex stood and cleared their places. She walked over to the deep, porcelain sinks that were nested into stark white marble countertops, and gazed through the expanse of windows that were present on that side of the kitchen. She had a good view of several fields and horse stables which lay in that direction. The stables looked bigger than her parents' house, and it was no small dwelling. She turned around, leaning on the counter and surveyed the room.

To her right were two large fireplaces, and she caught a flash of herself from the past bending over one checking meat turning slowly on a spit. She noted the modern touches that had been added. Several Sub-Zero refrigerators were lined up on the wall opposite her, and to her left there were multiple industrial grade ranges and ovens. You could certainly feed an army from this room, she mused to herself.

Ahadi came over and rinsed her plate, then placed it in one of the many dishwashers to the right of the sinks. She turned and lounged against the counter as well, crossing one ankle over the other. "Do you remember this room, Alex?" she asked. Alex found she loved the cadence of Ahadi's accent, lilting and lyrical.

"I do, though I picture it with far less stainless steel." They both chuckled at that, and Ahadi nodded her agreement. "But I suppose there's something to be said for modern appliances," Alex noted. "May I ask you a question, Ahadi?"

"Of course, Alexandria, you may ask anything of me."

"Is it awkward for you to have me here? I mean, I'm not exactly the friend you knew, and I don't want to detract from your memories of the time you spent together. Is it really alright that I'm here?" Alex could not believe she had voiced this worry so early in the morning, but she had thought about how the others must be reacting to her presence on and off again through breakfast, so the words had tumbled forth.

Ahadi set her coffee mug down and turned to face Alex directly. "When you love another so much that they become a part of who you are, you relish any moments you can spend together. I have missed my friend for many years, and yesterday she walked back in our door." She stepped forward and held Alex's hand in hers. "You may be called by another name, but you are my friend. You look the same, you sound the same, and you even smell the same!" Ahadi smiled over Alex's shocked expression at her last statement.

"And your aura is the same, Alex," she said, respectfully.

"Archimedes mentioned that when I saw him in a memory upon first entering the castle yesterday. What do you mean?" Alex pressed.

"Ah, the aura. It's one of your first lessons. When a new immortal child would come to you for training, you would teach us how to spot another *Nephilim* at a glance. There is an element within each of us that is passed down from our angelic fathers, and we learn to see that with our eyes and feel it with our intuitive abilities. You can do this now. It shouldn't be hard for you to remember this."

"Stare at the edges of my face, Alexandria," she said encouragingly. "Now, exhale slowly, and let your vision go out of focus when you do. Let your heart pick up on the rhythm of my heart, and feel the blood pulsing through my veins." Alex could indeed feel Ahadi's pulse, and her breathing slowed to match the pace of her friend's. "Now, feel the power that pulses through my veins as well, surging through every fiber of my being. You have power to match and then some, Alexandria. We are kindred. You know me, and you see me."

And Alex heard Ahadi's words resonate deep within her, vibrating like a harp string and stirring an ability long since forgotten, laying dormant until a time when she was ready. She inhaled slowly and saw a shimmering red, gold, and a yellow so bright it appeared almost white, wave rolling away from Ahadi's face and body. It looked like she was on fire, but from within, and the Light was looking for any means of escape.

Alex stepped back and whispered in awe, "Oh, Ahadi, you are so beautiful, so glorious." Tears were once again gliding down her cheeks, but not from pain or tragedy, but in quiet supplication for what she was witnessing. She looked around the cavernous kitchen and found that so many more *Nephilim* had made their way into the space, as word spread of what Ahadi was attempting.

She saw them truly then. Her initial meeting, paled in comparison to this introduction. Every color of the light spectrum cascaded from their bodies, and it was so magnificent, so enchanting. She walked forward and touched Heath's purple, maroon, and blue shimmering Light and felt it tingle under her touch. He chuckled at her reaction. She moved silently through the room, touching and glorying in the angelic presence she felt in each one of them.

Energy such as Alex had never known filled her senses and it was a heady rush. She paused at the far end of the island and held her own hands up in front of face, and had to blink several times to take in all the colors pouring from her body. Where the other *Nephilim* had one, two, or as many as four colors, she possessed them all. She was every color and then a few that she could not exactly name. Her eyes looked to Ahadi in amazement.

She came to stand in front of Alex, her eyes glistening as well. "Yes, you are every color, because you possess every ability that an immortal child can have. You were the first, the great experiment to see if we could be here on Earth with humans. Because of your love and guidance, we are here also. We owe everything to you, Alexandria. Can you feel that affection emanating from us towards you?"

"Now you have the true answer to your question, my friend. We are kindred and we know one another," Ahadi said, reverently.

"Yes, yes we do," said Alex, nodding her head. She was most assuredly one of them, and she felt blessed and humbled now that the veil had been lifted. The world was so much brighter and richer with this new sight she had been gifted with.

Alex closed her eyes and felt the others' presence now. She could feel where each one was in the kitchen and she could sense those who stood just outside in the hall. She cast her mental net wider and felt that John and Archimedes were in the library, far away from the gathering she was a part of. She let it go further still, and knew that there were three *Nephilim* at the stables and one coming back to the castle from the lake. Her eyes flew open and she pursed her lips trying to stifle a giggle, but it bubbled forth anyway.

"Pretty cool stuff, huh?" Heath asked, smiling at her broadly.

"Absolutely brilliant!" she exclaimed, and the others laughed along with them, enjoying the blissfulness of the moment. Her eyes searched for Jackson, and she found him toward the back of the crush, leaning up against one of the large fridges. He was smiling from ear to ear and looked very proud of her again.

"Good job," he mouthed at her, and she felt her cheeks go crimson.

She looked back at Ahadi and Heath, as Rohan came into the room. He walked over to her and studied her for a moment. "So you can see us now, huh? Well, that's good. It'll keep you sharp, and help you spot one of Kronis' trash before they can get to you. You up to some sword play now?" he pressed.

Rohan was all business, and Alex appreciated his no nonsense tone. What you saw with Rohan was what you got, and that meant she could trust him absolutely. Because if he was displeased or in disagreement with her, she knew now, that he would tell her to her face. If a battle was coming, she wanted someone like Rohan at her side.

She smirked up at him and planted her hands on her hips, widening her stance as if for battle. "Bring it," she said, issuing the challenge. He raised a single eyebrow at her audacity and nodded at her show of courage.

"Well alright, then. Elrick," he called over his shoulder, "go get my longsword!"

Whatever bravery Alexandria had felt when she toyed with Rohan left her, along with all of the color in her face. She noticed Jack straighten away from the refrigerator and begin to make his way over to her.

Benen sighed loudly as he said, "Rohan, don't scare the poor girl before she ever lifts a sword, gracious. Don't you worry, Alex. We won't let him near you with that thing. At least not until you're ready, alright? Come on now, we'll get you all set up."

She nodded mutely, wondering what was in store for her. Once Jack had regained her side, she began to file out of the kitchen with the others in the direction of a door which led to one of the estate's vast lawns. She felt Jack's hand on the back of her elbow again, and took comfort from such a small bit of contact. She looked up into his face as if to voice her thanks; and he, reading her thoughts, nodded back at her.

He winked, and leaned down to whisper his encouragement. "You'll be just fine. Remember, I still have my Glock," he smirked, and they both laughed at the thought.

They arrived on the lawn closest to the castle's left side. There was a stone terrace with trellises overhead that held vines and climbing plants during the spring and summer. Several overstuffed chairs were scattered about, but thick plastic covers were draped over each to protect them from the snow. Alex and Jack walked over to the area and greeted Daiki and Nassor, who were already set up and waiting on her to arrive. Nassor clasped both of his hands around Alex's to greet her, and Daiki gave her a very respectful bow to indicate his pleasure in working with Alex.

"Alexandria," began Nassor, "you will find that in today's world there are many weapons that can stop a *Nephilim* mid-stride if we allow them to. You will learn how to disable such weaponry while you are with us, I hope. But your first lesson will be with the weapon we all began with, and the one we still prefer in battle." He reached for a gleaming curved sword which appeared to have a delicate pattern embossed on the metal, and a bone grip which looked smooth after much handling and prolonged use.

"This is Damascus steel. Some would argue it is the finest in the world, and it was created by humans long ago under our tutelage. It is incredibly light and easily wielded by both men and women. It can cut through other metals and it is very accurate when thrown from a distance, most often hitting its mark and protecting its bearer. This actual sword contains original Wootz steel, and another metal that most humans don't know about, one that our fathers gifted us with ages ago, called Inonya. Take it and feel its weight."

Nassor placed the sword into Alex's hands and she felt the light and subtle balance of the weapon. Its blade reflected a rainbow of colors as she turned it over in the sunlight. It was not too heavy for her, and she was sure that she could use it if she were faced with another like Bertrand.

"You're right," she nodded at Nassor, "this does feel light."

He smiled his approval at the way she was already adjusting her stance to hold the weapon aloft. It felt right to stand that way, so she followed her instincts. She handed the weapon to Jack to let him appraise it. He nodded and also turned it over, watching the color display that the sun's rays ignited.

Jack looked to the two immortals, questioning them. "Won't she begin with a wooden sword, instead of something so lethal?"

Nassor shook his head, "No guardian, she will not. No one will harm her in training. This will come as easily as breathing to her, like an adult returning to a bicycle they've not ridden since youth. Trust us, you will see." Jack handed the sword back to Alexandria, trusting Nassor to know her limits. Daiki gestured for her to follow him over to a few stitched dummies that were hanging from poles.

"Alexandria, you must first learn which areas to strike on an immortal child. Though we can repair most damage instantaneously, we are not immune to severe organ or blood loss. If the heart or head is separated from our body, we cannot live. So, you will take the heart out of this first mannequin and you will take the head off of the second. Will you try?" he gestured towards the dummies.

She nodded and looked around to make sure Nassor and Jack were standing a fair distance from her, noting the many *Nephilim* who were perched either on or beside the low rock wall which enclosed that section of the grounds. She approached the first target and aimed for the area that would house the heart. She took the sword's grip in both hands and was about to plunge the end of the blade into the artificial chest, when the dummy shifted sideways and she missed.

Alex looked around confused and saw Daiki's slow smile. So, *Nephilim* can move things with their minds as well, she thought to herself.

"You don't think we would just stand there and wait on an attack to come directly at us, do you?" he shook his head in mock disapproval. "Again!" he commanded, and she turned back to the target.

Alex concentrated on its center and approached it once more. She narrowed her eyes, watching for the first sign of movement, and was beyond shocked when it flew forward at her and she fell hard on the ground, losing her blade in the process.

Daiki's voice echoed out across the lawn a second time. "We will fight back, Alex, and disarm our opponents. Again!"

She stood and nodded at him, to indicate she understood. She brushed her pants off and picked up the blade. Alex walked forward and, looking at the mannequin once more, closed her eyes. She felt the wind whipping by her face, heard the sound of horses braying in the distance, and then she let her ribbon unfurl towards both Daiki and Nassor. She had not tried to connect with two minds before, but she wanted to know what their strategy was.

"Ah," she thought. She smiled, opened her eyes, and raised her blade. Alexandria leapt up, higher than she knew she could, and cut a quick diamond in the first dummy's chest as it spun sideways on his pole through the air, releasing its fake heart within. The second was already in motion and she sank to her knees then rolled low on the ground, coming up behind it and sliced its head off with a sweeping downward motion. Both mannequins fell to the ground, looking like gingerbread men who had been snacked upon.

She looked up at Daiki and Nassor who shared a smile between them, and then gifted her with one as well. Elrick made his way over and praised her efforts.

"Alexandria," Daiki began, "you carried a sword for longer than all of us have been alive, so this should come back to you quickly." He gestured towards the mutilated dummies on the ground saying, "These pose no honest challenge for you. I am very glad to see that you have already figured out that reading your opponents' thoughts can show you what strategies they plan to employ. But some of our kind are also able to use that technique, and they are very, very fast."

"You will have to read their thoughts, block others from reading yours, and fight another who has speed and agility the likes of which you have not yet witnessed in your brief human life." Daiki continued, "This morning, we want you to concentrate on your swordsmanship and later this evening we will work on your ability to shield your mind. One skill at a time, Alexandria." He turned and gestured for Benen, Iain, Jaqen, Abdalla, Tomoko, and Elrick, who was still close by, to join them.

Daiki made a gesture with his hand and they all fanned out in front of Alex. She saw now that they all carried a sword of some description. Some looked quite heavy while others looked sleek and lithe, like the one she was holding. She scanned the field before her and the spectators, and now saw that Rohan reclined against the stone wall looking bored with the proceedings. His eyes were so hooded, he might actually be catching a catnap, she thought.

Elrick called her attention back to the six standing in front of her. "Alex, we're going to take this slowly, so don't worry, okay?" She nodded her understanding. "We will each take turns moving forward, and we'll engage you in the center. We'll show you various strikes and blocks that you can use for offense and defense, but we'll go in slow motion first. Feel the way your arms and body adjust when you raise your hands and let your muscle memory guide you. Ready?"

She willed her feet to move forward and tried to stamp down the internal panic she honestly felt. Never in a million years could she have imagined a New Year's Day such as this. Because Elrick was standing apart from the group when he spoke to her, he moved up first. He showed her how to bring her sword up to his much larger one, and block a downward sweeping strike. He repeated the motion slightly changing the angle each time, so she could learn to turn her blade and meet him strike for strike. Even with the light blows, she felt them reverberate all down the length of her arms.

He finally backed away and Jaqen stepped forward. His approach was more graceful, like that of a stalking panther. He asked her to raise her sword at him and when she complied, he quickly used his to tap all of the areas she had left exposed and vulnerable when she lifted her arms. He showed her how to bend her elbows and pull them in closer to her body, in an effort to protect her core even if she were going to lead the attack. He nodded his approval and backed away, giving Tomoko her entrance.

"Alex, we are close in size, though you are several inches taller than me. I will show you how one smaller than you can use balance and your weight against you, to disarm you." She bowed slightly, then proceeded to knock Alex off of her feet three times, before Alex learned how to anticipate Tomoko's shifts and quickly changing angles of assault. If this

175

was slow motion, then Alex knew she would be in trouble once Tomoko picked up the pace.

Abdalla was the next to stand before Alexandria. He explained that sword play was like the fine art of dance. That once one found themselves facing an opponent, they were locked in a delicate, but deadly ballet. She would have to be light and ready on her feet if she hoped to survive. He instructed her to watch the way his body moved and how his arms followed through in full, graceful arches to complete a swing of his sword.

Alex became mesmerized by the beauty in Abdalla's style. She felt her breathing slow again and his movements began to appear in slow motion as well, so finely attuned to his body did she become. She saw him indicate that he could strike at her feet and heels and she slowly jumped to avoid his blade, amazed that she felt almost suspended for a moment before gravity reclaimed her.

Before he could back away she thanked him for the dance, causing them both to blush a little. Iain came forward and she noted, as she had in the ballroom the previous day, that he was tall and muscular like Elrick. And now she could also see that he carried a very large sword. His eyes looked down at her, and he smiled at her appraisal of the large weapon.

"This is a claymore, Alex. At least that's the name the Victorians gave it. To me, it's just my sword," he said, as he grinned a boyish, lopsided smile at her. My this one was handsome, she thought, and then hoped no one around her had heard her internal dialogue.

Iain instructed Alex to come at him. "Choose your path of attack wisely. Think of me as a side of beef, and which parts you want to carve off." She wrinkled up her nose in disgust at his words, and shook her head at him.

"I don't want to think of you like that, that's cruel!"

"Might be cruel, but effective. And trust me, none of the Fallen's children will look lovingly at you," he advised.

An image of Kronis standing before her on the cliff, with tears streaming down his face came unbidden to her. Alex still wondered if Arianna was not right to try, and perhaps there was still a chance to save him and the other lost children.

"Alexandria?" she heard Iain's voice calling her from her reverie. "Hey, are you, okay? You turned as pale as a ghost." He stepped forward but stopped, when he felt the tip of her raised blade touching his shirt right above his heart. His eyebrows rose in surprise as he looked first at his chest then at her face. His slow smile told her he was not angry at all.

"Well, I'll be damned, look at you! Well played, young lady. If you can fight coming straight from a memory or vision like that, then you stand a good chance of winning. Never let your guard down, you understand?" he asked her, his voice filling with tight emotion. Why, she wondered. Perhaps, because she had once before, and she had paid the ultimate price. She nodded her understanding, and he stepped back allowing Benen to stand before her.

He smiled warmly down at her and praised her progress and patience thus far. Then he told her he was going to make the instruction a bit more challenging. "You see, Alex, we all possess different abilities which allow us to, at times, call on the elements or cause false images in our opponents' field of vision. This can distract and, ultimately, help us defeat our enemy."

"That's not playing fair, is it?" she asked, not liking where this was headed.

"No, it's not fair, and we don't usually fall to such dirty tactics, but think about Bertrand. Do you think he would meet you fairly on the field of battle, or do you think he'd pull out every trick he had up his sleeve and hurl them at you and the ones you love?" he pointedly asked.

She winced at the memory and narrowed her eyes at Benen. "You're right," she said softly.

He reached forward and touched her arm, "Hey, I'm not trying to be cruel; I just want you fully prepared by those who love you and who are going to be honest with you. I don't want you surprised or hurt again, okay?" His piercing gaze bore into hers, and she finally patted his hand.

"Thank you," she acquiesced.

He instructed her to stand back and be ready. "Don't trust your eyes, Alex. This won't be real." His words caused her concern and then she felt the hair on the back of her arms and neck begin to rise. The air around her became charged and felt brittle. She tasted metal and heard a faint buzzing sound in her ears. She looked around and saw no one, not Benen, not Jack, not another *Nephilim*.

She heard a slow menacing laugh and saw the edges of a dark, shadowy form to her right and she spun in its direction, but there was no one there. She felt a finger slide down her left cheek and she whirled in that direction, but again there was no one about. Simply reacting like that was getting her nowhere, she acknowledged to herself, so she stopped and stood completely still, her sword raised in front of her. Alex closed her eyes and remembered the feeling she had experienced in the kitchen earlier once she discovered the *Nephilim's* auras. Each one gave off a distinct signature; she imagined it was similar to what human soldiers saw through night vision or infrared goggles. It was that Light that she concentrated on now.

She began to see each of the six standing before her with her mind's eye. She no longer needed her human eyes to show her the way. And as before in the kitchen, she began to note where each immortal was both there on the lawn, and around the estate. She found Jack and noted that he looked like a cool blue form shimmering behind her, steady and calm, like crisp, clean water.

She stopped hearing the demonic laugh that Benen was creating and heard his true laughter, erasing her fear of the unknown. She focused all her concentration on his figure, studying her opponent.

"I hear you Benen, and I know you are 1.4 meters to my left. Your right foot is in front of your left and your sword is at your side. Which means…," and before she could finish the sentence, she raised her sword so fast that she caught him unawares and had her blade at his throat in an instant. Alex opened her eyes and took in the look of pride in his eyes.

"Well done, friend," he praised her. She nodded at him and the two moved apart.

Nassor walked the short distance downhill to her side and conveyed his congratulations at a very productive training exercise. Alex thought that they were about to take a break, when he called for them to put it all together. She gave him a surprised and incredulous look, but he merely laughed at her astonishment.

"Alexandria, a battle will not pause and wait until you feel less winded and tired. You're thinking like a human, child. Stop concentrating on how sore your arms and muscles feel, instead begin to feel the restorative power that all *Nephilim* share."

"The power of our angelic parents courses through every cell in our bodies. We can call on that strength to fortify us when we engage an opponent. You will find you won't tire like Mr. Campbell over there, you won't feel like your arms are about to fall off, and you can use your father's strength to land blows you might not think possible. Because, you see, for a human, this prolonged, immense strength is not possible. They all reach a point at which exhaustion takes over. You won't succumb to that, if you use the part of you which is your father within. Try, please," he asked kindly, and so she agreed.

Alex looked at the six and smiled. "Take it easy on me to begin with, okay?" she asked, as she once again tried to quell the nervousness she felt within.

She caught their nods and moved forward to engage. They were slow at first, letting her catch on to the rhythm and timing as they swapped off, one to another, against her. Eventually, the blows began to come harder and faster as she spun, dove, and volleyed with each one.

Her arms were really aching now and she stepped back, trying to call on this strength Nassor had spoken of, but Iain gave her no quarter. He continued to increase the strength by which he struck and she felt her arm cramp and lose the blade, as her sword slipped from her grasp. Everyone paused instantly watching her to see what she would do.

Alex bent to retrieve the sword, when she saw Rohan straighten away from the wall and begin to walk in her direction. His stride was purposeful and he seemed angry.

"To hell with this," she heard him say the scant second before he lifted his longsword with both powerful arms over his head, and he hurled it directly at Alexandria.

15

Time stood still for Alex. She noted that everyone around her had a look of shock or outrage painted on their faces. Jackson's arm was outstretched as if that motion in and of itself could stop Rohan's sword from a distance. She saw the six she had been sparring with to her left in various poses as they raced to intercept the weapon.

Then she felt a familiar tingle and a slow smile spread across her face. Ganymede appeared at her side and smiled broadly down at her. She embraced him, so very happy to feel the peace, love, and contentment she experienced in his arms. His kissed the top of her hair and smoothed it away from her face.

"You are doing so well, my child. I am so, very proud of you." She smiled back basking in his praise, noting that he had referred to her as his child.

"You are uncovering gifts faster than the others expected, but I think Archimedes' analogy of a dam springing leaks was correct. Now that you are tapping into what lies within, your abilities, gifts, or whatever you choose to call them, will continue to present themselves in rapid succession."

He gestured towards the longsword now stuck in midair. "I see Rohan took the most direct method to bring this ability to the surface," he said, somberly shaking his head.

"What was he thinking?" asked Alex. "He could have killed me!" She had no idea what Rohan could have hoped to gain by trying to cleave her in half.

Ganymede chuckled. "Why, Alexandria, he achieved this," he said, sweeping his hand before him to the frozen landscape. "Rohan knows that you, and you alone of all *Nephilim*, posses this ability. You can essentially freeze time and space, put them into suspended animation briefly. I cannot say that I agree with his methods," he said reproachfully, "but he wanted you to remember that no matter what you face, you can stop it and control the outcome."

"How…, wait, I did this?" she spluttered, thinking that Ganymede had caused everything around her to come to a standstill when he appeared.

"Yes, this was all you. You have done this only a handful of times in all the ages you have lived on this earth, because you recognized it as the ultimate betrayal of free will. It is no small act to take another's choices away, to manipulate them whilst they are unawares. And, well, it gave you such a feeling of distaste and disgust that you rarely, if ever, called on the ability."

"Ganymede, if I could do this, why then did Arianna allow Kronis to kill her? Can any of the Fallen's children do this as well, or cancel out the ability in any way? Is that how he got to her?"

"Ah," he exhaled slowly. He looked far off in the distance as if searching not over the land that lay directly ahead, but through the years witnessing her fall. "I was hoping that your mind would not make that leap just yet, but you are my daughter too, so I should have expected it," he smiled now at her, though it did not quite reach his luminous blue eyes.

"When I say no other has the ability, I mean those of the Light or of the darkness. I do not know why Arianna chose not to utilize this ability to save her life. She could have saved herself, but in the last few moments she chose to fight Kronis conventionally, and it was her undoing. This is a question that the other immortal children have struggled with since she perished, and one that we all hope you can help us answer as you embrace her presence within yourself."

"You can feel her as you feel me within you. The strength that Nassor told you to call on is within you, Alexandria. That is where the aura comes from. It is the sheer power of your immortal parent within, radiating outwards, which causes the light display. Close your eyes," he instructed, and she obeyed him.

He stepped forward and placed his long fingers on her temples and slowly exhaled. Alex felt warmth filling her and then a sharp jolt passed from her head to her toes. "Alexandria, keep your eyes closed. I want you to begin feeling this energy within. It has been there all along, but it is awakening, as if from hibernation. Concentrate on the surge of energy you just felt. Where has it traveled to in your body?"

She turned her mind inward and felt her upper arms, forearms, and thigh muscles acting as repositories for the energy burst. She began to push against it and felt it spread out to every fiber of the muscles, tendons, and ligaments. She pushed further until it was saturating individual cells. In response to this effort, Ganymede continued to instruct her.

"Now feel what this power does to those cells you just refortified. It is like armor plating around your very essence, and it is hard for a cell to degenerate from age or illness if it is protected in such a way."

Alex slowly opened her eyes and said in wonder, "This is how we achieve immortality. We shield our cells from the decay age brings to bear and we strengthen ourselves from within with the pure energy our fathers have. Does this mean that I am completely immortal now, Ganymede?" Alex was unsure why, but panic gripped her, and she was not prepared for what that meant for her future.

"No, Alexandria, not now. You are feeling me within you and this will make you stronger. To truly embrace the immortal life that is yours to claim, you will have to allow part of your subconscious to begin healing yourself continuously. And you will have to speak the words to me, acknowledging that you want to be fully, and completely a *Nephilim* again. Be their leader," he gestured around them again at all who were assembled, and still frozen she noted.

"Until you want to be as you were, and as you will be when you choose this for your path and your destiny, it cannot and will not be forced on you. For now, begin to meditate and commune with the power within your body and let it strengthen you for the coming days of trial." He leaned over and kissed her forehead and smiled disarmingly down at her.

"So tell me, what shall you do with Rohan's challenge?" he asked, as he rubbed his hands together in anticipation.

"Wow, a mischievous angel! Never thought I would see that in all my days," she laughed at him, shaking her head. "Okay, so let's decide. I definitely don't want this going anywhere near anyone else, so let's take it down." She walked forward and plucked the longsword from the air. Then she decided that she would surprise Rohan by moving behind him and gain the advantage. Now she had the weapon and the element of surprise on her side.

When she was all set, she looked up at Ganymede and smiled. He nodded his approval. "Just think about how everyone was in motion the moment before they paused. Remember them in action and will them to be so again." She nodded back and thought about everyone's bid to run and save her from the blade in her hands.

She heard their shouts, and then saw the confusion that registered as they began to realize they were running to a place where she no longer stood. Jackson's eyes found her and he altered his course to intercept her. Alex took the flat of the blade and smacked Rohan on his backside, causing him to whirl around and face her.

"Oh, no, you don't," she scolded. He gave her an appreciative smile.

Jackson reached their side and tried to put Alexandria behind him. "What in the hell do you think you're playing at, man? Do you usually try to kill your friends before lunch?" He was shouting directly at Rohan and she could feel the tense energy billowing off the immortal. Other *Nephilim* were coming to separate the two, when Ganymede cleared his throat.

Every immortal stopped and fell to one knee, or bowed their head to show him their fealty and respect. He acknowledged their silent vow and gestured for everyone to rise. He walked over and stood beside Alex, wrapping a protective arm around her shoulders. Alex saw Jack's lips part in wonder, but he quickly recovered.

Ganymede's voice increased in volume so that all might hear his words. "I am most pleased that my daughter had been welcomed back into this gathering with open arms. She has yet to speak the words, but I still recognize her as blood of my blood. I am also grateful to see her progressing so well as her talents and abilities re-emerge. Rohan, I would suggest a little more caution, if you please." Rohan paled a little, and nodded at the angel before him.

In a quieter voice he said, looking down at Alex, "I will come again, as you need me. Do not hesitate to call on me, Alexandria. I mean that," he vowed, squeezing her again. "Goodbye, my child," he whispered, and he was gone.

Alex looked around and realized they all seemed a bit shocked still. She decided to take control and lighten the mood. She stepped closer to Rohan and peered back into his face.

"So, nice lesson, but don't do anything like that again, okay? I'd hate to have to do more than just smack you on your backside." She extended the sword back to Rohan, and when he reached for it, she clasped his forearm. "Thank you, my friend."

"You're welcome," he said, genuinely.

Nassor came forward and offered everyone a break, which Alexandria gladly accepted.

Jack asked her in which direction she wanted to go, and she opted for a light snack and then the stables. Since they had arrived, she had been itching to get down to the horses and possibly ride if she could. They walked back to the kitchen and found an assortment of different cheeses, crackers, and various fruits under small glass domes on the butcher block island.

Sabina came in while the two were enjoying a quiet moment between bites. Alex was in deep introspection about Ganymede's words and Arianna's choice, and Jack was lost in his own mind as he wondered if he would really be able to fulfill his vow and keep her safe. He seemed heavily outmatched in skill and strength there, and that was a feeling that he was unaccustomed to experiencing. But he could not imagine not trying, because he felt she was more worth his effort than any other charge he had ever endeavored to safeguard.

"I thought I'd find you two here," Sabina commented. "Where are you going after you eat? Have Archimedes and John given you a plan for today?"

"No," said Alex, "Nassor and Daiki had me working through the paces with swords, as you saw, and Nassor mentioned that I would work on mental blocking later, but I think I'm still on break right now. I was actually hoping to head down to the stables. Would that be alright, you think?"

Sabina's face brightened considerably and she clasped her hands together. "Oh, I was so hoping we would get to ride together soon. This was one of our most treasured pastimes together. It gave us such release and freedom, and took us away from our worries and troubles. You and I used to strike out and ride for hours, sometimes at a slow, sedate pace, and at other times," she smiled wistfully, "it felt as if our mount's hooves never even touched the ground. Total freedom. Did you bring riding clothes with you?"

"I brought everything but a helmet. Do we have to wear those?" Alex had been schooled to always ride with a helmet, but now that she had the possibility of near indestructibility coursing through her veins, she wanted to try a ride without one on, and really feel the wind in her hair.

"You can wear one if you want, we have them for some of our human guests who visit from time to time, but you don't have to. If you were to get hurt, you could heal yourself or one of us could heal any injury you sustained within reason." Sabina turned her attention to Jackson. "Do you ride, Mr. Campbell?"

"I know enough to be dangerous," he smiled crookedly. "But I didn't bring any gear with me to ride."

"Not a problem. We have extra clothing here as well. I will go fetch you some, and then we'll all have a pleasant ride together. I'll place the garments in your room within a few minutes, Jackson." She turned and left in search of an outfit for Jack, humming an old tune to herself.

Alex tried to remember where she had heard that tune before, but she could not quite place it. She shrugged and popped another grape in her mouth, studying Jack's face. He really was very good looking. She wondered how many hearts he had broken along the way. No, she scolded herself, do not think that way. She tried to think of something to change the direction of her thoughts.

"Jack, if you aren't comfortable riding, I'm sure I'll be safe with Sabina. I can even ask another immortal to go along if you wish."

He pointed the small cheese knife he was using in her direction and wagged it back and forth. "Oh, no. Don't even think about trying to ditch me, Alex. I'm sure I'm not as proficient as you or Sabina, but I can hold my own on a horse. I've had a few lessons."

Alex noted that he blushed at his last comment and she narrowed her eyes at him. "Why are you blushing, Mr. Campbell? Come on, spill it!"

He rose and cleared their small plates away, placing them in a dishwasher. He started for the doorway of the kitchen and called over his shoulder, "Keep up, if you want to hear my secrets, Miss Groaban!" She ran after him, thoroughly intrigued to hear the whole tale.

They mounted the stairs together and he told her how he had experienced a crush on a girl in high school who liked to ride horses. So as a way to spend time with her and impress her, he had gone with her on weekends and a few evenings after school here and there to take lessons, too. He told Alex that he had not completed the training because, sadly, he discovered that the girl liked the horse she mainly rode more than him. It was a sound blow to his budding manhood.

She laughed at his dramatic retelling and shook her head. "I don't think your masculinity is in danger, Mr. Campbell. You are quite the specimen and it is her loss, not yours." Alex wanted to die of mortification right there and then. She could not believe that she had been so forward. When they reached the doors to their bedrooms, she turned to him, hoping to find some way to recover from her loose-lipped blunder.

"Jack, I'm sorry, I shouldn't have said that just there on the stairs. That was too informal of me. Please accept my apology," she said sincerely, and extended her hand in his direction.

He took it, but did not shake it; rather he squeezed it to get her to look up at him. "You English, you're always so formal and worried that you might have overstepped some imaginary line," he laughed. "Alex, you don't have to apologize to me. I like hearing that I'm not too bad a, what did you call me? A specimen. Does the ego good."

"Besides, I think you're right. It was her loss, not mine. But get this through your head, you can say anything to me, tell me anything and we're going to be fine with each other. Got it?"

"Got it," she nodded. Thank goodness he was not ready to run for the door yet, she thought.

"Now go change, and I'll meet you back here in the hall in a few." He turned her in the direction of her bedroom and gave her a gentle shove to get her moving. He need not have, because she was changed and ready before he was. She stood back in the hall studying the artwork there while she waited, still amazed at the eclectic mix throughout the home.

Home. She mulled the word over in her head. It was the first time she had thought of Aeoferth Hall as a home. But it was, was it not? It was enormous in size and scope, and she had not taken a good look in all of the rooms yet, but it felt like a home, especially with so many *Nephilim* about. Lots of love, family, and friends made any structure into a home. Yes, she decided, most certainly it did.

Jackson came out of his room and looked around until he spotted her. They both silently appraised the other, and then he held out his hand to her. She walked forward and took it, and together they made their way down to the stables.

16

Sabina met them at the entrance to the stables looking beautiful in her grey riding breaches, crisp white shirt, and polished black riding boots. Her long raven hair was unbound and she looked exquisite breathing in the cold winter air. Her jacket was draped over her arm as she leaned against the railing of one corral while she waited for Alex and Jack to join her.

Alex called out a greeting to let Sabina know they were approaching and she motioned for them to come to her. She pointed to a young mare that was running around exercising with an immortal named Reuben. She was spirited, but he was helping her channel that spirit into a desire to run with an immortal astride her, not from them, in fear of the saddle.

"Are we able to communicate with them directly?" asked Alex, astonished.

"Some of us can. You most certainly can. Come, let me show you," said Sabina, inviting them into the structure ahead.

It was the most beautiful of stables that Alex had ever beheld. If money and time were no object, this would be the kind of stables she would have built, she decided. It, too, was several stories high, with windows high above the individual stalls so that light and perhaps air could be let in. The main structure was built of stone, with room for over a hundred horses, and dark polished wood abounding inside.

The stalls were immaculately clean, and large enough to hold two or three horses per compartment. But there was only one mare or stallion assigned to each, if the name plaques on the doors were any indication. She was happy to see each had so much space to move around in. Alex felt heat and asked Sabina if the building was now climate controlled, and she confirmed that the horses had seemed most happy when that new invention was added. There were mahogany benches down the center for riders to sit on either before or after a ride, or just to take in a little time with the animals there.

Sabina showed them the rooms at the back of the stables which were equally impressive. They had their own veterinary clinic, in the event they had to perform any surgeries or procedures to keep the horses healthy. There were tack rooms and a large room dedicated to shoeing the steeds. She went on to point out changing rooms, restrooms and a large, gourmet kitchen devoted to the preparation of the horses' meals.

Alex had started opening doors along the tour and she found she could pick out elements which felt new to her, things that had changed since she last walked through the structure. Coming back to the horses, Sabina led them over to two stalls housing glorious white mares. Both animals were at least sixteen hands tall by Alex's estimation.

"Alex, these two beautiful ladies are actually some of the stock we have which are descended from mares and stallions you rode over a century ago, when your soul lived as Arianna. They were bred to keep the best attributes of their ancestors in the line. You will find them gently spirited and very strong. They can carry a great weight, and they have incredible stamina. This is Eimhir and this is Aileas. I'll ride their brother, Helion, today."

Sabina stepped forward and opened the stall doors, then looked back at Alex. "You can speak aloud or with your mind. It won't feel like a two-way conversation, but you will feel vibrations of what the animal feels. You once told me you were able to see through the eyes of any animal and gain insight from their perspective. Imagine riding them and see what they think. Ready to try?" she encouraged.

Alexandria stepped forward and held both hands out in front of her, with her palms facing up. The light from the windows overhead dappled her hands with shadows and patterns. Aileas' muzzle brushed against one of her palms looking for a treat. She looked into first Aileas', then Eimhir's eyes. She decided to speak aloud so that Jack could hear her and have a better understanding about what was transpiring.

"Hello, I am Alexandria. Before I was here and before you were here, there were others in our places. An immortal stood where I am and your ancestors stood ready to aid her when she needed their legs and speed. But like you, I feel the one who came before still here with us, standing in my place along with me. So should you feel those you have descended from. Shall we see if we remember?"

Alex stepped forward and touched a cheek on each horse so that she was sandwiched in between them. The two mares leaned in closer and she could see their wide eyes taking her in, and she could feel their breath warm and steady on her forearms. She looked into those dark pools that were their eyes and saw herself reflected back. Her image began to change and she saw herself as Arianna standing before horses in the same stables, talking to them before she placed a blanket, then saddle on their backs.

She saw them exit the huge double doors at the entrance and saw herself on their ancestors, laughing and racing through a path in the nearby forest. The wind in her hair and in the horse's mane, rejuvenated them both. It felt so good to fly like that, so free. "Shall we?" Alex whispered with her mind. Eimhir snorted and then reared up on two legs as if she, too, was ready to feel the air in her mane.

Jack looked startled, but Sabina reached out to reassure him. "She's fine, Jack. Alex, I knew you could commune with animals before, but I've never seen you enter into a memory with an animal like you just did. That was incredible!"

Eimhir was back on all fours, but pawing the ground now, indicating her impatience. They all laughed at the mare's reaction.

"I suppose I don't know what the limits are. I'm just feeling my way along as I go," shrugged Alex.

"Well, there is certainly nothing wrong with what you just did. It was just amazing, that's all," she laughed. "Let's take our cue from Eimhir and have some fun. Ready, Mr. Campbell?"

"As I'll ever be," Jack smiled. Riding was not his favorite pastime, but if Alex was heading out, then so was he.

Sabina's excitement fueled Alex's, until they were both grinning like school girls. They quickly brushed, blanketed, and saddled the horses with the help of two other immortals, Leaman and Raeburn, who had already bridled them. Alex thanked them for their help, and stepped onto a small stool designed to help her achieve Eimhir's saddle alone. She watched Sabina jump and propel herself into the saddle gracefully.

"Let me guess, we can mess with gravity too?" quizzed Alex.

"Some of us can," smiled Sabina. Jackson climbed onto his stool and seated himself astride Aileas. The three headed out of the enormous double doors at the stables' entrance and breathed in the crisp winter air.

"We'll have snow tonight," said Alex, looking up into the sky. "Let's fly while we can."

"Hold on, Alex. It's been years since I've ridden, so can we take it slowly to begin with?" asked Jack, hoping he was not cramping her style.

"Oh, of course, Jack. I'm sorry." She looked pointedly at Aileas then. "Be careful with him, please," she thought. "He cannot ride well, so don't unseat him, Aileas." Aileas brayed and stamped her foot in compliance.

"Did you just say something to my horse?" he asked, feigning shock.

Alex smiled at him and nodded. "She'll keep you safe, no worries."

Jackson just shook his head and leaned forward, stroking the mare's neck. "Thanks, Aileas."

The three rode slowly through the upper lawns and then through the lower meadows. Alex marveled that so much land could be hidden away and that no GPS had spotted them yet. Sabina shared several stories of Arianna's past with them, noting the work the two had done in Israel and the surrounding Middle East over the last two thousand years. She also told a few embarrassing tales which had Alex and Jack in stitches.

As they turned and made their way back, Sabina asked Jack if they could pick up the pace just a bit. He felt ready, and found that it was not as bad as he had remembered from his high school days. Though they were going much faster they still were not letting the horses run completely without restraint. It was not until they were within sight of the castle and stables that Sabina felt secure enough to turn the steeds free.

"Jackson," she said, looking around Alex to address him, "you may not attempt what Alexandria and I are about to do. We are close to the castle and stables now and there are *Nephilim* everywhere, so Alex is safe. Come back to the stables behind us, but know we're going to go a bit faster now." Her words sounded like a command and left little room for argument.

Still, as much as Alex wanted to set Eimhir free to run, she looked to Jackson waiting on his consent before she left him. She did not want him to feel like she was ungrateful for the effort he had put in that afternoon, no doubt becoming very sore, just so that she could ride.

He nodded at her, letting her know he appreciated her consideration. "Have fun ladies," and his words were all the permission Alex needed.

Sabina looked at Alex. "You first, Alexandria," she encouraged.

Alex leaned down and looked into Eimhir's eyes, thinking back to the memory of Arianna flying on a mare through that stretch of land. "It will feel so good, won't it, no one holding us back? Let's go, my friend," she intoned. She did not even need to use her heels, because Eimhir was ready. She opened up her legs and the power of her muscles thundered over the land.

Alex closed her eyes and willed herself to see through Eimhir's eyes. She felt the cool sting of the winter air on the mare's pupils, and felt how her nostrils flexed as she took in huge lungfulls of air to support the pace they were keeping. There was a horse jump up ahead built into the fence, and Alex encouraged her mentally to go for it if she wanted to.

The two soared over the gate and barely made a divot when her hooves hit the earth. Alex could feel the horse's glee at this feeling and she reveled in it as well. Eimhir picked up the pace even more, and now Alex could feel the blood racing through the mare's veins and her heart keeping steady pace with the exertion. The horse was not bothered by it, so Alex did not worry. Finally, Eimhir began to slow and Alex leaned back into the saddle and opened her eyes. She had not realized she had moved herself so far out of the saddle and up the mare's neck.

Alex hugged Eimhir and whispered her thanks. She had never in her lifetime ridden so fast, with such carefree abandonment. It was incredible, she thought with utter delight. She pulled lightly on the reigns so that the mare would turn and she could see Sabina and Jack. She thought Sabina would be right behind her, but she was still far in the distance next to Jack, both horses standing still. They finally began a trot and made their way to where Eimhir was now turning figure eights to pass the time.

"Hey! I thought you were coming with me?" asked Alex, teasing Sabina.

"I wanted to, believe me. But that was something I have not beheld in such a long time, that I had to see it from a distance and appreciate the full scope of such splendor. You were one with the wind, Alexandria. It was a moment of beauty and grace. Just splendid my friend!" Sabina's eyes looked moist, but fiercely proud. Her appraisal made Alex blush.

She looked to Jack, and he caught her gaze in his. "That was either the most amazing thing I've ever seen, Alex, or the most reckless. But it did seem like you and Eimhir were having a blast."

"Thank you, Sabina," said Alex, nodding gratefully. "I think I should do this every day. What do you think?" she chuckled. Eimhir reared up to voice her agreement. Sabina and Alex giggled, but Jack placed a hand over his heart.

"Don't know about tomorrow, Alex. Let's give my heart a few hours to recover, then we'll talk about it, okay?" he asked, chuckling softly to himself.

"Okay, Jack," she agreed.

The three made their way back into the stables, and Alex nodded her greeting to many *Nephilim* along the way who had apparently come out to watch her final run in. She saw so many smiles and looks of pride among their faces. Perhaps she was doing well with all of this after all, she thought.

They helped Leaman and Raeburn take off all of the riding tack and cool down the horses. Alex had always loved to brush down a horse, whether she were getting to ride or not. The slow arching sweeps of the brush were soothing to her and she loved having the time to just be, not really having to think about anything in particular. Apparently, all three of these horses like to be brushed as much as Alex liked doing it.

When they were finished, they turned the horses over to the care of the stable masters and began the trek back to the castle. Jackson was already walking a little stiffly, and Alex knew that his leg muscles would pay him back for the exercise he had just engaged in. Often people who were very fit were surprised to find riding worked their legs out to the degree which it did, and they had been riding for quite a while.

Sabina was apparently noticing too, because she addressed him regarding his uneven gait, and Alex was mortified.

"No, Alex, do not be embarrassed. It is good that we can take away the pain and discomfort of others. Healing is a great gift, and it is one of the few abilities that we all share. It helps our work with humans, for wherever we find suffering, we can ease it. May I, Mr. Campbell?"

"Um, sure, I guess?" Jack's voice sounded very unsure, however. He did not know what Sabina had in mind, but he also thought denying her would be futile.

Sabina stepped closer to Jackson and extended her hands in front of herself. She concentrated on Jack's legs and then closed her eyes, breathing slowly. Alex's eyes never left Jack's face, and he finally lifted his gaze from Sabina's hands to look back at Alex. He shrugged his shoulders to try and muddle his way through the awkwardness.

She smiled at him and then looked at Sabina. Alex began to concentrate on Sabina's aura of silver, red, green, and royal blue. She watched as the shimmering flow of energy cascaded from her friend's hands towards Jack's legs. She started to sense the intention of the flow, moving in and chasing away the muscle strain and building lactic acid in his muscles. There was a warming sensation massaging the tenderness away, and then it spread upward working on his back and finally out through his arms. When Sabina was satisfied that she had erased all of his soreness, she lowered her hands and stepped back, opening her eyes.

"Wow," he whispered, "I've never felt anything even close to that. It was like a massage, from the inside out. Thank you, Sabina."

"You are very welcome, Mr. Campbell." She turned to Alex and patted her on the shoulder. "Come, you look hungry. Shall we make a sandwich for ourselves?"

In answer to her question, Alex's stomach grumbled loudly. "Yes," she laughed, "I think that sounds like a good plan."

Several other *Nephilim* were in the kitchen when they arrived, as preparations for a large New Year's dinner were underway. They collected the supplies they needed from around the kitchen and sat at one end of the island eating and talking, at ease in each other's company now.

Once they had cleared their places, Alex offered to help with the large meal's preparation, but was shooed away. Sabina told them that she was going to head back to her room for a shower and that she would see them again later in the evening. She stepped forward and gave her friend a tight hug before walking away.

"Alexandria, I so enjoyed our ride. We shall do this again soon, yes?"

"Absolutely, wild horses couldn't keep me away from the stables now, no pun intended," laughed Alex.

"Good. Until later, Alex. Jack," Sabina nodded at both, as she turned and began walking away. Alexandria heard Sabina humming the same tune she had earlier in the day, when she had left to find Jackson some riding clothes to wear. Alex paused and tried to recall it. It was an old melody, she was sure, but her mind was still searching for its origin in her memory.

The music swirled around in Alex's head and she tried to remember where she had heard it before. It was familiar, but not to her current lifetime. She caught a glimpse of herself coming down a staircase in a burgundy gown that was fitted across her chest tightly and hung delicately off of her shoulders. Fine black stones were woven into the dress' bodice and it was long enough that she had to lift it to walk safely down the stairs. She was entering a grand room where people were dancing, and men were dressed elegantly in black tie and tails.

She was searching for someone, and she could not seem to find him. She could not even remember his name to call out for him among the crush. More and more people pushed in on her from all sides and she started to have trouble breathing. But did they not understand she had to get to him? Where was he, and why did he not come to her, Alexandria questioned. He must know she needed him, Alex thought, as her unease began to build.

The heat, tight corset, and ornate dress became too much. Alex felt herself tilt and her vision began to fade, when she heard him. He was calling her, panic clear in his voice. He had come for her, and it was like water to her parched lips. But this voice was not the one she had expected. She was confused, and she tried to understand why another man was looking for her, too.

"Alex, open your eyes, baby. Alexandria, can you hear me? What do I do?" He sounded so anguished, she wanted to reach out and end his torment, but if she went with him, how would the other man find her? She looked around, still not seeing him and decided to go with the one who was calling her. Perhaps he could help her find the one she was truly seeking.

Alexandria willed herself to open her eyes. She was lying on a couch in the library with a cold compress on her head. She noted how heavy her limbs felt, and her mouth was dry as the desert sands she had touched as a child in Egypt.

"There she is. See, Mr. Campbell, I told you all would be well. Where did you go to this time, Alex?" asked John. He had pulled a chair up beside her, and was checking her pulse and timing it with his old Rolex.

Jackson had also pulled up a chair to John's left and was holding the compress on her head, just as he had done the night before. But unlike the previous night, she detected panic on his face that had yet to retreat from his features. She reached for his hand and took it in hers.

"I'm okay, Jack," she said, trying to sooth away his worry, but the dry smacking sound her mouth made did not aid her at all.

"Here, drink this," said John, as he pressed a cool cup of water with a straw to her lips.

"Can you talk about it yet, dear?" Archimedes asked. She had not noticed him in the room. He walked closer and pulled up a chair for himself to John's right.

"Um, yes, just let me sit up," she started, but Jack did not let her finish. He just placed a hand on her shoulder and shook his head, as if he was not going to entertain her sitting up just yet.

"No," agreed John, "let's have you lie still a little while longer while we all talk. You were about to tell us what you saw."

"We were in the kitchen talking with Sabina, and as she left she was humming a tune. I'm getting better at remembering things from Arianna's past and placing them specifically where they belong in her timeline, but this melody seemed just out of reach somehow. It was so hard to focus on it, and I almost lost it, but then I remembered hearing it at a ball."

Alex looked away from their faces and let her eyes lose focus. She could see the scene right in front of her as if she were watching a movie that a projector was displaying in front of her eyes. It was surreal to watch herself go through the memory, which she had just experienced firsthand.

"I was walking down the staircase, trying to lift the heavy burgundy gown I had on. I remember seeing water through the windows, perhaps we were close to a river or lake, I don't know. But I was desperately searching for someone and I couldn't find him. The longer I looked, the hotter I became in the heavy dress, and I finally felt myself starting to faint. That's when I could make out someone calling my name, so I tried to find a way back to that voice. Was it one of you?" she asked, looking back at the three.

"It was me," breathed Jack. "You took the longest time coming 'round. And you didn't just faint away as I have seen you do now, you actually shook and had tremors. I'm just glad you're with us again," he said intensely, placing the cold cloth back on her forehead.

"I'm here," she answered, patting his hand. She noticed that Archimedes and John were sharing a look that she now knew meant they were conversing only with their thoughts.

"Stop that, both of you," she scolded. They both looked down at her in surprise at her censure. "Don't talk like that while we're here. Spill it!"

Archimedes chuckled over her brashness and answered her call for information. "Very well, we were speculating that this was not a memory at all, but rather a dream tied to some of Arianna's memories. She never, to our knowledge, experienced a faint at a ball as you described seeing. She would have been able to heal herself if she were taking ill, as well. So, perhaps, the tune you heard triggered some feeling that Arianna might have experienced and your mind was struggling to work it out for her."

"Maybe. I don't know though, Archimedes. This felt like she was desperately searching for someone and greatly panicked when she couldn't get to him. She expected him to come for her and he didn't. I just don't know."

"Well, I am sure that we'll work through this in time. No need to worry yourself, Alex. Now, there's some time before we all celebrate New Year's at dinner, so why don't you take a little nap and then have a bath before you come down?" John proposed. It sounded like a good plan so she agreed.

"I'll stay with her," Jack offered, and the two took their leave.

"Jack, I'm...," but he would not let her finish her statement.

"If you apologize again, I swear, I'm going to throttle you," he said, with no real force behind his empty threat. "Alex, I know you have no control over this now; that will come in time, I hope. But it seems to be taking quite a toll on you. I just want to make sure your body can handle it all, and there's no way to really know."

He was slowly stroking her hair back from her forehead as he confessed his worry to her. She doubted he was aware of the tender way he was comforting her, even though he seemed to need it more than she did in the moment. It was making her very drowsy.

"Have you ever been with someone else like this, Jack?" Her eyes flew open, in surprise that the words had come unbidden from her lips, and met his. He looked surprised too, but not angry.

"What do you mean, Alex?" he asked softly, deliberately forcing her to explain her question.

"I mean, have you ever had to protect someone who needed you around so much?" Now she knew she sounded like an idiot. How else could he protect someone if he was not around them, she asked herself. Alex wanted the floor to swallow her up.

He chuckled at her poor choice of words. "I think what you're trying to ask me, is have I ever gotten close to one of my clients before. And the answer is, no. It breaks the trust between the security team and the person or persons we are monitoring. We can't be objective and at the ready if we're not focused on the task at hand."

Alex could feel her face fall. What in heaven's name was the matter with her, she mentally chastised herself. This was the correct answer, and she knew it, but for the first time in her life she found herself actually attracted to a man. And as her luck would have it, she liked the one man she could not begin to pursue.

Alexandria felt the need to put some distance between herself and Jackson. She stammered out an apology for being so forward, despite his warning for her to stop the habit, and began to push herself up off of the sofa. She could nap in her room just as well as there in the library, she decided.

She had just gained her feet and was turning to head for the door, when he reached out and took her hand, halting her in her tracks.

"Alex, look at me," he softly commanded.

She really did not want to turn and face him. She was so embarrassed and hurt, and she could not explain it to him. She honestly did not want to see the rejection in his eyes.

"Alex," he squeezed her hand again, "look at me." He slowly enunciated each word, letting them hang in the air between the two of them. She finally turned and when she saw his slow smile, she almost turned away again, but he reached out with his other hand and took her free palm, so that she could not retreat and leave him.

"You asked if I have ever been close to another charge, and I answered you truthfully. I have not. But there is a first time for everything."

Her eyes shot up to meet his. Her lips parted, but she did not know what to say. What was he telling her, she asked herself.

"You are the most amazing person I have ever met, with or without all of this," he said, and gestured around the large library with his head. "You're graceful, smart, stubborn, accomplished, and so very brave. You're in such a precarious position right now, trying to find yourself and take care of everyone you love, but you're not running."

"Alex, I have lived through live fire fights, and I have seen some of the toughest warriors I've ever known want to turn and run. It's a natural inclination when faced with death, for self-preservation to kick in. I haven't seen that in you, not once. You're here, no matter the cost to yourself."

"Quite frankly, I'm in awe of you. I couldn't walk away from you right now if I tried. I'm glad I'm here with you to see who you will become through all of this. It's just a joy to see you awakening, for lack of a better term."

"And, Alex," he said, reaching up and tucking her hair behind her ear, then letting his fingers trail down her cheek, "I'd be blind if I couldn't see what a beautiful soul you are inside and out."

Tears pricked her eyes at his tender words. Never had anyone really noticed her in that way. She had never really tried to have a relationship, but Jack had snuck up on her and worked his way into her heart so quickly.

"Shhh, don't cry, Alexandria," he whispered.

He stepped forward and cupped her face in his hands and used his thumbs to brush away her silent tears. He hesitated for the briefest of moments, as if warring with himself, and finally closed his eyes, giving in and losing the battle. His lips met hers, tentatively at first, then more fervently. They wrapped their arms around each other, he holding her body to his, and she gently touching first his neck and then letting her fingers climb into his hair.

This was all new for Alex. She had only let two boys briefly kiss her throughout adolescence, but this passion was new and full of promise. It consumed her and she felt her hands shake. His hands reached up for her face again and he angled her head to give him better access. He rained kisses down her cheek, onto her neck and back up to her lips. Alex felt like she was melting and on fire at the same time.

When finally they pulled back, they both were breathless and amazed.

"Oh my Lord, Alex. I've never," he panted, and could not finish his sentence.

"Me either," she smiled, reaching up to trace his lips with her fingertips. Such a simple piece of flesh that could make them feel this way. No, she was kidding herself, it was not just these lips. She had passed by many a handsome man before, and never thought about sharing something such as that with them. It was her growing affection and comfort with Jack that made these feelings possible, she told herself.

"I should hope not," he smiled. "Are you okay?" he asked, with worry in his tone.

"I've never been better," she giggled. "Oh, Jack. What are we going to do?" she asked, as she reached up to run her hand back through his hair. It was so soft and given to curl at the ends.

He hugged her tightly and rested his chin on the top of her head, slowly rocking her. "I say we do what we're doing. Seems to be working, wouldn't you agree?" he breathed out a contented sigh.

"I've never let anyone hold me before, either," she whispered shyly.

"Lots of firsts on this journey, then." He pulled back and looked down into her eyes, one hand on her lower back and the other gently stroking her face. "This won't change my focus, Alex, I swear to you it won't. I'm still going to do my damnedest to keep you safe, okay? With everything I've got," his expression was so serious, as he pledged himself.

"I know Jack. I don't doubt you. But know this too: I'm just as concerned about your safety right now," she confessed, as he drew back and narrowed his eyes at her slightly.

"No, don't give me that look, you know what I mean. We know now that some very angry immortals are most likely seeking me out to finish some old business. For the same reasons I worry about my family, I worry for you, too. I would never forgive myself if you were caught in the crosshairs and harmed because of me." She shivered all over thinking of what someone like Bertrand would do to Jack. He would most definitely fight back, and they would crush him.

"Well then, we'll look out for each other. But if it comes down to it, Alex, you let me do my job, okay? No heroics," he pressed.

She opened her mouth to argue that his way of thinking was quite backwards, as it should be she who should do the protecting, but he leaned down and kissed her again, effectively cutting off any arguments she had.

17

Alexandria was up to her neck in a warm, foaming bath, and she thought surely this was what Heaven felt like. The bathtub was the largest old clawfoot tub she had ever seen, and it was the most beautiful as well. Its delicately carved feet were silver or pewter, she was not sure which, and the handles and faucet matched. Someone had added a high-tech mat to the bottom that could be adjusted to produce a current and jetted spray, essentially turning it into a sculpted Jacuzzi.

She had been lying there long enough to have wrinkled fingers and toes, but she did not care at all. There was no way she was getting into fresh clothing, or the bed's clean linens later on, with sweat and the smell of horse all over her. And the bubbly bath was making her muscles feel so good.

Alex closed her eyes and thought about all she had learned that day. Auras, sword fighting techniques, what riding really felt like, and communicating with animals. And she had been kissed, really kissed, for the first time in her life. It had been the best New Year's Day she had ever had in her twenty-one years.

She reflected on her conversation with Ganymede and his advice that she should begin meditating on the power within her. She draped a hand on the edge of the tub and looked out of one of the bathroom's large windows. Snow had begun to fall after all, steady and thick, blanketing the ground once more that she and Eimhir had flown over earlier. She looked down at her wrinkled fingers and concentrated on what lay beneath that skin.

She closed her eyes and felt the blood coursing through her veins and the cells that made up her muscles, organs, and skin. Everything about her had some of Ganymede within. She felt her way through each part of her body taking stock of all her internal components, and she was amazed at the sheer ingenuity of how seamlessly all of a human's parts worked together to keep a person alive. She studied herself down to the last molecule. God is an amazing engineer, she mused silently to herself.

Then she studied the plating and armor that Ganymede had given her. It reminded her of the way the Roman army of Caesar's day would lock their scutum, or shields, together in a pattern to protect the soldiers marching behind them. Only this defense was far superior, and blanketed each building block of her body seamlessly.

She slid down into the water and let it engulf her, so that she was weightless and suspended, free of gravity. She had seen Sabina all but bound atop her mount that day not letting gravity control her movements, and Alex felt certain that she was the one who had taught Sabina how to do that.

Hmmm, she thought, she had slipped again and thought of herself rather than Arianna when she thought of the past. But, this past was hers as well. It really did not make sense to her how this could be so. Yet, standing on that cliff with Kronis and feeling the power of the love she had offered him, as she tried to bring him in from the cold and shelter his soul, was enough to convince Alex that she and Arianna could be one and the same. Somehow, she would find a way to bring the past and present together, she told herself.

She could use these talents and abilities to help so many. She remembered a comment Ganymede had made in her parents' garden then, about how a long time on this earth could wear on a soul. Could she do that, she wondered. Could she be here for hundreds or thousands of years, trying to help humans without interfering to the point of changing their destinies and their desires?

She thought back further to the night Ganymede had visited her in Egypt when she was a child. He had told her how different her brothers would seem to her if he changed but one or two things about their personalities. How wrong it would be to play God, she thought. How cruel.

Then Alex recalled Arianna's words to Kronis about the constant struggle she, too, faced to not give in to the power within. She might have wanted to sway human behavior in a different direction, but she fought her own internal battle to stop herself from overwhelming humans' minds and compelling them into choices only she approved of.

Alex's mind wandered to all of the despots and leaders throughout history who had maimed, destroyed, and murdered entire groups of people. All of the genocide and pain inflicted by people filled with hate and venom, like Hitler and Pol Pot. Would she be able to stop herself from hopping a plane to some of the regions in Africa that still knew great conflict, and annihilating those who would destroy their own, she wondered. God help her, she could see that this was going to be a very emotional journey, and one that she hoped she was strong enough to see through.

Alex heard Ahadi's voice calling her and she rose up in the tub to answer her. She was just opening the door and sticking her head in, when Alex's head broke through the surface of the water.

"Alexandria, you are well?" she asked, looking around the bathroom.

"Um, yes. Why? Did you think I wasn't for some reason?" Alex knew that Ahadi would not normally come in on someone in the tub if she did not have cause for concern.

"Mr. Campbell called upon me to come in and verify you were safe and sound. He has been calling you for many minutes, but you did not answer. But you are well I see, so I will tell him you are just finishing your bath. I will see you at dinner." She smiled at Alex and took her leave.

Alex wondered how long she had been underwater. The water was very cool now, almost cold and she was beyond wrinkled. She sat up the rest of the way and pulled the tub's plug. She got out and dried first her body, then her hair, and finally pulled on some warm cords, her sweater and shoes before leaving the watercloset.

When she entered her bedroom, Jack was standing in front of one of the windows watching the snow fall. He turned as she came out and watched her walk over to him.

"I'm sorry if I scared you, Jack. I was underwater for a little while thinking about things. I guess I didn't hear you calling me."

He put one arm out offering her the chance to step into his embrace if she so chose, and she did not hesitate to step forward and soak up his warmth. They stood there silently looking out of the window together in companionable silence for some time, each with an arm around the other.

"What were you thinking about under water for so long, Alex?" he quietly asked.

"Oh, you know, the usual stuff. Inner armor plating, indestructibility, how an immortal can help without overtaking mankind, flying with a horse. Just a normal day, all in all," she smiled, still looking out at the snow.

He leaned down and kissed the top of her head, inhaling afterward. "You still smell like the wind out there from our ride earlier."

"I did wash my hair tonight, though," she started to explain that she did not how that could be possible, but he inhaled again.

"It stuck with you somehow. You looked really happy and carefree out there today. Like someone your age should. Hang on to that." Jack was quiet for several minutes.

"I was worried," he said softly, breaking the silence.

"I know, but I'm okay. Apparently, I can hold my breath for a really long time, but I wasn't even aware I was doing it."

He pulled back a little and looked down into her blue eyes, which looked so relaxed in that moment. "No, Alex, no apologizing remember. It's me who has to adjust to the changing landscape here, not you. You're not doing anything wrong. So far, I'd say you're right on target. I'm trying to not let my worry get in your way." He started chuckling and shook his head.

"Hell, I almost knocked your bathroom door down, but thought better of it and got Ahadi. I'm glad I did. I think if I trust in this more and stop trying to fit it into the reality I know, I'll be less troubled."

Alex nodded her head. "Sounds like a good plan, Mr. Campbell. Are you hungry?"

His eyes took on an all together different look and then he smirked at her. "Yes, I am, Miss Groaban. Let's get you down to the dining hall, while all's as it should be."

Alexandria had an inkling of what he was alluding to, so she pulled away and made her way in the direction of the door to her bedroom. She started to give him a smart little comment, but lost her balance and caught herself by grabbing an old quilt stand that was near the foot of her bed.

Once her hand touched the wood, she was no longer in the room during her time, but in the far distant past. Sunlight was streaming in through the windows and she heard music from somewhere below in the castle. It was the same tune she had heard earlier when she collapsed that day. What was this piece, she asked herself.

She started for the door, hoping to run downstairs and find out who was playing it, when she heard a cough behind her. She stopped and turned around cautiously. At first, she saw no one, then realized there was a man out on the balcony with his back to her.

"Hello," she called out, but he did not turn. He leaned forward and rested his arms on the railing looking out over the estate below. He was tall, she could tell that and he had chestnut brown hair, she thought. He seemed slightly in shadow despite the bright sunlight.

She looked around and noticed a letter on the bed, so she walked forward to look at it, hoping it would give her a clue as to what time she had arrived in and who he might be. Just as her fingers made contact with the parchment, she was thrown backwards with such a force, that it knocked the wind right out of her.

She registered out of the corner of her eye that the man was turning, but he was fading away. She felt the familiar tug back to her own time.

"Who are you?" she whispered, but no answer came.

"Hey," whispered Jack, "welcome back."

"How long this time?" she asked, knowing he understood her meaning.

"Just about five minutes, actually, so not nearly as long as all the others I've seen. Where'd you go?" He had laid her on the bed while she was unconscious, and he was sitting on the edge looking down at her, waiting for her response.

"I was here, actually, in this bedroom. But I think it was quite a long time ago. There was a piece of parchment paper on the bed and I was trying to look at it. There was a man on the balcony and I was hoping if I could look at it, I'd know who he was, because he wouldn't turn around when I called out to him. He seemed lost in thought."

"When I touched the paper, I was thrown backwards somehow and it took the breath right out of me. I think that's why I came back so quickly." She noticed the crease in his brow at her last statement. "What?" she asked, wanting to know his concern.

He shook his head. "Have you ever gotten hurt in a memory or a vision before, Alex?" he asked quietly.

His question was a sound one, and she thought back through her earliest visions in which she was always a silent spectator, then the transformation they had undergone since she had called on Ganymede at Christmastime.

"Not that I can recall. Though I never felt what I am feeling now, because I always seemed off to the side of the visions. Now that I'm seeing true memories associated with Arianna, I'm experiencing things first hand."

"But the man you saw from a distance didn't hear you this time?" he asked, trying to get an exact accounting from her.

"No, he didn't. What are you thinking, Jack?"

"I'm just wondering if any of the others here have considered that you can be injured while your mind is somewhere else. I mean, if you're hurt there, what does that do to you here?"

"Well, when I fell, I came back here pretty quickly, so maybe I cannot be hurt while my mind and soul are traveling." Alex sat up on the bed so that she could face him. This was the closest she had been to his face, for when he was standing he was much taller than she. She reached up with one hand and used her fingers to trace his worry lines away.

"Let's talk to Archimedes and John about this once dinner is over. I'm supposed to have a lesson tonight to help me shield my thoughts, remember? That should be a good time to go over our concerns. Okay?" she encouraged.

He nodded slowly in agreement. "Sounds like a good plan, Miss Groaban," he said, speaking her earlier words back to her.

His eyes lowered to her lips, and it was all the encouragement she needed. She leaned forward and placed a chaste kiss on his lips and then slowly leaned back to look into his eyes. He growled low in his throat and reached forward, cupping the back of her head in his hand, pulling her to him once again. This time he would not settle for a chaste kiss.

"Are you trying to be coy, Miss Groaban?" he whispered against her lips, smiling.

"Maybe just a little. I'm new at this remember?" she whispered back. He deepened the kiss until she was completely breathless. It was only when he heard her whisper his name, that he pulled back and took in her passionate expression.

"We had better stop. Everyone downstairs will know exactly what we've been up to if you go down looking like this." She was pleased to note that he sounded out of breath too, and his lips looked very pink.

"I find I rather like kissing, now. But just you, Jack," she confessed.

His eyebrows rose with her statement. "I'm glad to hear that, more than you know." His eyes searched hers, and then he gave her one last quick kiss before he stood and offered her his hand. "Come on, we still have about fifteen or twenty minutes before we eat. You can use that time to walk around and see some more of this castle. And I will use that time to get myself back in line." He grinned at her like a schoolboy who had been caught skipping class, and she laughed at his smile.

Alex and Jack wandered through the first level of Aeoferth Hall for the next twenty minutes playing a game Jack invented with her emerging abilities. They would pause outside of a room and he would ask her to tell him what the room was used for, and if there were any immortals inside. If someone was there, he wanted to know how many and who it was.

Jack had only one rule: no touching anything. He did not want her to fade away on him again. Alex decided not to remind him, that she did not seem to need to physically touch an object anymore to trigger a memory or a vision. She decided it was better to hold her tongue though and play along.

Alex picked out all but two of the rooms' names or functions, but in all fairness, the two she incorrectly named had changed purpose since she had last been there. She counted all *Nephilim* correctly and though she did not know everyone's aura initially, once she associated their color spectrum with their name and face, she knew she would not forget them again.

Heath caught up with them in the pool room, to lead them on to dinner. Alex narrowed her eyes at Heath and pretended to scold him for not telling her there was an Olympic size salt water pool housed in that end of the castle. He laughed at her surprise.

"Oh, come on, Alex, what was it before?" he asked, trying to push her to remember.

She looked around the large two-story room which had Roman murals painted on the ceiling, intricate tile frescos on the walls, and life-size marble sculptures standing equidistance between immense stone columns. The supports ran from floor to ceiling down both sides of the room. The end of the room was a solid expanse of windows and the bottom of the windows were doors, so that fresh air could be allowed in. Key elements of the pool room reminded her of the ballroom. There were benches along the walls and loungers for relaxing in between laps.

She inhaled the salt water smell and remembered that once there was the smell of fresh water in the room. She closed her eyes and saw Arianna swimming with nothing on, gliding through the water at a leisurely pace. She swam over to the edge and folded her arms under her chin. She was looking off in the distance as if she was talking to someone with her mind and not her voice. Alex turned in the direction, but the edges of the memory were so out of focus she could not tell who was there.

She saw a cloth, reminiscent of a modern towel, sail over her head coming from the area she could not make out. It landed squarely on Arianna's face. Her peals of laughter brought a giggle to Alex's lips. She opened her eyes to find both Jack and Heath standing before her, each holding one of her arms. She grinned gratefully at them.

"I'm good, thanks," she said, pulling out of their hold. "It was a Roman bath, wasn't it?" she asked Heath.

"The finest I ever saw. I always thought that if any of the Caesars ever glimpsed this place, we would have a full-scale invasion on our hands. Back in the day, you diverted a small stream and had it constantly feed this pool. The water stayed fresh and cool, and it was well circulated," Heath reminisced.

"Well, it still looks beautiful. I'll be in this soon enough," she proclaimed.

They took their leave of the room and headed to dinner together. When they entered, they were warmly greeted and placed in the same seats they had occupied the night before. There was so much food, and such a wide variety. Food to satisfy the meat eaters, the vegetarians, and the vegans in the gathering. There were Kosher and Halal dishes, and food from almost every continent.

What impressed Alex, were the portion sizes of the offerings. While the selections were vast, there were not great quantities of anything. It was as if those preparing the food had made specifically what they knew would be consumed, and did not make enough to waste. Dessert was a welcome treat, because she had been craving chocolate all day, and she was offered a small chocolate lava cake with vanilla ice cream on the side.

Jackson turned and looked in amazement. "You gonna eat that whole thing by yourself?" he asked incredulously.

"What? It's not so much! Besides, you should know I'm always hungry. Wallace and Conner say I can eat them under the table!" she laughed. "Did you want some of this?" she offered.

"Not a chance. That would take me a month to run off."

"Okay," she said, shaking her head, "your loss." And she proceeded to devour the entire dessert one scrumptious bite at a time.

Once Alex was finished with her meal she told Jack she was going to mingle. He nodded and sat back in his chair so that he could see her. She went to as many immortals as she could, talking and making sure she connected with each one. Their names and auras were becoming rote memory to her. She laughed at some of their stories, and found that she could actually interject an occasional fact, impressing her friends greatly.

After an hour and a half of talking, Alex moved over to where Archimedes sat. She asked him if it would be a good time to convene in the library for her training, and who would be involved. He assured her it was a perfect time, and that he, Benen, Sabina, Nikolaj, and E-We would assist her that night.

"Can I ask John to come as well? I had another vision this afternoon after I left the library, and it was equally as strange as the one I traveled through earlier in the day. I'd like his input," she said.

"But of course, Alexandria. Nothing is set in stone. You can bring along whomever you so desire."

She nodded her thanks and moved on to John to ask him to join them if he would, and explain why he was needed. Finally, she made her way back to Jack and told him they were headed to the library.

"We've got just a few minutes. I want to step up to my room to go the watercloset and grab my phone," she said.

"Yep, gotcha," Jack answered, and got up to follow her.

She was quick in the watercloset, snagged her mobile from its charger, and headed back to meet Jack in the hall. He had detoured into his room as well, but he was back out quickly and they began to head downstairs. However, Alex stopped briefly on the second landing and sat down. Jack had gotten just a few steps ahead of her, but he turned quickly scanning the hallway looking for a threat. My, he was quick, she mused to herself.

"Alex?" he started to inquire, but she held up her hand to reassure him.

"I'm fine, Jack, honestly. I just wanted a moment before we joined the others. I have a feeling this is going to be really intense and I, well I just wanted a moment."

She looked very vulnerable in that moment to Jack, and he wanted to take her in his arms as he had done while she cried herself to sleep the night before, soothing her while the demons passed by. He sat down beside her instead and took her hand in his, giving her what comfort he could. His thumb traced a circle on the inside of her palm, absentmindedly.

"You know, when I was in Afghanistan on my final tour, we had to go into this small village where we knew the Taliban were hiding in the homes of the citizens, using people for cover," he said quietly.

Alex was astonished that he was telling her this, and she looked closely at his face to see if the recollection would be too much for him to relive.

"We had a few main targets we were after, but my unit was tasked with protecting the local people, while another unit went after the few bad apples. It was not the safest of missions, but I was glad to take it. I thought about my little brother the whole time. And I thought that if someone came into my town, into my home, and used my brother as cover, I would be praying that someone like me was on the other end of the rifle coming in their door. I knew that my men and I would use restraint and actually take a look, before we did anything rash."

"I used their eyes, Alex. They say the eyes are the gateway to the soul, so I made damn sure I looked into people's eyes before I decided their fate. We saved so many, and found those few bad apples we were looking for."

"You can do that too, you know. Look these *Nephilim* in the eye, see into their souls and decide just how much or how little you're going to give them. Luckily, they're all good to the core, but a few are going to have to play the bad guy tonight to awaken this ability in you. It won't matter what they try to pick or take from you in training tonight. What you give or receive is entirely up to you. Your memories are your own, your choices are your own, and you can share them at your pleasure."

"Remember, use your eyes and the rest will follow, okay?" He ended his almost reverent remarks with a squeeze to her hand.

"Thank you, Jack," she whispered, afraid to upset the fragile atmosphere he had created around them. "I'm glad you were there, too. You probably saved lots of innocents that might otherwise have been hurt or killed. Now who's amazing?" she smiled at him.

He leaned over and bumped her shoulder with is, "Oh, I don't know about amazing. Just careful and cautious. Ready to give this a try?" he looked at her expectantly.

"I'm ready," she nodded. He stood and pulled her up, then continued with her down to the library.

18

They entered the library to find Archimedes, Benen, John, Nikolaj, Sabina, and E-We all talking quietly among themselves waiting on Alex and Jack. Eight leather chairs had been pulled together in a circle under the large windows of the library, and lamps both tall and short had also been placed on the floor and nearby antique wooden tables to soften the space nearest them. Benen gestured for Alex and Jack to come forward and take a chair in the circle.

"Alexandria," Archimedes began, "tonight will be an exercise in restraint and control, as well as power. Your mind, like ours, is tapped into a completely different level of thought and consciousness. Humans on this earth are three dimensional beings who can perceive their own dimension and those of lesser dimensions."

"As the children of angels, we can see things from our fathers' perspective occasionally when we concentrate and focus. Our Lord and His hosts are beings far greater than just three dimensional souls, so they can see more, observe more, and impact timelines in ways humans never could."

He leaned forward and began to spread out a few napkins that were sitting on a side table between his chair and Alex's. "Observe. If we lay two or three napkins out on a table we can see each one from above and we can observe all of its features and measurements. It appears as a two dimensional object, so as we are more than two dimensional creatures, we can see all of it and perceive all of it."

"Now, think of this paper napkin," he said, pointing to the one closest to him, "as our past. Think of this one," he gestured to the one in the middle, "as our present. And think of this last one as our…,"

"Future," she said, along with Archimedes.

He tapped the side of his nose and winked at her. "Yes, our future, Alexandria." He produced a pen from inside his dinner jacket and drew a square on the first napkin, a circle on the second, and a triangle on the third. He gestured to the shapes and looked back up at Alex, watching her reaction to his words.

"Now, if I asked you what shape occurs in the past, you would say a square. If I asked what shape occurs in the present, you would say…?" he paused, waiting for her to complete his statement.

"A circle," she responded, "and in the future, there will be a triangle."

"Not exactly, *will be*, Alex. There *is* a triangle in the future. As time exists now," Archimedes gestured to all three napkins, "the triangle is there and clearly visible to our eyes. Now if I did not want that triangle there," he reached forward and swept it away, replacing it with a new, clean one, "I could wipe the old away and replace it with a new one that is basically a clean slate."

"But couldn't you just erase it if you had used a pencil, and not have wiped the whole napkin away?" she asked.

224

She noticed the group's smiles and their nods at her observation. "Ah, my smart girl," praised Archimedes. "You could try, but not effectively. You see while that triangle was on that napkin, it was part of a much larger landscape." He bent and picked up the original napkin with the triangle drawn on it, and laid it beside the new blank one. He began to draw multiple triangles all over the napkin, crowding all around the original shape, some touching its edges, others completely overlapping it.

"If I were to decide to erase one, the others would perceive that something had been removed or altered in their reality as they know it. If the other triangles' lines were intersecting with or interacting with the first triangle's space, it could cause the others to lose their placement on the napkin as well, causing a shift."

"Ah, like Jenga," said Alexandria. "It's an old game that my brothers and I would play from time to time when I was younger. The object was to build a tall wooden tower with small building blocks and then take turns removing one piece at a time, trying to keep the tower structurally sound so that it did not fall. If you removed the wrong piece, it all came crashing down. But sometimes, you couldn't tell which piece was the right one and which piece was the wrong one to take away."

"Very good!" praised Archimedes. "You are taking the leap from a two dimensional demonstration to a three dimensional example. And your observation is spot on, too. Although we can see all three perspectives, we have to be very careful not to look too closely at the future and alter what exists there. The repercussions of such interference are far reaching, even more than we can perceive at times."

"And though all of the *Nephilim* can see into the future to some degree, none of us can to the degree which you can, Alexandria." He stood and picked up the napkin with the triangles and walked away from them until he was standing a good three meters away. He angled the sheet under a lamp and turned back to look at Alex.

"To most of us, this is what the future looks like. We can see it, kind of make out what the shapes are. And if we employ our keen eyesight, we might start to discern the placement of some of the shapes here. But for you, Alexandria," and he paused, then walked back over to her and held the napkin directly under her nose, "this is what the future looks like, for you."

Alex's eyes grew large and she lifted them up in surprise to gaze at Archimedes. He moved back to his seat and looked at her gravely. He was deadly serious, the most serious she had yet seen him.

"If the future is that close to my vision, what power must that kind of knowledge entail? And what restraint it must take to refrain from using it?" mused Alex aloud. She reflected back to her earlier thoughts in the bathtub regarding how one might stop humans who would harm or decimate their fellow man.

"Precisely," said E-We in response to her. "You are the most powerful of us all, as your father was the most powerful in the great host of angels who was allowed to marry a human. Your foresight knows no bounds, and there are many among the Fallen's children who would like to steal a glimpse into what you can see. They would love to find those humans that they could nurture and add to the chaos and destruction of the Lord's people."

"And they would love to use it to bring about our destruction as well," said Nikolaj. "Imagine if you knew where everyone of us was, and when we would be in that location. It would give the Fallen's children the biggest checkmate they could ever have. Alex, all of us can see into the past and observe the present quite well. Most of us can see a little into the future, but it's a brief glimpse of the most immediate future usually. Because many of us can also view the minds of others, we have to constantly shield from eavesdroppers."

"You have to stop someone else from looking in and discovering battle plans and strategies. Stop them from knowing what only you can perceive. When we have to battle another, we all throw up this mental barrier so that we cannot be taken unawares or our comrades besieged because our knowledge of their whereabouts has given them away. It could be as simple as what angle you plan to swing your sword in next, or as complex as where we are all positioned. No one, can know what you know," Nikolaj concluded.

"There is one more part to this Alex, before we allow you to try to block us," said Benen. "You are also the only immortal child who can see past all of our barriers, no matter how strong they are. We cannot defeat you, but you could crush us."

She gazed at him in wonder. "But, Benen, I love all of you. I mean, I know according to my timeline we've all just met, but I've known all of you, all your lives. I've only to concentrate and I can recall your lives in vivid detail. I feel that love and that connection, and I would never in all my days harm any of you, ever." She reached a hand out to touch him, trying to make him understand what she was feeling towards the *Nephilim*. It felt like the love she had shown Kronis on the cliff, as well.

He leaned forward and smiled at her warmly, taking her outstretched hand in between his. "No, I didn't mean to imply that you would ever hurt any of us. I was trying to explain how very instrumental your ability has always been in keeping our group safe and whole. You know what we cannot, you see what we cannot, and though we don't always comply, you've loved us regardless."

"You know what we're planning, either by looking directly into our minds, or by chancing a glance into the future. I have never seen you abuse your power, and I've never seen you look in on us unless we needed your guidance. You mostly let us be and trusted us to make the right choices. Free will was one of your top priorities," he said, then squeezed her hand to reassure her, and sat back again.

"So," smiled Sabina, "what we propose is for us to start with the here and now. Let's have you think of something mundane along with a few of us as well. We won't tell you who is thinking of something and who is trying to look in on your thoughts. We'll allow you to experience what the intrusion feels like, and we'll mentally converse as we instruct you and help you build stronger barriers if needed."

"But, Alex," she added, "remember that you have done all of this before. You taught us, so the more we do, the easier it will become. Think back to that armor plating you said Ganymede told you about this morning. You have it metaphysically, as well as physically."

"Okay," breathed Alexandria, "here goes nothing."

She looked over at Jack and saw him point to his eyes. She nodded her understanding, and looked at the six before her. She took slow, calming breaths and began to think of Dudley, curled up on the bed by her side. She was slowly petting him and rubbing his shiny, clean coat.

"Hmmm, so you have a yellow lab named Dudley," mused John aloud. "I saw him at your parents' home, but I did not know his name."

Alex looked up at John's bland expression and stopped thinking about Dudley. She looked straight into John's eyes instead and thought back to her ribbon. Perhaps, that was not the right name for this extraordinary ability, but she thought the analogy fit the feeling. She allowed it to unfurl.

At first she thought about the Roman shields again, and heard Nikolaj say, "Roman shields, hmmm," and then she began wrapping her mind's ribbon in that same shield formation. She imagined the plating wrapping around her mind, too. Not her actual brain, that was already protected from her concentrated effort in the bathtub earlier, but her mind. All of her thoughts, expressions, and emotions could be shielded with Ganymede's power.

Again, she heard Nikolaj speak. "Alex, don't think of yourself in the bathtub," chuckling under his breath.

Alex heard Sabina censure him, and she smiled back. Their voices were becoming fainter as she began to hear their internal voices becoming louder and overtaking what her ears were picking up on.

Alexandria stared into Sabina's eyes and saw that she was thinking of a vineyard just north of Rome. She was walking among the rows of grapevines, talking with an older man who was in charge of the other laborers who tended the vines throughout the year. She was congratulating this man on his attentiveness and dedication. Alex began to tell Sabina's thoughts aloud, and received an approving nod from her friend.

Next, she turned her thoughts to Nikolaj. His thoughts were sad and pensive. He was aboard a very old ship, sailing out to intercept a whaling vessel in an effort to negotiate restraint on their part. Too many whales were being taken for profit, not for actual need and he hoped to put a stop to it. The air was so cold, that she felt the skin on his face chapping and cracking in places. She spoke his thoughts aloud, and he praised her.

Alex concentrated on John. She could feel that his mental defenses were better, stronger than the previous two. His plating felt more like scales on a fish. She was able to hook her ribbon on the edge of one specific component and peel it back. She pried and pulled until she had opened a large enough hole for her ribbon to enter through.

She saw that he was thinking of a very pretty young lady who wore a nurse's uniform. She was in an army hospital helping to treat those who were brought in from the front lines. Many were burned and battered beyond recognition, but she was gentle in her care. John walked over to her and chatted with her about one particular young man's bandages. The way she looked up at John, Alex knew they were more than just colleagues. They were friends, perhaps even lovers, and then his memory shifted to one where he was holding her and kissing her. Alex felt that she was intruding where she had no right to be.

"John, I'm sorry," she said, regret sounding thick in her voice. "I shouldn't have seen that."

"No," he shook his head, "I wanted you to see that. That was Marie. I loved her so much, and she was my wife until she died. I wanted you to see what it feels like to see such a personal memory. There will be times when you see far more explicit thoughts than that, and I don't want you to hesitate or pull back. Knowing and seeing it all, can mean the difference between life and death, so don't hold back even if you feel shocked or embarrassed. If one of us was being held or a human was being hurt, you would need all the information you could gather to help. Do you understand, Alex?"

"Yes, John, I understand. Did I just hurt you? I couldn't detect pain, but I was working my way in there," she inquired, hoping that the peeling back of his defenses had not caused him discomfort.

"No," he said, shaking his head, "you were not doing so with any malicious intent, Alex. If someone wants information and they do not do so with care and love, it can hurt dreadfully though. Think of it as an intense migraine that attempts to cleave your mind in two."

"Yes," interjected Archimedes, "let's move on to that now, shall we? Now, Alex, I was trying to get at your mind the entire time you were connecting with Sabina, Nikolaj, and John, and I was unsuccessful. I think you have figured out how to lock us out quite effectively. Can anyone else tell what she's thinking right now?" he asked, looking at the small group.

They all looked pointedly at her, but shook their heads one after the other in denial. No one could get a reading on her thoughts it seemed, and Alex smiled victoriously at them. She was proud that she had figured out this most critical of defenses. It would hopefully help to keep her family, the *Nephilim*, and Jack safe in the future.

Archimedes took a deep breath, as if preparing to impart a bit of unpleasant news, and he moved forward in his seat until his knees were almost touching hers.

"Alex, look at me, dear," he said softly. "What we are about to do will not seem kind or loving at all, I know. Please understand, that you cannot really be completely prepared unless you experience the reality of what it feels like to have a *Nephilim* from the Fallen try to tear into your defenses. They are not gentle, so we must not be now."

"Arianna was always able to shut them out. So, too, can you. I am going to ask Benen to begin first. He will try to worm his way in with illusions, which as you saw during your sword training, he is particularly skilled at. Try to hold to what is real and true, and ground yourself. I'm sorry it has to be this way, but we must. Are you ready?" he asked, regret sounding in his words.

Alexandria reached out and squeezed Archimedes' hand. "I understand, my friend, and I'm ready."

"Mr. Campbell, be ready to grab hold of her if you have to."
Archimedes nodded at Benen and Alex turned her attention to his face.
His eyes looked sad and filled with regret, and then he closed them. So,
too, did she, preparing for the coming onslaught.

"Give me strength, Ganymede," she prayed to him.

Alex concentrated on the feeling she had experienced in the tub
early in the evening, and again as she secured her ribbon and mind. She
was sure that she was protected, and imagined herself standing in the library
looking out at the moonlit night. Alex imagined that her body was her
mind, and the library was the armored walls surrounding her, keeping out
the demons.

That is when she saw the first one. A large, rabid looking version
of a wolf stood outside the window. He was so much larger than any wolf
she had ever seen, and he began charging the glass trying to shatter it and
gain entrance. Alex held up her hands and allowed her aura to stream forth
in cascading waves, coating the glass. The glass shimmered in a rainbow of
colors now; colors and Light that she knew came from Ganymede. The
wolf was not coming in, even though he continued to try.

The whole room suddenly felt as if it were shaken from a mighty
earthquake. She heard footsteps walking across the roof, and then she saw
a crack appear in the ceiling's mural, as whatever was above began forcibly
jumping up and down with its heavy weight.

"No!" she screamed in her mind. She did not want to see such
beauty destroyed. Alex raised her hands now to the painting, and began to
use her aura to mend the cracks. She blanketed the artwork with her colors
as well, feeling the power within her holding up the great expanse overhead.

She breathed in slowly, looking around for the next assault. She thought she heard a slight rattle, and then turned quickly realizing it was the doorknob turning and twisting.

"Oh, very clever," she said.

How like someone to just try the door. It was probably John, she mused, being very logical about the whole process. She went over thinking to use her aura there as well, when the door bulged in toward her.

Alex slammed her shoulder against the door and tried to brace herself, locking her feet in place. It felt like someone had a battering ram with a full legion behind them. The jarring was so intense, she felt her teeth chatter and her bones screamed at her.

She looked about trying to see if there was anything she could wedge against the door in place of her body, but she saw nothing. She saw her Light flowing from her fingertips and she wondered if she could change the consistency of her aura, make it thicker.

Alexandria turned back around and began to let her energy flow in huge waves now, willing it to thicken and harden around the door. She was essentially building a wall, but one stronger than any manmade material. It was impervious, and more substantial than the walls of a military bunker, but creating it made her feel weaker.

The battering at the door continued, but she knew now that no one was coming in through there. Three down, three more to go, she thought to herself. Alex heard a hissing next and she looked for the origin of the noise. She saw a fine mist rise up from one of the vents in the room, and panic swept through her body like a wave.

"They cannot mess with my air, can they?" she asked herself.

Alex knew that she would not be able to run from one vent to another fast enough, so she imagined them all closing and threw her hands out willing them to do so. They all closed abruptly, and she allowed her aura to now flow like a mist and blanket the floor of her imaginary library to stamp out the enemy vapor that was pooling there. There was enough in the room, though, to make her nostrils burn and her eyes water.

She was panting now, and shaking from fatigue. She wondered just how much energy flow she could produce and how much she had already expended. She began to take stock of this artificial library, thinking to play more on the offensive now. The windows, roof, and door were secure. No tainted air could come in. What could be left, she wondered.

"Think!" she admonished herself, trying to plan ahead.

She looked over at the large fireplace thinking that the chimney was most certainly an opening into the room. Alex walked over and began building the same thick wall from her aura around the fireplace, which she had created at the door, when she heard a whooshing sound. Fire was beginning to rain down the chimney chute at an alarming speed. She hurried to secure the opening, but the flames were lapping up and over her wall faster than she could complete it. She knew she was getting burned, but she kept her hands up until she had completely fortified the entrance.

When she had contained the fire, she looked at her hands and arms, and saw the severe damage the flames had inflicted. She was badly burned and in terrible pain. She walked over to the sofa in the room and sat down gingerly. She held her arms in front of her face and thought about the healing power Ganymede had said she possessed. And though he had said she would begin to heal herself each moment of each day if she accepted the gift of immortality, she knew she had to end the acute discomfort she was currently enduring.

"I've not promised to be an immortal yet, but I have to end this pain, please Ganymede," she pleaded.

Her thoughts turned inward and she began inspecting the skin and tissue that was blistered or melting away. She channeled her aura into the blood vessels and breathed deep, cleansing breaths as a cooling sensation began to creep into the mutilated membranes. Her skin was slowly replaced by new, pink skin and she no longer was in agony. When she looked up, she saw that the room still looked heavily coated in her essence and she was still safe.

She was so glad to see that diverting her attention long enough to heal herself had not given the last of the six time to get to her. Alex got up off of her imaginary sofa, and began walking around the room looking for signs of the last assault. For what seemed like the longest time, she could find no new attack. She checked each of her barriers and waited.

Just when she thought she might stay there all night, she heard a sound that she could not believe. Pure dread settled in her heart as she took in the sounds of Wallace and Conner calling out to her. But no, she told herself, they were not there at Aeoferth Hall, they had stayed behind in Oxford. Where were their voices coming from, she wondered, and she began to search for them in earnest. Alex stopped in front of the large windows and beheld a sight that made her heart stop.

Wallace and Conner appeared to be outside, both tied to stakes, both badly beaten and Bertrand stood between them smiling at her.

"No!" she shouted. "Not them, anything but them!" She screamed and cried, wanting to go outside and rescue the two.

Conner looked up at her, begging her to stay inside and not come out. But Bertrand moved forward, hitting him so hard that Alex could hear his ribs shattering. Conner tried desperately to breath, but something had punctured a lung and now he was drowning in his own body.

Wallace was taunting Bertrand, calling him every vile name in the book. Bertrand sneered at her eldest brother, as he grabbed Wallace's arm from his binding and snapped it like a twig. Wallace screamed in pain, sobbing out incoherently. Alex knew she had to get to them, and there was not a second more to waste.

Alex was raising her hand to remove part of her shielding from the window, when she heard Ganymede behind her.

"Alexandria, be careful. Are those really your brothers out there?" he gently inquired.

"Oh, Ganymede! It looks and sounds like them, and they're being tortured. We have to do something. Please!" she begged.

"Think, my daughter. Is this the real library in Aeoferth Hall, or a construct of your mind?" he pressed her.

She heard Conner scream out again, and she looked from the window to Ganymede. She was so torn, and she did not know what to do. The room was beginning to shake again, and her aura on the ceiling flexed trying to hold the mural and roof up.

"You do know what to do, Alex. Assaults come in many forms and in many disguises. Look closely and you will see that those are not your brothers out there, but someone trying to tempt you into letting down your guard. Wallace does not have that scar on his left cheek, and Conner's hair is not that dark. Look into their eyes. Look and think, Alexandria," he compelled her.

She took a step closer to the window and really examined the two men she loved so. Through all of the blood and the abuse, she could see what Ganymede had pointed out. He was right, these were not her brothers. Their eyes were dark and twisted, haunted even. Not the carefree men she knew.

She turned back to him shaking her head, "No, they are not Wallace and Conner." A small sob escaped her mouth and she covered it with her hand, trying to quell the emotion.

"It is alright, my child. You are handling this very well. I know you do not like to witness suffering, but there are no people out there right now being harmed. It is only an illusion." He looked overhead and around the room at all she had created to keep the evil away.

"Most impressive, my dear. You wondered to yourself a little while ago how much aura you could produce. There is no limit to your stores, Alexandria, for it is, in a way, coming from me. I serve The Great I Am, who has no beginning and no end. Therefore, as long as it shall please Him for me to be in His service, my powers and thereby yours, shall have no end either. Now, expel these demons and be free of this place," he said, with fierce pride shining in his translucent blue eyes.

"Ganymede, thank you for stopping me," Alex said sadly, shaking her head at her near folly. "I was heading straight out of that door there. But I see your meaning, now. I'll try to stay focused and let logic prevail. And you're right," she sighed heavily, "I'm ready to end this."

"Very good. Until I see you again, Alexandria," he said, moving forward to hug her goodbye, and then he was gone.

Alex stood in the center of the library and lifted her arms. She wanted to return to the present and she needed all barriers removed that were in her way. She took one last look at her brothers' and Bertrand's imposters, and threw a burst of energy out of herself so great, that it obliterated everything she had created around her for the training scenario. It blew back the imaginary demons and the suffocating mist. Her aura wave rolled the fire back and the image of her brothers melted away like a mirage in the desert.

She slowly opened her eyes to see her friends in their leather chairs looking amazed and in awe of her. She did not know what to say, so she sat there numbly, trying to process what she had just experienced.

"Alex? Hey, look at me," said Jack, taking a handkerchief out of his pocket. He was standing next to her chair, and when she looked up, he clamped down hard on her nose. She winced, then noticed that she was soaking his cloth through with blood.

"Sorry, I'm not trying to hurt you, but you're bleeding pretty steadily here," he said regrettably.

She noticed that little crease back in his forehead, but she could not smooth it away while he was trying to stem the flow of her bleeding.

"Here, let me do that," offered Sabina, and she moved forward next to Jack, using her aura to stop the flow.

"Sorry, Alexandria," she whispered. "Are you alright?" and as she asked, she smoothed Alex's hair off of her face.

"Yes, I'm good. Which one of you tortured Wallace and Conner?" she asked, still congested and sounding far less severe than she hoped to. Jack's eyes hardened at her question and he turned to look around the group.

"I did," said Archimedes. "I am sorry I had to do that. But the *Nephilim* of the Fallen will use the ones you love against you, and they have no care whatsoever for whom they hurt." He reached over and patted her hand as a means of apology.

They each explained their tactics and means of assault, trying to get through her barriers. Benen had fabricated the wolf, Nikolaj had tried to bring the ceiling crashing down on her to crush her, John had indeed tried the door before he sought to ram it in, E-We used the poisonous mist,

Sabina created the fire, and Archimedes had conjured Bertrand to torture her brothers in front of her.

They further discussed her response to them, and all were very satisfied that she had been triumphant in her approach to the mental warfare they had just engaged her in. It appeared that they were about to adjourn for the evening, when Jack asked if he could bring up a topic of discussion. All sat back in their seats and waited to see what was on his mind.

He recounted Alexandria's earlier vision in the afternoon and how it might tie into the one she suffered through after their horseback ride. He posed the question of Alex's safety and physical well-being while in the throws of a memory, dream, vision, or whatever they wanted to call it. Watching from the sidelines was one thing in his book, but being thrown about, burned, and nearly choked on poisonous gas was quite another.

They all had opinions about her safety while her mind or soul was out traveling, and the more they discussed and debated, the more frustrated Jackson became. John admitted that they had no good answer. What Alex had just experienced had not really harmed her, though he could not account for the nosebleed, or the tremors she had experienced earlier in the day.

Finally, it was Alex herself who called a halt to the discussion. She held a hand up quietly, and looked at everyone as she sighed from her weariness.

"When I was small," she began, "I was constantly in danger of slipping back in time by touching things. The slightest little thing, a mirror, an antique pillbox, a jar, would send me back in time. And it didn't happen with every object, so I had no way to control it, and I had no way to stop it.

Not until Ganymede helped me to prevent it, by halting my ability to see into the past altogether."

"After tonight's lesson, I see now that was what I was doing: constantly connecting with the past. And let me tell you, for a child with no frame of reference, you can only imagine what it was like when I touched something like an old knife or ax at a museum. I saw some pretty frightening scenes."

"Wallace and Conner were always there, making sure I didn't fall over and hurt myself while my mind took at trip. And now I have all of you here, so I know I'm safe," Alex added, and smiled briefly over the memory of her brothers' constant guard.

"But I seriously doubt that when Arianna looked backwards or forwards in time she lost consciousness with each mental trip. Ganymede told me to start meditating on the power within and fortify myself from the inside out. I got a good taste of that tonight, but I think the more I try my hand at this the easier it will be in time. Not necessarily pleasant, but controllable and bearable. And maybe, now that I understand what is transpiring each time my mind travels, I can work on staying more grounded in the present to protect myself."

"Why don't we leave it there for tonight, and we'll talk about it later? I'm really, really tired," she suggested, though it was less of a request, so much as it was a statement regarding her intentions.

They all agreed and then stood to hug Alexandria goodnight. Alex and Jack made their way back upstairs, walking slowly, because she found she was exceptionally fatigued. When they reached their doors, she hugged him goodnight as well and made her way into her room. She changed into soft, warm pajamas and brushed her teeth.

Finally, she climbed into the bed and texted her brothers, parents, and Jameason. She told them she had experienced a very purposeful day and was grateful to be there. Alex said that she missed them all, and conveyed her love before turning the phone on silent so that she could sleep.

She snuggled down and was almost adrift when she heard her door open. She could not imagine who was coming in, so she reached over and turned on the bedside lamp.

"What are you doing?" she chuckled, at the sight before her.

"What does it look like?" asked Jack, heading for the sofa again, this time with a pillow and blanket from his bed. He had on pajama pants and a t-shirt with a gun holster strapped across his chest.

Alexandria rolled over to face him and propped her head up on one hand so she could watch him.

"You're not really going to sleep with that thing strapped across you, are you? It can't be comfortable," she admonished, shaking her head.

"Do it all the time," he grinned back at her. "Turn off the lamp Alex, and go to sleep. I hear Rohan has plans for you in the morning. Trust me, if it involves him, you're going to need your rest."

She flopped back onto the bed. "He better not throw that sword at my head again," she groaned. They both laughed aloud at her statement. Finally, she turned off the lamp so that only the crackling fireplace lit the room. Jack was settled and already looking peaceful.

"Jack," she whispered, hoping he was not one of those who could doze off in an instant.

"Alex," he drawled back at her.

"Thank you," she said.

"You're most welcome, Miss Groaban. Now go to sleep," he commanded in mock seriousness. And she did just that.

19

Alex was having the most interesting dream about riding Eimhir. It was a cold, winter day and she sat atop the mare on a high hill. They were looking down over a valley which had a frigid, grey river snaking through it. The wind had sleet and ice in it, and it stung her cheeks as it whipped around her head.

She was looking for something, scanning the land for it, but could not find what she sought. Her heart constricted at the longing, and the horse stamped a hoof in agitation as well.

Alex leaned forward and stroked Eimhir's neck to calm her, and spotted movement to her right. There! Coming across a field adjacent to the river was a man on horseback, riding as if his life depended on it.

Alexandria spurred Eimhir into motion and the two raced down to intercept the man. It was a punishing ride for both horse and rider, but it seemed that the mare understood her panic and raced with all of her might, her great flanks heaving with the strain.

The closer she came to this unnamed rider, the more she felt like she had seen him before. It came to her then. With his chestnut brown hair and large build, he looked like the man who had stood with his back to her on the balcony from her vision.

She squinted against the sleet and now snow that was coming in torrents, trying to make out his face and features, but she could not. She was close enough now to call out, but when she yelled for him, no sound came forth. She tried again in vain, and still she could produce no words at all.

She pulled on Eimhir's reigns, but the horse lost her footing and went down hard. Alex felt herself go down as well, and she was trapped under the immense weight of the mare. She tried to use her new found strength, but she was as weak as a mortal. She had no strength and no voice to aid her.

She heard the man's horse braying nearby. He was looking for her, but in the torrent of snow and ice a white horse would be nearly impossible to locate.

"Please," she cried out in her mind, "I'm here! Find me and help us, please!" She heard his horse moving in now. By some grace, he had realized where she was and he was coming.

Alex felt someone tug her arm. It must be the man getting her out from under Eimhir's crushing weight she thought, and sighed from the relief she felt. She felt him rubbing her arm, but that made no sense to her. Where was he, why could she not see him, she wondered in irritation.

"Alex, you can't see me, because you won't open your eyes, sleepyhead. You're talking in your sleep, so I know that brain is working. Come on, open those eyes," coaxed Jack, sounding very close.

She slowly left the dream world behind, feeling very frustrated that she had once again lost an opportunity to see his face. She looked up into Jack's blue eyes looming over her.

He smiled. "Must have been some dream. I've been trying to wake you up, but you wouldn't budge. I let you sleep in, made Rohan mad as hell, but he's getting really impatient now. You feel like getting up?" he asked.

"You told Rohan, no?" she asked, surprised that he dared to defy the largest *Nephilim* on the estate.

"Yeah, and I wish you could have seen the look on his face. I thought for sure he was gonna deck me, but he just said something under his breath and stalked out of the kitchen. That was an hour ago, and I think he's run out of patience now."

"You've been down to the kitchen already! Goodness, what time is it?" she asked, trying to focus in on the clock sitting atop the mantle.

"It's about half past nine. I brought you some breakfast up and put it on the table in the sitting room. If you're really awake for good now, I'll leave you to get ready and come back to check on you in about thirty minutes, okay?" He stood from where he was perched on the side of the bed and headed for her door. "Sabina left you thicker riding clothes in the bathroom. She said you're going to need them. Don't fall back asleep," he said, as he headed out.

After he was gone, Alex lay in the bed mulling her dream over. She still felt irritated, as if she had unfinished business from the dream's abrupt ending. She rolled over slowly, wallowing in the warm bed, and luxuriating in the feeling of being completely comfortable. She looked over at the balcony from where she lay on her stomach and imagined the man standing out there, his back to her.

She slid over to the other side of the bed and pushed the covers back, taking her time sitting up. Once her equilibrium had settled, she got up and went over to the balcony doors, unlatching each and swinging them wide. A blast of cold, arctic air greeted her, and she realized she needed her robe.

But rather than fetch it, she stepped out in her bare feet and approached the railing. She willed her feet to feel less susceptible to the cold, and remarkably they complied with her silent command. She raised her head and closed her eyes, breathing in the winter breeze as she had in her dream.

He had been standing in that exact same spot, she thought, opening her eyes. She leaned forward and placed her hands where his had rested, brushing off the snow so that she could feel the stone below. She closed her eyes again, picturing his back. There was something about the way his shoulders flexed out under the material of his shirt that looked so familiar.

With her eyes still closed, she imagined herself back in the vision before she had reached to pick up the parchment. He had been there, just not hearing her. She began to walk forward until she was standing in the doorway of the balcony, looking at his broad back. She studied his hair, thick and chestnut brown, just long enough to touch the top of his collar.

She took a tentative step forward with her hand outstretched and touched his back with the tips of her fingers. Alex felt as if she had been struck by lightning. Once again, she was thrown back with a force that might have killed a mere mortal. She had trouble seeing and she smelled singed hair all over her body. Her eyes lost focus and she lay back on the floor of the bedroom, deciding that it was a very good time for a nap.

"Alex, what are you doing?" asked Jack incredulously. "You'll freeze out there in your bare feet." He moved out onto the balcony and looked at her sternly, until he took in her dazed expression. He put his hands on either side of her face and looked searchingly into her eyes, trying to ascertain if she was with him or off in another place in her mind.

"Alex," he all but whispered, "can you hear me?"

Alex blinked and regained focus, staring up into his intense blue gaze. She breathed out and watched the cloud of vapor that escaped her lips in the cold.

"I'm here Jack, and I'm fine," she said.

"Come on, let's get you inside where it's warm." He led her over to the sofa by the fire first, then returned to shut the balcony doors, blocking out the frigid air. He added another log to the fire, then came over to sit beside her. He pulled her feet up into his lap and began to rub the cold away and restore life to her toes.

"I did that, Jack. That was my fault," Alex said tentatively, gesturing towards the balcony.

He continued to rub her skin, but tilted his head to the side and studied her. It was the same way he had looked at her in her parents' sitting room before she came to Aeoferth Hall.

"Tell me about it," he said, sounding too calm.

Alex proceeded to tell Jack about her dream that morning and how she still could not see the man's face. She described what she did to try and force the issue, and the electrifying result she received for her effort. She stopped talking and watched Jack slowly rubbing her feet.

"Are you mad?" she asked, surprised that he might actually be.

"Why would you think that?" he asked, looking back at her.

Alex pulled her feet out of Jack's lap and sat up on her knees, facing him. "You are angry, aren't you? Why?" she pressed.

He looked over at her face and sighed. "No, Alex, I'm not mad."

"Then what is it?"

"Ughh," he said, running his hands over his face. "I can't believe I'm gonna say this. The thought of you searching for some unknown guy just doesn't sit well with me, especially if you have to go through that," he said, gesturing towards the balcony, "to get answers."

Alex was so astounded by his revelation that she sat back on her heels and stared at him for a moment before she could speak. "You're jealous?" she asked in amazement.

"Yes, I guess, I am. Though now that I really think about it, if you truly have lived for thousands of years, I guess it's kinda naive to think you never were loved by anyone before."

"But even if that's true, I'm still Alexandria. I'm still single. I don't date, I don't anything," she shrugged.

He smiled at her and chuckled at her choice of words. "You don't anything? I think I remember you doing something, and quite well if I might add," he replied, tucking her hair behind her ear. "You had better get your shower now. Rohan's going to come after you himself soon."

Alex started to stand from the sofa, but he caught her hand and pulled her off balance, causing her to fall across his lap and right into his arms.

"Just a quick kiss," he breathed, "so you won't go off chasing shadows on me for a little while." And he proceeded to really take the wind right out of her lungs.

Alex got ready in record time. Once Jackson released her and she released him in turn, she hurried through her shower, dried her hair, dressed, and inhaled her breakfast. She grabbed Jack from the sitting room, after she brushed her teeth, and they headed out to the stables to see what Rohan had planned.

He was already on his horse waiting for them out in a nearby pasture. He was joined by Iain, Elrick, Nassor, and an immortal named Thomas, all on mounts so large that Alex knew they had to be destriers. Sabina waited in the stables until Alex and Jack were astride Eimhir and Aileas once more, then she, too, rode with them to the pasture.

"Have a nice lie in?" Rohan called, as the three approached.

"Oh, do hush!" Alex scolded him. "I was tired. So what are we doing today?" she asked, trying to redirect his bluster.

Iain leaned forward in his saddle and laughed at her censure, shaking his head. "Just as bossy as ever," he said, causing Alex to raise an eyebrow and turn her gaze his way. Iain only winked at her in return.

Rohan pulled her attention back to the matter of training. "We're going to put some of your different talents together, and it won't be easy. Sword fighting takes place while we're on horseback quite often, and at high speeds. You're going to have to block our attempts to figure out your game plan, too. Don't worry about getting hurt, though. Either we'll heal you or you can heal yourself. Ready to begin?" he stated, rather than asked for her agreement.

Nassor began to ride forward and handed Alexandria the sword she had trained with the previous day. He bowed to her in his saddle, before turning his mount and trotting back to the others.

Alex looked to Sabina for her advice.

"Is this something I'm ready for?" she asked, not hiding the worry in her voice.

"Yeah, I'm not so sure about this," added Jack, moving Aileas closer to Alex now.

Sabina tried to assuage her friends' fears. "Alexandria, I have seen you bound off of a stallion while it was in full gallop before and use the air to cushion your fall, never once getting hurt. You're also the reason those five brutes over there know how to do what they're about to show you. Use your muscle and sense memory and let it all come back to you. You really can do this."

Her words imbued Alex with the confidence she needed, and she nodded her head. "Okay, let's give this a try, then." She reached over and touched Jack's hand. "I'll be fine," she told him.

"I know. Don't think about me right now, just concentrate on them," he nodded at the five.

Alex put Sabina and Jack out of her thoughts and concentrated on the five *Nephilim* before her. Each was incredibly muscled and much bigger than she, but she began to draw quiet strength from Ganymede's Light and power within her. She thought of Tomoko's lesson, that size advantage does not always signal victory. The field seemed to come into sharper focus as she concentrated on their auras now, taking in the internal strength of each. She checked her armor plating inside and found it still intact. Finally, she spoke to Eimhir with her mind.

"They're not going to hurt us, they just want to play a very rough game I think. I am letting you inside, but only you, so when I think about moving, you take me in that direction. Will you stay with me through this exercise?" she asked, not wanting to force the animal into a frightening situation. Eimhir brayed loudly, and that was all the answer Alex required.

"Then let's go," she whispered, and the mare began to steadily approach their opponents.

Elrick raised his sword first and approached her at a slow gallop. "Just like yesterday, Alex," he called. He finally met her and she moved her sword to her left side so that she could block Elrick's downward stroke. She heard the singing sound of steel meeting steel in the otherwise silent morning.

"Very good," he praised, and turned to come at her again.

On his second pass, she stood up in her saddle to initiate the strike and came down over his head. He blocked her effectively, then came over to her side. "Watch your eyes, Alex. I can't get a read on what you're thinking, but your eyes gave you away. You were looking at my head before you raised your arm. I could tell what your plan was before you put it into motion."

She nodded her thanks at his instruction and the two came at one another again. She could feel the difference in her muscles from the previous day. She was barely registering the vibration that the clashing swords produced within her arms. Elrick brought his horse close and began to volley with her, slow deliberate strokes to show her how to defend and also to look for openings in which to strike.

He finally nodded his approval and spurred his steed into a gallop away from her, joining the others. Iain and Thomas approached her together, and they illustrated how she might have someone on either side trying to press their advantage in numbers. They worked through how she could use her aura as a shield against one while volleying with the other. *Nephilim* did not depend on conventional, man-made shields it seemed, as their own internal armor was far superior.

Their instruction lasted for a long time and when they broke away, Nassor and his solid black stallion moved in. His horse was a magnificent specimen that cantered and danced under his weight. She recognized it as a Friesian, but it was the largest of that breed she had ever beheld.

"Remember Abdalla's lesson yesterday," Nassor began. "There is art and finesse to swordplay. At times, some of the Fallen's children will use that grace and movement to mesmerize you, distract you. It can be a smokescreen, so look beyond the show to the plot behind the movements. Ready?" he asked calmly.

Alex nodded her assent, and moved forward to engage. Nassor fighting with a sword was, without a doubt, one of the most beautiful sights Alexandria had ever beheld. She had always admired the balance and grace with which a dancer moved, and Nassor's body moved in such a way, full of poetry and formidable splendor. Alex released Eimhir's reigns, just as Nassor had done with his stallion's, and used her thoughts and leg muscles to command her horse's direction.

They were close to one another and swinging their swords with purpose and power. Alexandria felt a surge pass over her and she saw herself in this same deadly dance with Nassor hundreds of years before, when it was she who was the instructor. She saw the same artful angles of their blades and the continued song of steel meeting steel. Yes, she could get lost in this ballet, she thought to herself.

Nassor's mount stepped too closely and she pressed her advantage. Alex raised her hand, letting her aura blind him, while she raised her sword with the other and placed it firmly against his neck. They paused and looked into one another's eyes, a feeling of mutual respect and appreciation of skill passing between them. Nassor bowed almost imperceptibly, and Alex removed her blade from his neck.

Nassor turned his stallion away, the two almost twirling together in the air, as they moved out of the way of Rohan approaching on his larger destrier. The ground shook as his horse thundered towards her.

"Steady," Alex whispered to Eimhir, "steady my friend." Alexandria began to feel the power in her legs, as she pressed her feet down in the stirrups and shifted forward ever so slightly so that she was almost standing.

She twirled her sword, feeling the balance and smoothness of the grip, and then held it with both hands to her side. She imagined the strength of her power flowing into the sword, down to the very tip of the blade. The strange metal within the folded steel, Inonya, a gift from their fathers, began to sing as it warmed under her energy flow. She could hear it calling to her.

Rohan's objective was clear. He wanted to overwhelm her with brute force, but she was stronger and she knew it now. She felt it as surely as she felt air in her lungs. He was almost upon her now and she exhaled slowly, intoning her aura to envelope and fortify her. She willed the atmosphere around her to shroud her back and brace her for the impact.

And then Rohan's blade met hers. In her mind, Alex imagined that this must be what it felt like for two trains to crash together on a track. Pure speed, weight, and supremacy were transferring one to another. She had tilted her blade at a slightly upturned angle just before the two collided, and in doing so achieved her desired effect. Her upward strike was propelled on by her internal power. Alex's strength and fortified wall of energy was too great. Her blade lifted his up, and Rohan went with his sword, up and off his mount.

He flew through the air for what seemed like too great a time, and hit the ground hard enough to leave a rather large impression. Alex swung her leg up and over Eimhir's back and jumped down to the ground, racing to her friend. She sank to her knees on the frosty, snow covered ground beside him and looked Rohan over from head to toe.

"Where are you hurt, Rohan? Rohan, talk to me!" she implored. His eyes were closed and he offered her no words, no indication of what might be broken or ruptured.

The others were in full gallop towards them, but Alex did not wait for them. She thought of how Ganymede had healed her after Bertrand's attack, of the pure energy she had felt pass from him to her. She closed her eyes and leaned forward, placing her forehead to Rohan's as Ganymede had done to her. She began to feel the flow of her energy sweeping down throughout first his head, over his chest, then on to his abdomen, and finally to his legs and feet.

She gasped as she realized Rohan had peeled back much of his own aura's shield before he charged her. He had deliberately allowed himself to be injured. She began to coax her aura to mend broken bones, too many to count, a ruptured spleen, bruised and torn kidneys, a shattered spinal column, and to place the internally spilled blood to the arteries and veins where it belonged.

She stayed bent like that, her head to his, until she was satisfied he was whole again. Then she willed air into his lungs, as she lifted her head and opened her eyes. Rohan stared up at her, with a lopsided grin on his face. He looked so young, up close like that.

"You stubborn old goat," she whispered, shaking her head slowly at him. She cupped his face and looked warmly into his eyes. Alex saw herself in much the same position on a battlefield from long ago, healing and mending him, while he was still learning to fortify himself.

"Why?" she breathed.

"You know why," he answered her gruffly. "There's so much for you to remember, and I don't want you to forget anything before it's too late."

"I'm not going anywhere, Rohan. I'm here, and I'm not going to let anyone take me away again. I believe that, so you trust in it too. Okay, my friend?" she smiled reassuringly at the concern she heard in his words and voice.

He winked at her and then turned his head to the circle of *Nephilim* that had come to help, but who had stood by watching the exchange and healing that had taken place between the two. He took in Sabina's exasperated expression and let out a deep, hearty laugh that shook his entire large chest.

Alex stood and offered him her hand. He took it, and with her still vastly fortified strength, she launched him from the ground so that he was upright before her much too quickly. He placed a palm to his head and blinked his eyes a few times until the lightheadedness passed.

"Oh, you're fine," she admonished him.

"I am now. Thanks," he said, clasping her forearm as she had done to his the previous afternoon. But he did not let go, only held her there and searched her eyes for a moment.

'What is it, Rohan?" she asked, wondering if she had missed something, and he was still in pain somewhere.

"Feel up to one more challenge?" he asked her quietly.

Surprisingly, she found she did. She had never felt so alive and so vibrant. She nodded her agreement, and he released her hand and then turned to the others. He signaled for the group to fan out away from their horses. Alex chanced a quick glance at Jack, and found him watching her steadily with the trace of a smile on his lips. He looked so proud of her.

She nodded in his direction before she turned back to the group and was surprised to see Sabina had joined in the circle.

More *Nephilim* were standing at the nearby fence and observing as they had done previously, and she had not even noticed them. She chastised herself for not being more aware. She scanned the group taking note of auras first, then faces. Satisfied that she knew where all possible players in Rohan's game might come from, she turned back to the immediate circle.

"Yesterday, you didn't get a chance to practice this skill very well, because someone threw a longsword at your head," said Elrick, cutting his eyes over to Rohan who just shrugged his shoulders in response. "Today, though, I think you're better prepared."

"Arianna taught us to handle more than one opponent at a time, to use our evolved senses and fathers' abilities to think outside of three dimensions to overcome one who would try to destroy us. We want you to try to defend against all of us, together. Do you want to try?" he asked, still leaving the decision in her court.

Alex thought of Rohan's words, "I don't what you to forget anything before it's too late," and knew she could not refuse their offer of training. Better to remember amongst friends than enemies, she decided. She raised her sword in front of her face and bowed in Nassor's fashion, then took a step back.

She called on Arianna's memories and saw herself standing in a circular formation such as that one, training her friends. The wind stilled as she drew in the memory and placed it over the canvas of the current training session. Then she inhaled, and thought about the future and what that exact circle would be doing a scant few seconds ahead in time.

Alexandria wrapped her aura around that picture of the future, so that none of the others could see it or know it. The future was hers.

As Nassor stepped forward, Alex closed her eyes and looked into her vision of the future and saw what was to come. She stepped into Nassor's strike and met his blade precisely with her own, as she saw it happening in her mind's eye. Thomas and Elrick approached and she volleyed with all three, her eyes closed to the entire mock battle.

She saw Sabina and Iain coming into the group, and she began to whip her aura into the thickening cloud she had created in her mind the night before to slow their progress. She was altering their movements through the air and space around their bodies, catching them in a quagmire of animated energy. To Alex, they all seemed to move in slow motion as their swords rang out again and again against one another's.

Jack had never imagined he would witness Alexandria in such a scene. She was twirling, dipping, and charging with such grace and finesse, and her eyes were closed the entire time. He watched in amazement as she took on all six of them, even easily handling Rohan's immense size and strength. She pushed off from the ground several times as Nassor's blade swiped at her feet, vaulting through the air, and to Jack, it appeared gravity was letting her have more time than a human should have to return to earth.

He was struck by the beauty and quiet authority that was contained within her, and even seeing it unleashed, he was in awe of her command of the power that lay within. What good she could work in the world with abilities such as those he had seen over the past few days, he wondered to himself. All of the war and fighting he had witnessed. All of the suffering he had seen in his travels, she could ease that, he thought. She and her kind.

And for all the good they could do, all of the hope that they could inspire, he imagined what the antithesis of that could do to mankind. A child of the Fallen they called them, hell bent on meddling in human affairs and destroying the *Nephilim* gathered there.

Alexandria had yet to completely tell him of the attack that led her to finally decide to accept the *Nephilim* and Ganymede's help. But, he thought, if she had been unprepared and one with the kind of power he was now witnessing had gotten to her, he could only imagine the pain and terror she must have suffered. He had never seen one so brave in all his life.

As she had the night before, Alex finally used her aura to subdue those she was sparring with and pushed outward in a great wave of energy, landing them all on their backsides. She stood from the crouched position she was in and released her hold on the future and then their bodies, finally opening her eyes.

Her face splitting grin told them all how she felt. She was so giddy from the rush of power and adrenaline, that she burst out laughing and threw her head back, relishing in the sweet feeling of victory. Not over her friends, but the feeling of finally coming to grips with what and who she was. She had fought this for so long, not understanding or knowing what she railed against. She felt the energy surging within and stretched her arms out letting it spread around her like a warm hug. This was her and this was Ganymede, and if she accepted his gift, she could feel this forever. She could do so much good with what he offered her, she realized.

Sabina came to her and enveloped her in true hug, breaking through Alex's silent reverie. Elrick and Iain piled on next, then Thomas and Rohan until she was sandwiched in the middle of them, laughing and celebrating with her friends. Just as they had done before, she was sure.

They finally stepped back one from another and Rohan touched her shoulder lightly.

"It's good to have you back, friend," he said, his voice carrying with it his heartfelt joy from his companion's return.

"I'm here," she whispered, and looked into all of their faces one at a time, reaffirming her vow.

Jackson approached and shook the men's hands, praising them for all that they had accomplished that morning and their skill in combat. Once Jack let it slip that he, too, had served as a soldier, Rohan, Iain, and Elrick took new interest in the human within their midst.

"Good," said Alex to Sabina. "Maybe now Rohan and Jack can play nicely with one another."

Sabina said nothing, but looked at Rohan just a little sadly. She offered Alex some lunch, so they called the men over to join them. As they were approaching, Alex looked into Eimhir and Aileas' large, soulful eyes and asked them if they would lead the other horses back to the stables. Eimhir brayed, and the mares and stallions began to trot away.

"Did you just do that?" asked Jack, coming up behind her.

"Yes. I just asked them to please go back to the stables and they seemed so inclined," said Alex, smiling up into Jack's face. "What is it? You've the strangest look on your face."

"Just mesmerized," he whispered. "That was quite an amazing show I just witnessed, Alex. I can't even begin to describe what I saw. It looked like something out of a martial arts film, they way you all came together. Simply amazing," he breathed out.

She smiled shyly, unaccustomed to such praise. Jack was the first outside of her family to really see her worth, but then again, he was the first one she had really let in. And it was all because Ganymede had insisted he come along. She offered up silent thanks to the angel for gifting her with this friend. In the days to come, she hoped she would always be able to talk to Jack and confide in him as she had done over the past few critical days.

20

Lunch was a loud and boisterous affair that afternoon. They ate in the dining hall, because so many immortals wanted to discuss and comment on the sparring they had witnessed. There were many old stories of training and battles waged throughout the ages told as well. And once Rohan started insulting the fighting capabilities of some of the others there, the tales grew bolder and, Alex thought, exaggerated.

From their discussion over the meal, Alex learned that Arianna had tried to teach the *Nephilim* restraint and moderation. Though they were all nearly invincible, she worked hard to instruct them not to interfere in mankind's wars and their bids for power. They were not to overwhelm and dominate their human brethren. It appeared it was still a hard lesson for some like Rohan and Iain to hold to.

She and Jack made their way to the library after lunch and they each did some exploring, discovering books and documents which would make the curators of the Vatican library weep to behold. The collection was so vast and well-rounded, that Alex mused a person could spend a lifetime just soaking up the knowledge that abounded within.

That thought led to an idea, which she had considered for a fleeting moment the first time she had entered the space. But it had fled from her mind that night with all the other pressing matters which had occurred. If Arianna had indeed orchestrated the collection and lived with these documents, transcribing many, then perhaps Alex could remember them now, she mused.

Jack had stretched out on a couch, the same one he had placed her on after her vision the previous day, and was reading a current newspaper he had found. Alex walked over to one of the bookcases located along the wall that contained the library's windows. Her eyes began to inspect the bindings that lined the wooden shelves. Some were new, but most were so very old. She let her eyes roam over the collection until she focused in on a volume wrapped in dark green velvet.

She hesitated for a moment, not wanting to have another vision pounce upon her. She was just too tired for that after her morning with Rohan and the others. Finally, she concentrated on just the memory of the book's contents and gingerly touched the binding with her fingers. There was no jolt, no jump in time, but more of a subtle view into herself peering into the book at one of the library's many tables, turning the pages slowly and making notes on a parchment to the book's side. Alex imagined walking up behind the figure of herself bent over the desk and looking over her own shoulder. She even began to read the pages, too.

She stood there for several minutes until she remembered what the book's contents were about. It was a volume from a friend, Galileo Galilei, who was sharing his thoughts and observations with her despite his house arrest under Pope Urban VIII. He had smuggled the work to her, hoping for a discussion of his theories about infinity and how one might accurately measure the flow of time. Alex could see she was actually writing him a letter on the parchment now, indicating her great pride in his achievements thus far.

She returned to the present and moved on to another bookcase, hoping for a similar experience. This time she touched a very small volume and saw John sitting under a tree down by the estate's lake, writing in the book. He was composing poetry, and the imagery he conjured up stirred her to great emotion. He compared the *Nephilim's* life to that of a great mountain. Strong, straight and majestic, but even so, they could still be worn down and weathered away over time. She was touched by his honesty and truthfulness.

Alex continued seeking out interesting bindings and reliving the books' contents for some time. She finally turned back to check on Jack and found that he was watching her with his hands stacked behind his head. She smiled and walked over to him, and as she reached the couch, he sat up patting the cushion next to him.

"Finished with your paper?" she asked.

"Long since. What have you been reading?" he asked, nodding his head towards the shelves.

Alex turned and drew her legs underneath herself so she could face him. She related her attempt to see into her soul's past interactions with the books there. And she described how, by fully concentrating on just what she hoped to gain by touching the bindings, she had been able to see into the books at different points in the volumes' pasts without having a problem.

"It's getting a little easier, I think," she grinned.

"After what I saw today on that field, I would say so," he agreed. He had one hand draped on the sofa's fluffy back cushions, and he raised a hand to smooth her hair behind her ear and then lowered it to trace the edge of her cheek and jaw. She felt so breathless at just the simplest touch from him.

"Jack," she breathed out, trying to distract herself from these new and powerful feelings. "Will you tell me more about yourself?"

"What do you want to know?" he asked softly, his eyes following his finger still playing on her jaw line.

"Everything," she smiled slightly.

"Well, that would take a while," he chuckled, and his eyes moved to hers. "There's not much to tell. I've already mentioned where I'm from, and that I have parents and a younger brother still there. You know about my military service, and what I do now. That's about it."

"No, I mean, I'm glad I know all of that about you. But I want to know more. I mean, I know you're strong, brave, and really kind-hearted," she said, leaning in and placing her palm over his heart, "but I want to know more about you. How old are you? What's your favorite color, football team, where do you live, what kind of car do you drive? What is your favorite food? What makes you happy?" She could have gone on all afternoon, but he raised his hand and placed it over hers still on his chest.

"You really do want to know a lot, don't you?" he asked in mock surprise. "Let's see if I can remember all of these questions. I'm twenty-eight, I like the color blue, and I got my Master's degree from the University of Georgia, so I'm a bulldog fan. I have a small flat in London that I live in when I'm not on assignment. I don't have a car here, my firm provides me with transportation when I need it. I love Italian food or a really good steak."

"Let's see, what else? Oh, you wanted to know what makes me happy. I've been pretty focused on my education, then my service, then getting established in this career. In my off time, I go home for visits or I travel, but I haven't left a lot of room for other things, really. But right now, here with you, I'm probably the happiest I've ever been," he said soberly, looking directly into Alex's eyes. "I'm very happy right now."

"I am too," she whispered. She leaned forward and placed her other hand on the side of his cheek. "I don't want you hurt, but I'm so glad you're here with me," she said sincerely, and she let her lips meet his.

Alex felt like this was where she wanted to stay for the next one hundred years, safe in Jack's arms, and she told him, trying to get the words out while she connected with him. And this was where he wanted her too, he whispered against her lips, safe and protected.

Finally, Jack pulled away and smiled gently, stroking her bottom lip with his thumb. "Why don't you lie back and take a nap, then we'll see what's in store for the remainder of the day." Alex did not want to let Jack go, but she finally agreed. Though she did not think she could sleep, her body surprised her by rapidly falling into a deep, dreamless slumber.

Alex opened her eyes slowly and stretched under the blanket she found herself under. She looked around and saw Jack sitting and reading an old book that looked to be a first edition <u>Lord of the Rings</u>.

"Hey," she said groggily.

He looked up at her over the pages he was reading. "Hey, yourself. Feel better?"

"Yes, I think. How long did I sleep?"

"About an hour," he laughed at her incredulous expression. "Don't be so surprised; your body's going through a lot right now. You need the rest."

"Well, so do you," she scolded, sitting up and rubbing her face.

"I dozed for about twenty minutes myself while you were sleeping, so I'm good. Got a proposition for you," he said. "What do you say to a little run?"

She wrinkled up her nose at the thought. Alex had never been one to go out running or jogging. Her knees always rebelled and it made her back ache. She usually settled for bicycling, horseback riding, or swimming. But she considered her newly reinforced body and decided that running now might not make her feel like an eighty year old lady.

"Is it that bad?" laughed Jack. "You don't have to you know, I was just asking."

"No, I had to think it over. I think I can go for a run, just don't leave me behind, I'm not so fast," she said, getting off of the couch and stretching as high as she could reach.

He stood as well, tucking his book under his arm and said, "That, you need not worry about, Miss Groaban. I'm not going to leave you behind." He reached for her hand and walked with her back up to their rooms so that they could change.

Alex and Jack both chose the same workout clothes they had worn the previous morning, because someone had already laundered them and brought them back to their rooms. Alex made a mental note to ask Sabina who was taking care of all the chores there. If it was a group effort, she needed to get her name on the list and start contributing.

Jack knocked to make sure she was decent, and she met him at the door, suggesting that they go get water bottles from the kitchen. He told her he did not normally run with water, but he would if that was what she wanted.

After fetching what they needed, they headed for a door and saw Ahadi on their way out. They told her what their intentions were, and she reminded them to stick close to the main house. Jack nodded to her and they made their way outside.

Alex zipped up her jacket and unrolled the fleece turtleneck below so that her mouth and nose were covered. Dragging the cold air into her lungs still did not feel too pleasant to her, so she protected her face. Jack started out at a slow warm-up pace, but eventually he really started moving. She found that she was not tired though, or even really winded. Her newly discovered strength was paying off.

They chatted a little at first, but ultimately each was lost to their own thoughts as their feet pounded across the ground. They ran down to the stables, then turned left and continued along the line of fencing that bordered the pastures from the forest. It was a beautiful afternoon, so pristine and quiet.

They ran for almost forty minutes, Aeoferth almost out of sight, when Jack began to slow. She slowed to match his pace until they had both stopped. He leaned against the fence and tried to regulate his breathing. Alex did not seem to need a recovery period like she normally did when she attempted exercise, but she kept quiet and open her bottle for a drink.

She looked around at the vast section of land. What an amazing secret this place was, she thought to herself. So beautiful, even covered in winter's bluster. Trees that were so ancient and tall loomed high overhead, and she thought that these old forests must have been like those which had inspired Tolkien to write about his Ents.

Alex turned back to Jack and noticed a movement behind him and to the left that was so fast, it seemed to not be real, like a figment of her imagination. Surely it had been a shadow, she thought, but there was no breeze she could detect that would cause the tree branches overhead to sway. In fact, there was no other movement or sound that she could discern. The forest was too quiet, even in the dead of winter.

Reality dawned then, and she launched herself at Jack trying desperately to reach him in time. But that second that she had hesitated, was one too many. Before she could get to Jack, he was grabbed and hoisted up and over the fence from behind, then dragged into the forest beyond.

Alex's fury and momentum gave her new speed and agility. She bounded over the fence, willing the air to buffet her across. She was running at full speed, and she caught sight of a dark purple aura up ahead moving in and out between trees. She was gaining on the dark *Nephilim*, but she did not know if it was enough.

"Please, God, let it be enough," she prayed.

When she felt that she was close enough, she threw her aura out with such a force that it toppled the dark one to the ground, but he did not relinquish Jack. Jack was still conscious and fighting with all his might. She ran until she was just a meter away, when the intruder gained his feet. He held Jack in one arm, choking him high enough off of the ground for his feet to dangle, and with the other he produced a long, curved knife. Dread settled in Alex's stomach.

"You want him, I'll trade you," he hissed at her, his head moving in a most unnatural way, slithering from side to side like a snake's head before it strikes.

Alexandria knew she should not look at Jack, but she could see him struggling out of the corner of her eye. She tried to stay focused on this Fallen one's child. His aura was so putrid and dank, that it felt suffocating to her. She began to remember this one and his game of toying with his prey first.

"You are Aagon, I remember you. You shall not leave this place alive if you harm one hair on his head. Release him, and deal with me! I'm what you came for, after all," she said, leveling her anger at him as her voice reverberated through the surrounding forest.

"Oh, yes! You. How *are* you here?" he laughed, as though they were old friends having a familiar conversation, and it gave Alex chills to her core.

"Kronis rid this world of your stinking carcass, and yet you stand here before me. When Bertrand told me he had discovered you yet lived, I thought he lied hoping to find power for himself in the tale. But when he didn't return, I wondered what or who might be keeping him," he said, as his voice lowered into a menacing tone and his eyes studied her.

"Imagine my surprise when I realized his story was fact, not fiction. How *have* you returned, or were you ever really dead at all?" His malicious laughter filled the air and set her hair on end. "So, if you have returned, how is your little council of twelve? I imagine one is overjoyed to have you back, safe and sound. Maybe now he can retire from stalking Kronis all around the world. Was it a happy reunion?" he asked, angling his head to one side and waiting for her reply.

Alex did not know what to say, but she had to get Jack out of Aagon's grip before he crushed Jack's windpipe or worse.

"What? No answer?" Aagon gasped, and then covered his mouth with the hand that held the gleaming knife. "Could it be that the great Arianna has not met all of her council this time around?" He hooted with laughter at her ignorance. "My, my, the good guys are playing dirty this time! Hmmm," he ran a finger across his lips contemplating his next words.

"Why don't you ask them what they've not told you, and then decide who you want to play for this time around. You might not want to be with *friends* like those, who don't trust you enough to tell you the whole truth," he huffed, and in one quick movement he crushed Jack's neck and flipped the knife over running it up Jack's abdomen, cutting deeply into his flesh.

Aagon tossed Jack's limp body at Alexandria and turned to leave, but she threw her hands out and froze them both midair, sending out such a shock wave with her anger and anguish that her ears popped, like a depth charge that carried on for as far as she could see.

"Oh, God, no!" she screamed. "No, Jack!"

Alex stood transfixed between the two, Jack hanging limply just a few feet from the ground and Aagon turned to flee. She did not know if she could only free one from her suspension. If she unfroze them both, she would not be able to save Jack and lay chase to Aagon at the same time. There was no choice who would get her attention first, so she had to deal with Aagon before she unfroze them both.

Crying aloud, she moved forward and took the knife, now soaked with Jack's blood, from Aagon's hand. She looked into his dark pupils and breathed heavily. She had never once thought she would have to take another's life so soon after her training had begun, but this malevolent being would run back to his compatriots and spread the word of what had taken place there in the wood. No one she loved would ever be truly safe again.

She raised the blade and sank it into his chest cutting in a diamond pattern, just as she had done to the training mannequin, until his chest cavity was open. And reaching in with trembling fingers, she took his heart in her hand.

"Why didn't you stop? Why? You could have been forgiven!" she screamed and sobbed. "You could have known grace!" She pulled back and took the heart some distance away, before she hurled it into the forest with all of her strength.

Alexandria felt completely ill and was shaking all over, but she steeled herself to look at the damage the demon had inflicted on Jack's body. He was so pale. His throat looked crumpled and he was slit from below his navel to his collarbones. And there was so much blood.

"Oh, Jack," she whispered, as she cried, "I'm so, so sorry. I wasn't fast enough, but I will heal you. I'm so sorry."

Alex lowered Jack to the ground so that he would fall no further. She knelt beside him and bent over his body, putting one hand over his stomach and one over his throat. She began to build up as much of her aura as she could, until she felt like she could create a tidal wave with it. When she knew she had enough to completely overwhelm his injuries, she leaned down and placed her lips over his, letting out a deep breath as she willed time to resume.

She released the wave she had stored over Jack and poured her very soul into her effort, willing all his fatal injuries to repair and Jack to be healed. Safe, and with her once more. She felt his organs, bones, skin, and blood resume their rightful places. Felt his neck begin to take shape again, and sensed his trachea become the tube it was meant to be. She felt his lungs inflate once more and heard his sharp intake of air, as he breathed her aura into his lungs.

She poured all the affection and gratitude for him into that flow, willing him to live. "Live, Jack, oh please live," she pleaded within her mind. "Don't leave me." She stayed connected with Jack, praying and transferring her energy to him, until she heard Rohan's yell.

"Alex, let me see him," he said. But she would not be moved. She stayed there beside him, her lips pressed to his. "Alex, I'm sorry," he said, and lifted her by her waist so that he could have a look at Jack's injuries.

She began to fight Rohan trying to get back to Jack, but she heard Jack cough and breathe in deep gasps of air. Rohan let her sink back beside him as he began to look over Jack's chest and neck. Jack's clothes were still soaked in blood, but he was completely whole again. She had mended him, and that realization caused her to sob aloud. She put her hand over her mouth to stem the emotion pouring forth.

She was aware of other voices then. Sabina, Elrick, John, and Benen were all there. John came over and looked at Jack as well, then took Alex's hand. "He's going to be just fine, Alex. You did well, my dear." But she could not look at any of them. She stayed transfixed on Jack's eyes willing him to wake, and John released her palm.

She knelt beside him, brushing his short hair from his forehead and staring at his closed eyes. She leaned down, putting her lips to his ear. "Jack, you have to wake up now. No more napping, I need you to look at me. Please, Jack, open your eyes and look at me." She leaned down and kissed his lips once again, not caring who saw her.

Finally, she registered some movement in his arms, then his chin shifted slightly up, and finally she felt him sigh against her lips. She pulled back and watched as his eyelids fluttered open, his blue eyes meeting hers.

"Hey, don't stop," he whispered.

Alex laughed through her tears and leaned down to kiss him once more, so happy that he was there again with her. "I'm so sorry, Jack. So very sorry you had to suffer like this," she cried softly.

"Shhh," he crooned, "no apologizing, remember?"

She laughed softly, "Yes, I remember."

Sabina came over and sank to her knees beside Jack, opposite Alexandria. She took Alex's hand and implored her to look at her. Finally, Alex allowed her gaze to turn towards Sabina and she saw tears streaming down her friend's face as well.

"Let's get him back to his room and cleaned up, so that he can rest. You have healed him well, Alexandria, but he will still need to recover for a little while. His body was very traumatized by Aagon," Sabina said, through her emotion.

Rohan came forward and knelt on the other side of Jack. He placed one arm under his knees and one under his shoulders. "Ready?" he asked. Jack gave a small nod and Rohan lifted him as if he weighed nothing, and then turned to head back towards Aeoferth.

Alex did not look back to see Aagon's body, she just walked quietly beside Rohan and Jack, with Sabina on her other side. The group finally reached one of the castle's side doors, and Sabina moved forward to hold it open. They moved through the halls and up the stairs, passing so many, but Alex could not look anyone in the eye. She just wanted to get Jack to his room.

Sabina once again held the door open and Rohan headed straight to the watercloset with Jack. He sat him gingerly on the side of his tub and turned the shower on, getting the water nice and warm. Alex moved forward and helped him remove his jacket and gun holster, then his tattered shirt, and finally she knelt to take his shoes and socks off.

"I think I can take it from here," said Jack smiling. "I just feel kinda sore all over, but I'm good." He looked up into Rohan's face and thanked him. Rohan nodded and left the bathroom.

Alex stood to leave Jack to his shower too, but he stood slowly and enfolded her in a hug. "Thank you," he whispered down into her hair.

Alex could not stem the flow, and tears ran hot down her cheeks touching Jackson's newly mended chest.

"Oh, Jack," she breathed, "I thought I had lost you. I was too slow, and I hesitated too long."

"Shhh," he said softly. "We're both here, thanks to you. That's what I'm concentrating on right now, and so should you." He pulled back and mouthed another thank you to her before he softly kissed her. It was not an urgent kiss, but one of tenderness and quiet supplication.

Alex was so grateful he was alive, and she tried to show him that through her touch. She held him to her so that she could feel his heart beating and know that he really had made it through Aagon's brutal assault. He was there, he was really there, she told herself over and over like a mantra.

At last she pulled away and looked into his eyes. "I'm going to leave, so you can have a shower. I'll be right back over, though. Don't worry," she said, hoping to reassure him, knowing he did not like to let her out of his sight.

Jack nodded, and she turned and left his watercloset. Sabina was still waiting in the bedroom and she came over to Alex. She brushed Alex's hair back and kissed her first on one cheek then the other.

"Alex, go have a shower as well and I'll bring some food up for you and Jackson, okay?" she suggested.

Alex felt so numb and cold inside, she did not have it in her to argue, so she nodded mutely and walked across the hall to her bedroom. She headed for her watercloset and started the warm water stream in her shower. While the water was heating, she turned and looked at herself in the mirror.

Gone was the joy she had felt earlier that morning, and replacing it was a pale, shell-shocked vacant look. She had Jack's blood all over the jacket and shirt she wore, and it covered her hands. She looked at the dried blood and felt the bile rise in her throat. She barely made it to the toilet before she began to retch. Again and again she was sick, until she thought there was nothing left in her stomach.

She began to pull against her clothes, struggling with them as if they had a will of their own and did not want her to shed them. Finally free of her bindings, she threw everything into the wastebasket and stepped into the shower. She sat on the shower seat and held her hands under the stream, watching the floor of the shower turn red.

It was Aagon's blood mixed with Jack's, and it made her weep again. Dear Lord, had this been what her brothers felt like after they had found her in Lord Lenley's library, she wondered. She knew now she would have to tell them everything. They could not be stuck with an image of her so hurt and not know the real reason why.

She continued to let the water flow until she saw red, then pink, and finally clear water at her feet. She dragged herself off of the shower seat and began to wash her body from head to toe, beginning with her hair. The thought that she was trying to push away worked its way back in, and she gasped and held her hands out against the tiled wall to brace herself.

She had taken a life. Not quickly, not with her opponent standing a chance to defend himself, but slowly and methodically until she was sure he could hurt no one else, ever again. What then did that make her, she asked herself. Alex began to retch again, but there was nothing left in her stomach to come forth. She cried and keened until her throat felt raw. But still she stood there, hoping that the water would somehow wash away her sin and make her whole again.

Alex finally pulled herself together enough to finish her bath, and stepped out to dry off. She gathered her robe around her and made her way out of the watercloset, intent on dressing then going back over to sit with Jack. When she entered her bedroom, however, she found him lying on top of the bed's comforter, fast asleep.

She stood watching him rest until she began to sway on her feet, and finally headed into her closet. She changed into sweats and quietly padded over to her bed, all while he slept peacefully. Alex did not dare pull back the covers, for fear of waking him, so she gently climbed atop the bed and lay next to him on her side so that she could watch his slow and steady breath.

He was alive, she told herself over and over, until her eyelids drooped. Just before she lost her battle to stay awake and watch over him, she prayed for no dreams. She could not see Aagon or what she had done to him, not now. Just not now, she prayed. Maybe later, when she felt less brittle and less dirty. And she finally let go and succumbed to rest.

21

Alex was warm and she snuggled down hoping to continue her bliss. She opened her eyes and found herself outside Aeoferth Hall with the warm summer sun beating down on her skin. She was lying on a blanket beside the lake, watching the ripples that the slight breeze produced across the lake's surface. Shimmering silver patterns danced and played before her eyes.

She looked into the patterns and observed that there were actually tiny reflections in the patterns, like microscopic pictures and images of lives lived and adventures too vast to be recorded. She moved closer to the surface and beheld that they stretched out as far as the eye could see. The harder she concentrated on the pictures, the more she could make out herself in the host of memories, for that was what they were.

Alexandria became aware that someone had come to stand beside her, and she turned, startled to find that she was looking into her own eyes. It was Arianna, come to gaze out across the ripples with her. Alex was shocked, because she had expected Ganymede. Arianna turned to look at her and smiled taking Alex's hand in hers, and then turned back towards the lake.

"There's so much to behold, isn't there, Alex?" she asked gently.

"All of this is you, your life?" Alexandria surmised.

"Yes, though I think this is only a small portion, a sampling if you will," she laughed, with such joy and mirth that Alex found herself smiling in response.

Arianna sighed, "So many events, and so many people I've known, so many I've loved. All of this is you now too, Alexandria. Though you've yet to decide whether to embrace an immortal life or not, you have access to all of this as well."

"I still don't really understand how any of this is possible or real, Arianna. I am growing and discovering here, but how are you me and I you? I have a family and I have my own name. I'm me, aren't I?" Alexandria pressed, wanting desperately to understand.

"Yes, you are Alexandria, and you are me." She smiled at Alex's confused face. "Come and sit with me, while we talk." Alex turned and followed Arianna to the blanket, and the two sat cross-legged and looked at one another.

"Alexandria, when I was here on this earth before, I lived alone for a long, long time. I grew and trained with Ganymede when I was young, and then after two hundred years, give or take a few, he returned to the Lord and I was left here to begin my work. I always knew I could call on my father, just as we can call on the one true God, but I had to find it within myself to endure."

"Humankind is full of promise and hope, but it is also weak and fallible. There needed to be a strong force of good, hope, and Light to lead man through some of his darkest hours when civilizations were first being created. Someone to guard over them and nurture them. I was that force. At least I tried to be," she shrugged her shoulders slightly.

"The more success I had in caring for God's people, the more I wanted to do for them. Because I didn't try to change them, only nurture what was good and right, it was determined that more *Nephilim* could join me. Finally, I wasn't so alone in this anymore."

"As the ages passed and the Fallen's children were born, our work became ever more difficult. It was because of them that I had to take my first life." Arianna paused and looked sadly into Alexandria's eyes. Alex instantly saw Aagon's face flash before her, and she bowed her head in shame and regret. Arianna reached forward and took her hand, offering comfort at a shared ache and lament.

"I know, Alex, I know. There are no words for the internal pain and damage it does to one's soul to take another's life. The regret and hurt never go away, no matter what the other did to provoke the act. And that, you see, is what sets us apart. We feel the pain and loss, and the Fallen's children do not."

"Or at least they pretend as if they don't, and it doesn't matter. I searched within myself, long and hard, before I offered Kronis the chance to repent. I knew it was a risk, but at my core I believed it was a risk worth taking. For how could I preach the message of God's enduring and everlasting love to humans for millennia, and not offer it to the most lost of souls I had ever seen?"

"When I lost my battle, all that I was and all that I am remained. It was, what was. All those events, all those actions of kindness," she gestured out to the scenes within the ripples, "they were and are true. They did come to pass."

Alexandria thought back to Archimedes' napkin analogy. The past was there, recorded and real for her to behold.

"Yes," nodded Arianna, "exactly like that. All that I was, all that I am, is still there."

"My absence from this world created an imbalance in the weight of immortal power on this earth. Once I was gone, and the Fallen's children knew that I was no longer here to hold them back, they became more determined than ever to cause anger, betrayal, murder, and war within mankind."

"My fellow *Nephilim* of the Light prayed that I be restored and help shift the power back. Once I was in God's presence, I did not want to be removed, but The Great I Am knew what was better for His people. I beseeched Ganymede that I might return as a human this time, and actually have a choice about my future."

"But if God sent you back," asked Alexandria, "how is there even a choice about any of this?"

"Ah, Alex. That is one of the most amazing gifts from our Lord. He gives us free will to carve out our own destiny. He's no grand puppeteer in the sky, pulling our strings for every movement we make. He allows us to seek out a path that, hopefully, will be filled with righteousness and goodness towards our fellow man. That is all the praise He could ever want; our love for one another and for Him."

Arianna looked out over the water and smiled at some of the ripples. She remembered past friends and humans never recorded in history, long since forgotten by the world, but not by her. Still looking at the water, she spoke again to Alex. "There is so much more that you do not know, so much more that you have yet to learn, and the coming days and weeks will be the toughest yet," she sighed heavily.

"Kronis and his brethren are seeking to annihilate all that we hold dear, your family and mine, and all those countless humans out there who will pay the price. A great deal has been held back, because I didn't know how much to give you without harming you."

Arianna stood and walked over to the water's edge, scooping up two handfuls of water and walked back over to Alex. She poured the water slowly into Alex's palms. Alexandria gasped as the water soaked into her flesh and pores, and she beheld flash after flash of different people's faces and lifetimes as they passed into her. The depth of just that little bit was overwhelming. Alex refocused her eyes and looked up at Arianna.

Arianna extended her hand and helped Alex rise to her feet, and the two faced one another again. She brushed Alex's hair off of her face and smiled at her lovingly. "The more you take in, the more you become me, Alex, for we are the same soul. Within you, my soul was reborn to a human family, with all my gifts intact, with all of the past, present and future full of endless possibilities."

"You can do so much good with what I offer, but understand it is an offer. You can say no to all those memories, all that you've seen and learned over the past few days and wipe the slate clean. We can take all of this away and you can just be human. The scale will have to right itself without you."

"Or you can embrace the mantel that is the greatest wealth of knowledge and power anyone has ever been offered, and see what good you can make of it. The choice is yours: mortality or immortality. It is the choice I never had," she smiled wistfully, looking back out at the water.

Alexandria turned back towards the lake too, thinking of what a blank slate would mean to all those who were depending on her being in her place and helping stop Kronis and his horde. What if Arianna had not been in those ripples, she wondered. How many would have been lost or harmed without her there standing guard through the ages, Alex questioned silently.

Finally, she spoke her thoughts aloud. "I can no more abandon them than you could, Arianna. It is not within my character to see harm come to others when I know I could have helped prevent it. I will embrace this, the best I can. I know I can find a way, though right now I am terrified."

Arianna turned to Alex and smiled at her, understanding and compassion flowing from her. So much so, that Alex could tangibly feel it. "You are about to leave me for now, but know that you and I will become more of one another everyday if you speak the words to Ganymede. We will flow, one to another, like this water, and you will be filled and fortified with my being. But you will still be Alex, with Alex's mind and free will, and the freedom to determine how you use these gifts and memories."

"Forgive me, Alexandria, and forgive the others for the memories and knowledge we have held back. Some things had to be presented to you as you were ready. You've come so far in such a short time, but you will receive more knowledge, the more you demonstrate you can handle the weight of it. I believe you're ready for the next step, and I pray peace and understanding for you."

She leaned forward and kissed Alex's head, and Alex felt herself becoming sleepy and lethargic. "Goodbye for now, Alexandria," whispered Arianna. Alex could feel that she was succumbing to sleep. She was drifting down towards the soft grass, but she never touched the blades.

Alex opened her eyes and found that she was lying on her bed. She was still atop the comforter, but there was now a blanket covering her, keeping her warm. She looked over at Jack to see if he, too, still slept. But his eyes were open and he was watching her.

"Hey," he said softly, reaching out a hand and smoothing her hair back. He let his hand come to rest on her cheek and brushed his thumb across her skin slowly.

"Hi," she whispered back. Alex felt her throat constrict, and she took a deep gulp of air trying to steady her emotions. "How are you feeling?"

"Remarkably well, considering," he smiled slightly at her. "I think that's the hardest I've slept in ages, but I feel okay. How are you, Alex?" he breathed out, and she could feel the gravity behind his question.

She drew in a shaky breath and closed her eyes in shame. "I killed someone Jack. I took his life, and I didn't save you in time."

"Alex, open your eyes and look at me," he coaxed her.

When she looked up into his kind gaze it was her undoing, and the tears began to flow again.

"How can you look at me like that? When you find out what I did to him, you'll hate me for it."

"No," he said reverently, still stroking her cheek now damp with her sorrow. "I could never hate you. You did save me, Alexandria, and you gave me everything you had to get me back here. I felt it you know, all the love and tenderness inside you, pushing away the darkness and pulling me back to the here and now. I could see your aura, and it was so dazzling. I couldn't have turned away from it if St. Peter and all the hosts in Heaven had been calling me on."

"You took a life, Alex, to save a life. I know what that feels like, and I'll bet that Rohan and the others do, too. When I had to take someone's life for the first time, I thought I'd never get over it. And I'm still not sure that I have or ever will," he whispered, sadness echoing in his words.

Jack's eyes looked moist as he continued, "It makes you feel less than whole, like their parting rips some of you away. But anyone who's ever faced war or battle knows that there are those terrible moments that seem to happen in almost slow motion, when you have to decide if your life or the lives of your team are worth the sacrifice of another who wants to destroy you."

"There is no good day after, and no happy feeling to write home about. There's just the silent gratitude that you were spared and you get to be here another day, to try to protect those around you. It's why they say 'war is hell' Alex, and why it feels like it."

"You've been through more in the last week than most people, even in my line of work, have to deal with in a lifetime. You've been attacked, watched your brothers tortured in Archimedes' mental training session, witnessed me almost die, and had to take another's life."

"I know you're hurting, but know, too, that you are one of the strongest people I've ever met. If anyone can find a way through this, it's you, Alex. Don't give in to it, baby, because the weight of it will crush you." He lifted his blanket and pulled her up to his body, wrapping his arms around her. Jack tried to give her what comfort he could offer, while she quietly cried and mourned the choice she had been forced to make when Aagon crushed and gutted him.

Alex did not know how long they stayed that way, and she did not care. In that moment she was safe, and so was Jack. She wanted to stay hidden away in their cocoon, but she knew that was not really an option. The ripples in the water called to her. There were so many others out there who might suffer needlessly as Jack had done, and she could not abide the thought of their pain.

She finally leaned away a bit so that she could look into his blue eyes, still moist from his own tears. She kissed his lips softly and briefly. "Thank you, Jack. Thank you for not judging me, and thank you for your friendship. Somehow, I feel it's what's fortifying and holding me up through all of this."

"I had not considered that all the training would have to be put into action so soon and so violently. And I've only just touched the surface of what's possible. But after Bertrand's attack, I should have been more prepared, less naive. I won't make that mistake again," Alex said somberly.

"Alex, don't harden yourself because of this," Jack cautioned. "It's one thing to have the kind of power and the abilities you possess, but another to wield it."

"I know, and I feel that now, Jack. I'm not going out on a crusade; I just mean that if another comes for my family or my friends, I won't hesitate again. I can't. You are all too precious to sacrifice." She raised her hand and placed it on his chest to feel his heartbeat, and what a gift it was. Alex looked back into Jack's eyes and took a deep breath before she found the words she wanted to say.

"There's more, Jack. More to what Aagon said and what Arianna shared with me."

"Oh? She's been here, too?" he asked, lifting his eyebrows.

Alex nodded against the pillow. "Yes, while I slept. I finally met her and got a better explanation from her as to what was and what is to come, if I so choose it," she said pausing, waiting to see if Jack really wanted to hear this.

"Why do I get the feeling it's going to make the last few days feel like child's play?" he said, sighing.

They both remained silent for several minutes contemplating his question and the gravity of all that lay before them. Finally, Alex cleared her throat and asked, "Jack, are you okay to talk about what happened with Aagon?" She did not know if it was still too new and fresh for a recounting for either of them.

"Yes, I think we need to, Alex," he replied soberly.

"Do you remember what he was saying before he…," she closed her eyes against the image of Jack's throat being crushed in Aagon's hand. Jack reached over to caress her face again, silently encouraging her to go on. "Before he hurt you so badly?"

"I was picking up most of what he was saying. I tried to hold onto the conversation, because he was cutting into my airflow so badly, I was afraid if I didn't hold on to something, I was going to lose consciousness. He asked you how you had come back and if you had met all of the council." Jack paused for a moment then added, "And he asked if you'd had a happy reunion with one in particular. That I remember."

"Yes, he was perversely happy that he had information I did not have." She looked pensively into Jack's eyes, hoping that her next words would not disappoint or hurt him. "Jack, Arianna came to me in my dreams this morning. She compared her lifetime to the lake we've seen near the castle, each drop full of people's lives she had impacted in one way or another. She poured some of that water into my hand, and it was overwhelming, the amount of knowledge and weight that just that small amount contained."

"She told me that most of it has been held back from me, so that the incoming wave of it all wouldn't drown me. I've been receiving abilities and her power, mine if I want them, drop by drop as I hold out my hands ready to receive it. She also asked me to forgive her for holding back some of the most important information that I've yet to learn, because she wanted to see me more prepared for it first."

She reached down and took hold of Jack's hand and held it tightly. "I think I have an idea what she was referring to now, after Aagon's words," she said softly.

Jack's eyes held regret as he answered her, "I think I do, too." And the words hung between them as they just stared into each others eyes, holding one another, and savoring the warmth and the quiet before the coming storm.

Finally, Jack voiced both of their thoughts aloud. "Are you ready, Alex, to go down and speak to the others?" She nodded slowly and he tried to pull away from her, but she held fast and kissed him with all her might. Jack moaned softly against her lips as if he was fighting desperately to stop the emotions that they both felt, but it was of no use. He had never felt that way for anyone, and now that he knew Alexandria, he doubted he would ever feel that way about another.

He gathered her body up to his and tried to give her what was in his heart through his lips and his touch, as she had for him when he lay dying in the snow.

"Alexandria," he pleaded against her lips, "I have to get you downstairs, I know I do. Please, Alex."

She found the will to pull back and she tried to catch her breath, worried that she had finally overstepped with Jack. He reached up and touched her bottom lip, which trembled under his delicate touch.

"No, baby, no more tears. Believe me, I want to stay up here and hide away too, but I can't be that selfish. You have to face this, if you're ever going to know which path to take," he said softly.

"I'm not leaving you, just trying to help you find your way. And to do that, I have to get you downstairs." He squeezed her tenderly once more, then added, "I'll be right beside you, Alex. We'll talk to them together. Okay?" He nodded slowly and encouragingly to her after his words.

"Yes," she nodded gradually in return.

This was going to be the hardest trek she had made down those stairs, she was sure, but then the day was early.

Alex and Jack got up and each went to their waterclosets to get ready. Finally, dressed and freshened, they met one another in the hall. Alex closed her eyes and imagined herself talking to the council members who were there in attendance at Aeoferth, calling them together. She knew that they had heard her summons, and she looked up at Jack.

"They'll meet us in the library," she said quietly.

He took her hand and squeezed it.

"Courage," he whispered, and together they headed down, down to face the new day and all that it held.

Alexandria and Jack made their way into the library and found all eleven assembled and awaiting their arrival. She quietly made her way over to a chair within their circle, and Jack took the seat adjacent. Alexandria looked around and felt the stillness of the group, felt as if they held a collective breath unsure what she might say or do.

She cleared her throat and began, not wanting to prolong the dreadful anticipation for them or for herself. "I am here this morning with a heavy heart. Last night, was most assuredly, one of the worst of my life. To be hurt by Bertrand was very difficult to endure, but it was me that he was hurting. Seeing the damage Aagon wrought on Jack's body made Bertrand's attack pale in comparison."

Alex noted that several bowed their heads then looked back to her. Sabina already had tears in her eyes.

"I have tried to begin learning what I could here over the last few days, but when it came to an actual fight, I faltered and Jack almost paid for it with his life. So I can falter no longer, for I cannot bear to see another suffer so."

Alexandria took in a deep breath and then recounted in precise detail what had transpired between she and Bertrand. Then she told them all of what Aagon had said and done in the woods. She heard E-We and Tomoko's sharp intake of breath as she repeated his insults word for word. And finally, she told them every detail of her dream and conversation with Arianna.

She let her words soak into the group, still feeling dirty and damaged from what she had chosen to do to Aagon, but sharing it nonetheless. She prayed they would forgive her and said so to them all. They all tried to reassure her that she already had it, though she did not require it from them, but she just shook her head at their denials.

She felt Jack reach over and take her hand, squeezing it gently, but she did not look at him, afraid she would not be able to go on with what she knew she had to do.

"I have had three dreams or visions this week about a man that I cannot see, but who appears to be tied to me in some way. Aagon was surprised that I had not yet had a joyful reunion with this twelfth council member, and I see that he is still not here. I cannot fight the wolves, if I don't know their game. And I most assuredly feel them encircling me," she breathed out, looking around the group and noting the looks of strain and disquiet gazing pointedly back at her.

"And though I understand Arianna's words that if all of the past were to come rushing in on me, it would be too much, this in one piece of knowledge I am ready for. Tell me, who is this man, this twelfth councilman and what is he to me?" Alex looked from one to another, and finally it was E-We who spoke.

"I came to this council, Alexandria, after Arianna's death. I held her place until her return, one that we all believed would come to pass. There is another who has been unable to stay with us, because his pain and grief were too great. He has used his time and energy to track Kronis, hoping to exact revenge for what was taken from him. His wife."

And E-We paused, gesturing to her temple with her hand, asking Alex's permission to share a memory with her. Alex's eyes were wide, but she closed them and slowly pulled back a piece of her internal armor and allowed her ribbon to connect with E-We's.

She inhaled and tightened down on Jack's hand as she found herself back in her room, standing just where she had before in her earlier vision. He was there on the balcony. She took a step forward then stopped, afraid of what she would see or how to handle this.

And then he turned, and she gasped for air so desperately she thought her lungs would explode. His face, oh God, she knew his face. He moved forward and stood before her looking down, his eyes shining brightly with love and joy now that she was with him once more.

He was beautiful in every way a *Nephilim* could be. He was tall with broad shoulders, dark chestnut hair that came to the top of his collar, just as she had noticed before when he would not turn. He had high cheekbones and a sculpted chin with a small cleft in its center. And his eyes, she knew those deep pools of blue and green mixed together. She knew that she had looked into them for so, so long.

"Gaius," she whispered his name, finding it now on her lips. Alexandria pulled her ribbon back in and restored her armor, more thoroughly than she had ever before. She opened her eyes and felt the silent tears rolling down her cheeks.

"Where is he now?" she asked softly.

"He is at your home, Alexandria. Your true home," said Sabina, silently crying with Alex. "You helped to construct Aeoferth Hall and lived here before you married Gaius. You built another home on the north eastern shore of Holy Island, Northumberland. The two of you would travel from that home to this one when you were in country."

Alex started to get a visual image of what the home looked like. She could see the drive leading up to a large, grey stone castle that had ivy and plant life clinging to its surfaces, softening the appearance of the hard stone. Cypress and sculpted hedges lined the lane in and trees held the castle away from prying eyes.

She knew that this place was slightly out of sync with the reality humans knew. Like Aeoferth, it was hidden away for them, a refuge and safe haven.

"Elysium," Alex whispered aloud.

"Yes," said Elrick, "that's what you both called your home, for the word meant a paradise in the ancient Greek and Roman cultures. Gaius is from Rome, his mother bore him there. Your home became your place of perfect happiness, you said. And when you went away there for small bits of time, you were in your own world together."

Alexandria looked at Rohan and finally understood his reaction to Jack. "Gaius is your closest friend, isn't he, Rohan?" And he nodded his head once, but did not comment.

Alex did not know if she could speak her next question, without her voice betraying the tremors she felt running through her body. Once she thought it would not fail her, she said slowly, "Will he see me?" Alex said no more, only waited to hear someone's reply.

It was Archimedes who answered for them all, and for Gaius in his absence. "He has been waiting a long time to see you, Alexandria. He knows all about what has been taking place here, and he's been waiting until you were ready to meet him once again."

He rose from his seat and came to kneel before her. "Alex, listen to me closely. Though this has been very hard for Gaius, he understands that you are no longer his wife. Yet as you can imagine, in his heart, he still thinks of you in that way. He has been counseled to show restraint and to not overwhelm you, with what was, in the past."

"He understands that the choice of immortal life and the path you choose is your destiny, to determine of your own free will. And with regard to that, whom you choose to spend your life with, rather it be a mortal or an immortal. But for him, Alex, he lost his soul mate, his wife of nearly two thousand years, and this meeting will be fraught with emotion for you both."

"Yes, he will see you. If you are really ready, I will go and let him know you're coming." Alexandria closed her eyes and saw his face once more. She had to know the entirety of the choice Arianna had laid at her feet.

She looked back into Archimedes' soulful eyes and nodded her agreement. "Tell him I'll meet with him. I'll come to Elysium." She looked to the others then, and asked that they leave her alone with Jack for a few minutes before she departed.

Once they had all taken their leave, Alex stood and turned to Jack. He stood as well and smiled down at her, his eyes looking moist again.

"I am so proud of you, do you know that?" he asked tenderly.

"I don't know what I'm doing, Jack. God help me, I feel so lost," she gasped, as she stepped into his arms. She cried quietly as he held her and stroked her back.

"Yes, you do," he said gently, pulling back and looking down into her eyes. "You are doing what you must, as all great leaders before you have had to do. You cannot let the Fallen's children harm you with knowledge from your own past. You cannot defend those you love, until you know them all by name, and aura, and heart. You have to continue on this journey, and today it is taking you to meet another."

He cupped her cheek in his hand and stared down into her face lovingly. "Alex, I'm not going with you to Elysium." At his words, Alex felt the world tilt off of its axis and she felt adrift.

"What? Of course you're coming! Why do you say this?" she pleaded, placing her hand over his heart. Oh, please do not leave me Jack, she silently prayed.

"Because if I go, I will stand in the way of what you need to learn next. I cannot distract you from what you are about to experience. And if I were Gaius, I wouldn't want me there, not at the initial reunion," he breathed out heavily.

Alex was shaking her head, trying not to hear his words. "But what about what I want, Jack? You haven't asked me what I want. No, you have to come." But despite her pleas, she could see he was resolute in his decision.

Jack shook his head at her, not willing to budge from his decision. "Alex, I'm not leaving you. I'm going to stay right here at Aeoferth Hall, and await your return, no matter what it brings. I'm not going to place any demands or restrictions on you, either."

"You go and be who you are meant to be, and know that I will always have your back, no matter what. I'm proud of you. Keep doing what you're doing and it will all work out in the end, I'm sure of it," he nodded. "Besides, it'll be fun to mess with Rohan a little while you're gone. I think he likes me a bit since I almost died," he chuckled.

"Oh, Jack," she whispered, "what did I ever do to deserve your friendship and trust? Thank you."

"Don't thank me yet," he whispered back, his eyes turning a lighter shade of blue. She stared into them, confused at his last words to her. Jack cupped her face in both of his hands and pulled her closer.

"God forgive me, Alex. I know this is childish and somewhat petty on my behalf, but please when you go, remember this and then I'll say no more." Alex began to ask him what he meant, but she could not get out the words as his lips settled on hers with such possession and passion that she could not think or breathe, only kiss him back in her desperation to not lose what was growing between them.

Again and again, they each thought to separate themselves from the other, but the attraction was too strong. It was finally Alex who pulled back. She traced his lips with her fingertips, trying to commit them to memory and smiled sadly at him. Then she turned and walked out of the library, not looking back, because she knew if she did, she would never be able to turn from him again and leave.

22

Alexandria made her way out of the castle and headed for the helicopter, which Heath was warming up. Rohan came forward and intercepted on the lawn. She looked up into his face, lined with regret.

"I wanted to tell you. I swear I did. But Gaius and the others forbade me. And my father, Eremiel, did as well. I'm so sorry, Alex," he said humbly.

"I understand, Rohan. I am not angry with you, just very confused." Alex looked back at the castle and wondered where Jack was at that moment. Was he still in the library or was he watching her leave from a window somewhere, she wondered. She looked back at Rohan and clasped his forearm with hers.

"Take care of him, Rohan. Don't let another like Aagon hurt him again. Watch over him for me, while I cannot," she said somberly.

"On my life and honor, I swear it to you. You have my word," he pledged to her. Alex broke her hold on his arm and hugged him farewell. Then she turned and boarded the S-92.

Archimedes, Sabina, and John were all aboard waiting to accompany her. She nodded at them then took her seat, quietly fastening her safety belt and looking out of the window at her side. Light was coming up across the estate now as morning bloomed in full.

Jack and Alex had risen just as dawn had pierced the sky, and their meeting in the library had taken such a short amount of time in Alex's estimation. Though the coming to terms with it all had felt much longer. Her stomach grumbled loudly and she realized she had skipped dinner the night before and breakfast that morning. But she felt so unsettled, she honestly did not think she could keep anything down.

Sabina moved forward and took some fruit and juice out of the small refrigerator and offered it to Alex, imploring her to try at least a few bites. She did as she was asked, and managed to keep it all down somehow.

The flight took no time, less than twenty minutes, and before Alexandria could worry about the impending reunion any longer she felt the helicopter bank and begin its descent. She tried to instill a sense of calm within herself, but found that her hands shook slightly. She closed her eyes and began to concentrate on her aura, trying to blanket herself with the restorative and protective power. Anything to hold on to, anything at all, she mentally reached out for.

When they were finally down and the rotor blades had slowed enough for the group to disembark, John moved forward and released the steps as he had when she first arrived at Aeoferth Hall. They all waited to see if Alex would want to leave first, so she took in a deep, calming breath and headed for the exit.

"Courage," she whispered to herself, as she made her way down to the soft ground.

Alexandria stepped a little distance away from the helicopter and looked around her. The castle was three stories tall and it faced away from the sea beyond. The ground now was covered in winter's blanket, but she knew, without trying too hard to recall the memories, that there were stepping stones made of old Roman glass nearby. They were just up the hill on the right, leading into a garden on that side of the estate.

She closed her eyes and breathed in the cold salt air that called to her in the distance. She caught a glimpse of herself laughing in the bow of a very small wooden sailboat with Gaius, teasing him because he could not catch the wind with his sail. She watched as they walked with Rohan and Elrick along the shore discussing strategy and defense, and she saw herself walking on the lawn at the other side of the structure with a great wolfhound and large stallion, talking to the two as if they were old friends.

All memories that spoke of happier times, times long since past. Alex looked up to see her friends waiting on her expectantly, but patiently.

"Take this slowly, Alexandria," cautioned Archimedes. "There is so much here to take in and the emotional connections will make it harder to control the flow of the memories as they try to work their way back in."

She did not trust her voice yet, so she gave him a tight nod.

They continued forward, and every few feet, she paused and looked inward as another memory washed over and through her. She thought to herself just how appropriate the analogy Arianna had chosen that very morning was, when she compared her memories and her past to water. All of this was flowing over her now, and she was trying to anchor herself to the world she knew so she would not be swept away.

Continuing forward, Alex finally made her way to the entryway. She paused and placed her hand against the wood, feeling the texture and remembering the tree that had given its life for the front door the day Gaius had cut it down. Fortifying herself, she opened it slowly and walked inside.

Everything there was more familiar and real to her than Aeoferth had been when she entered it just days ago. She was careful not to touch anything, because she did not want to be swept away, not there and not in that moment. She just stood in the foyer seeing flash after flash of herself with and without Gaius.

Opening the doors to welcome other *Nephilim* into their home for celebrations, walking in after a long horseback ride across the estate, both of them splattered with mud, and one scene that made her smile just a little as they ran inside after being caught in a deluge of summer rain, both of them soaked through and through, but laughing hysterically.

Through that last vision, she saw his face become real before her eyes as he walked quietly into the foyer and stood before her. He was so close she could reach out and touch him, but she dared not, unsure what physical contact would do to her or him for that matter.

She stood openly taking him in, trying to understand how she could not have remembered him. With all that had been coming through, why not him, she questioned. Because this was too real and too much, even now. She looked up into his serene blue and green eyes, bluer now than in E-We's memory.

Her eyes looked first to his hair and she remembered the feel of it, like silk under her fingertips. She remembered cutting it, too. She saw a slight bit of stubble on his cheeks; he had not shaved in a few days, she mused. His broad shoulders she remembered touching, and his arms when he had lifted her time and time again to carry her. His waist, which she had put her arms around and hugged him, sharing her love with this man who was her husband.

Husband. The word was not hers, and she could not use it. He was hers, but he was not, and she did not know if she should look away or continue to stare and remember. Finally, Archimedes came forward and softly broke through the reverie to introduce them, but he need not have.

Alexandria breathed his name aloud, "Gaius Alexander Marcus," and he inclined his head, never breaking eye contact with her. She noted his hands were clasped behind his back, and she wondered if he did so to stop himself from reaching out. She became aware that she had knotted hers together in front of herself as well.

"Alexandria Grace Groaban," he said quietly, stating her name back to her as if it were a prayer. "Will you walk with me?" he asked gently, gesturing towards a hall that led on beyond the main staircase.

Archimedes interjected, "Perhaps now is not the time for that, Gaius. Possibly we could have a bit if breakfast first, then Alex can walk with you at her pleasure."

Gaius' eyes never left Alex's when he listened to Archimedes' attempt to keep them separate. "What would you like to do, Alexandria?" he asked, making no attempt to hide the fact that he was not going to heed their friend's suggestion.

She finally tore her eyes away from his intense stare and looked to her friend. "I think I will walk with Gaius, Archimedes. You all start breakfast without us and we'll be along shortly." She nodded to let him know that this was what she wanted. She could not hide from any of this now, and going straight to a meal felt like she would most definitely be hiding.

She looked back at Gaius and asked him to guide the way. He led her out of the entryway and through the home, past rooms which she tried not to look in for fear they would distract her. She was also careful not to get too close to him, all too aware that their elbows were dangerously close to brushing up against one another. They paused for a moment at a door leading out of the back, and he leaned forward to open it for her.

Alexandria stepped back to give him room and then entered the frozen gardens with him at her side. They walked for a short distance and he led her to a gazebo enclosed in glass which would shelter them from the wind and frosty temperatures. She moved forward and looked at the metal sculptures within that whimsically held plants and pots, an artful collection that she felt sure she had had a hand in collecting. Finally, she turned and looked up at him, waiting to see what he would say to her.

He was standing not far away, taking in every part of her with his eyes. "Thank you for coming with me and giving me these few moments alone with you. I know that this is not easy, for me it is an internal war right now," he said, running his hand through his hair and she remembered that he did that frequently. His eyes bore into hers, and he stepped closer coming within inches of her.

"Alexandria, please answer me truthfully. Do you know me? Do you remember us at all?" His breaths were coming heavily in and out of his chest, and she could see such deep emotion in his eyes. But she closed her eyes for a moment to put some distance between them.

Inside, she knew she could not lie. This process and these choices demanded honesty. She looked back up into his face and saw the raw emotion there right at the surface. "I do." And with that simple statement, his entire body and aura visibly relaxed. He became less rigid and stepped back from her just a fraction.

"Though not in the way you might think," she quietly qualified. He angled his head to look closely at her face, and she saw his eyes narrow just a fraction.

"Please explain what you mean, Alexandria," he said softly.

"I was not given the knowledge of you until just a short while ago, but once you appeared in my mind, of course I knew you. I recognized the estate before we ever arrived, and I am sure I can close my eyes now and tell you about every room down to the last detail."

"I'm getting flashes of memories of us together, but I know they're only the tip of the iceberg. I know that the more I try to remember, I will, and I'll remember the emotions behind us, too," she said.

He nodded his head as if willing her to go on, knowing she had more to say to him.

"But, I want to make sure that if I feel these feelings, that they are mine and not just the memories of another. I want to make sure that I, Alexandria, choose this path. Does that make sense to you?" she asked hesitantly, hoping her honesty was not hurting him further.

He smiled down at her. "It does," he replied. "I want you to know me for what was *and* what could be, and I promise to try not to force any expectations on you. I've had a long time, much longer than you, to process these emotions and be ready for your return, and I still feel a mess inside. I can only imagine what you are going through," his brow creased with his obvious worry and concern.

"Quite frankly, I feel like I'm being tossed about by gale force winds and I'm just trying to find an anchor to hold myself down. So much that's new and unexpected has happened in my life within the last week. I suppose I'm just trying not to lose sight of who I am in all this, as I struggle to make the correct choices," she shrugged, out of words to describe her feelings.

"Then hopefully, I can help and provide answers you need for the road ahead. Would you like to eat now or remain here to talk?" he asked.

"I think I'll eat, if that's okay, and then you and I can talk more. Would that be alright?" she asked, wanting his input as much as he wanted hers.

He smiled a bright, dazzling smile then at her that took her breath away. "Of course, it's alright. Alexandria, I am so very glad you came," he said, holding out his hand to her expectantly.

She was so afraid to take his hand that she hesitated, and looked back up into his eyes trying to decide what she should do.

"I will not harm you, Alexandria. I would never, nor could ever, hurt you in any way. You are safe with me, always," he vowed sincerely.

She took a steadying breath and placed her hand in his, and was blinded for a moment as their auras surged and overlapped across one another's hands. She was in the center of a cyclone and she looked to see if he was feeling the effects as well. His sharp intake of breath told her he was. His eyes looked moist and he closed them, as he bowed his head forward.

She wanted to take her hand and run it through his hair, as she knew she had done in the past, but she held her other hand firmly in place at her side. She just stood in quiet reflection at the immense power surge that was occurring between them, and was in awe of the many colors within his Light.

In his aura she saw a deep blue like the blue in his eyes, green like the grass on the mountains in Scotland in the summer, yellow to match the sun reflected off of the sea, purple as she had only seen in sunsets, and a shimmering silver that reminded her of shooting stars. It was so beautiful, and she found it made her feel a deep sense of calm.

Finally, he lifted his head and released her hand. "I have missed you, so much. And if having you here causes you discomfort in any way, I expect you to tell me. Do you agree, Alexandria?" he stood over her, waiting for her agreement before they left for the main house.

"I agree. I will tell you how and what I am feeling," she nodded slowly, unsure if she had to put what had just passed between them into words, she would be able to. She was not hurt, but she was very overwhelmed.

"That is all I could ask. Shall we?" and he stepped forward once again and held the door open. Alex walked by his side to the main dining room, and together they entered to eat with their friends. Sabina and Heath had gone into the kitchen and prepared a light meal while Alex and Gaius talked outside. Alex took the seat to his immediate right, where she knew she had sat for hundreds and hundreds of years before.

All of them tried to make light conversation, but time and again, Alex found herself staring into Gaius' eyes, seeing memory after memory come to present itself. She had not seen so many in such rapid succession, except perhaps on her first night in the ballroom, when she became reacquainted with so many of the *Nephilim*. But even that night did not carry the weight of this meeting.

They were finished with their meal, just passing recollections around when Alex noticed a small red circle on the table in front of her. She squinted her eyes trying to decipher what it was and then there were two, not just one. She looked up to see if anyone else noticed them, and saw that no one else had. She tried to focus on Sabina's face, but she was looking through too many memories and Alex could not find her in the confusion.

Alex decided that she should speak up, but found instead that she was beginning to slide out of her chair, headed towards the floor. She looked back into Gaius' face and noticed his alarmed expression, and heard his shout as he launched himself from his chair to catch her. She gave into the dark pulling sensation she felt, and closed her eyes to follow it.

Gaius was out of his chair with his arms around Alex before the others knew something was wrong. He stood and cradled her against his chest as John ran over and held a napkin to her bleeding nose.

"Tilt her head back for me, Sabina," John instructed, while he used his aura to stop the flow. He took Alex's pulse and then opened her eyelids. John looked to his friend and said, "Gaius, take her and lay her down somewhere, quickly."

Gaius turned with her and vaulted up the steps to the third floor, taking two or three at a time. He was trembling, not from fatigue, but sheer terror when he laid her upon a bed. He had to forcibly make himself let go of her. It took all he had within him just to complete the motion. The others followed in behind, and John sat next to Alex checking her pulse again. He nodded, looking a little more relaxed, but only slightly.

"What is going on?" demanded Gaius, still greatly shaken.

"We don't really know, Gaius," said Archimedes. "Both she and her family have recounted that Alexandria experienced memory flashes when she was a child, but her family called them visions not knowing what they were. Since she has returned to us, she's had quite a few spells like this, varying in length and severity. She has experienced a few seizures and one other prominent nose bleed, but she has recovered from each episode."

"And no one thought to tell me this when you were updating me on her progress?" he said, in a deceptively calm voice.

"No," replied John, "because we have no information about it for you. She knows now how to heal herself and we can heal her as well, so

I'm not concerned about irreparable damage. But I cannot stop the episodes. It's not as if she has epilepsy and we can treat it, Gaius."

"What have you been doing for her?" he pressed.

"We monitor her to make sure her heart rate and blood pressure stay steady, we make sure to give her water when she wakes to keep her hydrated, and we stay with her in case she were to call out for us and connect to her with our aura to calm her and bring her reassurance," John answered.

Archimedes continued, "Each time she has awakened, she tells us of the memories and insights she has uncovered. It's all coming back in, and rather rapidly I might add, though Ganymede has told us he's holding so much back. I think somehow Alex's mind is finding ways around that to assimilate her past anyway. It's a lot for a mortal mind and body to handle," he said sadly, reaching out and patting Alex's head.

Sabina had returned from the watercloset with a cool, damp cloth in her hand. She stood by the bed, listening to their remarks and when she heard Archimedes' last statement she turned sharply to stare at him.

"What are you saying, Archimedes? Speak plainly to us now," she compelled him, hoping he would divulge what he was thinking.

Gaius' eyes narrowed, and he finally turned away from Alex to stare down at his friend now as well.

"What I know, is that the greatest immortal's power ever to be created is now housed in one young mortal's body. What I wonder, and do not know, is how much longer that body can continue to try to contain it before it becomes too much. Alexandria is accessing her aura and building shields within, but she is not healing herself from within as we do every second of every day."

"And until she claims her right as the immortal she was meant to be, she's burning out a very short fuse much too quickly. We cannot force her to choose this; she must want it for herself. But my friends, I just don't know how much longer she can sustain this. Weeks, months, perhaps a few more years, and then I would say Alexandria will reach the end of her journey as a mortal here on this earth."

No one said anything as they each weighed the gravity of Archimedes' words. She had just returned to them, yet unless she chose what life she truly wanted for her future, she was destined to leave them just as quickly as she came it seemed. And no one felt the pain of that potential loss more than Gaius.

"I have lost her once. I'll not do it again," he said, through a constricted throat. He turned and extended his hand for the cloth, and Sabina relinquished it to him. John stood and instructed Gaius what to watch for, and then they all took their leave, allowing Gaius to keep the vigil.

He sat beside her and slowly stroked her brow with the cloth, watching her face for any signs of awareness. He set it down on the bedside table and beheld the person whom he had loved through the ages. She was exactly the same as she had been before.

She had the same hair, the same startling blue eyes, the same nose, and delicate features. Her eyelashes were still darker than her hair color and long. Her lips were still softly pink on their own, and he was so glad to see that she refrained from painting her face with cosmetics. Alexandria needed no adornment he thought, because she was beautiful in her own right.

He had already witnessed for himself the steel within her that gave her the courage to face all of this, when she walked with him and gave him her truthful answers. And unbeknownst to Alex, through the years of her life, he had silently kept watch over her as she grew from child to woman.

Gaius had never told the others, not even Rohan, that he had tracked Alexandria's aura and located her when she was but two. He, and he alone, knew her so well, and loved her so much, that he had located her and guarded her from afar. And in the times between his watch, he used his energy to track Kronis. He had kept her safe until now, and he would find some way to convince her to take the mantel before it was too late.

He reached forward and did what he had wanted to when she first arrived. He cupped a hand to her cheek and ran his fingers down her jaw to her lips. He traced her lips with his fingers remembering all the times he had held her and loved her.

Gaius moved his hand up and ran it through the long length of her golden hair and leaned down until his face was right over hers. His eyes searched her face, as he whispered to her, "I know your heart and soul, Alexandria, now let me know your mind. Come back to me." And he lowered his mouth to hers, kissing her gently, wishing that she were awake and with him truly.

He pulled back and lifted the cloth, holding it once more to her brow. Slowly, he began to build his aura and spread it out across her like a blanket, protecting and comforting her.

"Come back," he whispered again.

Alexandria slowly opened her eyes to see where she might be, not knowing if she was experiencing another memory or if she was looking at the present she knew to be true. She turned her head and saw that Gaius was seated next to her on the bed where she lay, but it looked as if he had fallen asleep where he sat. She tentatively reached out a hand and laid it on his leg. He stirred immediately, looking into her face with concern.

"How long did I sleep?" she asked, her voice cracking.

He looked at a clock that sat on the bedside table, and told her that she had slept for the last three hours. He reached over to retrieve a glass of water that Sabina had brought to him some time ago. It was barely cool, no longer cold, and then he altered his plan.

Before she could protest, Gaius moved forward and put an arm behind her back and one under her knees, and shifted her up on the bed placing an extra pillow behind her so that she could sit up and try to drink the water. He handed the glass to her, and his hand covered hers in the transfer. She thought he was trying to ensure she did not drop the glass and make a mess, but she was hesitant to look into his face.

"I don't know why I lost consciousness," she stated reluctantly. "Each time that has happened this week, I get a good look into the past or a vision about you. But I'm here with you, and I didn't dream anything just then. It was just peaceful sleep." Alex could not get a handle on what her body was up to, and it certainly was not consulting her.

"You've had visions about me this week?" he asked her softly, hoping to coax more information from her.

Alex could feel her cheeks heat, and she shrugged her shoulders. "I never saw your face, but I knew that there was a man looking for me or someone I was trying to find. I didn't see your face though until this morning, when E-We gave me a direct image of you and then, well it seems the floodgates opened." She paused and looked into his eyes earnestly, trying to decide if she should be completely honest with him.

"What is it, Alex, if I may call you that?"

"Of course, you may. Gaius, I need to tell you what has happened this week, so that you will understand it from my perspective. I know Archimedes and perhaps some of the others have been relaying information to you, but I need you to understand what I'm thinking and where I am right now." And she faltered for a moment, not sure how to proceed with her next thought.

"And you need to tell me about Jackson, is that what you're thinking of?" he inquired, smiling down at her.

Though she was shocked, she was glad that he did not look angry or jealous. "Yes, I assumed the others mentioned him to you. Gaius, I don't want to be the cause of hurt to anyone, but I have to tell you everything, or we can't proceed. Will you hear me out?" she paused, waiting for his agreement.

"Of course, Alex. I want to hear you tell me what's in your heart and on your mind. From what I have heard, you've been through an extremely harrowing week. And I am very sorry that I could not be there to help you through it. I understand Mr. Campbell was, and I will be forever grateful to him, because he did what I could not: comfort and guide you."

She looked into his eyes, truly looked, and saw no malice or ill will when he mentioned Jack's name. Could it be that he was not threatened by the newly discovered attraction and deep abiding faith she had in Jack, she wondered. She knew nothing of men or relationships, but she had thought men would feel jealousy like many of the girls she had known at university had when they discovered they had a rival.

She nodded and began the retelling of her tale. She started with the early visions and her family's reactions to them, and moved on to how Ganymede had visited and stopped the memories for a time. She told him a little of how she felt finally going to school and on to university, where she excelled but still wondered when the visions would begin again.

As she moved into her adult life, she explained her work at the U.N., and her feelings about living alone in New York City. He smiled occasionally as he listened and nodded encouragingly. She progressed to her return for Christmas and of Bertrand finding her and locking her in Lord Lenley's study at the ball. This was still a raw and painful memory, so she made mention of the assault, but left out the traumatic details for the time being. Gaius moved higher on the bed so that he could sit closer to her, though he did not touch her.

She told him of her decision to move forward and call Ganymede for long awaited answers. She felt tears form in her eyes when she told him of coming to Aeoferth Hall and meeting the *Nephilim*, who she truly recognized and remembered. And she shared the memory of herself with Kronis on the cliff top, watching as Gaius hung his head in sorrow at what that memory wrought.

She paused and reached forward to touch his shoulder and felt the current pass through them again, but she did not remove her hand. Rather she tried to send her regret and compassion through their connection, recognizing his loss. He looked up at her and his eyes were bright with unshed tears for the wife he lost at Kronis' hands.

As they continued, she related each of her training sessions and how she had felt freedom for the first time ever on Eimhir's back as they thundered across the snow covered fields. He smiled brightly, and told her of other days when she had ridden bareback and gone so fast that it had left him breathless.

She paused seeing the images as well. Alex shivered when she told him of the mental exercises she had endured and how she felt watching her brothers be tortured. She noted that his brow creased significantly when she told him what Archimedes had created within her mind, just as Jack's had that night. They finally were able to laugh over Rohan's decision to hurl his longsword at her head, and how he had removed some of his own protection to remind her how to heal.

"Rohan never has developed patience. Goodness knows we have both tried to teach him over the centuries," he said, laughing and shaking his head. She chuckled too, but less enthusiastically, noticing his use of the word 'we'.

Alex then began to tell him about Jackson. How he had come along, but quickly related her brothers' interference and how he adapted to the changing landscape before him with grace and humor. She told him how Jack had really been the first friend she had ever confided in, and then she told him of Aagon's brutal assault. How she had been forced into a situation where she chose to take a life, in order to save Jack's and everyone else she cared about whom he would have surely targeted next.

Gaius never moved or wavered when she told him how she breathed life back into Jack's body, or how they had lain atop the bed just the night before, seeking comfort in the proximity of one another. And sadly, she told him of her parting from Jack that very same morning.

Alexandria ended her recitation of her dream just hours prior to her arrival at Elysium, in which Arianna appeared to her and offered Alex the full depth and wealth of her memories, abilities, and talents. If she wanted them, and if she wanted to commit her life to the service and protection of mankind.

When she finished, she was overwhelmed by all that the week had brought to her life. So many firsts and so many new opportunities, but also great pain and conflict.

When she voiced her last thoughts, she could feel the tears trailing down her cheeks, but she stayed silent waiting for his words. Would he judge her for Aagon's death, or her feelings for Jack, she wondered.

Finally he spoke, turning to face her and he braced his arms on either side of her legs so that he could look directly into her eyes. "Alexandria, I am so very, very proud of you, more than you may ever know. I am touched and humbled by all that you have shared with me, and I can feel the uncertainty you hold about your future still in the words you share."

"You have come so far, so fast, and it is no surprise that you are confused and frightened. I would be too, Alex. Your feelings for Mr. Campbell are nothing to be ashamed of, because you have, for the first time, felt real love. And love can be a powerful and all consuming emotion when you are with the right person," he said sincerely.

"With all the emotional twists and turns you experienced this week, I have no doubt that you needed a calm place in the midst of the storm, and he has been that. But know that I wanted to be there to shelter and hold you as well."

He raised a palm and touched her cheek, gently stroking her skin and wiping her tears away. Alex felt a slight current running along her face from his caress.

"You know your fledgling feelings for Jack, but you should also know what I offer you as well. I offer you an eternity of love, one that will go on through the centuries, and will never tire or fade away. It will never ask more than you can give, and my love will always support and nurture you in your tireless work yet to come."

"Alexandria, if you will let me, I want to offer for your hand as well. I want to know you in the here and now, in the hopes that there can be a future. If you choose this immortal life, you will need a partner who will stay by your side through the ages."

"I have no doubt that Jack is a very good man, because I don't think you would be drawn to anyone who would not love you and respect you. But think of his life in terms of a mortal life. He will live for another sixty or seventy years and then God will call him home."

"If you choose him or a mortal like him, you will not be able to spend an eternity with them and you will not grow old as they age. It would be most painful for you both, and I would not wish that heartache for you, even if you do not choose to spend the rest of your days with me."

Alexandria had not thought yet in those terms, because she had yet to declare love for Jack. She knew she felt something very powerful growing between them, but was it love, she could not say at that point. And could it survive in the outside world she wondered, with her running about the globe with the *Nephilim* if she chose that path, and he stationed who knows where guarding unforeseen people.

Yet, what if she did not choose an immortal life, she thought. A future with Jack might be achievable, but would he still want her if she turned her back on Ganymede and refused to help others with the gifts she had been offered, she pondered. He seemed to value honor and service to others highly, as did she.

Alex looked into Gaius' steady gaze and whispered, "I'm so confused, that I cannot tell you what I want right now. I don't even begin to know how to handle this," she said, shaking her head.

"Then let me help you. Will you let me try as well to show you how I feel?" he asked, pleading with her through his earnest gaze and his hand which still cupped her face.

"How can you help me?" she questioned him mournfully.

"Like this," he whispered, and leaned down meeting her lips with his own.

Alexandria immediately felt a shift in the atmosphere and she felt her lips tremble. There was so much, and she did not know how to process it. She could feel his aura flowing into her, and he was showing her without words the depth of his love and devotion. There was so much beauty and hope.

"Forgive me, Jack," she thought to herself as she allowed Gaius to deepen the kiss, consuming her. As much as she had felt with Jack, this was something all together different. This was a love that had already endured so much, and she was just catching a glimpse of what an eternity of his love might feel like.

He wrapped both arms around her and pulled her to his chest giving her all that he held within his heart, moving his hands up into her hair, and willing her to remember what such a life could mean for them both. "I would love you for centuries like this, Alexandria," he whispered against her lips. He rained kisses down her neck and back up to her cheeks and eyelids.

He pulled back and saw the haze in her eyes, and then came back to her lips once more. He gently touched her lips again and again with his, and then deepened his embrace once more.

"Please," he pleaded. "Tell me you feel something, anything," he quietly begged.

Alexandria's tears silently continued to flow, so staggered was she by all of the splendor and power she felt between the two of them.

"Yes, Gaius, God help me, I do," she breathed, as he held her to him. "I feel like I'm betraying Jack and you at the same time. But, yes," she said, leaning back and looking into his eyes, so radiant and so alive.

314

"Did you promise Jackson a future together already, Alexandria?" he asked her, smoothing her hair back with both of his hands.

"No," she said, shaking her head, "and I cannot promise one to you now either, Gaius. I can most certainly feel the connection between us, and I can see that there is something to explore. But I cannot give you anything more, than that we will try, as I have to try and decide where Jack fits into my future, too."

"That is all I had hoped for today, that you would at least consider me for your future. That you might remember and want this in the days to come. Thank you, for giving me hope," he said solemnly. He kissed her tenderly once more on her lips and gazing into her eyes, he forced himself to stand.

"I'll leave you to freshen up and rest a bit more if you would like, then I think you should come down to eat, Alex. I've kept you up here a long time and you need nourishment. Shall we try the dining hall again?" he smiled down at her, waiting for her reply.

She nodded her agreement and he walked over to the door. Gaius paused for a moment to look back at her and she could feel their auras still reaching out for one another, straining to connect across the small distance. He finally tore his gaze away and left her sitting alone, trying to calm her breathing and her heart rate.

Alex slowly got up and tested her legs by walking around the room. She visited the watercloset, and walked over to a cushioned window seat by the bedroom's large bay window. She gazed out through its panes, and again began to see flashes of herself walking on the lawn below. She looked away and closed her eyes.

Was this her future, or was this her past, she asked herself. She could not deny what had just passed between herself and Gaius. It was the most astounding revelation she had yet to have; that that amount of love, passion, and respect could endure for so long. It was a miracle in and of itself.

He had asked her to please consider him, and she would have to now. He knew what his touch would awaken, and she was now all the more confused for it. She had been able to talk to Jack all week as big shifts and changes like this were occurring, but Jack was not there now, and she was sure he would not want to hear the details of Gaius' ardor.

Still, she took out her mobile and briefly texted her family to let them know she was safe and well, then she sent a message to Jack.

It read:

'Thank you for supporting me, Jack. I am well. I will remember.'

His response came quickly:

'Courage, Alex.'

Alex put the phone back in her pocket and as she headed out of the door, she offered up a silent prayer to Ganymede. "Please, help me find the right path. I feel so, very lost right now. Please, be with me." And with the hope that he was with her, Alexandria began down the stairs ready to give the dining hall another try, as Gaius had phrased it.

23

Their early dinner was more relaxed than breakfast, as their conversation seemed less rigid and tense than it had earlier in the day. Alex noticed that someone had cleaned her drops of blood off of the table, as she knew now that was what she had been looking at before she fainted.

After their shared meal, Archimedes suggested they all adjourn to Elysium's library, as there was a particular book he would like to look over once again. Heath and John offered to clear the table and clean up, and Sabina and Archimedes left in the direction of the library. Gaius stood and came over to pull Alex's chair out for her, allowing her to stand and decide in which direction she wanted to go.

Alexandria found she actually did want to talk with Gaius. If she were going to know him as he was now and in his past, she could not deliberately avoid his company. Instead, she decided, she would try to know him as a friend and ally first, and then see what the future held.

She asked Gaius if they could sit and talk, and she smiled slightly at the delight she witnessed in his eyes in response to her request. He lead her to a large, but cozy den, and it reminded her of her father's favorite gathering room at her family's estate. It felt very much like home.

Alex entered first and slowly walked around the room, looking at objects that called to her and harkened of trips to lands both near and far away. She saw a small bowl, and she remembered an elderly man had gifted her with it in China. She, Gaius, and many other *Nephilim* had traveled there centuries ago to help set right his village after earthquakes had decimated their homes and buildings. She reached out and touched the bowl with her fingertips, and saw a vivid image of the old man's toothless grin. It made her smile.

She moved over to a bookcase holding old bound books which contained maps, and she remembered that she had charted some of her earliest voyages across the Atlantic before the Vikings or Europeans had endeavored to do so. Gingerly, she took one down from the shelf, hearing its binding creak and protest as she slowly opened it.

Alex ran her fingers over the papyrus she had acquired from Egypt and used to draw her journeys. She saw flash after flash of herself at the helm of a small, but sturdy sailing vessel. She saw a whale breaking the surface near her as she lay on the deck, the stars shining and reflecting off of the calm, dark waters of the sea. The whale's large, soulful eye gazed at her, and she at it, as she silently communicated with the great animal.

Alex closed the book and moved her fingers down to a small, glass box that was pale pink and adorned with hand-painted flowers across the top. She closed her eyes and remembered the day in northern France that Gaius had purchased it for her. He had brought it to the farmhouse they were staying in, and she could see him approaching as she turned away from the room's large window, the curtains billowing in the slight breeze.

He looked down at her with such adoration and presented his gift to her. When she lifted the lid, there was a pair of pearl earrings, small and perfectly formed. They were tastefully mounted on silver wires, and so simple. She had loved them. She remembered throwing her arms around his neck and hugging him tightly, then she saw him pull back and lean in for a kiss.

Alexandria removed her fingers from the box and closed her eyes for a moment trying to calm her breathing. She slowly turned and found that Gaius was still standing just inside the room's doorway, watching her. She moved forward, and gestured to a large fabric sofa which faced an expansive stone fireplace. He moved forward as well, and started a fire before he joined her.

They sat for several minutes, before Gaius turned towards her and asked what she would like to talk about or know.

Alex turned towards him then too, and crossed her feet in front of her body so that she could look into his eyes. "I would like to know about you and what you're life is like now," she answered. "I have heard that you are actively pursuing Kronis, but is there more to your life?" She sincerely hoped he had not thrown his days towards vengeance solely for the last century.

"There is now," he breathed. "I was so lost when you...," he breathed deeply, his nostrils flaring, as he sought to compose himself. "I could not eat or sleep. I had no direction but one. I wanted Kronis' life for yours. I wanted him on his knees, begging for his life so that I could deny him it. And I have looked endlessly for him, but he knows I hunt him and he has gone to ground." Gaius looked into the fire for a few moments reflecting on his tireless search.

"What more have you done?" she asked gently, hoping to pull him from his sorrow. "Have you continued the work?"

"I did try, but it was hard, Alex, so hard," he said, shaking his head. "Rohan came and demanded I snap out of my grief. He even picked me up one day and threw me out of the front door," he smiled, somewhat embarrassed.

"Yes, I can see Rohan doing that," she chuckled, and pushed her hair behind her ear, letting her arm settle on the back of the sofa. "I told you he threw his longsword at me a few days past."

He nodded with a slightly stern look on his face at her question. "Yes, and I'm going to have a few words with him, when next I see him."

"No, don't be too hard on him. He's just very…," and she searched for the right word, but Gaius answered for her.

"Blunt."

"Yes, so don't be upset. I've come to appreciate his no nonsense way of getting things accomplished. I'm glad he's on our side, one of the good guys."

He smiled, and nodded his head slightly.

"Tell me more, please," she encouraged.

"I eventually did try to go out with some of the others to various places and help with disaster or famine relief, but I just felt hollow. The one thing that gave me any satisfaction was tracking Kronis. So, eventually I came back here and restarted my hunt."

"Well, that is, until a little over twenty-one years ago," he paused and looked at her intensely, hoping that she could discern his meaning.

Alex narrowed her eyes at him, whispering, "What do you mean, Gaius?"

"We were all informed by our fathers that our pleas had not gone unheard, and that you were returning a century after you left us, but as a babe to a mortal family. I could not understand what was at play and why such a decision had been made, but on the date I lost you a century ago, you were reborn to this world."

"I put the search for Kronis aside and began to look for you, Alexandria. I was told, in no uncertain terms by my father and yours, that I could not go near you. But still, I sought you. After two years, I finally worked through the veil that our parents had hidden you under and detected your aura. I found you, Alex."

Gaius spoke the last words so softly, that it took Alexandria a moment to process what he was telling her. She searched his eyes and saw that he was speaking the truth to her. She was stunned that he had endeavored to look for her when she did not yet know who she was to be.

He lifted his arm until it rested along the back of the sofa, and his fingers touched hers. She immediately felt the connection and spark as their auras began overlapping. She looked from their hands back into his eyes.

"I watched over you, on and off throughout your childhood, and occasionally I would leave to further search for Kronis. It was hard to leave, because I did not want any of the Fallen's children near you. I could tell you struggled as a child, but I never spoke to you, never wanted to frighten you."

His eyes now seemed so intense to Alex, as if he was warring within himself. Finally, he cleared his voice and spoke again. "It was a night not long ago, that I was feeling very close to where I thought Kronis skulked away, in southern Portugal, when Rohan called me to impart the news that Bertrand had found you and what he had dared to do."

"I wanted to tear my heart from my chest, and I made my way back here as quickly as I could. But when I came to your home, others barred my way. My father, Haniel, and Ganymede, along with Rohan, Iain, and Ahadi were all there to stop me from coming in to get you and bring you back here."

Alex was astounded that this had been kept from her, but on some level she understood that with no frame of reference, a *Nephilim* barging in to take her would have been as frightening as the attack. She would not have gone with him. Quite the opposite, she would have run from him with everything she had.

He could see the recognition of the tragedy that would have been, had he not been held from her side just days ago, registering in her eyes. He slowly nodded his head.

"Yes, you see now. It would have been too much and too frightening for you. And though I am loathe to admit it, my race to get to you was not the right course. Ganymede knew what was best for his daughter."

"You have been with me all along?" Alex asked, astounded that he had witnessed her entire life unfold up until that moment.

"I have, Alexandria. I have seen you walk and play in your parents' gardens, watched you graduate from university with top honors at such a young age, and I have witnessed you meander into the public library in New York never noticing all the men, young and old, who stop and openly stare at your beauty."

"You've grown into a remarkable and accomplished young lady. And I see one who is so brave, given the courage you are displaying to see you through all of this. It was my honor to stand guard, and my deepest regret is that I was away seeking revenge for your loss, when you were hurt and needed my protection most desperately. I am so sorry that Bertrand got to you, Alexandria," he said solemnly.

"I do not fault you or anyone else for what transpired, Gaius. I refuse to let you shoulder the burden of that guilt. I mean it," she said, looking sternly into his face, until finally, he nodded in her direction.

"I've been learning a thing or two about free will this week, and it was Bertrand's choice to do what he did, just as it was Aagon's to attack Jack. They each will have to account for what they did, but not to us," said Alex.

"I want to help defend the others from attack, and somehow, I can't tell you how I know, but Kronis and the others are coming. I feel it Gaius, like a gathering storm. And I don't think this will all be laid to rest until Kronis and I deal with one another, not you or anyone else against him."

Gaius began to protest her last proclamation, but she raised her hand that had been lying in her lap and placed it over his lips to stop him from speaking.

"I haven't really focused on my last moments with him, I think because I've been afraid of what I would see. Ganymede told me that no one understands why I didn't defend myself better, why I let my guard down. I have no idea, but I think that perhaps I will try to look into this particular corner of my past, so that we can better guard the future. What say you, Gaius?" she asked, removing her fingers so that he could speak.

He grabbed hold of her hand and brought it back to his lips, placing light kisses on each of her fingertips before he lowered her hand and held it firmly. He looked imploringly into her eyes and said with great conviction, "Alexandria, if you were lost to me again, I could not bear it, I swear I could not. You went at this alone before with Kronis, and I do not

323

want you making that same mistake again. You must survive, do you understand?" he said breathlessly.

She nodded and could feel the desperation that now surged through his aura. He lifted his hand from where theirs touched along the sofa's back and took her hand in his, intertwining their fingers so that both of her hands now comingled with his. She gasped at the concern he felt, as he showed her as only a *Nephilim* could.

"I will take every precaution and the utmost care, I promise, Gaius. I'm sorry my soul's past decisions caused you so much pain. I am so sorry you have hurt for so long," said Alexandria soberly.

"It is no small thing, to meet the one other soul who connects to yours like no one ever had or ever will again, Alexandria. And to have had that as long as we did, for almost two thousand years, well, it was a paradise I could never fully articulate. Your love and our friendship gave this world meaning for me, helped me endure through the ages," he said softly.

"Oh, Gaius, you have my friendship, and perhaps someday more. But I cannot speak to that now. Now, I can only thank you for your watch through the years, and tell you that I am willing to consider you as well. How could I not, when I feel this?" she questioned softly, looking at the light display between their hands.

They both watched as the power grew and surged, and Alex could feel her breath coming in shallow gasps as she struggled to maintain her hold on the present. When her vision began to blur, she slowly pulled her hands back.

"I think I shall turn in for the night, Gaius. I feel a bit tired. Perhaps we can take a ride along the shore in the morning. I would like that, I think," she suggested.

He smiled at her proposal, and stood offering her his hand so that she could rise. "That sounds like a very good idea, Alexandria, and I look forward to it. I'll collect you from your room, then?"

"Yes," she said, standing. She once again had to force all of her attention on removing her hand from his. "Until then," Alex said quietly.

Alex could tell that his eyes searched hers with the hope of more, but she smiled and then turned and took her leave. She did not go to join the others in the library, nor did she go up to her room. Instead, she turned and headed for the back door that she and Gaius had walked out of the home through that morning. She pulled a coat from one of the many hanging on pegs near the door, and walked out into the cold, refreshing night air.

She needed to just be alone for a few moments, and sought solitude there in the barren winter landscape. The grounds, though asleep for the season, were still lit with small lights hidden in the hardscape and amongst the shrubbery and trees. Alex walked until she found a second gazebo, and unlike the one she talked with Gaius in earlier, it was not enclosed.

Alex sat on one of the seats in the softly lit space, and began to meditate as Ganymede has instructed her to do. She thought about all that Gaius had told her and how much restraint he had shown throughout the years, as he watched over her, yet never presented himself. He had acted as a guardian, though she never knew he stood watch, and the thought greatly touched her heart. How badly, she thought, he must have wanted to come to her.

She began to take in slow deep breaths, and she thought of herself once again on the cliff with Kronis. She felt the wind pick up and could see herself sharing her aura, and the taste of freedom and forgiveness with him.

She concentrated on that connection, when her hand touched his face and she poured her plea straight into his being.

The longer she stayed with the flow, the more she began to detect what his aura felt, smelled, and tasted like. It was bitter on her tongue, and her mind rebelled against the acidity of his thoughts and desires. So much dark energy, so much hate and animosity, and her aura had tried to push that back.

She wondered if she could track the knowledge of his true essence through all those ripples in Arianna's lake of memories, now that she knew what she was looking for. Could she find him on the day she died, witness that, and discover the way in which he had defeated her, Alex questioned. Was she strong enough to do this, she silently wondered.

Alexandria searched her soul for the courage to try. She feared that this might be too much, too soon. But something told her time was drawing near to a day when she would need this knowledge to save her friends, and her family. And it was her love for them, which compelled her to search for answers.

She imagined herself back at the lake's edge staring into the abyss of past emotions, experiences, and loved ones. She stepped forward and closed her eyes, smelling and tasting the wind for a sense of where Kronis and Arianna's last moment might lay within the waves.

She extended her hands, letting her aura flow out over the water's surface, hunting and dipping through the ripples. There was so, so much to behold. Alexandria felt the memories lapping up and over her aura, threatening to pull her under, but she resisted until she felt that she was more than halfway across the water, pushing and extending herself yet further.

There, she thought, as relief and hope bloomed in her heart. Just there, she smelled him, tasted the raw hate and desolation, and she moved in the direction of that particular undulation. She steeled herself, and then imagined her aura diving below the surface to be at one with the water and the memory.

But what she expected to see and feel was not willing to allow her access. It pushed against her aura, denying her. How could her own past fight her in this way, she wondered. Alex pushed harder throwing as much of her aura as she dared against the black wall of water she found herself against, and felt herself falter.

She grimaced slightly as she admitted to herself that she had dared too much, and so she tried to pull back from the water and return to her body on the shore. But the water was holding her, as though it was tar, and she could not shake the resistance. It began to envelope her, and it was such a cold and suffocating sensation.

Desperate now to return, she started fighting in earnest, pulling and kicking, but to no avail. Was she to drown here, she thought frantically. She urgently needed to return, but how to get free, she did not know.

Alex was ready to admit to herself that she was in a desperate situation, when she smelled a very familiar scent. It reminded her of grass on a Tuscan hillside in summer, of horses running across the ground, of leather and spices from the orient. It was a smell she knew and she tried to work her way up to it.

She felt her aura being lifted from the quagmire and it was gently supported on its way to the shore by another's. This aura she knew as she knew her own, and he had come to rescue her as they had done for centuries together.

As she felt her spirit reconnect with her person once more, she stepped back from the lake and willed her eyes to open. She looked up into Gaius' eyes as he held her in his arms, so tightly that she was amazed she could breath. There was such a tumult in his gaze and she reached up to touch his face with her palm to sooth him, hoping her aura could reassure him that she was alright. But her aura felt tired just then, so she settled for her flesh to his.

"Thank you," she whispered. "I was unsure if I would be able to free myself, and make it back to shore."

"Oh, Alex," he choked back a sob, and lowered his head to kiss her with all the emotion behind the fear and near loss he had just experienced. "Where did you go? You were so far away," he breathed against her lips, as he tried to restore some life into her cold body.

"I had to try," she breathed back, and thought to pull away, for she was not sure if she was ready for such intense contact. But she was so comforted and so at home in his arms, that she could not deny him or what she truly felt.

He felt her lose her resistance and gloried in the feel of her back where he thought she should be, in his arms and at his side. He sent his aura pouring over her to warm and restore her, and to bind her to him. When he finally straightened away from her, he could tell that they were both shaken.

Her eyes were so large as she searched his face and trailed her fingertips across first his brow, then down his straight nose, over across his stubbled cheek, to his chin, then back across his lips, still red and swollen from his passion. She moved her hand down his neck to the dip between his collarbones and over to his shoulder, eventually bringing it to rest on his arm that still held her across his body.

Finally, she raised her eyes back to his and realized they were both holding their breath as she explored the terrain of a body she knew so well, yet not at all. He was hers, if she gave him the words that she wanted him again. She leaned up, and he gently met her lips with his, tenderly.

Gaius pulled back and squeezed her, imploring her to tell him. "Alex, why are you out here? You said you had to try. What were you attempting?"

She told him what she had tried and how she had found what she believed to be the memory. Alex said regretfully that she had not only found it denied to her, but that it had attempted to pull her under and trap her. She said she did not understand how this could be.

Gaius shook his head slowly at her. "No more right now, Alexandria. Do you understand, no more? I cannot lose you, and this is too much. Please, will you rest tonight?" he whispered, and the anguish in his voice was her undoing.

"I didn't mean to hurt you, Gaius, I was trying to help," she tried to reason her way out of his distress, but saw him only shake his head again.

"No more. I am taking you to bed and you will rest." And she was given no more chances to talk, as Gaius was determined she pause in her pursuit of answers. He stood, taking her with him and holding her against his chest. He made his way back into the house, walking slowly up the stairs with her and glancing down at her intermittently. He turned and used his back to open her door, and walked into the watercloset with her.

He sat her on the bench within the bathroom and bent over the tub, plugging it and beginning a warm water flow. He reached over and put bergamot and coriander in the water to lightly scent it, then he turned back to her. Alex's eyes widened, not sure what he was planning to do next.

Gaius leaned over her and put a finger under her chin. "Alex, you are precious to so many, and you must take care. You cannot chase the demons alone, and you cannot fight this battle alone. I want you to rest here in this warm water, and I will send Sabina to check on you in a few minutes. No memories, no mental excursions, please, Alex." His eyes bore into her, willing her to listen and take heed.

"I will rest, Gaius, thank you," said Alex earnestly. "Thank you for finding me."

He smiled gently and leaned closer to her face.

"Oh, Alexandria, I will always find you, of that you may forever place your trust and faith. Now please, relax here," he said, gesturing to the tub, then he turned and walked out, closing the door behind him.

Alex stood and started undressing, then made her way to the warm, fragrant water. She realized then how very cold she was, as her body adjusted to the water's temperature. Alex slowly sat down and tried desperately to hold to the here and now.

She thought of Wallace and Conner, remembering past pranks that they had played on one another. Her mind drifted to her parents, and her mother's insistence that Henry was a good prospect. And she thought of Jameason, and how he was never embarrassed to put her mother's pink, frilly apron on, and rebuke them while wearing it.

She imagined them all doing something they liked, smiling and laughing together. As she ran a soapy cloth over her body, she tried to let the tension in her muscles roll away. And she then thought of Dudley, and how much she would like to have him to snuggle and keep warm with.

Eventually, her thoughts turned to Jack, and she wondered what he was doing at that moment. Was he in the library reading Tolkien, was he arguing with Rohan, or was he out target practicing and imagining the bullseye was Aagon or Gaius, she wondered. That thought made her smile and chuckle to herself.

When she felt cleansed and warm, she rinsed off and let the water out, watching it swirl away. It made her think of Arianna's lake and what would happen to the great repository if she said 'no' to an immortal life. All that wisdom, power, and energy would be lost to the world. Most was not recorded, because the everyday man who usually went unnoticed was the kind of man Arianna would have helped.

Alex shook her head and tried to pull herself back to where she was. She concentrated on drying off and readying herself for sleep. She pulled on a robe she found hanging from a hook, and then realized her luggage was still at Aeoferth Hall, so she had nothing to sleep in.

She came out and saw that Gaius had built quite a fire, so she moved over to a large, overstuffed leather chair before it. Alex let the flames warm her, as her mind continued to drift. She was just nodding off, when Sabina knocked softly and Alex motioned her in.

"Alex, your clothes are in your luggage. Heath placed your bags in the closet over there, after we arrived this morning. Do you want me to get you something to sleep in?" she asked, gesturing to the closet behind where she stood.

"No, thank you, Sabina. You are too kind. But I would be very grateful if you would sit with me for a while." Alex hoped her friend would sense that she very much needed her presence at that moment.

"Of course, Alex," she said smiling tenderly, moving to an adjacent chair, so that they both were in front of the fire and angled towards one another. "How are you holding up?" she asked, and Alex let out a deep breath that turned into a nervous chuckle.

She ran her fingers through her hair and pulled her legs up underneath her body. "Sabina, I don't know. I am completely adrift here, and I don't know which way to turn." Alex shook her head despairing her choices, and she propped her chin in her hand as she rested her elbow on the arm of the supple leather chair.

Sabina nodded solemnly. "That I can understand. Gaius has been like a force of nature to hold back once he knew Bertrand had gotten to you. Though he had promised to go slowly with you, it seems he's doing anything but that."

"He's not doing anything I'm not letting him do, Sabina," said Alex honestly. "I just feel like this reunion cannot take place in front of all of you. And I hope I did not make Archimedes angry this morning when I didn't go along with his plan for an immediate meal, so soon after we walked through the front door."

"He is just trying to do what he thinks is best," Sabina shrugged, "but then, we all are with this. We've never experienced an immortal returning and it's new territory for all of us. We want to follow your lead in most things, so if you say you want to be alone with Gaius, then that's what you'll do. No one is going to pressure you or judge you, Alex. We all love you."

"I know you all do, and believe me when I say it is returned. I feel like you are such a part of me now, and I guess that's why I am pushing so hard to find answers and abilities. So I don't leave you all at the mercy of those who would harm you. Because of me," she added quietly, but Sabina would have none of that way of thinking.

"Alexandria, look at me," she said a little too forcefully, and Alex glanced at her, startled. "You will not sacrifice yourself because Arianna offered Kronis absolution. We will all find a way through this for you and us, because that is what families do, they stick together. You are the sister of my heart, and together, as family, we will prevail. I have all faith," she said, nodding firmly.

Alex found her first real laugh of the day from Sabina's firm tone, and soon they were both giggling like school girls. Their laughter became hysterical, and both had tears streaming down their faces.

When Sabina could finally stop herself from laughing, she stood to let Alex change and get into bed. She walked over and smoothed Alex's hair back from her face and kissed her forehead. "Goodnight, my friend," she said tenderly, and left Alex for the night.

Alexandria sat for another thirty minutes or so in front of the fire, letting the flames mesmerize her. When she felt herself nod, she stood up and found her sleeping clothes and finally climbed under the sheets. She felt so bone weary, and was lost to slumber almost immediately.

Sometime after she had fallen asleep, Gaius came into the room. He checked the locks on the windows and he made sure the fireplace was set for the remainder of the night. He picked up one of the leather chairs and moved it to her side of the bed, just close enough so that he could reach out a hand and touch her fingers that lay atop the bed's comforter.

He stretched out his long legs and leaned back in the seat. Then he rested one arm on the bed and touched his hand to hers. She moaned softly in her sleep, but she did not wake.

"No dreams tonight, Alexandria," he whispered. "Just peaceful, gentle sleep, my love." He began to send his aura out to hers, letting it coat her as he had earlier when she slept from her faint. He closed his eyes and let sleep take him as well. It was the most calming rest he had experienced in over one hundred and twenty-one years. The nightmares were held at bay, and neither of them dreamed that night.

24

Alexandria felt so happy and content, more than she had in ages. She could feel the sheets under her and over her, so she remembered where she was, but she did not want to open her eyes. This was bliss, she told herself.

She stretched and rolled over to her stomach, and then registered the smell of eggs, bacon, and pancakes. She realized she now had a very good reason to open her eyes. Alexandria opened one slowly, and beheld a small table, laden with food. It was placed between the two leather chairs in front of the fireplace, where she and Sabina had chatted the night before. Alex moved to the side of the bed closest to the delicious smelling meal, and made her way out of the warm cocoon she had created for herself.

She sat and saw a small card leaning against a bud vase which contained a single, yellow rose. Her favorite, she mused to herself. She noticed that her name was elegantly written in script across the front, and she opened it, then slid out a simple white card embossed with a silver border. It had an undemanding message written to her on the inside:

Alexandria, I hope you had a restful night. Please enjoy breakfast, and when you're ready, I will meet you in the stables. Clothes are waiting for you on the window seat.

Yours Always,
Gaius

Alex smiled at his thoughtfulness, and his succinct choice of words. She sat and indulged in all that was offered before her. There were fresh strawberries on the tray, as well as a tiny container holding slightly warmed syrup. She had come to appreciate pancakes while in New York after having them at a small delicatessen near her apartment. Did he know that too, she wondered. She savored each bite and drank the orange juice, which she preferred to coffee any day.

After she had finished her meal she stood and stretched, feeling her body so relaxed for the first time in days. She turned and padded over to the watercloset and freshened up, braiding her hair and brushing her teeth. When she looked in the mirror, Alex noticed that there was finally some color back in her cheeks, but there were still slight dark smudges under her eyes.

She came out and found the clothes Gaius had alluded to in her note. They were not hers. They looked closer to what Sabina had worn at Aeoferth, but the well-worn boots were hers. She dressed and made her way downstairs. Alex saw no one else, and so she stepped out of the door at the back of the kitchen and closed her eyes, trying to picture the horses. She remembered in which direction the stables lay, so she opened her eyes and began to walk in that direction.

As she approached the stables, she saw that it, too, was made of stone, but was not as large as the structure at Aeoferth. Its size was appropriate to Elysium though, and she made her way in through the substantial, heavy wooden doors, which were both pulled back. She looked around and found Gaius talking with two very large stallions, both solid black. She walked slowly up to them, not wanting to break the moment they were sharing.

Alex allowed her ribbon to unfurl, and she heard Gaius' sharp intake in breath as he felt her make contact with his flow of thoughts. He was telling the two of the day he had planned, and asking them to watch over Alex and himself as they rode and threw caution to the wind. Both stallions stamped their mighty hooves and looked him in the eye.

Finally, he turned and smiled a warm welcome to her. He held out a hand and said, "Come."

Alex moved forward and placed her hand in his. They stared into each other's eyes and she felt a calm wash over her, just like the feeling she had experienced that morning when she woke from her slumber. He squeezed her fingers gently and turned, leading them out of the stables, and the horses followed of their own accord.

Alex noted that though the horses had bridles and reigns, they had no blankets, saddles, or stirrups. She raised her eyebrows and he answered her unspoken question. "They have agreed to let us ride without any encumbrances today. We're going to make a day of just having some fun, you and I. No immortal business, no training sessions; just be with me, in the here and now, Alexandria," he said softly.

He moved closer to her and tucked a stray piece of hair that had already worked its way free of her braid behind her ear, and she felt that now familiar energy at his touch. "You are so young, Alexandria. And this should be enjoyable for you, not fraught with such pain and torment. Will you set it aside and spend the day with me? Just be with me today?" he asked her gently.

Alex was very moved by his words and most grateful for the reprieve. She needed a day away from the struggle her body and mind were having. So she answered him truthfully, saying, "Yes, Gaius. I would very much so like to be with you today. And perhaps, we can get to know one another better." His smile lit up his entire face and he turned, motioning the horses closer.

He put his hands around her waist and told her to jump high. She did as he asked, and was atop the mount in one swift motion. She touched the horse's neck and felt the sheer strength of the magnificent animal pulsing under her hand.

"Are you ready to fly?" she asked him, and he cantered sideways telling her that he was more than ready.

Gaius was promptly on his steed, and he turned to her, still smiling a boyish grin. "You are riding Arvan today, Alex, and I will ride Boaz." She thought through the languages in her head, and found that both names meant swift, fast, or strong in their native tongues.

"Are we going to ride swiftly?" she asked, teasing him.

He guided Boaz over, so that their horses were alongside one another.

"We are going to go at whatever pace we want, Alexandria. Are you ready?" She nodded her agreement, and they began to ride along a wide path that led out of the back gardens and snaked across a snow covered and rocky field. They passed by no one and nothing, seemingly in their own world.

Alex remembered that they were slightly out of sync with the rest of reality when they wanted to be, so perhaps they would not encounter any tourists during their ride. Gaius chatted with her, as they moved along, about her riding experiences. He asked about her childhood lessons, and how she found riding now that she knew she could communicate with her mount.

She told him about her success with the sport, but that she never pursued it as anything more than pleasure, not wanting to enter any kind of formal competitions. Alex stated that would have been too public, and too uncomfortable for her. But she was in love with riding now after her experiences with Eimhir, she gushed. They finally reached the coastline and paused, looking out across the North Sea.

Alex closed her eyes and smelled the cold, salty air rolling in off of the waves. She remembered that smell, of that specific sea and those waters. She had ridden there for so long, and she felt it coming back to her senses.

"Alex," Gaius said softly, pulling her back to the present. "Do not think of what was, right now. Concentrate on you and I, together today. Experience this, in this moment," he nodded slowly at her to gain her agreement.

"Yes," she breathed out.

They turned and began to ride gradually at first, then picked up speed. She looked over to Gaius and saw him nod his assent, and she leaned over Arvan's long neck and whispered for him to turn loose. He rocketed across the sand and she laughed aloud at the freedom she and the stallion felt together.

There were no words to describe how she felt in that moment. She could feel the steed's muscles flexing and his sides expanding and contracting, but she could also feel his joy at the way they moved together as one. She was no burden for him to carry, and he was in bliss just as she was. Alex could feel the rhythm of his hooves in her chest and she closed her eyes and gloried in the sensation.

"Faster, if you dare," she prodded him, and he gave her an additional burst so that the two were flying across the sands.

Eventually he slowed of his own accord, and they turned to watch Gaius speed toward them with Boaz. He was a sight to behold. She tried to hold to the present, but she saw a flash of him riding across a valley trying to stop a child on a horse that had broken away. Another memory came of him on the same beach on a dappled mare, riding with longer hair, and the wind lifting it off of his shoulders.

Alex ran her fingers into Arvan's mane trying to anchor herself and she whispered to him to help her return. She was able to stop the flashes and see Gaius as he was, not as he had been. She breathed slowly, and smiled at his apparent joy as he and Boaz came to a stop in front of her. Both horses were breathing heavily, but neither was overly exhausted.

He lifted a long leg and slid down off his horse, and then came around to her. "Would you like to walk?" he asked, holding his hands out for her to slide into. Alex swung her leg over Arvan's neck and head as well, and traveled down into his outstretched hands and arms.

He did not hold her long, just lightly squeezed her waist, and then he turned and the two walked together for quite some time, talking and laughing together. He wanted to know about her career and how she liked her colleagues. He asked about the time her family lived in Egypt and what her favorite historical sites in the region were when she was small. She recounted how she had actually tried to avoid most of the history the area had to offer, because of the visions at the time, and she noticed his frown as he looked out ahead of them.

She turned the topic to music then, asking if he liked current music, or pieces mainly from the past. Alex found that he was surprisingly well versed in the pop culture of the present. Gaius told her of movies he had seen and books he had read, trying to pass the time over the last few decades. He told her that he had actually given some thought to installing a home theatre room in Elysium, and she laughed aloud at the thought.

He pretended her laughter had wounded him, and placed a hand over his heart, but he began to laugh as well. He told her of his love for a well turned phrase, and thus he still was a fan of poetry. An image of her sitting on a blanket in tall grass came unbidden and she saw his head in her lap. He was reading sonnets aloud, and she had one hand behind her holding herself up while the other slowly trailed through his soft hair. It was most serene.

Alex felt Gaius' fingers intertwine with hers, pulling her out of the memory. She looked up into his eyes, and he said softly, "Just us here, right now, Alex," and she nodded. Alex looked back over her shoulder and saw that both horses were a little distance behind, but still following them.

Gaius led her over to the water, and they stood watching the waves lap up onto the sand.

"It's so peaceful here, so beautiful. I can see why we'd never want to leave," she said quietly. He turned, and she saw the surprise on his face as his eyes roamed over hers. "Yesterday morning when I learned of you, Elrick said that we would come here and take refuge, not wanting to leave for portions of time. I can see why. This place is very restorative." He nodded, not trusting his voice to answer her.

Gaius stepped forward and his hand hovered just over her hair, waiting for her permission to touch it. She nodded almost imperceptibly, and he took both hands and ran them down the length of her braid until he reached the end, then he unfastened her tie. He slowly worked her hair free of the pattern she had woven it into, and massaged the length of it and her scalp, until she closed her eyes and succumbed to the bliss he was instilling in her.

She reopened her eyes and saw the longing in his. He slowly took his hands from her hair and trailed his fingers around the edge of her hairline that framed her face.

"Would you like to ride back now?" he whispered.

"If you'd like to," she whispered back.

"No," he laughed softly, "this is your day. We're riding or not riding, whenever you say so."

Alex could see he was giving her an out, a way to break the contact between them, so she gratefully accepted. Though she found it very hard to do so. "Let's ride, and you can show me more of the land," she said, and he nodded, stepping back and calling the horses to them silently.

They spent the next hour meandering about and continuing their time alone. Gaius wanted to talk, and Alex found that his inquiries were his attempt to understand her thoughts or emotions behind specific events in her life that he had witnessed when he guarded over her. It was oddly comforting to know that he knew so much about her, and cared for her well-being.

When they turned back from the beach he looked over to her with a dimple in his cheek and a mischievous glint in his eyes. "I'll race you home," he said, grinning from ear to ear. Alex immediately accepted the challenge and leaned low over Arvan, showing him with her mind how good it would feel to leave Gaius and Boaz in their wake.

The stallion reared up slightly and launched himself across the ground, just as Eimhir had done. Alex's hair flew behind her like a yellow piece of silk, billowing in the wind. She closed her eyes again, and was filled with joy and freedom from this new way of riding. She laughed when she thought of the heart palpitations she would give her parents and Jameason if they could see her like that.

Alex and Arvan roared into the courtyard in front of the stables, and the two had so much momentum that they continued on past and down the lane. They sprinted across the lawn at the front of the estate where the S-92 still sat. Finally, the steed slowed and she found that Gaius was right behind her, bringing Boaz to a stop. They were both of them laughing and grinning, and Alex felt so light from the experience.

She rode over to his side, their mounts facing in opposite directions. Alex tried to catch her breath to thank him, but her smile was all the thanks he needed. "You were glorious out there, your hair trailing you. It is a delight to see you so in the moment," he said. "Can I interest you in some lunch?" he asked, trying to still his breathing as well.

"Lunch, sounds good. What are we having?" she asked playfully.

Gaius gave her his devilish, young man's grin again and said, "Oh, I have a surprise. Come." And he turned Boaz, leading the way back to the stables. Heath was waiting inside to take over the care of the horses, so that they could go on their way. They both thanked him, and he brushed off their words nonchalantly.

They walked back towards the house together, both sated from the invigorating exercise. Gaius strode ahead a few steps and held the door open for Alex to enter the main house, and told her he would meet her in the foyer in thirty minutes or so, so that they could both freshen up.

She made her way back to her room and decided on a quick shower. She pulled on jeans and a warm, powder blue cashmere sweater that her mother had given her two Christmases ago and dried her hair as quickly as she could. It was still damp at the edges when she made her way back downstairs.

Gaius was just coming back in the front door and he walked up to her, smiling appreciatively at her choice in attire. Alex blushed, but tried to meet his eyes.

"I would like to take you away from here for a little while, Alexandria. Would you come away from the memories for a time, and perhaps we can create a few new ones together?" he asked.

"I would like that very much," she agreed. Alex thought that the chance to escape the constant stream of the two of them together was a good way to see Gaius as he was now, and as they possibly could be. He held the front door open for her, bowing and gesturing her forward. She had no idea what he was up to, but she walked out of the front and down the steps to find she was looking at a very expensive, new quantum silver Aston Martin. She looked back at him aghast at the machine in front of her.

He laughed out loud then and made his way over to the passenger side, holding that door open for her as well.

"Are you coming, Alexandria?" he asked, teasingly.

She shook her head and made her way over, giving him an exasperated look before she slid into the soft cream leather seat. He closed her door, then made his way around and slid in beside her. He started the car and its engine roared to life.

Before he put the car in gear, he looked back over at her and laughed, saying, "What? We drive cars now, too." But he did not wait for an answer. He just drove them away from the estate chuckling to himself and she soon found she was as well.

They made their way across the island to its lone village, and Alex found herself completely speechless as she watched Gaius use his aura to melt snow ahead of their path to give the car a way through. He kept his attention focused until they had reached the tiny town and he had found a place to park.

He looked over at her and asked her if she was ready for a little adventure. She nodded and found that his happiness was spilling over into her mood as well. Gaius helped her out of her side, and held her hand as they walked along the streets. He pointed out the few shops and eateries the place offered, and finally led her to a little restaurant called the BeanGoose. Alex chuckled at the name on the sign and walked in beside Gaius.

It was warm and toasty inside, and he led her to a booth in the back, positioning himself so that he was facing the restaurant's entrance. A lady in her mid-fifties perhaps, asked them what they wanted to drink and she welcomed Gaius back to their establishment.

"So good to see he finally has a lady with him," she laughed. "I'm always trying to get him to date my niece, but he's never taken the bait. What's your name, dear?" she asked, as she delved for information.

Alex chuckled at Gaius' embarrassed expression, and told the lady her name. She left them to retrieve their drinks and let them look over the menu together.

"Her niece, huh?" whispered Alex, laughing at his obvious discomfort.

He shuddered all over. "You laugh, but you've not met her. No, Alex," he replied, looking up from his menu into her eyes, "there is only you." And she felt her cheeks warm at his direct words.

She turned the topic by asking him what was good to eat there, and they both settled on lobster bisque with some of the restaurant's organic greens and fresh baked bread on the side. When it arrived, she found it delicious, and actually finished her portion before he did.

He caught her eyeing his bowl, and he raised his eyebrows in mock surprise. "Do you want some of mine, Alex?"

She flushed, embarrassed that she was actually still hungry. Her mother would probably have something to say if she ate his food right out from under him, she thought to herself.

"No, I'm good," she said, and he did laugh then.

"No, you're not. You are always hungry," he said, shaking his head and she felt her mouth open slightly at his comment.

"How do you know?" she asked in amazement.

"Because, you have a lot more power and energy running through your body than even the rest of us, and it burns through what nourishment you take in rather quickly. It is nothing to be self-conscious about; it just is what we all deal with." He reached forward and laced his fingers through hers. "Alex, do not be embarrassed by what you are and how your body reacts to the power within," he said sincerely.

She glanced down at their hands, and watched the growing light display as their auras began to dance and move in unison. Alex looked back into his eyes, so warm and encouraging.

He nodded, "Right, another round then." And he looked over, signaling to the lady who was taking care of them that they would like another portion. If she was surprised, she did not let on, and soon Alex was feeling full and satisfied. Gaius left to pay, and Alex realized for the first time she had not even thought to bring her wallet along.

He stood beside her and offered her his hand, and she slowly slid her palm into his. Gaius gently squeezed her fingers as she stood, and she walked by his side out of the restaurant. He led her through the quiet streets for a little while, pointing out different buildings and telling her what lay within.

She began to remember the churches and monasteries that existed there on the island through the ages, when she knew it as Lindisfarne. Images of how they had worked with many of the monks who had come there to build first one monastery, and then another after Vikings destroyed the original, filtered through her mind. And when the past threatened to sweep her away, she was pulled back by Gaius' aura.

He still had her hand firmly in his and he was not letting go. Alex had no desire to lose consciousness on the street in front of witnesses, so she stayed anchored to him. She shivered once and he broke contact long enough to put his jacket on her, then gathered her hand in his and placed it in the bend of his elbow, pulling her in closer.

They walked into a Celtic craft shop and talked about the souvenirs and artwork inside. The place brought back recollections of their travels across Ireland, and the one specific trip they took to bring Benen back to Aeoferth after his mother passed away and his angelic father had to return to the Lord. Alex felt her eyes cloud at the memory of Benen's grief from the loss of one he loved so much.

Gaius brushed her cheek with his fingers and hugged her, causing several shoppers and the clerk to smile wistfully at the beautiful young people before them caught in an impromptu embrace. He pulled back and tucked her hand back inside his arm, then led her through the store's offerings. He paused by a case which held silver jewelry, featuring various rings, bracelets, and necklaces. He looked back at her for a moment as if considering something of gravity.

"Alexandria, would you allow me to purchase something for you? It would give me great pleasure. A token to mark a very happy day," he said, and to Alex, he seemed to hold his breath awaiting her answer.

"If it is a small reminder of our day, then I accept," she said quietly, unsure what he was thinking or planning. She had tried to stress the word 'small', and she hoped that he had heard it in her voice.

He nodded and exhaled slowly. He then turned and asked a young lady who worked there to please remove a simple, silver ring from the case. She did so, and tried repeatedly not to openly gawk at Gaius' handsome face and his beauty. Alex smiled at the young girl's struggle, as she felt slightly sorry for her. *Nephilim* could be very intense to humans, thought Alex, and apparently the young lady was susceptible to their pull.

He turned and reached for Alex's right hand. He slid the ring, a Claddagh ring, onto her ring finger with the heart pointed toward her wrist. It fit perfectly, and his jaw flexed slightly as he appraised it on her hand.

"Will you wear it?" he breathed. Alex nodded her agreement, and thanked him for the unadorned silver ring. He nodded tightly and then moved forward to pay for it.

As they walked out of the shop and along the street, Alex stopped and pulled on his arm to halt him from going any further. He turned quickly and looked to assure himself she was alright.

"Alex?" he said, in question.

"Thank you, Gaius, for today. I didn't realize how much I needed this, but you did. You do seem to know me very well." She looked off in the distance for a few moments, and then back up into his eyes. "I would like to give you a token too, but I didn't bring my wallet along," she shrugged her apology.

"I don't need anything more than what I have right now, in this moment, Alexandria. You are safe and whole and happy. That is all I need," he replied, and reached forward to smooth her hair back and away from her face. "Come, I have one more place I want to take you before we head back." He turned and led her to a little coffee shop called the Pilgrims Coffee House, and ducked his head under the doorframe as they walked in.

Alex could smell the sugar before she had even taken a moment to look around, and she knew her face must be telling him of her obvious excitement. He laughed softly, and pulled her forward to a small table for two. The unique eatery specialized in a wide variety of cakes and scones along with gourmet coffees, and she smiled as she read over the menu.

Alex opted for a large slice of triple chocolate cake with hot chocolate on the side. Gaius ordered coconut cake for himself and a cup of black coffee, with no cream or sugar. She watched him raise the cup to his lips and wrinkled her nose.

"What? Still not a coffee drinker?" he asked playfully.

"Not at all," she answered him. "Sometimes I can stomach the smell, but I don't like it, in any variety or flavor. Some mornings, just the aroma of someone else having a cup nearby can make me feel nauseous. Do you drink it often?"

"Every day," he replied. "But I'll remember not to get it too close to you." He looked down to gather a bite of cake on his fork and did not notice Alex's look of surprise over his last comment. It sounded to her that he assumed they would be together most days in the future. She looked down before he registered her expression and concentrated on the food before her.

When they had both finished, Gaius paid the ticket and they made their way back through the village. Each seemed lost in their own thoughts and Alex was surprised to look up and find that they were already back at the car. Gaius said nothing, but held her door open for her and closed her in before taking the driver's seat. He drove them slowly back to Elysium and parked the car to the left of the main house, just outside the kitchen.

He turned in his seat and looked at Alex, taking her right hand in his and lifting it to his lips. He kissed the back of her hand, then the silver ring he had given her. Gaius continued as he turned her palm over and brushed his lips across it, softly and gently.

Alexandria closed her eyes and felt the current pass from his lips to her hand and travel throughout her skin and body. Even the top of her scalp was singing. She opened her eyes to see his burning into hers.

"Gaius," she whispered in warning, not trusting herself to what was building between them.

"I know," he whispered, feeling the charged atmosphere that he had initiated as well. "Your mind is torn, as is your heart. There is Jackson, and there is also me. I only ask that you don't shut me out, because I was held back from you for a few days, but consider me also. Please, don't shut me out, Alex," he breathed, and leaned into her, touching her lips with his.

He slowly coaxed her into responding, holding her head in his hands as his fingers shook slightly in her hair. He continued his gentle play until she sighed and he deepened his embrace. Again, and again his mouth slanted over hers, taking and giving all that he felt for her and wanted to offer her.

"Oh, Gaius," she said, almost crying, so at war was she within herself.

"I know, Alex, I know. I'm so sorry I was late," he said, with anguish and regret.

Alex felt swept away and tried to fight it, but it was of no use. She felt as if this man knew her body better than she, and he knew exactly what would make her respond. She caught a glimpse of them on another day, in such a passionate embrace as that, and tried to pull away from it before she saw too much.

Gaius felt her tremble, and he pulled his head back and shook it sadly. "Alexandria, I am so sorry. I promised myself I would not do this today. I wanted to give you one perfect day. I am so completely and utterly yours, that being physically apart from you is very difficult for me. I've missed you so much; I cannot ever begin to express it fully to you." He ran a hand down her cheek and his thumb traveled across her swollen lips.

"And now you're here, and I am trying. God help me, I am. Please, Alex, forgive me," he said, still sounding winded and leaning his forehead against hers, getting his eyes as close to hers as he could.

She looked into his blue and green irises and sighed, knowing that she could not lie to him or herself. "There's nothing to forgive, Gaius. I can only imagine what your battle is like for you now. And believe me when I say, I feel the connection too. I just need to slow down a little, so that I'm not so consumed by what was, and I know what *is* for me, right now."

"I honestly don't know that we can, because all I have to do is look at you, and my aura reaches out for you, I can feel it. I'm just afraid I am going to be led by it more than my own mind. Do you understand?" she asked, pulling back and looking imploringly into his eyes.

He nodded his head slowly, in response.

"If you asked me, do I like the man I see before me, I'd be a fool to say 'no'. I see not just this beautiful exterior, but I see your goodness and kindness. It flows off of you like a river. I can also feel how much you've tried to care for me since I arrived. Today was exactly what I needed, and you saw that and made it possible." His shoulders relaxed slightly at her last statement.

"You think I'm beautiful?" he asked, smirking at her.

"Of course, and so did every other female who looked at you today. The poor girl whom you purchased the ring from had a hard time completing her sentences. I actually felt sorry for her," Alex chuckled, causing him to completely relax beside her.

"I am sure, given time, I can make sense of my emotions, but I really must slow down. I can say though, that I do know one thing for certain now," she paused, making sure she had his complete attention. "Henry will be devastated to know that he finally has competition." She smiled at the way his eyebrows shot up in question to her remark, and she laughed using his surprise to allow her a quick escape from the car.

She squealed when she saw him come swiftly out of his side, and he began to chase her towards the house. Alex beat him inside, and ran as fast as her legs would carry her through the castle, down corridor after corridor, until found herself within the same den they had been in the night before. She came to a stop in the center of the room and turned just in time to see him come running in behind her, panting and smiling broadly that she had initiated such play.

He quietly walked over to her, and she took two steps back until she bumped into a table and could retreat no farther. He came to stand before her and she saw such delight run across his features. He leaned forward and braced his arms on either side of her, causing her to lean back on the table. His eyes moved slowly from the top of her face, down her nose, to her lips, then back up to her eyes, drinking her in.

Alex was still trying to catch her breath, when he leaned down until he hovered over her mouth. "Who," he whispered, "is Henry?" He stayed there waiting for her response.

She smirked at him and chuckled before giving him her answer. "The young man my mother thinks would be a good husband for me." She tilted her head to the side, waiting to see what he would say.

His slow smile let her know he was not really worried at this new competition. "Well then, we'll just have to let her meet me and see if I measure up to good old Henry. Will you let me meet your parents, Alexandria?" he breathed, still not touching her.

"Yes. They've met Jack, so it's only fair that they meet you, too," she said softly.

"Good, I look forward to it. I enjoyed our day together, Alex. I hope that there will be more like it to come. Many, many more," and he leaned down kissing first her lips chastely, then the tip of her nose, and finally her forehead. He looked back into her eyes as he said, "I would like to share some poetry and writings with you tonight. Will you join me in the library in another hour or so?"

She nodded her head and watched as he straightened to his full height, then turned to walk away. Gaius paused in the entryway and looked back at her briefly, and then finally left the room. When Alex trusted her legs to support her again, she straightened away from the table as well.

Being with Gaius when he was looking at her as he just had, completely clouded her view of everything else, she thought to herself. She knew she would have to work harder to guard against the pull. She ran her hand through her hair and walked over to a fabric-covered chair by a window. She sat down, and looked out across the frozen earth before her.

Alexandria began to search her soul for answers. Not about Kronis, but about Jack and Gaius. She recognized her attraction to Jack as a slowly emerging friendship and possible romance. She knew that he would be a slow and steady constant at her side, and he would give her perspective, guidance, and acceptance. He would love her no matter what strange lights shot out of her hands.

But if she chose an immortal life, he would grow old in front of her, and she doubted he would ever have children. She had been smart enough to observe there were no children at Aeoferth Hall, and no pictures of descendants anywhere in the castle that she had noticed. She decided to talk to John and ask for clarification.

Then there was Gaius, with his complete understanding of her life, both as Arianna and Alexandria, now that she knew he had watched her grow and mature. They had spent a very enjoyable day together, their conversation coming easily and already comfortable. She knew if she gave him the okay, he would have her as his wife and the rest would come in time. He would not want to let her slip away again.

But she could not say 'yes', because deep down, she loved Jack, too. She put a hand over her mouth, realizing she had confessed her feelings finally to herself. She loved Jack, and could feel the already established love between herself and Gaius. What if he had not been held back from her days ago, she questioned. Would she have ever allowed herself to go into Jack's arms for comfort? No, she told herself, she would not. She would have found Gaius' embrace waiting on her, and sheltered there.

Alexandria looked down and studied the ring now on her hand. She knew that the hand it was worn on and the direction it sat on the finger held special significance, but she could not remember at the moment. She used her thumb to spin it around on her finger, feeling its smooth surface.

Finally, she looked back outside and saw a memory of herself as Arianna walking across the lawn. But Arianna gazed back at the house, looking at the windows as if she was hoping to take her leave without being detected. Alex stood and moved over to the window, trying to see what she was doing in the past. She looked closely at herself as she mounted a tall mare. She was wearing the same outfit she had been in the day she met Kronis on the cliff.

Alex noticed a pack behind the animal's saddle, and she knew it held her luggage. This was the moment she left to offer him a way out, she told herself. She felt very dizzy and slightly sick to her stomach, knowing what was to come. The image began to dissolve in front of Alex's face, and she decided to let it go, as she thought she had seen all she needed to from that particular scene.

She decided to go up to her room and lie down for a little while, but felt an odd burning sensation in her nostrils. Alex then registered something wet on her lip, and knew what was happening. She moved her hand up in time to catch the next few drops, before her nose began to freely run blood. She grabbed her face, and bolted up the stairs before anyone saw her distress. She made it to the watercloset and got a handful of tissue, then tilted her head back.

Alex had never been prone to illness much and certainly never suffered from nosebleeds before. Now, in this one week, she had experienced several. She stayed like that, nose pinched and head back, trying not to let the metallic taste on the back of her throat make her ill.

Perhaps, she thought, the stress of the week was finally getting the best of her. She sat on the bench and got new tissue and noted that the flow was decreasing. When she thought it had finally ended, she flushed all of the evidence away and washed her face gingerly.

She made her way out and fell across the bed, not even bothering to take her boots off. She just let her feet dangle off of the edge, and succumbed to an exhausted sleep. She felt something tug at her, but also a warm soothing sensation that reminded her of Gaius' aura, and so she stayed under.

Gaius had come down the hall towards his own room and paused at Alex's door, which she had left wide open. He noticed her lying across the bed, and he was unsure why she had chosen to lay in what looked to be an uncomfortable position.

He moved forward to ask her if she was alright, but realized she already slept. He pulled off one of her boots then the other, and then he gently lifted her until she lay with her head on a pillow. He closed his eyes and sent his aura to her, willing her to rest well. Then he left her to her nap, sending a prayer her way as he departed.

25

"Alex, sweetheart, can you open your eyes?" It was John asking, and she opened them slowly to see him sitting on the side of the bed to her left. "Hey, there, sleepyhead," he said, smiling down at her.

"How long did I nap?" she asked, with no real frame of reference. She looked over and noticed that it was now completely dark outside her window.

"Oh, I'd say about two hours," he paused at her alarmed expression. "Now, Alex, don't worry yourself. You need it, trust me. We're all going to have dinner in a few minutes. Do you feel like getting up and eating something, or would you like for me to bring your food here?' he asked, sounding calm and unruffled by her long lie-down.

"Oh, I'll come downstairs. Just let me freshen up and I'll meet you in the dining room."

"Very well, I'll see you there," he said, patting her leg and stood to take his leave.

Alex rose and visited the watercloset again to make sure there was no evidence of her earlier nosebleed, and then walked out of her bedroom.

Rather than turning towards the staircase, she turned towards her left and walked over to the bedroom next to hers. Its door was slightly ajar, and she knew that is was the bedroom she had shared with Gaius.

Thinking him downstairs preparing for dinner, she walked over and put her hand to the wood and slowly pushed it open. She had to hold on to the door for support, as the past's images began to rush in on her quite quickly and with such force. She closed her eyes and thought of the door she grasped, willing the inanimate object to pull her back to where she really was.

Finally, when the flashes subsided she moved forward into the space and stood at its center. This was truly her area, more so than the room at Aeoferth. She saw paintings on the walls that were so familiar. Alex noticed a balcony that she had stood on hundreds, if not thousands, of times. And she beheld furniture that she had commissioned crafted just for their space.

She moved tentatively forward and paused at a large dresser that would make most museum curators speechless to behold. The artistry of the minute details along its edge, and the like new condition it was in, made her smile wistfully. She ran her hand along the edge, and saw the faces of the two old men who had constructed it so very long ago. Alex saw their smiles of pride as well, when she praised their craft and skill after its completion.

There was an ornate silver chest on its surface and she leaned forward, opening its lid. Inside was a staggering collection of jewels, some set in rings, others on bracelets, necklaces, or broaches. She had only seen pieces of that quality and size in magazines or in museums her family had taken her to when she was growing up.

There was one ring in particular that called to Alex, and it was slightly smaller than the others. It was an intense blue stone, most definitely not a sapphire she told herself. A topaz, perhaps, she wondered. The stone itself was cut into a triangular shape, and it was set in yellow gold with two little sweeps of gold on either side of the singular center stone. It was breathtaking.

Alex reached in and pulled the ring out, holding it up to the light from a lamp which had been left on atop the dresser. She felt the ring vibrating within her fingers, almost as if was begging to tell her its story. She was preparing to allow herself to see into the past, when she felt Gaius' hand close over hers. She turned and saw his surprised expression.

"Alexandria," he said, slowly and deliberately, "what are you doing?"

"I'm sorry, Gaius, if I overstepped," she said, trying to return the ring to its resting place. But he would not let her move away, as he placed his hands on her shoulders and held her in place.

"Of course, you have not overstepped. This was your room once, too. I'm just surprised to find you in here," he said, searching her eyes.

"So am I," she confessed in a small voice.

He removed his hands from her shoulders and placed them behind his back. He nodded in the direction of the ring she still held. "Do you remember this?"

"I was actually about to connect with a memory when you touched my hand. I feel that it is very important to me, but I cannot tell you why? Will you tell me?" she asked, looking up into his eyes, and saw his slow smile appear.

"Gladly, Alexandria. It was your wedding ring." He paused letting his words sink in. "I purchased the stone from a trader who had recently returned from India. It had such fire and was so clear, like I knew my road ahead with you would be. I asked a stone cutter to cut it with three sides, and he thought I was mad," Gaius laughed at the memory.

"From our birth, all *Nephilim* know of the Trinity that came to pass: the Father, the Son, and the Holy Spirit, no matter what time we are born to. I thought the shape would remind you of that, and of me each day you wore it. I always thought it went well with your eyes, too," he said, smiling wistfully.

"What kind of stone is it?" she asked.

"It is a blue diamond," he responded.

Alex stepped over and replaced the priceless ring back into the chest and closed its lid. She moved over next to him and looked back around the room. She remembered trading for a small statue of a horse in full gallop that sat on the mantle. She had thought it reminded her of a mare she had once loved, named Ina. Alex looked at a framed sketch standing in a small easel, and she remembered da Vinci drawing it of her horse and its musculature, as a gift for her.

And then she saw an image of them walking hand in hand over to the bed, and she gasped softly. It was covered in a quilt, not the comforter she saw upon it now, and she could see the passion in his eyes as he turned her towards his face. Alex blinked trying to clear the vision and pulled back with all of her might to see him before her in the moment, and not in such an intimate memory from her soul's past.

"Come, let's leave those memories in the past, Alex, and join the others for dinner," said Gaius softly, taking her hand in his and pulling her from her reverie. He did not release her hand until he had her downstairs and was leading her through the entrance to the dining room. He pulled her chair out for her, and Alex noted that they were the last to come to the table.

Alexandria was embarrassed, because she had been raised to come to the table on time and be seated with everyone else. She offered her apology for being tardy, but the others brushed it off. She made eye contact with Sabina, who smiled at her, but Alex noticed that her friend's eyes traveled to Gaius, no doubt wondering why the two were late together.

As they ate, both John and Archimedes asked about their day together. Alex did not know if Gaius wanted the details shared, so she let him lead the recounting of their excursions. He told them what a delight it had been to ride that morning and feel the cold, salt air in his lungs. Heath affirmed that the horses were extremely happy and replete when they came back to the stables.

Alex felt safe to interject that she had never ridden bareback before, and they all shared a laugh at that statement.

"Let me guess, I used to do it all the time?" she asked dryly, and they all chuckled once more.

Gaius leaned forward and said proudly, "Well for a first time, this time around, you looked like a seasoned professional. It was a thing of joy to behold." She smiled back at his praise, and then took an extra moment to study placing her piece of beef on her fork.

"That's how I felt, too, watching her ride at Aeoferth," said Sabina, and the two shared a smile at the experience.

Archimedes asked about their trip into the village. Gaius admitted that he had avoided taking Alex to the different museums and holy historical sights that gave the island its common name. He wanted her to visit the present, so he told them about their lunch and how good the lobster bisque had been and about their dessert at the coffee house.

Archimedes started recalling the first time he had ever tasted coffee, and the others joined in to add their recollections of their own experiences as well. Alex felt the ring still on her right hand with her thumb again, and wondered why he had skipped that part of the afternoon. She looked over at him, and he gave her a slow wink as if he were reading her mind. Her cheeks colored slightly, and she turned back to the conversation before her.

Once dinner was over, they all decided to adjourn to the library together. Alex offered to help John clear the table, hoping to talk with him in private regarding her earlier thoughts about children. Heath, however, shooed her away and took over the task. She tried not to show her displeasure, but Gaius lifted an eyebrow asking her silently why she seemed dismayed. She only offered him a smile in answer, and turned to follow Archimedes and Sabina to Elysium's library.

Alex had not entered the library there yet, and when she did she felt like she was back in Aeoferth, only on a slightly smaller scale. They had incorporated a mural there as well, but this one featured mainly angels and majestic scenery. Dark, wooden book shelves climbed to the second story ceiling. There were comfortable chairs scattered here and there, with tables and desks to work on as well. She stopped just inside and Archimedes came to stand beside her.

"You always did love a library, Alex," he mused. "You said to me once, that if you could have saved the great Library of Alexandria, you would have felt you had accomplished more in your life. It was a great regret of yours," he said, rocking back and forth on his heels once more. She smiled at the action.

"Alexandria," she whispered, thinking of her name and the once great repository of information and knowledge.

"Yes, but don't worry, we actually have copies of most items the library contained scattered throughout our own collections. You just hated seeing it being lost to the masses."

Something else was lurking in her memory. Something she had heard herself say when she spoke Gaius' full name to him in the foyer. She looked over and saw that he watched her from a sofa where he had placed himself.

"Your middle name is Alexander?" she asked, surprised that she was just now focusing on this.

He nodded. "My mother chose my second name after Alexander the Great. I am not entirely sure why she felt compelled to do that, but it is who I am. I kept the name in her honor." He finished his remarks by gesturing to the cushion next to him.

Alex thought that perhaps she would be less likely to completely fall under the influence of Gaius' aura with an audience, so she agreed to sit close to him. Sabina and Archimedes took seats opposite them and they all read quietly for a while, while they waited on John and Heath to rejoin them.

Alex had picked up a book of Shakespeare's plays from a stack on a nearby table. She was skimming through Hamlet, when her eyes locked onto an all too familiar passage:

> *"And therefore as a stranger give it welcome*
> *There are more things in heaven and earth, Horatio,*
> *Than are dreamt of in your philosophy."*

Alex closed her eyes and let his words sink in, and she felt the power of his character's observation. There is so much to behold in the heavens and on this earth, she mused to herself. If humans knew a fraction of what she had seen over the course of the last week, could they handle it she wondered. No, she thought, as every frightening alien or ghost movie she had ever been forced to watch with Wallace demonstrated. In her heart, Alex knew that humans do not easily think outside of what reality they know to be true and definable.

And how would they perceive the *Nephilim* en mass, Alex pondered. Through wide-scale panic and fear to be sure. But if they were there on the sidelines, quietly protecting, healing and nurturing, they could effectively hold humanity together. They could strive to establish the principles by which their fathers and the Great I Am created all peoples, of all races and creeds. Through the bonds of love and compassion for someone other than yourself, Alex thought quietly to herself.

It was an awesome and breathtaking responsibility. She contemplated how wrong the Greeks had gotten it in their mythology. The image of the Titan, Atlas, being punished and forced to hold up the celestial spheres, and people's images of him now holding the earth up, came to her. It was an inspiring possibility to help mankind, not a punishment from what she could imagine. Though the weight of the years might begin to weigh heavily, if one was fighting the likes of Bertrand and Aagon.

Alex wondered if that was what Gaius had tried to tell her, when he held her in her bedroom after her first faint at Elysium. Having someone by your side could make the centuries bearable, because there was another to support and share in your triumphs and mistakes. She then thought back to reading John's mind at Aeoferth and seeing his wife. His human wife.

He had loved her so much, and he had so little time with her. Could she do that with Jack, she asked herself. Have him for a little while, and then mourn his passing for the ages. She retreated from the path her thoughts were leading her down and sat back against the cushions, opening her eyes once more.

Heath and John were just coming in, and they moved two more chairs over to create a small circle as she had seen them do at Aeoferth several times now. She wondered if they were the ones who had taught Arthur the value of the round table, everyone visible and on an equal footing. Archimedes placed his book down and cleared his throat to get their attention.

"I would like to bring up a topic for discussion, if everyone is willing," he paused and looked around. John waved his hand in the air, as if he were urging Archimedes to go ahead without so much formality.

"Alex, Gaius told us what you attempted in the gazebo last night," Archimedes said, and she drew in a deep breath at his words so casually spoken.

She looked over at Gaius sternly, showing him her disapproval, but Archimedes drew her attention back to himself.

"Now, now, Alex don't get angry with him. He only shared it because he is very worried about you. Gaius would not betray your confidence; he just doesn't want you hurt." She nodded tightly to signal she understood his reasoning.

Gaius said nothing, but draped one long arm on the back of the sofa so that his hand was close to her head and neck. She felt him shift on his cushion, but did not look his way again for a moment.

"The reason I bring it up, is because I think you had a very astute plan. One that might eventually help us to track Kronis and end this standoff, once and for all." As he finished his words, everyone began talking at once and they were all voicing their reluctance to see her put in such jeopardy and peril. Gaius was the most in opposition to such a plan, and his hand lowered to the back of Alex's head as if his touch would keep her mind from traveling.

Archimedes held up his hand to stop the arguments, and finally everyone quieted down. "Hear me out friends, please. I don't suggest that she try this alone. Gaius, you saved her by finding and holding fast to her aura. You essentially were the beacon home, and she found her way."

But Gaius interrupted him, "No, Archimedes, that is not true. I did not shine a light for her to follow. I felt her aura and essence being forcibly pulled away, and I fought whatever it was with everything I had just to get her back here. I almost did not," he breathed.

Alex finally looked back over at him, and realized now why he had been so panicked and shaken when she came to in his arms. Had he saved her from dying, she wondered. She laid her right palm out close to his leg and he reached across his lap taking it with his free hand, so that he could keep his left in contact with her head. Sabina looked at their hands and smiled to herself.

"Well, I for one think it's too risky," said John. "If Alex is not in this physical realm, there is no way to predict how long she can be safely gone. And whatever this malevolent force is, it is mired deeply enough in Arianna's subconscious that we won't have any way of knowing its intent, or which powers or abilities to advise her to employ against it."

"I can most certainly tell you its intent," said Gaius, in a deceptively calm voice. "It wants her dead. She is not going back there anytime soon," he said, hoping to close the discussion. But Archimedes was not ready to let the topic go just yet.

Alex squeezed Gaius' hand to try and calm him. He looked down at her and nodded slightly, letting her know he understood her intent.

"What I think is, that if we, as a collective, used our auras to hold to Alex's aura as she travels to this memory, then the sheer magnitude would be great enough to keep her from harm. It could work if we were all together. We could call more of our numbers back from the field to try." Archimedes let his last thought hang between them, waiting to see if they might concur that it was possible to get at the truth together.

Finally, Sabina answered. "It just might work. I'm sorry, Gaius, I know you don't want to try again, but it could succeed with all of us there to support the effort. We all know Kronis leads and sometimes guides the others when they will let him. Arianna's death was his one reason for the ultimate power he now has over the Fallen's children. He won't let Alex live for long if she is a threat to that power. So we will have to know how he defeated her, one who should have been far greater than he."

She paused and looked at Alex next. "Again, Alex, this will be your choice. But I think Archimedes is on to something. We will have to find the full story to stop him from taking you again."

At that statement, Alex felt a pure jolt of fear from Gaius and she turned to stare into his eyes. "I'm not going to try this search again without help, Gaius. I promise. Please know that I have no desire to see my mortal or possible immortal life come to an end. I *will* fight for my family, my friends, and myself. No one is taking me away again, I promise." She placed her left hand on his cheek and felt her aura flow to him.

"I promise," she whispered.

He nodded and breathed out slowly, taking in her aura to calm himself. Alex smiled at him, and then asked, "I'll bet you are one formidable soldier, aren't you?"

"You have no idea," he said, with an ominous tone that let her know he would most certainly protect what was his.

Archimedes rubbed his hands together as if in anticipation of a new project he could put his mind to. Alex could tell he was already plotting and planning, and she caught Heath shaking his head at Archimedes' eagerness. She and Heath looked at each other and grinned.

All six of them sat together and tried to steer the conversation into more neutral territory. Alex found that she still held onto Gaius' hand, and she was rubbing slow circles on his palm with her thumb, trying to calm him. When she finally stopped, she felt him begin a similar pattern on the back of her head and it made her groggy.

The last thing she heard was Heath saying that they should have some sword practice in the morning, and Gaius and Sabina agreeing to the plan. Sleep claimed her then and she readily gave in to its call.

Gaius felt her go, and continued his contact with her, willing her to stay put. He did not want to disturb her, so he chose not to pick up his book of poetry again. He just held to her instead. He felt Sabina's keen eyes on them, and he looked up smiling briefly at her.

"She's so very at peace right now, Gaius," she whispered in awe. "More than I have seen her at any other time this week. I look at her as my friend and sister, yet I know how fragile she still is." She paused and watched Alex lightly breathe in and out. "I'm glad she came to meet you finally. Please, go easy on her," she pleaded for her friend's sake.

"I have no intention of hurting her, Sabina," he responded quietly. "I want only what's best for her, whether that is me or Jackson. But, I am not going to let someone else pry her away from me without a fight," he qualified.

Sabina sat back in her chair and smiled knowingly at her friend. "Of that, I have no doubt, Gaius."

The group continued reading and talking in hushed tones until the hour grew late. Then as they began to take their leave, Gaius stood and bent over the sofa, lifting Alex in his arms. He settled her against his chest and inhaled her familiar scent. As he turned to leave with her, Sabina asked if he needed help getting Alex settled for the night, but he shook his head.

He carried Alexandria up to his room and placed her on the bed, taking off her shoes and pulling the covers up over her. He moved a chair over and once again connected with her hand, settling back for restful slumber.

"Goodnight, Alexandria," he whispered.

And in her sleep she whispered back, "Goodnight, Gaius."

He looked over at her, surprised by her words. Gaius then closed his eyes, falling to sleep with a contented smile on his face.

26

Alexandria felt so at peace, so calm. She looked to see where she was and she was atop the cliff once more. She was alone this time though, no Kronis, no one as far as the eye could see. She sat and crossed her legs, taking in deep breaths of the salty air. She remembered the feel of Kronis' aura meeting her own, and she felt the sorrow and pain attached to the darkness on display. He was fighting against her so hard, but drop by drop she was rolling the darkness back.

The feeling gave her an idea that had yet to occur to her. Perhaps she could seek out Kronis, not in Arianna's lake of memories, but in the here and now. She might stand a better chance of getting to him before he hurt her or the ones she loved the most.

She stayed in her meditative pose and began to let her aura flow out in waves as big as she could build them, and then she cast them into the currents of wind that flowed high overhead. She imagined her aura swirling away like the sky in van Gogh's painting *The Starry Night*, twisting and spreading across the land. She had to breathe deeply and focus, because the effort was taking so much of her strength.

She sat like that, generating wave after wave, until she felt a faint prickle of the acidity she now knew to look for. She let her mind follow the currents, and over valleys, rivers, and mountains she soared. The world rushed by at such a pace and then her consciousness began to slow. The terrain became more familiar. Trees and pastures, gardens and a terrace came into view.

Terror such as she had never thought possible seized her, as she beheld Aeoferth Hall come plainly into her view. It was dark, and night was upon the castle. Everyone inside was a part of her now, someone she cared about. And Jack, she thought with alarm. He could not stand the attack of another dark *Nephilim*, that she knew with all certainty.

She knew she had to warn them, had to save them all somehow. Alexandria looked within herself and offered the one thing that she had which they would all recognize. She sent out a substantial burst of her aura and willed it to spill into the windows, chimneys, and crevices. Alex could feel it diving, churning, and twisting around Aeoferth as it found its way into the mammoth structure, and she pushed it forward so that it touched the hearts, minds, and souls of the immortals within.

"Wake up!" she screamed. "Please, wake up my friends. Kronis is coming!"

Alex felt Gaius' hold on her, and heard him calling to her mind, so she began to struggle to return to where she knew him to be. She begged her aura to retreat into her body on the cliff top, and then implored her eyes to open. Her heart and soul knew that they all had to hurry back to Aeoferth, and she fought with everything she had to reseat her aura within her physical body once more. When she finally managed to force her eyelids open and see him, he was holding her up and rubbing her hair back from her eyes, sending his own aura flowing over her to heal and restore her.

"Gaius," she breathed, "we have to hurry! Kronis is coming to Aeoferth, I felt him. Please," she pleaded.

"Yes, Alex, I saw what you saw. Somehow you sent the message out to us all. You are burning up though," he said, looking at her with great concern.

"I don't care! We have to go, now!" she declared, and started to struggle in an effort to stand.

Gaius lifted her swiftly off of the bed and carried her back to her room, straight into the watercloset. He told her to freshen up, that they would be leaving in minutes. Dashing out of the room, he called out orders to the others who were already up because of Alex's warning.

Alex took care of her basic needs, and then ran to get her phone. She was just coming out of her room, when Gaius met her in the hall carrying two large swords in their scabbards and a duffle bag. He grabbed her with his free hand around her legs and once he had lifted her, he began to run down the stairs. All Alex could do was hold on to his shoulders tightly, and hope that he did not drop her. He sprinted out of the house and into the helicopter, which Heath had ready to go.

Once Alex and Gaius were aboard, John closed the door and they lifted off, banking hard and away from Elysium. Alex sat and took her mobile out, then called Jack. He answered on the second ring.

"Jack, please tell me you all heard my SOS, and everyone is getting ready?" breathed Alexandria.

"We did, Alex. I don't know how you did it, but even I and the horses heard you. We're manning all battle stations now, and believe me, they've got this place covered. How are you after that?" he asked.

"I'm good," she said, aware that several pairs of eyes were looking keenly at her. "Jack, you listen to me. I am not there, so there's no need for you to play hero. Just hang back and do what Rohan tells you to do, do you understand?" she pleaded with him.

"I'm not going to do anything foolish, Alex, stop worrying about me. Why do I hear what sounds like a helicopter in the background?" he asked slowly.

"We're on our way," she replied, a little too quickly.

"Oh, no you're not, Alexandria. You get back to Elysium, right now! Put John on the phone!" he shouted, but Alex ignored him.

"You're breaking up, Jack. We must be going through a bad patch, I can't hear you," she lied and ended the connection, sitting back in her seat and trying not to shake. The mobile began to vibrate almost immediately, but she just canceled the incoming call and ignored it.

John moved over to sit opposite her, and put his hand across her forehead. She watched as he took her wrist between his fingers and checked her pulse. He looked at her with concern clearly painted on his features, but she tried to shrug off his worry.

"I'm good, John, really I am. Just let me go to the restroom," and she rose, not looking at anyone, then quickly made her way to the back of the helicopter.

She stood in front of the mirror and felt herself still shaking. She was pale and had sweat beaded across her brow. Alex found a cloth in a cabinet under the sink, and wet it with cool water. She turned and leaned against the small vanity, and began to wipe her head and neck gently.

And then she tasted metal at the back of her throat and knew what to expect. She quickly got tissue and balled two tiny pieces up, and then stuffed them up her nostrils to stop the blood from running out. She held her head back, pinching the bridge of her nose tightly. Alex heard Sabina knock and call to her to see if she was alright.

"I'll be right there, Sabina. Just a few moments, please," she said, trying not to sound nasally. She heard Sabina retreat from the door, and she continued to pinch her nose. Finally, she replaced the tissue with another dry set, and flushed the first. She made her way out of the bathroom and sat back in her seat.

John looked her over, and pursed his lips. He extended his hand and she cautiously placed her palm in his. He sent his healing aura to her and she began to feel her fever lessen, and her nose stop its flow. She quietly voiced her thanks and he smiled back, then looked over her shoulder and nodded to Gaius. John stood and the two swapped places. Gaius took her hand in his and sent her his energy as well, but with much more of a surge.

She tried to pull back, afraid that he would need all of his strength for the coming battle, but he clamped down hard and slowly shook his head at her. She gave up her struggle and allowed him to share his power with her.

Heath was pushing the S-92 for all it was worth, and they were rapidly gaining on the castle. As the first rocks and small mountains came into view that signaled their approach, Alex could feel every one of the *Nephilim*'s auras begin to increase in size and strength. The angels within were becoming more dominant, and it was overwhelming in the confines of the small cabin.

Alex leaned over, and looked out of the window closest to her seat. She saw that the castle was lit up from every corner and crevice, and shown like its own city below. She could not tell if the battle had begun yet or not, but she was praying that she was ready for what was about to transpire before her. No matter what was coming though, she knew within her heart and soul she was ready to stop those she loved from being harmed.

Heath swung the helicopter downward quickly to the ground, and there was a noticeable bump when they touched down. It was not one of his usual smooth landings. As they all rose from their seats, John paused and sent his aura out searching for danger. When he felt their passage was safe, he released the door and steps, then turned to beckon them forward.

They all disembarked rapidly, and Gaius kept one hand on Alex as they ran for the cover of the castle. Rohan, Iain, and Elrick met them mid-lawn and ran the rest of the way in with them. Once inside, Gaius released Alex's hand long enough to step forward and embrace his friends with a quick slap on the back.

Alex turned and saw Jack approaching, and she ran to him. He lifted her off the ground and hugged her tightly. When he set her back on her feet, he grabbed both sides of her face with his hands and looked into her eyes.

"What are you doing here? You have no business coming back to Aeoferth, Alex! What are you thinking?" he shook his head at her, exasperation lining his brow.

"I have to be here, Jack. I can't let them all get hurt," she pleaded with him to see it from her perspective, but she should have known his training would kick in and he would try to put her out of harm's way.

But she had every intention of helping.

"No, you're going to let them do what they do best and you are going to sit this one out, do you hear me?" he stated, rather than asked, and moved his hands down to hold her arms.

"Jack, you can't ask me not to help. Please, don't demand this of me," she whispered.

"Yes, he can, and he should," said Gaius, coming up behind her. He offered Jack his hand, and Jack released Alexandria to reciprocate. "I am Gaius. Nice to meet you, Jack. I've only heard good things about you," he stated.

"Same here," responded Jack. "How do we handle this?" he asked Gaius, getting straight to the point.

Gaius smiled in appreciation of Jack's direct approach. "One moment at a time," he replied steadily.

Alex rolled her eyes, knowing what they were referring to, and they both looked down at her and smiled at her impatient look.

Gaius looked back to Jack, and said, "Right now, let's both keep her safe."

"Sounds like a good plan," answered Jack.

Rohan stepped forward and told them that everyone had gathered in the dining hall when they heard the helicopter approaching for a war briefing. He gestured them all forward, and they made their way down the hall in that direction. Alex was keenly aware that she was walking with Gaius on one side and Jack on the other, but she said nothing and touched neither of them.

The thought of a battle coming there made her feel nauseous, but she willed her aura to still her shaking knees. She looked up at Jack and he mouthed, "Courage," to her, helping her to fortify herself for what was unfolding before her.

Rohan called everyone together from their smaller groups and individual conversations. He welcomed the party of six back and asked Alex to tell them what had led to her signal. She recounted her dream and told them how she was learning to track Kronis through the memory of the contact between Arianna's aura with his. She had felt it all around the castle and knew that they were in danger.

She had sent as much of her aura as she could, calling out a warning, hoping that it would reach them, and she told them how grateful she was that they were all okay. After that, Rohan simply nodded and began to go over the different stations each *Nephilim* would take based on their strengths, powers, and past successes in battles with the children of the Fallen.

One by one, they left the dining hall, most hugging Alexandria and thanking her for buying them time to be ready, until it was just she, Rohan, Gaius, and Jack. She looked expectantly at Rohan, willing him to bypass Jack and Gaius and give her something to do.

He took one look at her face and shook his head at her. "Oh, no you don't," he scolded. "Don't you give me that look. You're staying inside with Jack. That's final, Alex, no negotiating." He nodded at her as if that should close the discussion, but she turned and started to leave the three of them standing there together.

She had made it to the door, so surprised were they that she dared to leave, but Gaius ran and caught her, lifting her off of her feet.

"Be still," he said in her ear, firmly enough that she took note.

She stopped wiggling to get free and shook her head at him. "Please, Gaius, you of all people know what I can do, what I'm capable of. Let me help. He's coming for me, and I don't want him cutting through all of you to find me." She searched his eyes, willing him to agree, but he shook his head slowly.

"Not this time, my love. Trust us; we've done this for so long, we can handle one more battle." He set her on her feet and called for Jack over his shoulder. Jack approached and looked down at her, in total solidarity with Gaius.

Gaius never took his eyes from Alex's when he spoke to Jack. "Take her to the library, Jack. Lock the door and keep her in there, no matter what you hear, until one of us comes for her. They can disguise their voices, so only if we give you a safeword."

He put his hand next to Alex's cheek. "What is a word that they would never know, but that means a great deal to you?"

She did not need time to think and said, "Dudley," almost immediately.

"Dudley, it is. I'll spread the word to the others." Gaius turned to Jack and clasped his forearm. "Protect her," he said firmly, and Jack nodded.

"With my life," he responded.

Gaius turned back and quickly kissed Alexandria, then left with Rohan headed towards the rear of the castle. Jack reached down and clasped her hand in his, and began to take her in the direction of the library without delay. As they were entering the grand room, Sabina ran up to Alex and handed her one of the swords Gaius had brought with them from Elysium.

"This is your sword, Alexandria. I pray you don't require it, but you need to be able to defend yourself and Jack." Alexandria nodded her thanks and the two embraced one another tightly, before Sabina turned and took flight.

Once Jack had locked the door, the two of them worked together to slide a heavy chest in front it. Neither thought the effort would do any great good, but Alex hoped that it might buy her a few seconds, with which she could save Jack. He took her hand in his and led her over to the familiar sofa, where they had sat together and she had slept before. He turned and brushed her hair back from her face, looking her over and checking her condition.

"You look like you have the flu, Alex," he said, voicing his concern.

"I think sending forth the amount of aura I generated, took a lot out of me. But John and Gaius tried to heal me on the flight over, so I feel better. Honestly," she qualified, hoping he believed her.

She looked away from him and picked up the sword that lay across her lap. She slowly withdrew it, and gasped aloud at the beauty contained within the plain leather scabbard which incased it. It, too, had the design of the Damascus steel blade she had practiced with, but she could feel that it had much more Inonya, the metal from their angelic fathers, forged within its folds.

The pattern gave off such an iridescent glow, that it was singing of its own accord without her aura yet connecting to it. Unadulterated power radiated from the sword. She looked at the hilt and found that is was pure Inonya, shining brightly like a star in its own right, acting as a conduit so that her aura had direct access to the blade. Alexandria realized she could fortify the weapon completely from her own power.

Alex silently thanked Ganymede for this gift, as she knew it had to come directly from him. She then began to offer up prayers for everyone there that night. She called them by their name and recognized them by their aura. Alex realized that Jack was slowly rubbing her back, trying to sooth her while she was lost in her own thoughts.

She opened her eyes, and looked into his clear, blue eyes staring back at her.

"Hi," she whispered.

"Hey," he said, softly back.

"Jack, I'm sorry…," but he would not let her finish.

He leaned down and kissed her briefly and tenderly, then whispered to her, "No apologizing, remember?" They both laughed quietly over his previous reprimand.

"Jack, if I can help from in here, I'm going to try. Please don't interfere," she said, staring earnestly into his eyes.

"Alexandria, you heard them. They said to stay out of it, completely. I think they meant mentally, too. Besides, you already look wiped, and I don't know if you can do anymore than you've already done. And believe me when I say, preventing an ambush is a very big help in any battle."

She kept looking at him, imploring him to see it from her perspective.

"Alex," he sighed, shaking his head, "you brave, sweet girl. What am I going to do with you? Try to be careful, okay?"

And it was all the permission she needed.

"Thank you, Jack. Oh, thank you," she said, reaching out and cupping his cheek. "You can help me. Keep one hand on me and keep me anchored to you, in this place. I think it will help me not drift too far off course." She let her left hand fall from his face and took his hand with it.

"Alex, at the first sign that this is hurting you, I'm calling Gaius. Do you understand?" He nodded at her slowly, until he received her nod in agreement.

Alexandria sat back and closed her eyes. She imagined that she was floating above the castle looking down, and set her mind free. She began to pour a blanket of her aura around the perimeter, so that the Fallen's children would have to pass through the barrier to get to her friends, hoping that would slow them down.

Then she began to register where each of her own *Nephilim* stood, awaiting the coming tide. She found Gaius with Rohan, Elrick, and Iain at the rear of the castle, and saw Sabina, John, and Archimedes together at the kitchen's entrance. Benen was on the roof with Ahadi, Daiki, Guymon, Weldon, Rawley, Paulus, and Tomoko, with not only their swords, but also with bows and arrows made with Inonya.

Nassor, Thomas, Tabor, Flynn, Braddock, Albion, and Abdalla were on horseback and riding out into the large lawn behind the castle, fanning out. Nikolaj led another contingent on horseback into the field nearest the library and lake. On an on she found them, one and all.

Finally, she began to search for Kronis' aura. She waited, tasting the air and willing him to find her, not another. She grew more and more frustrated as time dragged by. Had she misread something in her dream, she wondered. No, she could not doubt herself; she had to trust that her aura would never lead her astray. But rather than sense Kronis directly, a strong and pungent smell began to fill her nostrils.

The odor was heavy and pervasive, and it spoke of death and decay. It was enough to repel her and send her senses fleeing, but she pushed against it. Instinctually, Alex sat up straighter, holding her sword tightly in her right hand. She knew this vibration in the air trying to overwhelm her and her comrades, because she had felt it so many times before.

Alexandria's eyes flew open and she whispered, "They're here!"

Every one of the *Nephilim* of the Light heard Alex's declaration. They felt it roll over them and through them, steeling them for the onslaught. Gaius turned to go back inside, knowing what she was doing and desperate to stop her, but Rohan placed a hand on his arm and called him back to his position.

"We cannot let them get to her," he said, between clenched teeth. "Ganymede will be with her. Focus Gaius, and push them back with me, brother." He felt so miserable demanding that Gaius not return to her, but he had to hold the line.

Gaius stared into Rohan's eyes for a moment and finally nodded his head. He turned back to the encroaching enemy before him, now fueled by a furry such as he had not felt in over one hundred and twenty-one years. No one or nothing would ever get to her again, he vowed silently to himself. It became his mantra and it became his mission. He turned to the fields beyond and waited.

Nassor and Nikolaj's lines of *Nephilim* on their horses became the first to engage the enemy. The initial dark ones came across Alexandria's barrier slowly, pushing against the Light which burned and scorched their skin. Many charged it, hoping that the speed at which they passed through it would save them. But the Light was trying to stamp out the evil it felt, and they were all touched in some way. Those who had come on horseback, tried to use their mounts to scale the wall of Light, but they were still singed by it.

The first line came running and riding in, and Nikolaj and Nassor met them with speed and strength. Swords rang out in the night, that now looked like day, due to all of the castle's lights and the *Nephilim's* own internal Lights shining for all to see. Nassor and his stallion danced with a Fallen's child named Trodon, Alex noted, and Nassor was not in the frenzied panic his opponent was. Rather, he was meticulously meeting him strike for strike and wearing Trodon down rapidly. As he tired from his initial burst of anger and speed, Nassor pierced his heart and then cut it from his breast. Trodon fell from his mount, no longer a threat.

Alexandria was still sitting in the library with Jack, and he now had one arm around her back and held her left hand with his other. He tried desperately to anchor her as she had requested. Though her eyes were open, he knew she was watching the battle and not aware of him at all, yet still he held firmly to her.

Alex's attention turned to Nikolaj and his riders. They were keeping a line of dark immortals from getting to the library where she now sat. And they seemed so very determined to protect her. She watched as Nikolaj and Conleth rode together to intercept a very large dark immortal, whom she remembered as Pulmaeous. They took him on either side, as he had a sword in each hand that rivaled Rohan's longsword. He was incredibly strong and he was a formidable opponent for them both.

Finally, Conleth got in a solid cut across Pulmaeous' abdomen, causing him to look down in shock that someone had actually dared to touch him. Nikolaj used the moment to swing with all his might and took Pulmaeous' head in one fluid motion. But they did not have time to savor their victory as another two approached ready to strike.

Alex sent constant prayers for her friends' protection up, and pleaded to Ganymede and the other immortal fathers to stand with their children and fortify them against the darkness. She saw Benen and Ahadi call for volley after volley of arrows to rain down, cutting many from the approaching line. Their arrows, made of pure Inonya, sliced through the hearts and minds of at least fourteen invaders which Alex counted before her attention was directed elsewhere.

She pulled in a sharp gasp of breath as she witnessed Rohan, Gaius, Elrick, and Iain run at full speed against a line of six dark *Nephilim* that had made it past Nassor's riders. She was amazed at the dexterity and conviction with which they fought. It looked as if metal was moving so quickly through the air to her, that silver arcs were hanging in visible sight long after the sword had moved on to another position. Gaius sliced the head off of one and forced another to the ground, taking his heart and then his head as well.

As Alex watched them push back the horde, she also saw Thomas falter and he was soundly knocked from his stallion to the ground with enough momentum to delay him from immediately rising. She knew she could not send out a call to save him, because it would cause the others to pause, and such a distraction could cost them their lives. She began to frantically search for an answer, some way to save him.

Alexandria grew warm all over and she felt her sword growing hotter in her palm. There was one gift that she had, which the others had relied on in times past. One thing that she, and she alone, could share with them. Without consciously ordering her body to do so, she stood, holding her sword at her side, her eyes still open to the battle.

Jack went with her and stood behind her, wrapping his strong arms around her, trying to hold her to the present as much as he could. He leaned down and whispered into her ear, "I've got you Alex, and I'm not letting go. I'm right here. I know you are helping, but come back to me and to Gaius as soon as you can, baby." He kissed her ear and held on for dear life, unable to do anything more.

Alex stepped quickly ahead in time and saw what was to come. She saw all of the dark rays in the field of battle and knew them by name, and knew their positions. She saw her beacons of Light scattered and locked, each one of them, in their own deadly struggles. She attached her aura on to her loved ones' auras, and began to send them the images she was getting of their opponents' next moves.

They had every advantage now, and they seized it. They looked through her eyes and began to cut down the enemy decisively. Braddock and Flynn moved to intercept a rider who was rapidly approaching, and stopped him before he could trample and then kill Thomas. Rohan moved in on one named Zimphadi, who actually laughed until Rohan closed his eyes and began to swing his longsword.

Alex saw Sabina, Archimedes, and John fighting with three who had gotten so close to the castle's kitchen entrance. Sabina was a marvel to behold as she used Alex's sight to take the vital organs from one so much larger than she, and then stepped in next to help Archimedes. Alex poured her love out to them all, willing them to come back to her unharmed.

She began to stretch what little corner of her own mind she could still hold to, in search of Kronis. He was nowhere to be found on the battlefield. She had felt him in her dream, so she knew he had orchestrated the battle encircling the castle. Where was he hiding, she asked herself in frustration. As her weakening aura searched, she felt the faint acidity on her tongue she had come to associate with Kronis' aura. Her consciousness turned to find him standing on the opposite shore of the lake.

She moved to meet him, her aura to his. But Alex kept this hidden from the others, so that they would not move to intercept him. He was hers.

Alexandria imagined that her aura could solidify and she could actually stand in front of Kronis. When suddenly she appeared at his side, he visibly jumped and gaped at her, bewildered. His eyes narrowed as he realized it was a specter of her, not actually Alexandria before him.

"Not the most effective way to challenge me Arianna, or should I say, Alexandria?" he questioned, sounding deceptively calm and amused. She detected a slight edge of nervousness in his tone, however. So he was not so confident after all, she discovered.

"Why have you come, to have so many of yours cut down? You know you cannot win against us. It is a battle that will always end the same way. Good shall overcome evil, Kronis," she said solemnly.

He laughed the same bitter laugh she had heard from him on the cliff.

"You always have all the answers, don't you? Well, not this time!" he yelled into her face. "*How* have you come back? I saw you destroyed!" He looked her over in bewilderment.

And rather than meet him with hatred and venom in return, Alexandria felt a shift. She truly felt what Arianna had so long ago. He was striking out, but his response was that of an abused child, rebelling against a love he did not know how to process or think himself worthy of. It gave her pause.

"Yes, I am here. This should show you what the Lord is capable of, Kronis. He healed me and returned me from the damage you inflicted, and you can still have His love, too. I know you still struggle, and I can help shelter your spirit if you will only let me. Please, don't turn away this time," she pleaded.

"Stop!" he screamed, putting his hands over his ears and trying to block out her voice. "Just, stop! I cannot take it anymore! Do you know what you've done to me? You made me feel, damn you! And I felt it all, too. Every life, every soul I ever did damage to. If there were demons in me before, it was nothing compared to now." He closed his eyes, and then opened them to look at her with pure, unadulterated torment and fury.

"I will end this, once and for all," he vowed, lethally. He looked to the battle beyond the water, realizing that the night was lost to him. He shook his head slowly in disgust, and then turned his haunted eyes back to her.

"You may try, Alexandria, to bring me into the fold, but I cannot and will not follow you. I am not one of your sheep, and you are not my shepherd," he spat, through gritted teeth.

Alex actually found she smiled at his choice of words, and she angled her aura's head at him before she spoke.

"No, Kronis, I am not your shepherd. The Lord Jesus Christ is your shepherd, and you would do well to follow Him." She let her words sink in as he stood gaping into her beautiful face, radiating love and sincerity directly at him.

He screamed and brought his sword up, slicing with all his might into her aura, and she felt herself dissipate right before his eyes.

Alexandria began to shake in Jack's arms. She lost her grip on the sword she held, and she lost control of her legs. He saw her collapse coming and lifted her up in his arms, then gently laid her on the sofa. Jack did not have to place his hand on her face to feel the incredible heat rolling off of her body. He realized whatever she had been doing had just caught up with her.

He knelt beside her and looked at her face, wishing he possessed an aura that could heal her and lead her back. Jack thought of what she had done for him when Aagon had attacked, and he leaned forward. He kissed her tenderly, but with all the love and hope he held for her in his heart.

When he lifted his head, she was still lost, and he whispered, "Come back, Alex. Come back as quickly as you can."

27

Every *Nephilim* of the Light felt the precise moment Alexandria left the field of battle. Gaius felt it so keenly, that he thought his knees would buckle. There were only a few demons left to dispatch and Alex's brethren made quick work of them. As one, Gaius, Rohan, Elrick, and Iain laid the last before them to rest and then turned, headed back into the castle.

Gaius did not bother with the safeword. His anguish gave him renewed strength and he burst through the library door, throwing the chest across the room as he entered. He was by Jack's side in an instant looking at her fevered body. He ran his hands through the air over her, looking for signs of life and aura.

"She's still with us, Gaius. But just barely, I think," breathed out Jack.

Gaius nodded at his words, then stood, gathering her up in his arms.

"Help me run a cold bath for her, Jackson," he asked, and Jack moved with him rapidly up the stairs to her room.

Jack ran into the watercloset and plugged the tub, filling it with cold water. Gaius sat on the seat by the large window, and began to take off her shoes, then her socks. When the tub was half full, he lifted her and placed her in. She shook a bit more from the tremors running through her body, but he knelt beside the tub and held her head up, so that she could breathe. Jack moved to the opposite side, ready if he was needed.

Gaius looked at him, and then nodded his thanks. Jack returned the gesture, and they moved their gaze to Alex's body.

"She still burns with fever," said Gaius, in anguish. "Jack, will you hold her head up for me? I am going to try to reduce her temperature."

Jack placed his arms in the chilly water and used his forearms and hands to support her head and neck. Gaius took both of her hands in his and closed his eyes. After several minutes, Jack began to actually smell a fragrance in the air. He knew that Gaius was using the full strength of his aura to connect with Alexandria, in the effort to heal her and bring her back to them. Jack wondered to himself, if his face held the same grief stricken look he saw on Gaius' countenance. He was sure that it did.

They stayed that way until Jack lost all feeling in his legs. Sabina, John, and Ahadi came in, and began to employ their auras also. Eventually, Archimedes, Rohan, Iain, Elrick, and E-We squeezed their way into the now crowded space, and began to work towards her healing as well. Jack was so touched by their love and devotion, that he had to close his eyes and bow his head for a moment.

"We must take her from the water now, Gaius," said Sabina softly. "Please, let us," she implored. When he lifted his eyes to hers they were red and haunted. "Please?" she asked gently again, and he finally nodded. Rohan helped him to his feet, and Iain stepped forward to help Jack up. A silent understanding passed between the men and the women, and all of the men left the watercloset together.

Sabina, Ahadi, and E-We moved forward and lifted Alexandria gently from the now frigid water. Ahadi held her while E-We and Sabina removed her sodden clothes and wrapped her in the robe that was still hanging on its hook by the shower. E-We dried Alex's hair with a towel and ran her fingers through it, willing the air to move and dry it further.

Sabina moved forward and opened the door, as Ahadi carried Alex through and over to the bed. Archimedes and John had already turned down the sheets to prepare it for her. Rohan, Elrick, and Iain had started a fire while Gaius and Jack stood numbly, trying to think and feel their way through.

As soon as Ahadi and E-We had her settled, they turned and looked to Sabina who took the lead.

"My friends, Alexandria is not lost to us, only overly taxed," she said, with unmistakable confidence in her voice. "We are all covered in the gore of battle. Ahadi, E-We, and I will stay with her while you all go and bathe yourselves, then you may take over the watch."

Gaius started forward, but she stopped him by holding up her hands.

"Go, Gaius, and make yourself clean. When she wakes, and she will wake, she doesn't need to see you like that. Go," she ordered him. He turned and stalked from the room, saying nothing to her command. Everyone filed out except for Jack.

Sabina turned towards him next. "Jack, go next door and put on dry clothes. You are soaked through from Alex's cold bath. Go, so that we can put her into a sleeping gown. We will let you back in when we are finished," she nodded her encouragement to get him moving. He walked out as well, and the ladies began to change Alex into clothing and tuck her into the bed.

Ahadi stepped into the hall to find Jack already changed and leaning against the door to his bedroom. She walked over and placed a hand on his shoulder.

"She will be well, my friend. Have faith," she smiled encouragingly, and he smiled slightly back. "You may go in now, she's dressed."

Ahadi walked away down the hallway, and Jack slowly entered Alex's room. E-We and Sabina were both beside her sharing their auras with her. Sabina looked back over her shoulder and smiled at him.

"Jack, come and sit on the other side of the bed. You can keep watch from there," she motioned him forward.

He walked over and picked up a chair, putting it as close to the bed as he could. But even there, Jack still felt too far away. Gaius followed closely behind Jack, and he came in looking freshly showered and changed, no more blood splattered across his skin or clothing. E-We looked at him tenderly and inclined her head at Sabina, then took her leave.

Gaius came to look down at her and nodded in Jack's direction, acknowledging him.

"I will go wash the blood away now too, Gaius. I'll be back with food for you both when I return," she said, and smiled tentatively before turning and leaving them with Alexandria.

Gaius moved forward and lifted what Jack knew to be a very heavy chair, and placed it where the women had just stood. He took Alex's hands in his and began to pass his aura along to her once again, trying to restore her, to mend her.

He finally looked up at Jack and said, "Thank you, for being with her once again. For trying to keep her safe."

"I'm not sure how much good I did, Gaius. She was so engaged in what you were all struggling through, I could only hold onto her and try to keep her anchored to something real and tangible," Jack breathed out, still filled with regret that he could not have done more.

"And that may have made all the difference, friend," said Gaius.

They remained silent for some time and both took turns eating while the other held Alex's hands; Jack for support, Gaius for healing and restoration.

Early in the morning, just as dawn was peeking through the windows, Jack spoke again.

"Gaius, I can only imagine what it would be like to have Alexandria as my wife, but you do know. You've loved and lost her, and I'm sure you don't want to lose her again. I don't want to come between the two of you, so say the word, and I'll take my leave," he said, in as even a tone as he could manage around the emotion behind his words.

Gaius looked into Jack's eyes and smiled sadly, then began to shake his head.

"No, my friend, but thank you for your words. If Alexandria wakes to find you gone, she would truly hold it against me. No, whether I find comfort in this situation or not, we are both in her life for a reason. She will choose her path, and the one she wants to share it with."

"But know this," Gaius added, "I truly believe she is mine. I have been her husband for almost two thousand years, and I will not give her up so easily. I never want to be parted from her again," he said, conviction and determination resounding in his voice and in his words.

"I understand, Gaius. I do," said Jack, looking back over at Alex who still slumbered, and who still looked too pale.

Alexandria was walking through a library, her bare feet striking the cool stone tiles softly. She could feel the heat on her skin from the hot Egyptian air, but the roof soaring over her head provided some relief. She slowed as she passed a small reflecting pool, which sat in center of the room she found herself in. She ran her fingers through the cool water, savoring the temperature and the texture.

Her sheer, white linen dress was perfect for such a climate, but she wished she could peel it off and get into the water to take some of the heat away. She looked around, and beheld many men with shaved heads. Each wore a linen wrap shendyt and they moved from shelf to shelf, some replacing scrolls, others removing them. She observed two men discussing the contents of a particularly large scroll they had placed on a table before them, using smooth stones to hold down its corners and edges.

"Ah," she thought to herself, "I know where I am." Alex felt her smile grow as she took in all that was before her.

"The great Library of Alexandria," said Ganymede reverently, as he came to stand by her side. He gazed out with her at the vast repository of knowledge that seemed to go on forever. "It was never really lost, you know. All this was once, and so it still remains. Humankind will never forget this place."

"Yes," she said. "I see."

She put one arm out and encircled Ganymede's waist. He, in turn, put an arm around her shoulders and squeezed her into his side. They stood together like that, holding on to each other and watching as the scribes and priests moved from shelf to shelf, until she pulled back and looked up into his eyes. They were bright, and shining with his love and pride.

"I am so proud of you, my daughter. You did well for your friends. They suffered no losses because of your bravery."

"I tried Ganymede, but I don't think it was enough. When I cast my aura out and use my mind in other capacities at the same time, it becomes too much and I feel stretched too thin. Shall I get better in time, you think?" she asked him.

"I think that you may become more at one with your powers, and thus, become skilled as you once were. You will be able to control more than one ability at the same time, and thereby protect more innocents." He looked down at her with concern etched across his forehead.

"Have you decided what you will choose, my child, for your future? Will you remain mortal or will you return to immortality?" he asked her gently.

"I have yet to decide, Ganymede. I've learned so much this past week," she laughed aloud at that thought. "Goodness, I can't believe it's been just a little over a week for me! I am truly beginning to see what good I might affect, but I need to learn more about the service that will be required of me, and what I will be sacrificing if I tell you, yes. Can I have just a bit more time, please?" she asked quietly.

He turned to look into her eyes, and answered her question truthfully. "Yes, Alexandria, you may have more time, but not as much as I would like to give you, my child. Time is drawing short for you, and you will have to give your answer sooner than you may like. It is the way it must be, though."

"You, my daughter, are like this great library you were named after," he said, extending his arm and gesturing to all the knowledge contained within its walls. "There is so much more to what you can accomplish if you agree to spend the ages here guarding and protecting, as these priests do with the scrolls. These parchments are like their children, their treasures. So, too, would humankind be to you. Think carefully in the days ahead and be ready with your answer when next I ask."

"I understand Ganymede, I do." Alex took a few more moments to look back at the never-ending documents displayed throughout the Library, while she considered what he was telling her.

"I thank you, for helping me save my friends. I felt myself falter several times, but you continued to channel your power through me. I only wish I could have reached Kronis more," she said quietly, sighing with regret.

"Daughter, I think you have done more for him than anyone had ever dared or dreamed possible. You gave him yet another opportunity, I know, and the Lord is well pleased. Do not doubt your gift to see what others cannot. Love knows no bounds, as you have once again proved."

She smiled, but raised a hand to her head to wipe the sweat off of her brow.

"I'm sorry, Ganymede. I am so very hot," she said, looking around for water to quench her thirst.

"You have expended much to save the other immortal children, Alexandria. Come, let me cool your fever and restore you. You must rest for the next few days before you attempt to use your abilities again," he said to her, searching her eyes with his.

He placed his hands on her temples and smoothed her hair back from her face. She felt a cool wind lift her hair, then what felt like crisp, healing water cascading from her head down and throughout her body. She felt Ganymede kiss her forehead, then she felt very drowsy and succumbed to sleep.

Alex felt cool, finally. She sensed sheets around her, so she thought herself to be in bed. She tried to open her eyes, but they would not cooperate. After much effort, she was able to pry one open and was surprised by what was before her. She opened both eyes then, and fully took in the scene. Jack was kicked back in a chair with his feet propped up on the bed to her right, and Gaius was in a chair to her left. Gaius' head was lying over on the covers, and his palms were encircling her left hand.

She did not want to disturb their sleep, so she lay there just watching the two. How had she ever become so blessed, so quickly, to have not just one, but two dear friends who would risk so much for her safety and well-being, Alex asked herself. Perhaps, she mused, because she was willing to risk just that much and more for them as well. She would do anything for those she loved.

She saw Jack shift a little, and his eyes lifted to see her staring at him. He smiled broadly and put a finger to his lips, pointing then at Gaius. She nodded and stretched out her right hand to him, and he gladly took it in his. He squeezed it, and mouthed "Welcome, back," to her.

"Thank you," she replied silently, as well. He winked at her and slowly got up and made his way over to the door. Jack looked back at her and smiled again, then left, closing the door silently behind him. It was just enough sound though to rouse Gaius.

His head came up quickly, and he looked first at the door then at Alex and saw that she was awake. His eyes became moist as he brought her hand to his lips.

"Alexandria," he whispered in quiet reverence.

"I'm here, Gaius. I'm here," she said, lifting her hand from his embrace to run her fingers through his hair. It was as silky as she remembered. He closed his eyes in silent surrender to her touch, and inhaled deeply. He slowly stood and came to sit beside her on the edge of the bed, leaning over her and bracing his weight on either side of her with his long arms. His eyes roamed over her face for a few moments before he spoke.

"What you attempted saved many, Alex, but it also cost you dearly. You must take more care, if not for me or yourself, then for all the others who love you. Still, I am very proud of you," he said, smiling. "Though I wanted to tear the doors down and come stop you, Rohan convinced me to stay and fight. You saved us all, my love."

She shrugged, embarrassed by his praise. "I saw you fighting, Gaius. I was so afraid for you, so afraid to lose you," she whispered, and his eyes widened a fraction at her comment.

"So there is hope for us yet, then?" he teased, and angled his head to the side.

"Of course there is," she laughed. "You look so young when you smile like that. Gaius, how old are you?" she asked quietly.

"You know that I am almost two thousand years old, but I stopped aging at about twenty-nine human years, as they measure the calendar now. Why?" he pressed for her thoughts.

Alex just shook her head, and he leaned closer to her, his lips hovering just over hers. "Why, Alexandria?" he breathed against her skin.

"Just curious, what my mother might think when she meets you," she giggled.

"I love that sound, Alex, the sound of your laughter. I am so glad you are here," he said, leaning in to touch his lips to hers.

400

It was an undemanding kiss. One that spoke of his adoration, but also his desire to not excite her, only sooth her. When he pulled back he smiled tenderly at her and moved a hand to trail it down her face. He gently caressed her skin and made her sigh, as his aura danced across the path his fingers traversed.

Finally, he paused and asked, "Alex, do you want to try to get up?"

She thought about her body's needs and agreed.

Gaius stood again and put his arms under her knees and back, then lifted her, taking her into the watercloset. He put her on the same bench where he sat holding her the night before, when he had removed her shoes and socks. He placed one finger under her chin and lifted it, so that she would look into his eyes.

"Alexandria, I am going to be right outside if you need me. If you feel faint or ill, call out and I will be right back in here by your side. Do not worry about modesty. There was a time when I cared for your body, as well as your heart and soul. Understand?" he said gently.

Her eyes grew large, but she replied, "I do. Thank you, Gaius."

He kissed her on the forehead, then turned and left her alone.

Alex stood and realized just how weak she really was. Jack's diagnosis, the night before, seemed appropriate now. She really did feel as if she were recovering from the flu.

She moved slowly and took care of her most immediate needs, then remembered that she still had tissue in her nostrils from the helicopter ride over. Alex removed each tiny ball, and flushed all evidence of them away. Then she glanced at herself in the mirror. She decided that a shower was called for and she got into the warm water, letting the seat support her while she bathed.

She tried not to remember the blood she had seen in the shower after Aagon attacked Jack, and the blood she had witnessed during the night as her friends fought their enemies. It was too much, and she closed her eyes against the mental images.

When she was finished, she stood and left the shower, reaching for her robe and thankfully found it on its hook. She chastised herself for not checking before. Alex found her legs were really beginning to shake by then, so she sat hard on the bench and tried to bring the room back into focus.

Feeling herself close to tipping over the edge, she called out to Gaius. He was there before she could finish his name. He came over and took one look at her, then lifted her, and headed back towards the bed. Sabina was there, as well as John. Gaius propped Alexandria up atop the bed, and began to place a few extra pillows around her in order to better support her. Sabina gently touched Alex's arm, and then handed her a glass of fresh orange juice to begin the process of nourishing her still weak body.

Alex tried to pull her robe around her, and she looked at John hoping for answers.

"John, why am I so weak?" she asked. "I feel like I've been very ill."

"Alex, you generated an incredible amount of mental and aura offense last night. Your muscles and body are reacting to the strain. You must take it slowly for the next few days, okay?" he asked expectantly.

"Yes, that is what Ganymede told me to do," Alex said, and snared an immediate response from Gaius.

"When was he with you, Alexandria? Last night?" he asked.

"I certainly felt him with me throughout last night's battle, especially when I found Kronis. But he was with me while I slept, and helped me to return," Alex answered, noting the looks of shock and dismay on their faces.

"You faced Kronis last night? How Alex, and where?" whispered Gaius, his expression unreadable.

"Don't be angry with me. I found his aura while I was giving you all access to their future plans. He was on the other side of the lake, standing back and watching everyone else fight for him," Alex said, shaking her head. "I just basically imagined my aura coalescing in front of him and I was able to talk to him. Is that not something I have ever done before?" she asked them all.

Gaius closed his eyes and sat back beside her on the bed. She looked around at their expressions and finally made eye contact with Sabina.

"No, Alex, it is not something you have ever done before to my knowledge," she answered. Sabina looked to the others, and then said, "I think we should all hear the details of last night from your perspective, Alexandria. If I helped you to dress, would you feel like coming downstairs to sit in the library, so that we may all talk?"

"No, Sabina. She doesn't need to be downstairs. She needs to stay right where she is," said Gaius, trying to quell her idea.

Alex thought she saw a way around the stalemate forming between the two, and took the matter into her own hands.

"Gaius," she said, touching his hand to draw his attention back to her. "I am hungry. Why don't I let Sabina assist me as I put some clothing on, and then you can help me downstairs to the kitchen. I'll eat something first to give me some strength and stamina, and then I can sit beside you all and tell you what happened. Will that work?" she patted his hand, hoping to gain his cooperation.

He gave her an exasperated look, then said, "You let one of us carry you, alright? No walking, running, or anything too strenuous. Understand?" he pressed.

Alex could not help but laugh at him just a bit, though she was trying so hard to take him seriously. Her laughter was infectious, and Sabina and John started to chuckle as well. Finally, Gaius gave up the struggle to maintain a straight face. He hung his head in defeat and softly laughed along with the three.

He peered up at her and shook his head in mock reprimand.

"Oh, Alexandria! You are just as bossy as you ever were," he said playfully. He stood and kissed her quickly, but firmly and headed out of the bedroom. John took his leave next, and Sabina began to help Alex dress in clothes she had brought upstairs from her own closet.

Alexandria was grateful that Sabina did not seem embarrassed by her immodesty, and it made it easier for Alex to disrobe in front of her.

"They stayed with you the whole night, Alexandria, both Jack and Gaius," said Sabina, as she was helping Alex into her undergarments.

"I know. I woke and found them both here, one on either side of me. What am I going to do, Sabina? I have feelings for them both, and I do not want to hurt either of them," said Alex, sounding so forlorn.

Sabina told Alexandria how they had worked together to place her in the cold bath, and how the others had helped to care for her body when she could not. Alex was deeply humbled and moved by the attention and concern they had shown her. Sabina concluded by telling Alex how Jack and Gaius had returned and taken over the watch, and how she felt the two had reached some type of accord.

"I have every faith that this will all work out as it should, Alex. Continue to follow you heart, and it won't lead you astray," said Sabina, straightening Alex's shirt for her.

"But what if my heart has affection for both, Sabina?" she pressed.

"Ah, Alex. The heart can love many different people in many different ways: mother, father, brother, sister, friend, husband, or wife. If you truly listen closely enough, you will eventually work out who is who in your heart, and you will follow it to happiness. I am sure. Now that you are dressed, let us do something with your hair," she said, helping Alex to stand and walk back into the watercloset so that she could assist her further.

"Thank you, dear friend," said Alexandria, looking at Sabina in the mirror while she took over the task of drying Alex's hair for her.

"No, it is we who are thankful, Alexandria. Thankful for your sacrifice last night, and your friendship today," Sabina replied, smiling at her friend and squeezing her shoulders.

They left the bedroom together and found Gaius waiting in the hall. Sabina just shook her head and went ahead down the stairs, as he lifted Alexandria and began down with her. She looked into his eyes, so blue and green, but still more blue that day than green. She smiled and held fast to his strong arms, as he took her into the kitchen and placed her on a stool.

As he straightened to retrieve a glass from a cabinet, Jack turned from the sink and came over, smiling, to sit on her left. He leaned into her and bumped her shoulder with his as he asked, "How ya feeling?"

"Like I have the flu," she smiled back at him, and they both chuckled. "How are you, Jack?"

"Never been better," he said, stretching his legs out in front of him. "The good guys won, and I saved the girl." And to that statement they both burst out laughing, causing others in the kitchen to laugh with them as well.

She shook her head, as Gaius walked back over and placed a tray of food in front of her. He lowered himself on a stool and took his place to her right. Alex let the two of them keep up the flow of conversation while she ate every morsel that was placed before her. She felt like she could eat another bowl of oatmeal, and Gaius, seeming to understand where her eyes were looking, got up and made her a second portion without comment.

After she had finished, she began to stand to clear her place, but both Gaius and Jack placed a hand on one of her shoulders. They gently pushed her back down on her stool. They were both shaking their heads, and she understood their silent message.

"Oh, good grief, you guys! I can walk on my own, I really can," she said, clearly frustrated with them both. She heard Rohan's laughter behind her.

"They giving you a hard time, Alex?" he asked. "Come here," he said, leaning down to lift her from her stool with such strength, that she grabbed his arms and yelped.

"Be careful with her," said Gaius in warning.

"Yeah, yeah," he replied, and started off with her in the direction of the library.

"You're calling me Alex, now," she said, looking Rohan in the eye. "I noticed when I left to meet Gaius."

"That's your name, isn't it?" he asked, walking her over to a large, leather chair in the library.

She swatted his arm and he pretended to drop her, so that she really had to hold on to him and she squealed with delight. They both laughed over his uncharacteristic play. She leaned up in his arms and hugged him.

"Thank you, Rohan," she whispered, and he turned gruff from her praise.

Slowly, they all came to the library and either found a seat or brought a chair in with them. Archimedes called everyone together. He asked that they all give Alexandria their attention, while she told them about her experience the night before.

Sabina stepped forward to avoid a tug-of-war between Jack and Gaius. She helped Alex to stand and guided her over to a desk, so that she had something to lean against. Alexandria told the immortals how she used her aura to build a fence around their perimeter, how she had tried to monitor their progress by locating their auras, and how when she saw one fall, she used her ability to see into the future to help them turn the tide decisively. All of this, she thought they knew.

Then she explained how she had focused a portion of her concentration and mind on Kronis' aura, and tried to locate him in the mêlée. She had finally found him on the shore of their lake, and she told them of her effort to solidify her aura and actually speak to him. She repeated their conversation, word for word, and told them how he struck out at her aura with his sword. Alex quietly related that it was that action which caused her to falter.

Finally, she told them that Ganymede had visited with her while she slept, and helped to restore her so that she might return. She did not mention that he had asked her if she was ready to transition, or her request for more time. Nor did she tell them that he had warned her, that her time was running out. Those thoughts she kept to herself for the moment.

"Alex, I don't know whether to think you are incredibly brave, or just plain crazy," said Elrick, coming over to hug her. "Girl, you've got some nerve, I'll give you that."

He patted her, then turned and leaned against the desk next to her. He stayed there while the group discussed Kronis' possible future plans, and one and all agreed that this felt like his attempt to test the waters to learn what Alexandria was capable of. Alex began to lean into Elrick's side and he put his arm around her, trying to hold her up.

Several members began to discuss plans to recall many more of their brethren from their stations around the globe and consolidate power. Strategies, and battle plans became the topic of discussion, and Alexandria felt her fatigue taking hold again. She leaned completely into Elrick and dozed off, still mostly sitting upright.

Elrick realized that she was no longer conscious, and continued his hold on her until Gaius came forward and took her in his arms. Upon returning to her room, he settled her into bed then brought his chair back to her side. Gaius extended his legs, then took her left hand in his right, and soon they were both napping together.

Much later, Jack came to the door and knocked softly. Hearing Gaius call him in, he entered and stated that he was just checking to see if either of them needed anything before he turned in for the night. Gaius feigned a need to step out for a while, and gave the watch over to Jack.

Alexandria did not know that they took turns keeping guard through the night, as she slept the remainder of her afternoon and evening away. When she woke the next morning, she felt much more refreshed and got out of bed before Gaius could stop her. She showered, and shooed him from her room while she changed into clothes that Sabina had brought in for her to borrow, since her luggage was still back at Elysium.

While she was getting ready, she made a decision about her immediate future which she needed to address. It was the one decision she could make and be completely at peace with, and it felt like the right time to do it.

She went to the bedside table and picked up her phone. She sent several messages, then made her way across the bedroom and opened the doors to her balcony. She stepped out and gazed across the estate, while the cold, winter wind played with her hair. Alex saw there were still some faint traces of red and pink in the snow, but that all other evidence of their struggle had been removed.

She closed her eyes, and tested the strength of her internal voice. She called to them, one and all, and asked that they meet her in the dining hall, as she had something of importance to tell them. She came back in then and closed the balcony's doors, locking them behind her.

Alex looked up to see Gaius coming back in her room, looking concerned. He walked over to stand in front of her, and took her arms in his hands.

"Alex, what is it? Are you alright?" he asked, studying her face and eyes.

"Yes, Gaius, I am much better," she replied, smiling up at him. "Don't worry so. I have made a decision, and I think you will find it to be good news. Come, walk with me downstairs."

Alexandria would not let him carry her, but they walked down together as all the *Nephilim* made their way to the dining hall to hear what she had to say.

28

Alexandria smiled and greeted each immortal as they came in, either with hugs or by shaking their hands. Jack entered the dining hall and stood by Rohan towards the back of the assembly, and she smiled at them both. She waited until she knew they were all with her before she began her remarks. When she was ready, she held up her hand to gain their attention.

A quiet descended over the hall and Alex began.

"My friends and family, I have asked you to gather here because I have made a decision, and I think you should all hear me together. You have all graciously welcomed me into this home and made me a part of who and what you are, with no reservations nor hesitations. You have begun to instruct me, cared for me when I could not care for myself, and placed my safety above your own."

"I have a human family who also loves me very much, and I have decided that it is time for me to bring them into the fold, so to speak. I will leave Aeoferth today and tell my family who I really am, and the choice which lies before me. They have raised me to be the person I am today, and being the loving, supporting people that they are, they deserve to hear the truth from me."

"Once I have been honest with them, I plan to return to Aeoferth Hall and continue to learn and grow with you, and help you find and defeat Kronis. I will only be gone for a day or two at the most. But if I am to consider an immortal life with you all, I must do so with my family's knowledge of where their daughter and sister is going, and what she is truly doing."

"I thank you all for the past week, and I look forward to many more when I return. Until then, my friends," she said warmly, and was astounded by the deafening applause that answered her heartfelt speech. They began to move now, hugging her once more, praising her decision to stay, and a few like Sabina, openly wept and touched her cheek or her hair.

As Alex was hugging Tabor, her eyes connected with Jack's. He was still leaning against the wall with Rohan looking relaxed. He nodded at her slowly and mouthed, "Courage," to her. She nodded her head in agreement. She would need lots of courage to see the coming weeks through, but she knew she could weather any storm now with the group before her.

She continued to speak with individuals, and looked over to see Gaius talking with Archimedes. He gave her a heart-stopping smile that made her grin in return. Once the gathering had dissipated somewhat, she moved forward and asked John, Archimedes, Heath, Sabina, Ahadi, Rohan, Jack, and Gaius to stay.

Alexandria addressed Heath first, and asked him if the helicopter was up for another run. He smiled, and assured her it was. She then asked the others if they would do her the honor of coming with her to talk with her parents, brothers, and Jameason. They all accepted her invitation, without hesitation.

"Good," she said smiling, "can we all be ready to leave in fifteen minutes?" If they were shocked, no one said anything, and at once they all left to prepare for the imminent departure. Alex reached out and grabbed Jack's hand as he started to leave, silently asking him to stay behind for a moment. Gaius smiled at her and left the room.

"Jack, I have a question to ask you, and I want to do it now before we have an audience again," she said, looking up into his face. "When we leave my parents' home, we'll be coming back to an active war zone. I intend to take over the security arrangements for my family; in fact, I plan on doubling or tripling the detail around them." His eyebrows rose at her statement.

"I know it sounds crazy, but I want Kronis' followers to think long and hard before they come after them, and I know at some point they're going to try. What I want to ask you, is do you want to come back with me, or stay with them?"

Jack smiled at her and lifted his hand so that it hovered over her cheek. She leaned into his palm and smiled back at him.

"I know what I'm asking is not fair, and it's not kind. But I still want you here, if you want to stay, Jack. I can't give you or Gaius more than that right now, but I know I need you both. What will you do, Jack?" she asked him, finding that she was holding her breath waiting for his reply.

"Alex, I can't say what the future holds either, but I know I trust my gut, always. And right now, my gut says I'm wherever you are. So if you're coming back here and want me around, I'm coming back, too," he said, and he leaned down and gently kissed her forehead.

"I'm so glad," she breathed out. "Go on and get your luggage. We're going to stay a day or two with my family, then come back to Aeoferth." He saluted her orders and chuckling softly, made his way upstairs.

Alexandria used the next few minutes to walk around the halls looking at all Aeoferth Hall had to offer. She hoped that someday it would be safe enough to bring her family there. Her father, Conner, and Jameason would probably never leave the library, and she smiled at the thought. She made her way outside to the helicopter as Heath was warming it up, and she turned her back to the snowstorm he was whipping up.

"Where is your coat?" asked Gaius, taking his off and putting it around her.

"Back at Elysium," she said. "All of my luggage is still there."

"Hmmm, that is an interesting dilemma, isn't it?" he chuckled. She shook her head at his teasing remark and entered the helicopter, taking a seat by a window. Within a few minutes the others were settled, and they lifted off.

The ride back was a quiet journey. Everyone seemed lost in their own thoughts, perhaps still sorting through the events of the last several days. Alex found that she was apprehensive about her parents' impending reaction when they learned that her abrupt departure with John to a retreat was but a ruse, and that it did not exist.

She hoped that their love would see them through this most unbelievable story. She had already decided that morning when she texted them, asking them to all meet her at the Manor, that she would show them her aura. If nothing else convinced them that what she said was true, then perhaps that would.

Alex was unaware that her leg had begun to nervously jump, until Gaius moved up to the seat beside her and placed his hand on her knee.

"What has you so anxious, Alex? I could feel it all the way in the back," he asked, looking down at her with concern.

"I'm just a little tense that's all. Everything is good, though," she said, smiling.

But he pursed his lips at her thinly veiled attempt to push her worries away. Gaius moved his palm off of her leg and took her hand in his, letting their auras begin to intertwine. Alex looked at the swirl of colors, then returned her gaze to meet his.

"Part of this connection lets me know when you're being truthful, you know," he smiled at her startled expression.

"Ah, you have forgotten. I see. Well, I can sense how you're feeling. I know if you are in danger, scared, or frightened. I also know when you are happy, feeling shy, or fulfilled. You do not have to be brave or give me false testimony, Alexandria. Always be truthful with me, as you have done so far. You will find that I can help you in ways you have not even considered yet," he said, smiling at her slow blush.

"Please, tell me what has you worried, Alex," he asked again.

She had to breathe slowly to think through the sensations his aura was sending into her hand and arm. But she managed to find her voice.

"I am worried that they will be hurt and disappointed that I didn't really tell them where I was going. I don't lie to my family, Gaius. In the past I have intentionally not told them things I've seen or experienced on purpose, to save them from being frightened of what I was going through. But I've never deliberately lied to them. This will be a hard confession for me," she said softly, hoping that none of the others could overhear her.

Gaius leaned in close, though he could hear her perfectly.

"I see. They may feel a bit shocked at first, but from what I have observed, your family is very strong. Your father and your mother will love you unconditionally, as it should be, and they will forgive you this one tale. We will make them see it together. All of us here today will help you, Alexandria," he nodded at her, to reassure her that she was not alone.

"Thank you, Gaius. I needed the pep talk."

"So tell me one thing," he said, playing with her fingers and intensifying the energy flow, "what do you think your mother will think of me?" He smiled slowly down at her, and she shook her head.

"I think Henry doesn't stand a chance anymore," she laughed softly.

"Good," he whispered, then kissed the back of her hand and released her fingers. Alex found that she actually missed the connection, because it was soothing her. But she put her hand in her lap, and did not reach out for his again.

When Heath landed at the airport in Oxford, Alex realized that she had forgotten to set up transportation to the Manor House. But she learned that Heath had taken care of it for her, and she voiced her thanks aloud for his care. There were three Land Rovers parked by the area where he had touched down, awaiting their arrival. An attendant from the field came forward to help them with their steps, and welcome them. The man was looking for the person in charge, and John stepped forward to assume the role, signing some paperwork and taking an envelope containing their keys.

Alex climbed into the second vehicle and rode with Sabina and Ahadi. John, Archimedes, and Heath took the lead in the first Rover, and Rohan, Jack, and Gaius took the rear in the third. As they made their way through the streets of Oxford, the ladies laughed that they had actually managed to get a testosterone free ride for once.

At last, they were pulling into the drive which led to her home, her true home. The pebbled lane crunched under their tires in an oh so familiar way, and it made Alex feel content. They gradually rolled to a stop and all began to climb out. Alex looked up, and saw her family already coming down the steps to greet them.

Wallace and Conner reached her first, both looking her over to make sure she was alright. Then Wallace had her up off the ground in a bear hug, that made her laugh without a care in the world. And for just a few precious moments, the demons were put to the side.

Conner smoothed her hair behind her ears, and then hugged her tightly as well. She moved forward, and her parents each had a turn holding her and welcoming her home. And then Jameason, who tried to act as though he was unaffected, hugged her as well and patted her back. She smiled up at them, grateful that if Arianna had chosen to be placed first with mortals this time around, that this was the family she got to spend her time with.

She remembered her manners then and began to make the introductions. Both her parents and Jameason gave pause to Archimedes' name, but said nothing. She saw Wallace and Conner sizing up Rohan and Gaius almost immediately. Alex was sure her brothers were trying to discern if one of them was a possible suitor, whom they would have to put the fear of God in. Everyone seemed impressed with Sabina's grace, and Ahadi's strong confidence. And as they had already met Jack, John, and Heath, they too were welcomed back.

Her parents had an early lunch prepared, so they led everyone on a brief tour of the Manor and then made their way to the dining room.

Wallace took Alex by the elbow and, not too subtly, led her over to a chair between himself and Conner. She sighed and gave him a knowing look.

Her mother led the conversation with ease and grace, trying to gently extract information from the assembly now seated around her dining table. Alex watched as one and all deftly avoided giving her a direct answer regarding any topic she brought up. The conversations kept going round and round until they had completed dessert, and still her mother had yet to learn anything of great importance.

Once it appeared all were finished, but politely waiting to be excused, Alexandria cleared her throat and asked her parents if they might all adjourn to the family den. She indicated there was some information she wanted to share with them, and that she really did not want to put it off any further. Alex asked if their guests could come along as well.

Her father nodded, concern growing in his eyes, but he stood and invited their visitors to follow him. He pointed out two bathrooms along the way, and Alex saw Jack and Rohan break off from the group and return with a few more chairs from her mother's music room.

As everyone filed in, Alex took a seat close to the sofa her parents sat on. Wallace and Conner pulled chairs up on either side of their parents, and Jameason came to sit nearby as well. Gaius moved and sat next to Alex on her right, and Jack placed himself directly across from her. Jack leaned forward, resting his arms on his legs, so that he looked like he could spring up at any movement. He nodded his head at her, and the word 'courage' came unbidden to her mind. She smiled at him, and then looked over at her family who were clearly nervous about Alex's unorthodox called meeting.

"Mother, Father, I have so much I want to share with you today. My last week has been unlike anything I have ever known, or could have ever imagined possible. I know that what I'm about to say will seem like a flight of fancy, or something from a fairy tale, but on my life, all I am going to tell you is true. Will you hear me out?" she asked, trying not to sound as nervous as she felt.

She felt Gaius' aura touch her back, and she was so very grateful for the added support.

"Alexandria," said her father, "you can tell us anything, and we will believe and support you. You are our daughter, and we love you. Tell us what's on your mind," he encouraged her.

She took a deep breath and began as best she could.

"When I was a child, I was very different, wasn't I? I saw and heard things that no child should. I knew details of things and people long since passed, and I could hear voices and repeat them in whatever language I heard during the vision."

Alex saw her mother's eyes look up in alarm at the assembled guests. They had never spoken of this outside of their tight family circle, and she did not know how to react to Alex speaking of it so plainly.

"It's alright, Mother," Alex encouraged her, "they know all about it."

"When I was eight, a guardian angel named Ganymede came to visit me and promised to take the voices away for a while, so that I might experience some peace in my childhood. I gladly accepted the offer and tried to tell you all that I had a grace period, essentially. My grace period ran out at Lord Lenley's ball," Alex said somberly.

"While I was there, you all thought that someone attacked me, but it was not a someone, more of a something. His name was Bertrand and Ganymede came and stopped him, and then healed my main injuries. I have learned that there are still beings once spoken of in Genesis called the

Nephilim who exist and live on this earth amongst humans." Alex paused and took in her family's shocked expressions, but she moved on.

"Some, like the ones you see in this room are the children of angels of the Lord, and others, like Bertrand, are children of the Fallen angels, those who were cast out. There is a struggle between the two groups that has gone on across the ages, and I have learned that I am one of them, reborn. I was the first, an immortal named Arianna, and she chose to come back as a mortal so that she would have the choice between a mortal existence and immortality in the service of humanity for the rest of her days."

"I am your child," she said, looking directly at her parents, "and your sister," looking to Wallace and Conner, "but I also am a great repository for everything she once was. I was offered the chance to go with the *Nephilim* and learn who and what I can be if I embrace this life, if I choose to be immortal. It is where I have been for the past week, and where I hope to return to continue to learn."

"Everything I am today, the person I have become, is because of your love and your care for me. I am sorry I did not tell you where I was really going, but I did not know the story then well enough to tell you all. I want to share my adventures with you, but to do that, I must first share this with you," and she stood, moving directly in front of her parents.

She asked Ganymede to be with her, and she began to will her aura to come out from behind the veil where it normally lies hidden from the view of humans. She saw her rainbow of colors begin to flow from her fingertips and then her pores opened up, so that she seemed a curtain of colors and Light. She began to let her aura move away from her and dip around the room, causing everyone it came near to smile. Alex finally willed it to return to her body, and she asked it to once again retreat behind the veil.

For what felt like an eternity to Alexandria, no one said anything or moved. Finally, her father and mother stood and looked openly at her. They were holding hands as if for support, or possibly just to touch something they knew to be real. Lord Errol reached his free hand out and cupped Alex's cheek, gently smoothing away tears that she did not even know were there.

"Alexandria, my beautiful, special girl. We knew when we brought you home from hospital that you were amazing, and over the years we've wondered what tale your life would finally tell us. Alex, the beauty and all the love you just shared, we felt it. I…," and finally at a loss for words, he looked to his wife.

Lady Juliana let go of her husband's hand and took Alexandria in her arms. The two embraced one other, and Alex could feel her mother's body shake as she cried silently. Wallace and Conner stood and came over as well, looking down at the two holding one another.

Finally, Alex's mother pulled back and held her daughter's arms as she studied her face.

"Alex," she said softly, "there are no words that I can give you to tell you what I'm feeling right now. Perhaps there is one though, from a mother to her child: love. I. Love. You. We *all* love you very much, Alexandria. And even if you hadn't shown us those lights, we would choose to believe you. I'm in awe of my own daughter," she whispered, looking up at her husband, and still crying softly.

Wallace moved to take his mother's place, and for once Alex found him speechless. Both he and Conner had tears in their eyes as well, and none of the three could speak. They moved in to hug one another and stood, the three of them in their own cocoon, holding on to the unwavering bond between them. For Alex, it was one of the most precious moments she had ever shared with her big brothers, these guardians of her childhood.

Wallace smoothed her hair and smiled, shaking his head slowly. His voice sounded strained when he said, "Do you remember what I told you the night you first mentioned Ganymede to me in Egypt? I said, 'I love you, Alexandria, all of you.' That still stands, for me, Conner, Mom and Dad. You have this in you, we see that. But we've known what's in you from the day you were born: strength, courage, honor, patience, and love. You have all those traits in abundance and more."

"That's right, sweetie," said Conner. "You don't have to prove anything to us. We love you and have faith in you, always. We are your family, and we've got your back in every way." He looked at Wallace and found his first laugh. "Oh, my word! Our sister is an angel, literally!" Both brothers started laughing then, and the assembly followed suit.

Someone cleared their voice quite loudly, and Alex's brothers stepped back to make way for Jameason, who was now working his way up to Alexandria. He shooed them back with his hands, and stood before her. He looked sternly at her, and she became very serious.

"I want to know one thing, Alexandria," he said. "Are you happy?"

She smiled a bright, infectious smile, and nodded slowly at the man she loved like a grandfather.

"Yes, Jameason. I have never been so happy," she confessed.

"Then why do you look so tired?" he asked, as only he could, getting straight to the care of his young charge. "I think there's more to this tale, and I for one would like to hear it," he stated, and his words brokered no argument.

Alex nodded that she understood his instructions, and she moved back to her seat. Her family followed to theirs, and she noticed Jack slide back in his chair and relax a little. Perhaps, she thought inwardly, this would all really work out in the end as Sabina had said. Alex smiled at her friend, and she received Sabina's nod of encouragement in return.

"Yes, Jameason, there is a great deal more to tell. Parts of this last week will not be easy to hear, so I hope that you will all keep an open mind and heart. I have learned that the greater good sometimes comes at a great price. The lives of the *Nephilim* are not without danger, because the Fallen's children would love to stop them, and by that I mean end them. I will tell you what I can, and I am going to ask my friends to help me tell the story."

Alex received her family's nod of agreement, and she began with Bertrand and what he had done to her at the ball, though she still gave scant details about the actual attack. She moved into her conversation with Ganymede in the family garden, and how that led to her trip to Aeoferth Hall. She told her family of the great estate and how she had helped to create it long, long ago.

Over the course of the next two hours, Alexandria and her new, extended family told her parents, brothers, and Jameason about the training she had undertaken, the abilities and powers she was awakening within herself, and of the immense struggles she had endured. She told them all what Jack had suffered at her side, and how much she now valued his friendship. When they came to the story of Gaius and his past with her, she tried to give as few details as she could. But she clearly saw from their expressions, that many more questions regarding the two of them would come up when she was alone with her family.

Alex was delighted to see how exited her father, Conner, and Jameason were to have access to Archimedes, once they realized that he was the true Archimedes they knew from history. And once their recounting was complete, the questions began to come tentatively at first, but then ran rampant. They wanted to know what Alex's transition might be like if she chose to be immortal, and how she was handling the power currently residing in her. Like all families, they wanted to make sure that she was well.

Though it was not easy to hear, John was truthful that this was the first time a *Nephilim* had returned and they were doing the best they could in these uncharted waters. Jameason left for a few minutes and returned bearing a tray with drinks for all, to refresh them while they continued the conversation. He leaned over and asked Conner what he had missed while he had been away, and everyone chuckled at his question.

Alexandria could feel her eyelids getting heavy several times, but she willed herself to stay awake for this most important of meetings. She was so proud of her family's strength and patience. They were handling the extraordinary news with grace and finesse. Hopefully, she thought to herself, if she chose to become immortal, she could do so with the same grace. She smiled silently to herself thinking that her parents had already placed that within her, as Grace was her middle name.

Lord Errol, Wallace, and Conner all begin to quiz the *Nephilim* on new battle plans, and Alex decided that she would step out for just a moment to wash her face and try to wake herself up. She stood and several eyes looked at her with surprise, but she held up her hands imploring them to remain seated. "Bathroom," she mouthed, so that they would understand she needed a few moments alone.

She did not walk to the facilities down the hall, but instead made her way up to her bedroom and rinsed her face off, then she came to sit on the edge of her bed. She was so tired, bone weary in fact, even though she had slept through the previous afternoon and night. Just hearing all that had happened in her life over the past two weeks, discussed and dissected, had made her see the enormity of the change working within her.

She knew Ganymede was right. She would have to choose her path soon, and whatever her decision, it had to be right not just for herself, but for everyone else, too. An opportunity this important to so many others, would have to be weighed in that broader context. Alex prayed for the strength to think outside of her own wants and desires when the time came.

Alex bent and put her head in her hands, trying to still her emotions. But she felt slow, silent tears spilling forth and she noiselessly let them fall. She felt a hand on her head, smoothing her hair back, and then felt the bed sink in next to her from someone's weight. She did not have to look up to know who was beside her. She smiled slowly, and turned to see Jack grinning down at her.

"Hey," he whispered.

"Hi," she whispered back.

"You did really well down there, Alex. You have one amazing family, I'll give you that. I'm not sure my family would have handled that kind of information with the same...," he was searching for the right word, and she completed his sentence for him.

"Grace. It's my middle name, you know?" she said, smiling wistfully as she tried to dry her face with her sleeve.

"Actually, I do," he replied, and watched her eyebrows rise in question to his statement, and laughed. "I know the name of anyone I'm protecting, Alex. It's kinda required." His lopsided grin made her smile as well, and she found herself chuckling at his response.

"There's my girl. That's a lot better than those tears," he said gently, and pulled out a handkerchief from his back pocket to finish cleaning her face. "I'll give you something else to smile about. You should have seen the way your brothers looked at me when I got up to check on you. But it was nothing compared to the look your whole family gave Gaius when they heard you two were once married. Now that was something to see!" Alex and Jack laughed over his observation, until her tears were completely chased away.

"Thank you, Jack," she whispered.

"You're welcome, Miss Groaban," he whispered back. Jack leaned over and kissed her forehead, then told her to lie down and take a nap. They would come and get her when dinner was ready, and he promised to let them know she was fine, just napping. He headed back downstairs and Alex was asleep minutes later.

Throughout Alex's nap, different ones came to peek in on her, but no one disturbed her. Before too long, Dudley came to nap beside her, cuddled firmly against her back. She slept the sleep of the innocents, and no dreams or visions interrupted her rest. When the dinner hour arrived, Gaius came up to retrieve her. He watched her for few moments than bent down, lifting Alex and holding her against his chest. Arianna had always been brave, but the courage he had witnessed that day in Alexandria, gave him hope that she would choose an immortal life with him in the future.

She opened her eyes, and was surprised to find herself being cradled. He slowly placed her on her feet and smiled down at her, kissing her lips gently.

"I am so proud of you this day, Alexandria. Coming home to your parents was the right course of action. It will make the coming days so much clearer for you," he said softly.

Without thinking, Alex reached up and cupped his face with her palm and he leaned into the gentle caress, closing his eyes and savoring the contact. When he reopened them, she took note of the passion in his gaze. She smiled up at him, and gradually took a step back. He nodded slowly, understanding her silent message, and offered her his arm to escort her to their meal.

Dinner was much more relaxed and social than their lunch had been. Wallace and Conner tried to steer Alex toward a seat between them again, but she shook her head in denial and moved to a seat between Gaius and Jack. Both brothers looked humored and laughed quietly at her refusal to be strong-armed by either of them. It was a step in the right direction, in Alex's opinion.

She found herself sitting back and watching all those she loved interact with joy and pride, more than she was actually participating in the conversations herself. Gaius and Jack kept up a steady dialog with Rohan and her brothers, and she was relieved to see everyone working together instead of pulling against one another. This was as it should be, she thought.

After their meal, Alexandria and her mother got everyone settled in a room of their own, and bid them all to retire when they were ready. Alex went back to the den and snuggled up on a couch under a blanket, and Dudley came to lie across her feet and legs. More and more people found their way into the room, and soon the discussions and conversations from earlier in the day resumed.

Though she tried to fight it, she once again fell asleep and no one disturbed her. Gaius had taken a seat closest to where her head lay, and he watched her more than he listened to everyone's comments and questions. Lady Juliana came over to sit in a chair by his side, and she smiled up at him in quiet approval.

"You must tell me once again how long you have known my daughter, Gaius. It confounds the mind, trying to process all of this," she said to him.

He shifted his weight so that he could look in her direction.

"Yes, madam, I am sure that is does. But to your credit, and that of your family, you are handling the news very well. And that can only help Alexandria, so I give you my heartfelt thanks," he said, placing a hand over his heart.

"In answer to your question, when she was on this earth before, we were husband and wife for almost two thousand years. I hope, in time, she will see me in that light, again," he said, smiling briefly.

"I know my daughter has never really let anyone court her, but it would seem that both you and Mr. Campbell have plans to change that," she said, giving him a knowing smile of her own.

Gaius laughed softly at her comment. "A mother does not miss much, does she? It is true; we both hold great affection for your daughter. As you can guess, I am hoping she chooses an immortal life with me, once more."

"So long as it is her choice, Gaius, we will support Alexandria's decision."

He understood her meaning at once, and leaned slightly forward in his chair.

"I will never do anything to cause harm to come to Alexandria, Lady Groaban. To do so, would cause me eternal pain and regret. No, she will choose. I just intend to make a very good case for myself," he nodded solemnly.

"I am glad to hear that, Gaius. You have, no doubt, noticed how Wallace and Conner watch over her. Just remember, they get that tendency from their parents," she concluded her thoughts.

"I do have one thing more I'd like to add, if I may, Lady Groaban. I understand there is the small matter of one named Henry to attend to. Perhaps you could help me remedy that problem?" he asked, his eyebrows rising in mock sincerity.

She laughed aloud at his question, and had to cover her mouth with her hand to keep from waking her daughter.

Alex slept on the couch for the remainder of the evening, and finally her parents came over and gently woke her so that she could sleep in her own bed. She made her way groggily up the stairs to her room and prepared quickly for bed. She welcomed Dudley in and the two curled up together and slept peacefully.

For the next two days, Alexandria, Jack, and the *Nephilim* stayed with her family. They shared so much, taking walks and meals together, and engaging in enlightening discussions about the truth behind many misrepresented historical periods and facts. It gave her family time to make peace with their daughter's imminent departure.

Alex took several walks with different members of her family, and they each tried to impart a special piece of advice or wisdom for her to take along, as she prepared to leave them. Her father told her to hold to the bond they had as a family and remember that whatever came, she had their unconditional love and support. Her mother advised her as Sabina had, to listen to her heart and it would lead her down the correct path. She wished happiness and safety for her daughter, and for her to take the utmost care in all she endeavored to learn.

Wallace and Conner reminded her how strong she was, now more than ever. They told her to never let another touch a hair on her head, and asked her to think through all of the ramifications before she accepted immortality. It was Jameason, though, who cut through all of the emotions she was feeling; when he took her hand in his and told her how proud he was of her, for she was the granddaughter of his heart.

They had been walking slowly through the snow covered gardens when he paused and said, "You know, Alexandria, there is a very appropriate verse that I shall share with you. It is found in Deuteronomy: chapter 31, verse 6. I memorized it years ago when I was a young man, really just a child, in the military. It says: *Be strong and courageous. Do not be afraid or terrified because of them, for the Lord your God goes with you, He will never leave you nor forsake you.'*"

"I believe that if you hold to the Lord, He will show you why He has chosen to place you here on this earth with such incredible choices laid before you. Be strong and true to yourself and Him, and you will work your way through this. I love you, Alexandria, as do we all. Be the young lady we have raised you to be," he said, in an uncharacteristically quiet voice. She hugged him and thanked him for his advice, both of them trying to squelch the knots in their throats.

Alex noticed as well that different members of her family found opportunities to speak to Jack and Gaius individually, but neither seemed the least upset by whatever was said. When she tried to ask Gaius one evening about what her brothers had said to him earlier in the afternoon, he just smiled broadly at her and walked away, giving her no information at all.

Before her departure, Jack, Gaius, Rohan, and Alexandria took time to sit with her parents and brothers, and made arrangements to triple the people guarding her family. Alex told them that she and the *Nephilim* were now covering the cost, and placing *Nephilim* among the human guards to deter Kronis from approaching them. Though her brothers did not want any guards with them, they acquiesced to take any added burden from Alex that might distract her from the challenges that lay before her.

The time had finally come for the group to leave. Alex had packed as if she would need everything she owned with her this time, and it took her brothers, Rohan, Gaius, and Jack to get everything downstairs and in the waiting Rovers. Alex stood alone for a few minutes in her bedroom after they had carried the last piece of luggage down, and looked at the space that she had always come back to and called home.

Though she had moved to New York, it had yet to feel like home the way the Manor House did. She ran her fingers along the wood posts of her bed and looked out of her window, onto the still frozen, rear gardens. She closed her eyes and tried to capture the image in her mind, then took in a deep breath and turned to head downstairs.

The *Nephilim* bid their farewells to her family and received open invitations to return at any time. They all moved into the SUVs to give Alexandria a last moment alone with her family. She hugged them all tightly and thanked them for their love and support once again. Alex promised to call or text regularly to keep them updated on her progress. Her parents finally walked with her to the vehicle and helped her in, shutting the door behind her.

Alex waved until they were all out of sight, and then turned in her seat looking ahead at the road. She was quiet as they drove back to the airport, reflecting on all that she had been blessed with. She was so very grateful.

Once the S-92 was loaded with her cargo, they all began to climb aboard. Alex thought to take her same seat by the window, when Heath called out to her from the pilot's seat. She angled her head at him in question.

"Alex, come up here with me," he called out, looking over his shoulder. She moved into the copilot's seat beside him, which until then had sat empty. "I want you to help me fly back to Aeoferth," he said, as if it were a common occurrence for her to do so. He chuckled at her surprised expression.

"We all know how to fly, Alex, and it's time you got your first lesson. You can read my mind, so let's start with you following my lead and doing what I am thinking, okay?" he asked, smiling at her.

"Get out!" she exclaimed.

"I assure you, if I get out, you get no lesson," he grinned, and she heard the light laughter of everyone behind her. Alex looked into the cabin and smirked at them all.

Alexandria turned back to Heath, and smiling, said, "I'm ready. Show me how to take us home."

Jack and Gaius looked at one another and shared a smile of their own. She had said, "Home."

Made in the USA
Charleston, SC
10 February 2013